The
Falcon's Heart

The Falcon's Heart

Poitevin Hearts

JOYCE DIPASTENA

A Note to the Reader

In the course of this story, my hero, Jevon, becomes enamored with thoughts of England, which he imagines as a "golden land." This is not intended to suggest my own feelings about the superiority of one country over another. Jevon's view grows out of his personal past and experiences. Other characters in the book love their homeland of Poitou just as deeply as he dreams of England. To me as their writer, each character is an individual shaped by their own unique histories and worldviews. I hope you will read this story with that spirit in mind.

CAST OF CHARACTERS
(IN ALPHABETICAL ORDER)

FICTIONAL CHARACTERS

Aumary de Laurant: baron of **Pennault Castle**; husband of Lady **Gwenllian de Laurant**; father of **Clothilde de Merval, Therri de Laurant** and **Heléne de Laurant**. Also appears in *Loyalty's Web* and *Illuminations of the Heart*.

Balduin de Soler: a knight of **Vere Castle**. Also appears in *Illuminations of the Heart*; hero of *Loving Lucianna*.

Baudri: a knight of Pennault Castle. Also appears in *Loyalty's Web*.

Beatris de Fores: one of **Gwenllian de Laurant**'s ladies-in-waiting at **Pennault Castle**; daughter of one of **Aumary de Laurant**'s vassals.

Clothilde de Laurant/de Merval (mentioned): elder daughter of Lord **Aumary de Laurant** and Lady **Gwenllian de Laurant** of **Pennault Castle**; married to Sir Fulbert de Merval of **Blancaval Castle**. Appears in *Loyalty's Web*)

Constantia de Ormande (pronounced *Con-STAHN-cha*/nickname *STAHN-cha*): one of **Gwenllian de Laurant's** ladies-in-waiting at **Pennault Castle**; daughter of Sir **Engerran de Ormande**, a vassal of **Aumary de Laurant**.

Damien de Brielle: knight and master of **Vere Castle**; father of **Triston** and **Etienne de Brielle**, husband of Aline de Brielle (deceased) and Osanne **de Brielle**. Also appears in *Loyalty's Web*.

Eda: a serving girl at **Vere Castle**.

Etienne de Brielle (mentioned): younger son of **Damien de Brielle** of **Vere Castle**; friend of **Therri de Laurant** of **Pennault Castle**. Also appears in *Loyalty's Web*; hero of *Dangerous Favor*.

Eudes: knight of **Pennault Castle** in charge of the gatehouse.

Franco de Marché: a knight of **Pennault Castle**.

Guia Doucet (pronounced GEE-ah): one of **Gwenllian de Laurant**'s ladies-in-waiting at **Pennault Castle**; daughter of one of **Aumary de Laurant**'s vassals.

Guilhem: sword master at Pennault Castle.

Gwenllian de Laurant (pronounced GWEN-lee-ahn in Poitou): wife of Lord **Aumary de Laurant** of **Pennault Castle**; mother of **Clothilde de Merval, Therri de Laurant** and **Heléne de Laurant**; of Welsh descent. Also appears in *Loyalty's Web*.

Hamo: one of **Hugh de Bury**'s men-at-arms.

Heléne de Laurant: younger daughter of Lord **Aumary de Laurant** and **Gwenllian de Laurant** of **Pennault Castle**. Heroine of *Loyalty's Web*; also appears in *Dangerous Favor* and *The Lady and the Minstrel*.

Hugh de Bury, Earl of Gunthar: an English supporter of King **Henry II**; assigned by the king to defeat the rebels in Poitou during the Great Revolt by the King's sons of 1173-1174. Hero of *Loyalty's Web*; also appears in *Dangerous Favor* and *The Lady and the Minstrel*.

Jevon de Cazalet: nicknamed "le Falquet" (the Falcon); a former squire of Pennault Castle; banished by **Aumary de Laurant** before he was knighted; son of **Vidal de Cazalet** and **Pelegrina de Cazalet**.

Llygad ap Dafydd (pronounced *LEE-gahd <u>in Poitou</u>*): cousin to Lady **Gwenllian de Laurant**; brought to Pennault Castle as a page from Wales when Lady Gwenllian married **Aumary de Laurant**.

Ned Woodville: English archer sergeant in service to **Hugh de Bury, Earl of Gunthar**.

Osanne de Brielle (mentioned): second wife of **Damien de Brielle** of **Vere Castle**. Appears in *Loyalty's Web* and *Illuminations of the Heart*.

Pelegrina de Cazalet: Jevon de Cazalet's mother; wife of **Vidal de Cazalet** of **Rouquard Castle**.

Peyre Mazel (pronounced *PAY-ruh*): huntsman of **Pennault Castle**.

Raimon Tirell: a knight of **Pennault Castle**.

Therri de Laurant: son of Lord **Aumary de Laurant** and Lady **Gwenllian de Laurant** of **Pennault Castle**. Also appears in *Loyalty's Web* and *Dangerous Favor*.

Triston de Brielle: elder son of **Damien de Brielle** of **Vere Castle**. Hero of *Illuminations of the Heart*; also appears in *Dangerous Favor*.

Vidal de Cazalet: Jevon de Cazalet's father; baron of **Rouquard Castle**.

HISTORICAL CHARACTERS

Henry II (mentioned): King of England 1154-1189; ruled over large sections of modern-day France, including Poitou and Aquitaine.

Richard Plantagenet: second son of **Henry II** and Eleanor of Aquitaine; created Duke of Aquitaine by Henry II in 1172; rebelled with his brothers Henry the Young King and Geoffrey in 1173-1174, demanding more power and respect from their father.

FICTIONAL CHARACTERS
LISTED BY CASTLE

PENNAULT CASTLE

Aumary de Laurant: baron of Pennault Castle

Gwenllian de Laurant: wife of Aumary de Laurant; mother of Clothilde de Merval, Therri de Laurant and Heléne de Laurant

Therri de Laurant: son of Aumary de Laurant and Gwenllian de Laurant

Heléne de Laurant: younger daughter of Aumary de Laurant and Gwenllian de Laurant

Constantia de Ormande: one of Gwenllian de Laurant's ladies-in-waiting

Beatris de Fores: one of Gwenllian de Laurant's ladies-in-waiting

Guia Doucet: one of Gwenllian de Laurant's ladies-in-waiting

Llygad ap Dafydd: cousin to Gwenllian de Laurant

Baudri: a castle knight

Eudes: knight in charge of the gatehouse

Franco de Marché: a castle knight

Guilhem: a castle knight; master-at-arms

Raimon Tirell: a castle knight

Peyre Mazel: huntsman of Pennault Castle

VERE CASTLE

Damien de Brielle: knight and master of Vere Castle; father of Triston de Brielle and Etienne de Brielle

Triston de Brielle: elder son of Damien de Brielle

Etienne de Brielle: younger son of Damien de Brielle

Osanne de Brielle (mentioned): second wife of Damien de Brielle

Balduin de Soler: a castle knight

Eda: a serving girl

THE ENGLISH

Hugh de Bury, Earl of Gunthar: an English supporter of King Henry II

John Lee: a knight and close friend of Hugh de Bury

Jevon de Cazalet: nicknamed "le Falquet" (the Falcon); a mercenary archer in service to Hugh de Bury, Earl of Gunthar

Ned Woodville: English archer sergeant in service to Hugh de Bury, Earl of Gunthar

Hamo: one of Hugh de Bury's men-at-arms

BLANCAVAL CASTLE (mentioned)

Clothilde de Laurant/de Merval (mentioned): elder daughter of Aumary de Laurant and Gwenllian de Laurant of Pennault Castle; married to Fulbert de Merval

Fulbert de Merval (mentioned): husband of Clothilde de Laurant of Pennault Castle; a rebel baron of Poitou

ROUQUARD CASTLE

Vidal de Cazalet: baron of Rouquard Castle; father of Jevon de Cazalet

Pelegrina de Cazalet: wife of Vidal de Cazalet; mother of Jevon de Cazalet

MAY 1167
POITOU
THE WOODS OUTSIDE PENNAULT CASTLE

His drubbing heart echoed the cadence of his silent curse as he shook the rain from his hair and bolted around another tree. This infernal rainstorm would make his footprints as easy to follow as a hare's in the snow. At least it also lent him the advantage of being able to hear the squelching of his pursuers' boots. Sadly, he knew a drenching would not slow them down. A reward of one hundred livres for his head was worth the discomfort of being soaked to the bon

The steady patter of rain softened the crunch of ancient leaves and twigs beneath his flying feet, but there were too many muddy patches in the grass and forest debris. Who chased him this time? A stranger, he hoped. Some knight or merchant merely passing through the county who'd heard about the thief lingering in these woods and hoped to capture the bounty. Less bitter to be brought down like a rabid dog by an unfamiliar face than one he knew and trusted.

"There he is!"

He swerved around another tree at the shout, pumping his arms to increase his speed. A puddle appeared up ahead. But so did a conveniently low tree branch. He launched himself from his sprint and latched his hands around the limb, swinging himself over the puddle to land several feet farther along the path. The rough wood burned his palms, but it gave him an idea. He zagged to another well-positioned branch and repeated the maneuver, once again pitching his body over the soggy patches of ground that would give his position away.

Only after a third leap and swing, launching himself so far it took his breath away, did he take shelter in a pocket of dryness beneath the leaves of a broad oak, granting his heaving chest a reprieve. He shivered a little at the clammy coldness of his drenched tunic.

I should have been more careful. I should have waited until I carved a working bow.

Instead, he had foolishly ventured into an exposed spot along the river to try to catch some fish before the rain clouds broke. He had grown tired of subsisting on berries, and most of the hares in these woods evaded his clumsy snares. His training hadn't focused on rigging traps. He'd tried to carve a bow from branches of hazel and ash, but both snapped when he drew them. He may have been Pennault Castle's best archer, but he was not a skilled bowyer.

"He cannot have gotten far. I saw his footsteps just a few yards back."

Squish. Splash. Slosh.

His heart jounced back into double rhythm. They were too close. Too late to try to use that branch overhead to vault his body through the air again. The only safe direction now was up. He bent his knees, then hurled himself at the branch above him. His hands scrabbled madly to catch hold, ignoring the fire in his bark-chafed palms as he hauled his body up.

Usually, his pursuers only sought him on the ground. They rarely thought to glance skyward—except for the Brown Hoods. The cowl of the man who appeared just below him looked nearly black, but that could be from the rain. Just to be safe, he quietly climbed up several branches higher, doing his best not to disturb the leaves and praying the hooded man blamed any rustling on the downpour.

Through the spaces between the leaves, four more heads appeared, all clad like the first. The five of them circled the oak like hounds fixed on a strong but abruptly truncated scent.

"His last footprint pointed this way," one said.

"And here." Another motioned at the ground. "The litter here is flattened by something heavier than a deer or boar. Do you see any other dents in the grass or mud?"

He risked worming his way still farther aloft as they rounded the broad oak again. When he shifted to prop his back against the trunk and looked down, he saw a face turned upward, gazing through the leaves.

Oh, saints! His breath froze in his chest even though he knew he was too high for anyone to hear his huffing and puffing. He did not recognize the features that peered his way, but the Brown Hoods always carried crossbows. If that man saw him, he would not be able to climb fast enough or high enough to avoid a crossbolt through his breast or between his shoulder blades.

I could do that even through the tangled tree limbs.

He shuddered. Surely men who stalked him as relentlessly as these men had for months possessed skills equal to his own.

He pressed his body against the trunk, hoping his wet russet hair and tunic blended into the bark. He waited. And waited. He could do nothing else. Even when one man said, "He's not here. Spread out and look for another print," he dared not relax. He had done so once, climbing down a tree to find them lying in wait to catch him. He had escaped by the merest slip of luck—a lesson he'd not soon forget.

His bones ached from his prolonged stiffness in his chilled, wet clothes. When a bit of pliancy finally seeped back into his muscles, his twenty-year-old joints groaned like old Father Dominic's in the depths of winter. He shook his hands to stir the blood back to life and bobbed a bit to loosen his knees before beginning his descent.

Halfway down, a ring of summery laughter checked him. This sound carried no threat—the party the merriment wafted from believed him long gone from these woods—but it did fall with a too-familiar blow upon his heart. He squatted on his perch and waited for the foursome to pass beneath him. Only when he saw them approaching in crisp, clean clarity instead of through a haze of rain or mist did he realize the storm had passed.

The little boy, his pale-blond hair darkened by the rain and no little amount of mud, carried two handfuls of the latter, which he appeared to be threatening to toss at his sister. A year younger but almost as tall as her brother, the girl swished her pale braid to her opposite shoulder and shouted, "Don't you dare! Don't you dare!" but she giggled as she did so.

The man and woman who shepherded them both laughed. Of course she would laugh. Everything was only a game to her. How had he not seen it for so long? How had he been so blind?

And how could it still hurt so much to hear and see it? He ran his hand over his cheeks where two months stubble grew and tried not to remember the soft caress of her fingers against his freshly shaven skin. He had wanted everything to be perfect that day. His tunic and surcote freshly laundered by Guia, the mud scrubbed from his shoes, his nails pared and cleaned, even a little powder made from cloves smuggled from the kitchen for him by Beatris and sprinkled along the back of his neck, all to encourage her to answer, "Yes."

And she had, the duplicitous vixen.

"We will all be switched when their mamma sees them like this," the man warned. Raindrops curled his dark hair into tight rings against his skull.

The little boy said, "Not you, Sir Franco. You're too big, and you're a knight now." The boy's teasing grin disappeared, and he sent an earnest look at the woman. "I'm sorry, Constantia. It will be my fault if Sybil switches you. I should not have jumped into that puddle."

The little girl slid her hand into her brother's, then wrinkled her nose when it landed in a squish of mud.

The boy responded by splattering his other fistful on the front of his sister's gown, saying when she squealed, "Don't worry, Heléne. I'll tell Mamma I pushed you into the puddle and got you dirty before Constantia could stop me. Then she will have Sybil switch only me."

"Your mama will never believe that," the woman said, echoing his own cynical thoughts as they stepped beneath his tree. "I will take you both in by the postern gate and clean you up in the laundry hut before we return to the keep. All your mamma need know is that we got caught in a rain shower."

The damp air frizzed her dark-brown hair, the bedraggled tendrils more unruly than ever. He refused to remember the exhilaration that seized him when those sinuous ripples engulfed his hands as he lifted her face to kiss her.

He lost the rest of their conversation as they passed beyond the boughs of the oak, only indistinct tones drifting to his ears now.

So Franco had supplanted him today. *Sir* Franco. His former friend would be knighted by now, like Raimon, who accompanied Constantia and the children two days ago.

He ignored the bitter tang in his mouth and climbed down through the remaining branches. When he reached the lowest, he jumped, the storm-mired earth beneath the leaf cover sinking with his weight. If the Brown Hoods came back this way, they would surely see the dint and know they had missed him. Then he had better not tarry. Had he a grain of sense, he would leave these woods altogether. He could reach the safety of Brittany in a little over a fortnight. Relative safety, anyway. The bounty was not in force there, but this—

He glanced at his hand, balling it into a fist. There was nowhere he could run to escape the shame of *this*. But he would not be actively hunted in Brittany's woods, as he was here. So long as he stayed away from men, they would stay away from him. He should go. Now. Today. Why had he stayed so long?

Because he wanted to see her one more time, then once more, and once more after that. As traitorous as she was, he wanted to hear her voice, watch the bounce of her rebellious hair, see her smile, even if she no longer smiled for him. Likely she never had. The double-hearted trickster.

He would go. Once he was free of Poitou, the memory of her would fade. Well, not that. He would always carry the shame of her lie with him. But the face he had loved, the lilting voice that had quickened his heartbeat, the memories of shared mischief, laughter, and even mirrored thoughts—all of that would dim with time and distance. No woman, however slyly she lured him, could haunt a man's dreams forever.

But it was too late to go today. The shadows between the trees had deepened. In the morning, then, if he survived another night without being caught.

"There! I told you he had probably gone up that tree!"

The Brown Hoods. He bolted like a stag at the baying of hounds, his heart hammering as he imagined that hunted creature's must. No one had sought him as doggedly as these men. The others who'd tried eventually gave up, but the Brown Hoods never tired of stalking him. He would never be safe in these woods. He had known it for months. Plague take them all!

It wouldn't, though. They would take him first if he stayed any longer. If he made it through this one last night, he would strike out for Brittany. He swore it by every oath he could summon between his panting breaths. *She will fade, she will fade, she will fade . . .*

But when his ribs began to ache as he veered around tree after tree after tree, his vow changed. *She* was the reason he ran for his life again. No, he did not want to forget her. He wanted to remember her betrayal forever.

AUGUST 1174
POITOU
THE WOODS OUTSIDE VERE CASTLE

"Ho, le Falquet. What do you see?"

Jevon studied the castle's gray walls through the oak branches before he answered. From his perch upon a sturdy limb, he stood level with the bored-looking arbalists milling in and out of view from behind the battlement's merlons. He could see the men more clearly than they would see him at this distance, even without his advantage of the oak's obscuring leaves. The arbalists' crossbows lolled lazily in most of their hands as they cursorily watched the open ground between the forest and castle.

"Nothing has changed from a fortnight ago," Jevon called down to Ned. He could not hear the arbalists' conversations and therefore felt confident they could not hear his.

"No signs at all that they are suspicious?" The archer sergeant sounded worried. "The sappers should be very close to the target by now. If the castle has heard scraping beneath the ground—"

It seemed doubtful. The sappers were not aiming for the foreyard, though it was always possible they might misjudge the distance Jevon had advised or that someone from the castle had ventured through the postern gate and heard the tick-tick-ticking of the pickaxes.

"I will climb higher," Jevon said.

He checked the arrow bag strapped to his waist to be sure it had not come loose as he'd scaled the oak, then adjusted the hemp bowstring across

6

his chest. As deadly as the crossbows were, reloading them was slow. Jevon could fire five or six equally well-aimed shafts from his war bow in half the time it took an arbalist to fire one or two. He maneuvered through the branches overhead until he stood balanced on a limb several feet above the walls. The summer wind whipped the leaves more wildly here, scurrying a gust up the back of his neck and whisking his hair around his cheeks. He pushed the wavy locks away from his face with his fingers before parting the branches to clear his view. From here he could see nearly everything about the castle, both old and new.

Sir Damien, the fox, had been busy since Poitou rose in support of Duke Richard against his father, the king. The castle's barbican jutted out farther from the castle's foreyard than the old gatehouse Jevon remembered. Two timber towers, lower than the four massive stone ones at the castle's corners, rose on either side of the barbican with abutting walls that stretched back to connect to the older ramparts. The water-filled moat still only curved around three of the four castle walls, but the barbican's palisades embraced a new outer bailey with a second moat so recently dug it had not been filled with water. Or perhaps Sir Damien intended for the steep-sided ditch to remain dry? Those wooden spikes projecting from its base would make any invader think twice about crossing it.

Any man except the English earl Jevon served. The hawk-faced Englishman would make Sir Damien regret his bold expansion of the castle. Jevon should not be so eager to see the fortress of a man he once thought a friend suffer the devastation he'd witnessed at Blancaval Castle. But if Sir Damien had not joined in the hunt for Jevon's head seven years ago, neither had the knight offered him so much as a crumb of compassion or aid.

Jevon watched the castle guards, shrunken to minikins from this height, strolling unhurriedly about the walls and courtyards. Once confident he had seen all he needed to, he prepared to climb back down the tree, but a movement caught his eye. A pair of riders approached on the road that snaked toward Vere Castle. They were still too far away for even Jevon's keen vision to make out. Did they come from Pennault? They rode from that direction.

He scuttled down the oak with a speed that would have been foolhardy for a man who had not spent so many months hiding in the ancient branches of these woods.

"What is it?" Ned asked sharply. Of course, Jevon's scrambling had alarmed him. "What did you see?"

"Nothing to worry about. No one appears to suspect anything. There is no digging going on in the baileys that might suggest listening shafts, no bowls of water on the ground that vibrations from picks might disturb. So long as the earl's miners aim exactly at the tower I told them of, they should meet with no obstruction."

Ned scratched his ruddy beard and fell in step beside Jevon as the latter strode away from the tree. "You could see bowls of water on the ground from this distance?"

Jevon shrugged, not wanting to boast. "Had there been any."

The vision men called "falcon sharp" and which earned him the byname "le Falquet" had been natural to Jevon all his life. His mercenary brothers ceased commenting on it years ago. But the English earl's men still found his vision for distances a novelty.

"Where are we going?" Ned asked.

"There are riders on the road. I might know them—or not. But I want to watch them as they ride by."

"Riders?" Alarm returned to Ned's voice. His sergeant held far less confidence in their skill as spies than in directing barrages of arrows in battle. "What if they bring word that Blancaval has fallen?"

"If they had broken through the tight perimeter the earl left around Blancaval, they would be riding hellbent from the north, not sauntering in from the south. What is more, Sir Damien left both his gates open—his new barbican's as well as the one in the old gatehouse. He must be sufficiently at peace with his neighbors that he sees no need to seal off the yard during the day."

"Or he expects the riders you saw."

"I don't think so," Jevon said. "It is a show of deliberate contempt for the king. If Sir Damien were at war with one of the other knights or barons, he would keep his gate shut and wait for the riders to announce themselves to his gatekeeper before raising the portcullis. Believe me, I know these men. When they fall to quarreling, they keep their gates shut tight night and day. The barons must think that so long as they stand united, young Richard will protect them or at least send them warning should the king turn his wrath from Normandy to Poitou."

"Which the king is too preoccupied to do at the moment, so he's sent Gunthar to subdue the rebels as quickly and quietly as he can before Duke Richard becomes aware. Once the young prince realizes he has lost his

Poitevin allies, he will have no choice but to surrender to his father." Ned stated the unspoken but clearly implied hope for the earl's army for this campaign into Poitou.

Ned scrubbed his beard, a rich ginger color that mocked the yellow straw of his hair. "If you are not worried, why are we striding so fast?"

Were they? Jevon slowed his steps, but only a little. Curiosity drove him. Would the riders be familiar?

"What else did you see?" Ned asked.

Jevon described his view of Vere Castle from the branches.

"What sort of fool digs a moat and stops at the back of his castle?" Ned said.

Jevon explained the strategy, which would be obvious to a knight but might escape a humble archer. "A moat on four sides would hem Sir Damien in if an enemy breached both gatehouse and keep. This way, he and his family can flee to the woods through the postern gate should his defenses fail."

Ned stopped. "There's a postern gate? Why did you not inform the earl when you told his sappers where to mine?"

Jevon reluctantly stopped, too. "Because the postern would do him no good. Sir Damien knows that wall is potentially vulnerable without the moat, so he keeps arbalists stationed at that quarter in peace or in war. Besides, vines and bushes all along that portion of the wall conceal the gate. The earl's men would be mowed down by a hail of arrows before they reached it."

"Not if they held shields over their heads and you told them where to find it. It is a short distance from the trees to the wall."

"I do not know where to find the gate. I spent time with Sir Damien's younger son when he was at play with Laurant's heir in the woods and when the boys fished at the river, but the only times I visited Vere was when I attended Laurant's wife as a squire, and she rarely let me wander from her side."

"You were a squire?"

Jevon bit his lip. He had not intended to make that slip. "My father sent me to Pennault to train for knighthood when I was a boy," he admitted. "I served the Baron de Laurant and his lady for thirteen years. I can tell the earl much more about Pennault Castle than I can about Vere."

Jevon started walking again, hoping Ned would drop the subject.

"You were never knighted?" Ned asked, joining him in motion.

"No," Jevon said tersely.

"Well," Ned said after a few moments of silence, "I suppose that explains that fancy bow of yours. You are sure I cannot persuade you to sell it?"

Jevon shook his head and merely kept walking. He could not blame Ned for his questions. Archers were usually men of middling rank, free farmers or townsmen who wielded powerful but utilitarian bows, not bows embellished with highly decorative nocks of antler, much less bearing one of Hywel ap Ioan's cunning epigrams for a bowyer's mark. Jevon liked Ned Woodville. The archer sergeant had treated him fairly since Jevon joined the earl's bowmen. But he did not intend to confide his past to Ned after he had concealed it from the earl, who'd hired him. The earl knew only that as a native of Poitou, Jevon's familiarity with the county and its barons could provide valuable tactical information, while Jevon's uncanny aim with the arrow was a skill the earl said he preferred to have on the king's side in a war.

Ned refrained from asking any more questions until Jevon waved him to a halt near enough to the road to view the travelers but deep enough in the trees not to be seen. As the riders approached, the wind blew the woman's veil across her cheeks. The man's profile was equally obscured by his arm arched over his head to prevent the gale from carrying his cap away.

"My wife is Poitevin, you know," Ned remarked as they waited for the riders to draw close.

Jevon glanced at him in surprise and caught the sergeant scratching his beard again. Jevon reflexively stroked his own, neat beard. The soft hair on his cheeks and chin never bothered him, but Ned clearly disliked his. Jevon saw the scrunch of Ned's eyebrows and lowered his hand lest the sergeant think he mocked him. He scratched the back of his hand instead. The leather gloves, with their fingers cut just above his knuckles, always seemed to itch, but it was safer to keep them on despite the discomfort. Too much sunlight had been his undoing more than once.

"You have been to Poitou before?" Jevon asked.

"Twice. The earl came to fight in the queen's tournaments and brought some of his best bowmen to compete in a contest of archers. I met Lunete, a bookseller's daughter, while accompanying one of the earl's knights to commission a book from her father. I fell in love the moment I saw her, but it took her longer to fall in love with me."

Ned rubbed his beard a little more cheerfully.

Hoofbeats warned them to silence. Jevon trusted his walnut-brown gambeson and russet hair to blend with the trees, but he placed his hand over the badge sewn to his shoulder lest the flash of silver on blue cause one of the riders to glance in their direction. Ned, similarly dressed, followed his example.

The two stood perfectly still between a rustling oak and a fluttering, glossy-leafed beech. The riders passed at a languid pace, giving Jevon ample time to study them. The woman turned her head so that her veil now gusted away from her face, while the man switched hands against his cap, baring his features as well. They would be strangers to Ned, but despite the years, Jevon knew them instantly.

He'd half hoped, half dreaded he would, for he knew not what emotion might strike him when the woman rode into view: longing or white-hot anger. It was anger, but blizzard white rather than scalding. The frigid rawness surprised him given how her warm, traitorous kiss lingered in his memory all these years.

"Think it over, Constantia." The wind carried the man's words into the trees. "Are you not sick to death of Pennault?"

The woman gave a tight smile. "It would be most unwise of me to answer that."

She had matured from the cheerful, rosy-cheeked girl Jevon had wanted to spend his life with. Her smooth skin still carried the light-bronze glow of a woman who enjoyed the sunlight more than was proper for a nobly born lady, but she was clearly no longer the impish companion of his youth. Her cloak and gown were several degrees finer than the serviceable castoffs Lady Gwenllian formerly clothed her in. The gold embroidery on the green band that held her veil in place sparkled like the spirited flecks of her forest-green eyes. She'd parted her dark-brown hair in the center and drawn it back into two sleek, coiled plaits that played hide-and-seek with the veil's blustery folds. Did sun-kissed ripples still dance amidst her rebellious tresses when she loosed them over her shoulders?

The man held his cap clamped against a tousle of indecisive locks that still could not seem to agree whether to be blond or brown. Raimon Tirrell. *Sir* Raimon. Jevon tried hard not to be jealous of the gilded spurs that flashed from his former friend's heels. Only ten more days and Jevon would have been knighted too.

Raimon leaned into the space between him and the woman, releasing his cap to reach out as though to take her hand. The blustery wind swept the cap from his head, sailing it straight into her arms. She laughed—a rich, summery sound that could thaw the coldest winter and chipped the tiniest crack in the ice around Jevon's heart.

She held the cap against her breast. "You are Lord Laurant's best knight. Not one of his men has defeated your sword since"—she hesitated the briefest instant—"he left. You will have to be very persuasive to convince the baron to let you leave his service. Where would you even go?"

The frown that twitched at Raimon's lips vanished in his familiar cocky grin. "You mean where would *we* go. To the tournament fields, of course, just as Franco and I always vowed we would. I will burn a trail of fame across Flanders and France with my lance and sword. Every knight will envy me, and when they see how I drape you in silks and jewels, every woman will envy you. Our troubadours will weave songs of my courage and immortalize your beauty. Our love will resound through the ages."

Their love? The punch in Jevon's stomach startled him. They rode out of range before he heard her reply.

My heart's twin, I called you once. And now you smile at him?

He had not fully fathomed how the merry, gamesome girl who could complete his thoughts before he finished speaking them would so completely vanish.

As the riders retreated, Ned said, "They did not sound as though they knew of Blancaval's fall or how near the earl is to Vere, so I suppose there is no need to intercept them. Did you know them?"

Jevon nodded. "Raimon Tirrell. I grew up with him at Pennault. The woman is Constantia de Ormande, one of Lady Gwenllian de Laurant's waiting ladies."

De Ormande? Or Tirrell now? Jevon shrugged. It did not matter who the faithless wench had wed. Or perhaps she and Raimon were not married after all. The troubadours did not exactly extol chastity in their love songs. And unless Constantia's father had unexpectedly decided to dower his youngest daughter after ignoring her for nearly fifteen years, only a lusty old widower with a brace of sons would overlook her poverty and consider her for a wife.

A stupid old man or a gullible boy so moon-mad in love that he'd fallen heels-over-head for a scheming vixen.

"Were you friends?"

Ned's question flustered Jevon before he realized that the sergeant's curiosity was for the knight, not the lady.

"Yes," Jevon owned. "We shared quarters and training as squires. He was good with the sword—excellent, actually. None of the others could disarm him, not even the older knights."

"What about you?"

"We had a friendly rivalry. I was better at archery." This time, Ned must have sensed too much humility in Jevon's reply, for the sergeant gazed at him until he added, "And the lance. And the sword. But Raimon was good-natured whenever I defeated him, unlike some of the other squires."

Llygad in particular. Lady Gwenllian's young cousin made clear his resentment of Jevon's ease with martial skills, while Llygad's clumsiness humiliated the baroness.

How had Constantia fared with Llygad after Jevon left? Well enough, no doubt. She had always made ridiculous excuses for Llygad's abominable behavior. No doubt she had found a better defender than Jevon in Raimon, given the easy, intimate way she rode at Raimon's side.

Ned scratched his beard again. "Perhaps when the earl attacks Pennault, you should remain in the tents."

Jevon raised his brows. "Why on earth should I?"

Ned's intense blue eyes looked steadily into Jevon's. "You said you have friends there. If you hesitate in your aim—"

"I won't." Jevon cut him off. "I have no friends in Poitou. The earl can burn every one of these castles to the ground, and I will not so much as blink in regret. I hope more than a few flaming missiles from my bow assist him in his goal. Did you see me flinch from his commands at Blancaval?"

"No. But Blancaval was not your home."

"Nor is Pennault anymore. I have seen how the earl deals with rebels. He is hard, but he is not cruel. I can serve a man like that. It is why I swore my faith to him. What reason have I given you to doubt me?"

"None," Ned admitted. "The earl is so impressed with your skill that he told me he might invite you to join his household archers when he returns to England. But do you not care that these men whose blood you share will call you traitor for helping the earl to spill it?"

"These men" had called Jevon enough other foul names and hunted him like an animal. No, he had no pity for any of them.

"Did *I* swear fealty to King Henry and then break my oath? No. That was Sir Damien de Brielle and Lord Aumary de Laurant. The earl will find me as staunchly loyal at Vere and Pennault as I was at Blancaval."

Ned nodded, seemingly satisfied with Jevon's stout response. "Then let us bring him our report."

Ned let Jevon lead the way through the trees. Jevon knew these woods and roads and fields as the English could not. It was one of the reasons the earl hired the mercenary archer to join the company of bowmen he'd brought with him from across the Breton sea. By proving his loyalty to the earl and the king, Jevon hoped to win more than justice. He expected to be rewarded. Only the king could wipe away the unjust shame that dogged Jevon in every county, duchy, and kingdom he traveled through, and if laying waste to the castles of his enemies was the price, it was one he was willing to pay.

VERE CASTLE

onstantia stretched her toes beneath the sheets, luxuriating in their smoothness and the well-stuffed mattress that cradled her. For once she woke to the sweet scent of beeswax candles instead of the muttony odor of tallow. At Pennault Castle, she slept in a small, cold chamber with Beatris and Guia. They, like Contantia, were daughters of some of the Baron de Laurant's vassals who waited on his wife, but their lack of dowries won his wife's scorn. At Pennault, the baroness dressed Constantia and her companions in dull, worn gowns and assigned them menial chores more worthy of common servants than the well-born ladies they were.

But whenever visitors stayed at Pennault, or when Lady Gwenllian sent Constantia on an errand to Vere Castle as she had yesterday, Lady Gwenllian clothed Constantia in a gown worthy of an honored, pampered lady so that her father might not learn of her demeaning treatment from their guests or neighbors. Especially now that Constantia's brother had died and Lady Gwenllian hoped to manipulate an alliance between her cousin Llygad and Constantia.

Muffled thunder rumbled through the shutters. Constantia sat up, pushing the thick tendrils of her hair out of her eyes. She sighed at the thought of Llygad. At least he was honest enough not to pretend he wanted her. Raimon's behavior baffled her. She had told Raimon she did not love him. Even if she did, unlike Llygad, Raimon's lack of fortune excluded him from her father's consideration for her hand.

All the same, she should not have said, "Fuddle!" when in his enthusiasm for his elusive tournament dreams Raimon had grown loquacious about the troubadours immortalizing her beauty. More likely, the poets would compose parodies of the peculiar woman with crumply, meandering hair and skin so browned by the sun she must be a demented virago.

On another roll of thunder, she swung her legs out of bed. The door opened, and a maid peered into the chamber.

"Oh, you are awake. May I help you dress, milady?"

"Thank you—Eda, is it?" The woman had helped prepare Constantia for bed last night, lending her a sleeping chemise of delicate lawn from the Lady Osanne's wardrobe. Constantia had never felt anything so soft against her skin.

Eda nodded. She picked up an ivory comb from the table next to the bed and ran it through Constantia's hair, immediately hitting a snag. Last night, Eda patiently worked through handfuls of snarls that strayed from Constantia's braided hair even before she'd removed the pins after dinner, but the knots returned while she slept. Constantia blamed it on the storm that yesterday's wind blew in overnight.

"How long has it been raining?" she asked the maid.

"The thunder began shortly after dawn." Eda repeated last night's ritual—slip-slide-hitch, firm but gentle currying until the comb slid a little farther, slip-slide-hitch. "It must be pouring for we have been told not to open the shutters."

Such a downpour would likely slow the Lady Osanne's return to Vere. "What is she like, your new mistress?" Constantia asked.

"She is very beautiful. Not as dazzling as Lady Gwenllian, but, then, her beauty is very different. Lady Osanne is sleek and dark, whereas the baroness glitters like a golden jewel."

If Constantia had mastered one thing in her years at Pennault, it was smiling in agreement at the extravagant praise of Laurant's dazzling baroness.

Eda coaxed out another tangle. "Sir Damien is quite pleased with her, but the castle has been very different since they married. Lady Aline was quiet, kind, and pious. You remember the little case she always chained to her girdle to carry her tiny prayer books?"

Prayer books, psalteries, saints' lives, Lady Aline had generously shared these with the only one of Laurant's squires who prized the reading lessons the baron imposed upon all his pages. Constantia had benefited from that squire's eagerness to share his knowledge with her. She spent some of her most gloriously happy hours at Pennault reading at his side. Now her memories, like all her memories of him, stabbed like splintered shards in the breast where her heart once beat so contentedly.

"Lady Osanne has no use for books. She wanted to sell them all, but Sir Triston would not allow it."

Triston, Sir Damien's eldest son, had been somber and quiet at dinner last night, drinking large amounts of wine and leaving the conversation to his father, who enjoyed regaling Constantia with stories of his new wife's vivacious charms.

Constantia took the comb from Eda, and with ruthless strokes that stung her scalp, distracted herself from the hollow emptiness the mention of Lady Aline's books stirred.

Eda clasped her hands together. "May I see the gifts, milady? Just a peek?"

Constantia hesitated, then set down the comb and stood. She smoothed out the blanket on the bed before unpacking and carefully laying out a series of beautifully embroidered veils—bride gifts Lady Gwenllian had sent with Constantia for Sir Damien's new wife.

"Look only," Constantia warned. "If we soil them, Lady Gwenllian will be —unhappy."

While the maid oohed and aahed over the gifts, Constantia donned her gown from the night before.

"Did your mistress say how long she intended to stay in Poitiers?" Constantia loosely plaited her hair at the back of her head. Without a mirror, any attempt to recoil it over her ears would be lopsided.

"No," Eda replied. "She loves new gowns as much as Lady Aline loved books, so she may remain there to shop for a good long while."

"And Etienne accompanied her?" Constantia missed the engaging seventeen-year-old at dinner yesterday. She had spent more time with Sir Damien's younger son when he played and fished with Laurant's heir than she had with Sir Damien or Triston.

"Etienne still grieves for his mother, but his father's happiness is everything to the boy, so he offered to escort the Lady Osanne to Poitiers, knowing it would please Sir Damien, especially as Sir Triston has been somewhat surly about the new marriage."

Surly, hmm? Perhaps an extended stay at Vere would not be as pleasant as Constantia had thought.

"Sir Damien left me with the impression that his wife would return within a day." What had Eda done with the pins for her hair? "That is what I told Sir Raimon to relay to the baroness when I sent him back to Pennault without me yesterday. If it is to be longer, I should send a message to explain my extended absence to Lord Laurant. Do you think Sir Damien would lend me a courier?"

"Of course, milady, just as soon as the storm passes. Let me show you to the chapel. Our chaplain will have some parchment you can use."

Constantia packed the veils carefully away before she followed Eda from the bedchamber. She would pin up her braid and don her own veil after she wrote to the baron.

Eda led Constantia past a stone stairway that descended from the upper floors to the great hall below. A gray-haired knight paced near the head of the stairs, hands behind his back. He appeared not to see the women as he muttered, "My sword was good enough to serve him for thirty years, and now he chooses that jackal Sir Oliver to fight at his side instead of me? What does he think I am—a ramshackle old man merely because my hair grayed faster than his?"

Eda curtsied. "Good day, Sir Balduin."

He acknowledged the women with a distracted nod.

"Is it still raining outside, sir?" Constantia asked. "I would like to send a message to Pennault as soon as the weather permits."

Sir Balduin looked surprised, raising a brow that mixed gray with his once-dark chestnut hair. "Rain? The sky is perfectly clear, my lady."

"Clear?" Constantia said. "But it has been thundering all morning."

A loud clap of thunder contradicted Sir Balduin's statement and confirmed hers.

Sir Balduin's soaring brows plunged into a ferocious scowl. "Those are siege engines, my lady, and it sounds like that hit may have broken through." His hand fell to the hilt of the sword at his side. "Orders or no orders, I am not going to stand here like a weak woman while the enemy tries to fight their way to the keep."

Constantia caught his arm as he swiveled to plunge down the stairs. "Siege? We are under siege? By whom?"

"By the king's men. Our walls were surrounded when we woke up this morning. Sir Damien refuses to renounce his loyalty to Duke Richard. He did not wish to alarm you and the womenfolk, so he ordered me to stay here to guard you and keep you ignorant of the threat. But if they have penetrated the walls, he will need my sword to help beat the English back." Sir Balduin must have registered Constantia's shock in her grip on his arm, for he added with a robust confidence, "Do not be alarmed, my lady. We will drive these English devils away. But"—he hesitated—"return to your chamber and bar the door as a precaution."

He freed himself from her hold and ran down the stairs. Constantia stared after him. Vere Castle under siege? Laurant had sworn fealty to Duke Richard as well. If the king's men were in Poitou, would Pennault Castle be next?

She whirled on Eda, whose cheeks drained of color. "Where is your postern gate?"

"The postern, milady?"

"I know you have one. Etienne used to slip through it at night to meet Lord Therri by the river to fish. He told me he watched at night for Lord Therri to climb out his window, then followed at a distance to be sure the boys did not come to harm."

Eda looked confused. "He?"

Yes, he whose name is too painful to speak. If she did, her shattered heart would piece itself together just so it could break all over again. She had learned that torturous lesson the hard way the first wrenching months after his departure.

"Oh, never mind," Constantia said. "Just fetch my cloak."

Hoping a page or squire could lead her to the postern gate, she hurried down the stairs while Eda darted off. She prayed Sir Balduin was right and Sir Damien repelled the attack, but that would not prevent the English from wreaking havoc on the next nearest castle. She had to warn Pennault. But first she had to find a way out of Vere.

She had overheard Therri tell his sister that Vere's postern opened nearly directly into the woods. It must be someplace at the castle's rear. There would not be room for siege engines there. If the attack were taking place at the forefront of the castle, perhaps Constantia could escape unseen through the postern.

The great hall was empty, no servants sweeping out rushes, no pages concealing their boredom while waiting for an assignment, not even a hound nosing about for an overlooked morsel from yesterday's dinner. Eda returned with Constantia's cloak in her arms. Constantia threw the cloak around her shoulders and hurried to the keep's exit. To her relief, the wooden stairs that led down to the bailey from this upper floor had not been rolled away from the wall.

She paused on the landing, initially thinking Sir Balduin must be wrong. Heavy, dark clouds lowered over the yard, dimming the sun. The "thunder" was only a rainstorm after all. She released the anxious breath she held, then gagged at the acrid fumes that stung her nose and burned her lungs. Tears blurred her vision. She wiped them away with her sleeve, then stared again at the sky. Like a scroll slowly unfolding across the sun, black clouds billowed over the gatehouse, casting the yard in a shadow more ominous than any storm. The gatehouse was on fire!

No, not the great stone gatehouse. It must be the new wooden barbican with its adjacent towers. Constantia pressed her nose into her sleeve to strain out the smoke and blinked until she squeezed enough water from her eyes to view the commotion in the bailey. Mailed knights and men-at-arms in thick leather gambesons ran about in a scene of organized chaos, responding to directions shouted by a tall, broad-shouldered knight with thick ebony curls. Three men paused to listen to him before two dashed off in one direction and the third in another.

The man giving commands wore a forest-green surcote with a gilded rose, emblem of the de Brielle house, over his mail. Sir Damien's son Triston. Constantia did not see Sir Damien. She guessed he stood somewhere on the walls, directing a counteroffensive to the siege.

She ran down the stairs, her steps echoing hollowly against the wood. She breathed as shallowly as she could to avoid choking on the smoke. Just as she reached the levelled ground of the gently sloped motte that lifted the keep above the yard, a great reverberating clap like the knell of a giant bell exploded in her ears. Screams rent the air as men scattered like a swarm of terrified rats under a shower of stone shards.

Horror jerked her hands away from her ears as the great stone wall collapsed. A thunderous splash accompanied the roar of shattering stones.

Men scrambled to reach the safety of the center yard, but those standing guard atop the ramparts had nowhere to flee. Her stomach seized as she watched for the inevitable pitching of bodies from the wall-walk to the hard earth below.

The walls on either side of the huge gap in the ramparts continued to crumble, but the hazy sky remained empty. Sir Balduin had known since sunrise that the "thunder" she and Eda heard came from the English siege engine's volleys. Any guards along that stretch of wall would have been trying and failing to deflect the attack. They must have known when to abandon their positions to avoid plummeting down with the wall.

Constantia choked over a smoke-filled breath of relief.

"The moat!" a man shouted. "The rubble has dammed the moat! Turn about! Turn about and fight! Triston, summon the arbalists! We need their crossbows here in the yard to cut down the English dogs when they come through the wreckage!"

Constantia looked up and saw Sir Damien, hands cupped around his mouth as he bellowed the order from atop one of the gatehouse towers. Triston hesitated, sword in hand, then lunged away from the fractured wall to round the keep. Were some of the arbalists stationed to guard the postern? If Sir Damien thought it safe to draw them away, he must believe that portion of his defenses safe from attack. Perhaps the English had not brought enough soldiers to completely encircle the castle. If so, while Vere's soldiers fought the enemy in the foreyard, Constantia could search for the postern gate at the castle's rear.

The English had taken Sir Damien by surprise, but with her warning, Laurant would have time to prepare Pennault for a vigorous defense.

Constantia sped through the springy grass atop the mound that supported the looming keep, but eventually she had to scramble down the motte, careful not to trip over her hem. She wound her cloak around one arm to shorten it, lifted her skirts nearly to her knees, and sidled down the slope to avoid pitching headfirst in her haste to reach the yard. The side of the motte was steeper here, less worn by people coming and going through the keep's entrance. Constantia began to slide, pebbles spraying into her shoes as she struggled to control her speed. She careened sideways with no way to break her fall and steeled herself for a collision with the ground.

She landed with a thud—not against dirt and gravel but against a hard, bracing body.

"What the blazes! Lady Constantia?"

She looked up, shaken but grateful, into Triston's dark eyes as his strong hands set her safely on her feet.

"What are you doing out here?" he said. "It isn't safe. Go back inside. We will route these English devils, but retreat with the servants to the cellar and bar the door until we do." He released her and ran until he was close enough to shout up at the wall. "Machon! What do you see?"

A man in a leather helmet and gambeson appeared between the merlons. "A pack of English wolves trying to make their way through the wreckage of the south wall."

"And from your side?" Triston called.

"All is clear here, sir. What would you have us do?"

"Come down. My father wants you to meet the English in the yard."

Machon gave a wave with the crossbow and retreated to relay the order.

Triston turned, then muttered a startled oath when he found Constantia behind him. "I told you—"

"I have to get to Pennault," she said. "You heard him. It is safe on this side of the castle. Show me where to find the postern gate so I can tell Lord Laurant what has happened here. He has been generous to your house, Sir Triston. Give him a chance to prepare our castle. He may even send some of his own knights to help you drive back the English."

Triston's mouth tightened. For a moment, she feared he meant to refuse. Then he grabbed her arm and pulled her toward the western wall.

He stopped so abruptly that her head snapped back.

"Do you feel that?" he said.

"Feel what?" As soon as the words left her mouth, the ground shivered beneath her feet.

The shiver became a shudder that rolled up through her ankles and legs. She had an odd sensation of standing on water, even though the ground looked perfectly solid. A quiver rippled through her belly.

"What is that?" Her voice came out on a shocked whisper.

"Oh, saints," Triston croaked as the western wall with its corner tower did a curious thing. They suddenly began to sink.

I am dreaming? Constantia told herself. *There can be no other explanation for earth that heaves like the sea and swallows stone towers. I am sound asleep in Sir Damien's guest chamber—or perhaps I never left Pennault. The fire and smoke, the destruction and panic, the slumping tower in front of me—it is all a nightmare from which I shall awake in but a moment.*

"Oh, saints. Oh, saints!" Triston shouted. "Constantia, run!"

His hand dug into her arm with such force it should have jarred her eyes open, but the nightmare continued. He dragged her back toward the front bailey, but his long strides could not outpace the upheaval of earth. Constantia did not know whether the lurching of the ground or the second deafening blast threw them both off their feet, but she felt herself flying eerily through the air. Pain exploded through her temple as a smothering weight crushed her against a hard, gritty surface. Then the nightmare became a hazy gray mist of nothingness.

"You were right," Constantia said. "Franco does drop his right shoulder a bit before he steps in for an attack. And Raimon shifts his eyes in the direction he plans to strike before he swings his sword at an opening he thinks he percieves. No wonder you can always disarm them!"

A breeze swirled just the barest trace of autumn crispness over her cheeks and stirred the russet waves of Jevon's hair. She had watched him at sword practice for years without ever noticing the subtle but telling gestures of his opponents. She marveled at his unerring ability to win every match, first with the other squires his age, then with the younger knights, and from the time he turned sixteen, all the older knights, even the baron. He would be the most splendid knight to ever fight on the tournament fields once he and Raimon and Franco were knighted. Her heart would burst with pride to hear the troubadours sing his praises. But it would also break when he left.

She turned toward the shaggy bushes that hid the forest clearing, refusing to let him see her sadness. They had only five months together before he turned one-and-twenty. Lord Laurant knighted the squires he fostered on their birthdays rather than en masse. Jevon's fell after Raimon's and before Llygad's and Franco's. Why Jevon troubled himself o'er the last seven years with a dowerless, insignificant girl three years his junior, however nobly born, she never understood, but he had been her lifeline to everything good that had happened to her at Pennault. He could never truly know how much his friendship buoyed her through Lady Gwenllian's dismal demands on Constantia as one of the baroness's waiting ladies. How could he, when there simply seemed no words to express Constantia's gratitude?

She glanced at him again. Jevon looked pleased that she recognized the signs he'd encouraged her to watch for when he trained, but his smile held something different today. His usual easy confidence felt . . . off. As though he were uncomfortable or nervous.

The hum of voices inside the clearing drew her attention back to the children playing inside the ring of shrubs, their favorite spot in the woods to romp safely distanced from their mother's impatient frowns. They loved the perceived independence of having their grown-up companion, Constantia, "wander away" for a while and leave them to their youthful games. She never went far, though, always within earshot should they need her, and she only strayed from her covert post just outside the shrubs when Jevon joined in her watch duties.

When their hands reached simultaneously to part the branches to allow them to peer inside the clearing, she and Jevon exchanged quick grins.

Two ten-year-old boys jumped and gamboled about, their wooden swords clattering together. Therri's smooth, pale-gold hair shone in stark contrast to his friend Etienne's tangled black curls.

"They are dancing about like puppets," Constantia whispered. "I thought you were teaching Therri proper footwork."

"I'm trying." Jevon matched her lowered tone. "But once Etienne gets carried away, Therri does too. It doesn't matter, though, because today is Tuesday. Look—Clothilde is about to say . . ."

Constantia and Jevon murmured along with the twelve-year-old fairy sprite who sat atop one of her mother's castoff cloaks spread over the tree stump that served as her throne. "Fight valiantly, Sir Knight. The prize my father offers you is great."

Clothilde's beauty fairly blazed in a shaft of gilding sunlight.

The two boys looked too engrossed in their sword battle to hear either Clothilde or the watchers through the bushes. And the tall nine-year-old with the pale-blonde braid standing at her sister's shoulder had allowed boredom to turn her attention to a squirrel dashing across the grass.

"Clothilde will have to poke her to get her attention," Jevon murmured.

"Heléne would be more interested in the game if she ever got to wear a pretty gown and play the princess," Constantia replied.

Clothilde, in her blue, embroidered kirtle, did indeed elbow her sister's side. Heléne dragged her gaze away from the squirrel and intoned her assigned line. "Only the bravest and strongest knight in all the land deserves the hand of a princess."

Etienne snickered at her humdrum chant, which made Heléne twinkle at him, lighting up her pointed, sallow face, but the beautiful Clothilde was too blissfully entranced in the game to notice either.

Constantia mouthed along as Clothilde clapped her hands to her breast and bade Therri, "My heart is true, Sir Knight. I pray you, do not let that villain carry me off! My father will reward you greatly—"

"—and you will win my abiding love."

Jevon's baritone joined Constantia's recitation. She glanced at him, expecting to catch another grin. Instead, a curious pink warmed his tanned cheeks.

His rich, acorn-brown eyes glanced away from her, back through the parted branches. "And now," he muttered, "Therri will say . . ." He paused, waiting for the manly roar at a ten-year-old boy's pitch, before repeating along with Therri, "Take that, you blackguard! And that and that!"

Therri "stabbed" Etienne three times. Etienne dropped his sword, clutched his breast, flung himself down with a great groan of pain, then rolled back and forth in the grass before he finally "died."

Tomorrow would be Etienne's turn to "slay" Therri. The boys alternated playing the hero. Today, Therri beamed in triumph.

Jevon let go of the branch he held. "Now Clothilde will pretend to dance with her rescuer while the boys ignore her and Heléne practices archery with an imaginary bow. They will be perfectly safe if we walk a little distance."

Constantia fell in step beside him, always happy for time alone with him. "It was kind of you to lend Heléne Therri's training bow and encourage Etienne to show her how to use it."

"It is safer for Etienne to teach her than me. If Lady Gwenllian caught me capitulating to Heléne's pleas, I'd never be able to crawl out of her disgrace, no matter how attentive I pretend to be when she gossips about our guests and neighbors."

"Has it been worth it?" Constantia asked. "Collecting coins from Llygad all these years to take his place at Lady Gwenllian's side?"

She would not use the insulting "Lady Gwenllian's lapdog" as Raimon and Franco had freely referred to Llygad before he bribed Jevon to trade places with him as his cousin's attendant squire. Jevon was too chivalrous to openly mock Llygad as the other squires did, even though he detested Llygad too.

"You must have raised enough from the allowance Llygad's uncle sends him to purchase a good portion of your tournament equipment by now," she added. She smiled bravely to mask her dread of the day he left Pennault.

He shrugged. "Not quite. If Laurant did not insist that I train daily with the others, Lady Gwenllian would never let me leave her side. I can only bear her prattle for so long, so when that chapman came to the castle last month, I bought a few trinkets from him to beguile her into allowing me a little time to myself."

Constantia could sympathize. "I know it is frustrating for you to sit at her side and hold her basket of threads while she embroiders when you would rather be practicing with your sword or lance or bow."

"It is her endless disparaging of anyone unfortunate enough to enjoy a night's hospitality from her husband that annoys me. They are not *all* nitwits, and none deserve to have their oddities and mannerisms ridiculed behind their backs to one of her husband's squires."

"Especially when that poor squire is forced to silently smile and nod as she does so." Constantia and Guia and Beatris did the same when Jevon was not available to attend the baroness.

"The monk who stayed with us a fortnight ago," Jevon said, "the one under a vow of silence. She still flaps her hands about in derision of his gestures."

Constantia remembered the holy guest who passed a few nights at Pennault on his way to his abbey.

"No matter how many times he did this"—she made an X with her forefingers, then dragged one of them across her cheek—"Lady Gwenllian insisted he only had an itch. Had you not unraveled the true meaning of his gesture, he'd have left us as distressed as when he arrived because his beard had begun to grow. None of his former hosts understood that his razor had broken and he wanted to borrow one to shave with before his abbot saw him again."

Jevon held his hand palm up and spread his fingers. "Do you remember this one?"

He made a scooping motion with his other hand from his palm to his mouth, then raised his brows. After the monk left Pennault, Jevon taught Constantia all the signs he'd learned. They'd turned them into a game when they waited upon Lady Gwenllian at meals, though from behind the high back of her chair. Constantia responded to his query, "What's for dinner?" by forming a fist with her thumb tucked inside, then wrapping her other hand around it.

"Pears?" Jevon asked.

She followed the sign by touching her tongue with her finger.

His face lit up. "With honey? I hope Sir Eudes leaves enough for his lady's squire to indulge in later." The dish was a favorite with both the gatekeeper and Jevon.

"I will try to save you some," Constantia said. "I'm practicing my table manners at dinner today. Guia will be serving Lady Gwenllian with you."

Jevon's expression fell. "Then I'm in for a dull time. Once, I whispered something that made Guia chuckle, and Lady Gwenllian glared at her. Now Guia will not even look at me while she holds the laver for Lady Gwenllian to rinse her hands between courses."

A twig caught in Constantia's skirt. She paused to shake it loose, but Jevon snatched it off before she could free it.

"I wish the other squires would take turns with me," he said glumly. "If I have to read Benoît's description of Briseida's golden beauty to Lady Gwenllian one more time—"

"Poor thing," Constantia cooed. "No wonder you were eager to fill the chapman's purse. What trinkets did you buy to persuade Lady Gwenllian to grant you an hour of peace?"

They resumed walking. "An embroidered fillet for her veils, a peacock feather tied with a silk ribbon, and a bronze, flower-shaped pendant. I could only afford one with glass for the petals, but it was the sapphire-blue that matches her eyes, so it still pleased her enough to let me spend an afternoon with you."

Constantia asked the same question she always did when he squandered his time away from the baroness with her and the children. "Wouldn't you rather spend your free time with Raimon and Franco?"

And he answered as he always did. "I see and hear enough of them every night while I watch them squander their coins at dice, then snore away in their beds."

The three young men shared a cramped chamber in one of Pennault's towers because Laurant did not want his squires reveling with his knights in the garrison until they were knighted as well.

Constantia's forehead crinkled. "How will you afford to go tourneying if you keep squandering Llygad's allowance on Lady Gwenllian?"

Jevon looked unconcerned. "Laurant is sure to change his mind once he knights us. The triumph of his knights in the tourney can only redound to his own reputation."

Jevon always used the plural when he spoke of his tournament ambitions, for he shared them with Raimon and Franco. Not with fumbling Llygad, though. Even if Llygad weren't so clumsy, Jevon would never forgive him for the names he called Constantia.

"Did you see how quickly I disarmed Sir Eudes yesterday? And Sir Baudri? And Sir Guilhem?"

It was not quite boasting. Jevon never boasted. But his chest did puff a little. A squire who could defeat the castle's best knights had a right to be just a little proud, didn't he?

"I will do the same on the tournament field. You will see."

He punctuated his crtainty with a slight upward thrust of his chin. Llygad mocked the cleft that lurked there, but to Constantia, the small indentation lent Jevon's face a quiet strength.

"No, I will not see it," she pointed out. "But I will hear of your fame. We all will, and Pennault will celebrate your victories, however far away you are."

Their feet crunched piles of amber and scarlet leaves as they strolled beneath a furrowed oak, its partially bereft branches gnarling up at a brisk blue sky. Jevon abruptly stopped.

"Stantia."

His glare whenever anyone else shortened her name ensured that his diminutive for her remained his alone. He did not immediately turn toward her, his earlier hesitance returning.

"I was wondering . . . You and I have been friends a long while, but sometimes . . . Well, lately I have been thinking . . . thinking about . . ."

He paused and drew a deep breath, then finally turned to face her. They both tucked their hands behind their backs, making her smile until he resumed his stammering.

"I-I suppose I should just come out with it. A few weeks ago while Beatris served Lady Gwenllian with me and you sat at one of the side tables between Sir Baudri and Sir Eudes and they were prating at you about who knows what, I looked down at you and . . . and realized that . . . that . . ."

His nervousness made *her* nervous. What could he possibly be trying to tell her that had him so unnaturally tongue-tied? She tried to break the tension gripping her stomach with a jest.

"Was this before or after you crossed your eyes at me over Lady Gwenllian's shoulder and nearly made me spew the wine I was drinking?"

He took up her quip with just a little too much playful relief. "It was after the third time you swiveled your head between the two knights and almost forgot which one you were smiling at and which one you were solicitously commiserating with."

She glowered at him. "Just wait until you are knighted and must sit at the table like the rest of us, enduring tedious conversations. Or no, you are a man, so you will be the one prattling at hapless women forced to listen meekly and mutely to your blather."

"I never blather," Jevon said.

"You are blathering now." She was not sure she wanted to know why, but since he would undoubtedly tell her eventually, waiting might be worse than forcing him to the point. "Jevon, what are you trying to tell me?"

He started to reach for her but jerked his hand back. Surely she only imagined the small beads of perspiration along his brow?

"Stantia . . . what I'm trying to say is—"

"Constantia!" A scrunch of hurried footsteps cut him off. Beatris rushed through dried leaves and withered grass to join them .

Constantia was not sure whether she was frustrated or glad of the intrusion. Jevon was acting so oddly!

Beatris paused to catch her breath. Constantia envied her buxom figure and the plump, pink cheeks that won her men's admiring gazes. Of Lady Gwenllian's three impoverished waiting ladies, surely Beatris was most likely to win a husband in spite of her fluttery nature. It was not that Constantia's seventeen-year-old body lacked curves, but she felt spindly next to Beatris. She hoped by the time *she* was eighteen . . . In spite of herself, her gaze slid to Jevon. Her chest panged again. But by that time, he would be gone.

Beatris snuffled. Constantia saw that the rims of her eyes were red. "What's happened?" she asked.

"Sybil is waiting to switch me." Beatris's dimpled hands crimped the lap of her skirt. "Lady Gwenllian asked me to fetch her father's brooch, but when I brought it, she discovered the clasp was broken and, of course, she blamed me rather than her own neglect, even though I *told* her it was loose the last time she wore it. Sybil was busy switching one of the page boys for some mischief or other, but she'll be done by the time I get back. In the meantime, Lady Gwenllian told me to find you and the children and bring you back to the keep."

"Why?"

"Because Lady Clothilde will soon turn twelve, and her mother says she must cease playing childish games."

Jevon interjected. "I heard Laurant tell Sir Eudes he does not want to marry his daughter off before she is at least fifteen."

Beatris pursed her pretty lips. "But it is not too soon for Lady Gwenllian to start thinking about potential marriage partners for her. Lady Clothilde will soon be of an age to dine on the dais, so Lady Gwenllian says she must stop romping about like a hoyden."

"But just this morning," Constantia protested, "I asked if I could take the children to play in the woods, including Lady Clothilde. Lady Gwenllian replied—"

"Whatever she replied," Beatris said, "she either does not remember or does not care. For goodness' sake, Constantia, you know what she is like!"

Yes, Constantia did.

"Very well. Jevon, will you go call them for me?" She slipped her arm around Beatris's waist. "When we get back, I will send Clothilde to distract Sybil. Sybil dotes on Clo and won't interrupt her chatter to switch you. And I will make Therri go up and confess to his mother that he's the one who broke the clasp on her brooch. He's been fascinated with the jeweled dragon ever since Lady Gwenllian's father sent it to her. I caught him taking it off her cloak just a few days ago. I made him pin it right back on, but I suspect it is not the first time he's removed it. He probably used it to play knights and dragon with the little wooden knights Jevon carved for him."

Jevon had started for the clearing but remained sufficiently within earshot to toss a repentant look at Constantia over his shoulder, even though they knew Laurant would not allow Therri, his only son and heir, to be switched by Sybil. Constantia was glad it was not Heléne who had fallen into mischief this time. The second daughter's relative lack of importance in the family left her more vulnerable to her mother's temper.

"Thank you," Beatris breathed. "If you want me to, I'll trade places with you on the dais today so you can stand with Jevon. I'm sure Lady Gwenllian will agree that I need more practice at the table. I dropped my spoon in my lap and stained my gown with soup on Saturday, and she called me a clumsy ninny."

"Then I must thank *you*," Constantia said as she and Beatris started for the castle. "Sir Baudri and Sir Guilhem left me nearly bored to tears last time." In spite of Jevon's silly grimaces at her.

Why had he acted so oddly all day? Maybe she could coax him to whisper whatever Beatris had interrupted while Lady Gwenllian twaddled her latest gossip into her husband's adoring ear during dinner. It was easy to engage in furtive exchanges with Jevon when they stood together behind the baroness's chair, waiting for Lady Gwenllian to ask Constantia to bring the laver of rose-scented water to rinse her hands or Jevon to refill her goblet from the decorative stand on the dais.

Or perhaps it would be better to keep Jevon silent and distracted with a game of *What will they choose?* using the monk's hand gestures to guess the diners' choices from the trays the servants brought them. Any subject that broke sweat across his brow and made him stammer like a man in the grip of a fever could not possibly be something she wanted to hear.

AUGUST 1174
VERE CASTLE

"Constantia."

The voice pulled her back to awareness. It seemed to come from the weight that pinned her down.

"Lady Constantia, are you hurt?"

Hurt? Her forehead throbbed too ruthlessly to be a dream. She spat out a mouthful of musty gravel. No nightmare tasted this foul. The weight that covered her, hard yet pliant—a body?—smelled of salt, sweat, and, curiously, fear.

His? Or mine?

"Triston?"

"Stay down. It isn't over yet."

As though she could move with him lying atop her. Yet his solidity brought her comfort, for the ground still shifted disconcertingly.

"What is happening?" A crash roared in answer through her ringing ears, the sound now horrifyingly familiar. How could the English possibly have maneuvered their siege engines through the woods?

"Just stay down," Triston said. "If the saints are kind, the wall and tower will continue to fall outward, toward the trees, instead of on top of us."

Outward? The wall in the foreyard had fallen inward when the boulders broke through. As devastating as that destruction had been, it had not caused the earth to shake and shake like this. Constantia slowly began to understand. This was not the work of an English siege engine hurling massive missiles until they broke a hole through the wall. This was something more devious, more horrifying because when done cunningly enough, the castle did not see it coming.

Mining. She had heard the baron's men speak of it, men burrowing through the earth like moles, digging tunnels directly under a castle's walls. Once beneath a tower's corner, the miners dug a chamber supported by wooden beams, filled it with brushwood, set it on fire, then ran for their lives as the flames destroyed the beams and collapsed the tower into the empty cavern, dragging the attached wall down with it. No wonder they had appeared to be dropping straight into the earth!

The empty gray haze that engulfed her might have been permanent had the masonry not fallen away from her and Triston. She realized he had covered her with his own body to protect her in case the Fates had chosen differently. His courage and chivalry stole her shivering breath. She must thank him if the ground ever stopped quaking.

Eventually the tremors slowed and the roaring dulled to a rumble. Triston lifted himself off her and helped her to sit up. Where a soaring square tower once stood, only a heap of rubble spewed into the woods behind the castle. Some trees lay snapped like twigs between the burly, broken stones, but a few of the most ancient oaks survived the onslaught with only dents in their massive trunks.

"Are you hurt?" Triston asked again. He stared as though transfixed by the chilling void of tower and wall.

She must have hit her head in the fall. "My temple aches, but it is nothing"—her voice broke, then resumed with a quaver—"*nothing* to what we might have suffered."

We could both be dead.

He grabbed her hand and pulled her up with him. A fine dust coated his hair and the back of his clothes, turning both almost white. She was merely covered with gray-brown dirt from the bailey.

"The English will be pouring through there soon," he said grimly. "They will already be in the foreyard by now. Vere is lost."

His bleak admission roused her from her shock. A sense of fiery urgency flowed through her. "I must warn Lord Laurant!"

"All you will do is run straight into the arms of the English if you try to go through there." Triston nodded at the deceptive lure of an escape through the void. "Come"—he took her arm again—"we must join in surrender and pray the English will prove as merciful as the saints were to us this day."

The earthshaking collapse of the tower and wall must have been heard and felt all the way to the foreyard, but the knights of Vere had not yet conceded as Triston predicted. Constantia identified the English knights by the blue surcotes they wore over their mail, the men-at-arms by the badges of blue and silver that flashed from the shoulders of their leather gambesons. Helmets concealed the blue knights' faces, giving them an advantage against the green-clad knights of Vere, many of whom, not expecting the castle to fall so swiftly, had not donned their helms before the enemy broke in.

"They will push toward the keep," Triston muttered. "You'll not be able to safely reach the entrance now. Stay as far away from the battle as possible. If they seize you, tell them you are Lady Constantia de Ormande of Pennault Castle. They will consider you too valuable to harm. Likely, they will take you hostage and try to use you to negotiate Pennault's surrender. You chose an ill time to visit us, but perhaps your misfortune will prove Pennault's deliverance."

However inevitable Vere's defeat, Triston felt obligated to join its defense. He drew his sword and charged into the fray.

If Triston knew her better, he would realize how misguided his counsel was. Laurant would never surrender Pennault for Constantia. Despite her title, she was as poor as a pauper with four sisters in the line of succession to their father before her. She'd had no communication with her sire since the day he gave her into the baron's care fifteen years ago. Her father was unlikely to care whether the English took her prisoner or not, therefore, neither would the baron.

Over the shouts of the battle and the clash of steel rose a high-pitched keening. A woman knelt beside a green-clad knight. She must have been trapped in one of the outbuildings—the laundry or well-house or stable—when the assault broke through. Now she grieved over the fallen man. A chill ran up Constantia's spine. How many more men would die this day?

An idea came to her. More of Vere's defenders lay strewn about the yard. They deserved mourners too. If she inched close enough to the broken wall, perhaps she could pick her way through the rubble unnoticed while the English fought to reach the keep and Vere's remaining knights strove to block them.

She pulled the hood of her cloak over her head, crooked her back, and shuffled forward, feigning the aspect of a slow and doddering old woman so that no one among the enemy perceived her as a threat. She wobbled from one sprawled, green-garbed knight to another, each with the gilded rose of the de Brielle house sewn to his shoulder. Some were bleeding, all were stunned or unconscious, but to her relief, all still breathed. She wailed over each one, her voice cracking in imitation of an ancient crone overwhelmed with anguish. As she sent up her laments, the war continued. Why had the knights of Vere not retreated inside the formidable stronghold of the keep, where they might hold off the enemy for weeks or even months if they had enough supplies and hope for relief from friends, like the lords of Pennault and Belle Noir?

She finally understood when she glanced up and saw two men battling atop a jagged remnant of the wall whose gap she surreptitiously hobbled toward. Sir Damien lunged and thrust his sword at a helmed blue knight who parried and counterthrust. A fragment of a broken stone, loosened by the sharp movement of their feet, tumbled over the side into the yard. No wonder the knights continued to fight. None of Vere's men would withdraw to the keep without the lord of the castle.

Constantia shuffled to the next wounded man. He moaned, rolled his head, blinked open dazed-looking eyes, then closed them again. His wits would be scattered for a while, judging by the lump on his head—she commiserated with him—but she saw no sword tears in his tunic, no blood-stains. She moved on. With the battle increasingly clustered near the keep, the path to the gap in the wall lay clear. Only a few more yards.

A harrowing scream bolted her upright. Sir Damien pitched from the wall, sword flying, arms and legs flailing. He hit the ground with a bone-shattering crunch that reverberated through Constantia's body even though she stood too far away to actually hear it.

Every man in the yard, green and blue alike, whirled to stare at Vere Castle's ill-fated lord. Constantia's stomach heaved. Sir Damien could not possibly have survived such a fall! But in the same instance as hatred for these murderous Englishmen choked her, she recognized opportunity. No one watched her. Now was her chance.

She picked up a sword some knight had lost in the skirmish, tucked it beneath her cloak, and quickened her steps towards the unguarded gap. The way through was not easy. Ragged edges of broken stones snatched her skirts and ripped the cloth when she pulled it free, but the flood of English who had poured over the fragments had pressed them down, making a rough but semi-stable, navigable pathway. The moat sloshed on either side of her, but the damming stones from the wall had flung much of the water over its banks, lowering the remaining water level and turning the open field where the mangon stood to mud.

The demonic siege engine looked deceptively innocent with its long wooden arm idly reclining, ropes slack, the huge wooden cup that hurled its infernal stones of destruction as empty and harmless as a giant spoon waiting to be dipped in an enormous bowl of soup. The handful of men-at-arms standing around some supply wagons and a depleted pile of hurling stones were more dangerous to her. Two were armed with bows, not the powerful but slow-loading crossbows but lithe, flexible war bows, the sort that could loose a dozen arrows at her before she counted to three.

At the moment, the men appeared distracted by an argument between an archer with a ginger beard and a burly, balding man with a sheathed sword. They pointed over one another's shoulders, at cross-opinions about something. Whatever it was, it held the other men's attention, but a single glance toward the gap would betray her. She stepped cautiously onto the mud and felt her slippers sink into the sludge. She could not stand here until they saw her. But which way to flee?

The road lay to her left, the direction of the burly man's finger, but they would easily see her there. To her right lay the vastness of the woods, where the ginger-bearded archer pointed, but Triston was right. English troops must have lain in wait in the trees, watching to see if the mining efforts succeeded, ready to swoop into the castle's rear yard if it did. But she had no other choice. Pray heaven the English would be so fixed on the collapsed corner that she could flank them on the south without them knowing she was there.

She moved to her right, raising and lowering her feet sticky-honey slow to minimize the sucking sound the mud made each time she took a step, until the ground gradually firmed. The woods' proximity truncated the moat on this side, so it had not spilled out as much water. The men by the wagons still argued. Ignoring her cold, slimy, pebble-filled slippers, she quickened her pace.

"Stop her!"

The blue-surcoted man who still stood atop the damaged wall where he had fought—and murdered!—Sir Damien pointed straight at Constantia. The men by the wagons all spun toward her. The ginger-bearded man's companion raised his bow.

She sprinted for the trees as though the hounds of hell were at her heels, expecting the sting of an arrow between her shoulder blades. The archer must have had second thoughts, for she reached the edge of the woods unscathed. But she heard the English devils shouting and their feet pounding after her.

Constantia prayed as she had never prayed before as she plunged between two towering oaks. "Please . . ." she tore around an ash tree " . . . carry me safely . . ." she swerved beneath a beech's verdant canopy ". . . to Pennault."

Her billowing cloak caught on the limbs of a sapling elm, snapping her into its branches. She frantically untied the strings and flew on without it, swiveling to change her direction. She whipped and wound her way through the dappled shadows that splayed across the forest floor until her chest began to burn. A stitch of pain stabbed her side. Fearful of betraying her location with her rasping gasps, she gritted her teeth, pulling breath after desperate breath through her nose.

She did not know how long she ran, zigging and zagging to lose her pursuers, ignoring the dull throb in her temple and the stinging pebbles inside her slippers. Her one advantage was that she knew these woods with an intimacy the English could not. Surely at some point they would give up and go back to Vere? She sped on until tiny sparks of light flickered across her dimming vision. Even then, she feared to stop until she stumbled over an unseen root and pitched into a nearby oak.

The impact briefly knocked the remaining breath from her. She splayed her arms across the oak's wide, ancient trunk and turned her face to the roughened bark to try to hide her ragged attempts to refill her aching lungs. Lines and arcs danced before her blurring eyes. At first she thought them blemishes left by errant arrows of endless hunts through these trees. But as her breathing slowed, her vision cleared, revealing a distinctive C traced into the bark. A vertical stroke slashed it in half, the upper line topped with a short crossbar, the lower half curling like a hook just below the C. She cursed the rent the interlocking J slit through her breast. That part of her life was dead, as he no doubt was by now.

The initials, tormenting as they were, helped reorient her to her position in the woods. She could not save him. But she could save Pennault and all those within if she could only outwit her English pursuers. She grew up in these woods. She knew its paths better than any English soldier or Norman mercenary, the only sort of men who would join the English ranks to battle the hot-blooded, freedom-loving barons of Poitou. She hoped they had ceased the chase, but she could not be certain. She had to press forward by the most circuitous route possible, just in case.

Her urgency helped force *him* back into that pocket of her mind where she kept his memory locked up tightly. Remembering always threatened to cripple her. She left the oak—scarred like her heart—with determined steps. It might be dusk before she reached Pennault, but she could not maintain her former pace without collapsing at her pursuers' feet. A slower but quieter pace would allow her to regain her energy and make it harder for the English to track her than continuing to crash through the dry, crumbling debris of the forest floor. She guessed the English would not abandon a castle they'd conquered mere hours ago to begin an assault on a new target. Even with Sir Damien's death—she flinched at the word—the English would require a few days to ensure they stamped out every last flicker of rebellion amongst Vere's garrison.

Her pulse jumped at a faint rustling nearby. She darted behind a broad-trunked elm, tightening her grip on the sword she had taken from Vere's yard. Someone slipped, quicksilver nimble, between the trees. Tall, short red tunic, long pale hair . . .

"Llygad?" She called the name without thinking.

The man paused and turned to look at her.

Fool! Those delicately pretty features did not belong to the baroness's cousin. The stranger's small, full mouth curled at the corners as his pale-blue gaze raked over her with a sensuous scrutiny that made the hairs soar on the back of her arms. She held up the sword to warn him off, but he vanished so suddenly she wondered whether she had even seen him.

She stood for several moments, too unnerved to move, ears pricked for his return or sounds of her pursuers. Reassuring silence stretched. Should she strike out in yet another direction? That would delay her arrival at Pennault past dark and without a lantern, place her at risk not only to the English but to the quicksilver stranger. She found little comfort in knowing he did not serve the English, else he would have seized her. His lewd gaze pimpled her skin anew. Was he an outlaw seeking shelter here, plundering hapless wanderers and ravishing unaccompanied women? Not all fugitives were as honorable as the man who had carved their initials in the tree.

An honorable thief. The contradiction almost drew a bitter laugh from her. She thought she knew him as well as she knew herself, but she never truly knew him at all.

She emptied the pebbles from her slippers, then rubbed her bruised temple. She had spent hours among these trees in the daylight, tending the baron's children at play during their childhood years, but she'd always shepherded them safely home before dark. Risking a night alone surrounded by predators, whether feral animals or lecherous lawbreakers, even with a sword, suddenly outweighed her fear of being captured by the English.

She moved with quickened steps directly toward Pennault, triply urgent now to reach the safety of the castle walls. A twig snapped some distance behind her. Perhaps it was nothing more than a deer, but she quickened her pace. A crackle of leaves spurred her into a trot.

Scrunch. Scrunch. Scrunch.

Footsteps. The kind only a man made. His gait sounded long-legged and forceful. Determined. The bestial stranger stalked her!

Constantia tore into another frenzied run, one hand wrapped tightly around the sword's hilt, the other hugging the blade so it could do no harm should a misstep cause her to fall. A swift scudding confirmed the hunter had found his prey. She swerved in and out of the trees again, hoping to shake him off her trail, but his stubborn tramping pounded in her wake. A lump of terror lodged in her throat, threatening to choke off what little air she could still drag in through the burn that spread through her chest again.

"Stop!" a man shouted.

English or quicksilver stranger, she dared not obey. She hurtled straight through the clearing where the children of Pennault and Vere once played together, emerging into a thicket of shaggy bushes. Surely she could lose him here.

"I said stop!"

She snaked through the close-grown shrubs, then sprinted when the space between the shrubs widened again.

"Last warning!"

It did not sound as though she had so much as slowed him down.

She ducked under a low-hanging branch, skidded past a gray-barked ash, and twisted through several sharp, random turns. Her breath scraped in such loud rasps it began to drown out his pursuit. Her gasps would keep him on her heels no matter how pell-mell she ran. When black spots swam across her vision, she knew she could run no farther.

Her only option was the sword. She had no training, but perhaps the sight of a woman pointing the weapon at his breast would startle him long enough to allow her to catch a few breaths. If necessary—she shuddered— she could seize on his surprise and shove the blade through his heart. She must show no mercy, for she knew from the way he'd looked at her that he would show her none.

She whirled, whipping out the sword and leveling it at where she last heard the dogged footsteps. All she saw were trees, their thick trunks swaying with her winded exhaustion. She shifted backward until she felt the reassuring protection of an expansive oak behind her. Slowly both her breath and vision steadied. She probed the shaded depths between the trees around her. Where was he? Could she have lost him in her twisting, turning flight after all?

The woods regained their solid majesty. The shadows were deepening. The afternoon was slipping away, renewing her desperation to do the same. She sought to reorient herself. Now that her heartbeat no longer drummed in her ears, she heard the faint babbling of a stream to her left. If she followed the sound, she would emerge into sunlight mottling the forest floor. From there she could identify the landmarks that pointed her to the sloped green hill where Pennault Castle stood.

This time, she kept the sword at the ready as she stepped away from the oak. Something whizzed above her head. The hair on her scalp hummed, the arrow sang so close, before it sailed into the trunk behind her.

"Stay where you are, my lady."

The harsh voice drew her gaze up to the branches of another oak a few yards away. A man stood on one of the lower limbs, half hidden in the leaves above her. All she could see of him were his leather boots and a pair of strongly muscled calves encased in buff-colored hose. The rest blended into the brown of the branches and green of the leaves. No glimpse of red—the color the stranger wore—or blue, the color of the English, peeked through. What she did see, very clearly, was the pointed steel broadhead of an arrow aimed at her.

"Drop the sword." His voice lashed across the distance between them with as much pity as a whip.

She reluctantly obeyed. The sword was of no use against an arrow. His knees bent slowly, then he sprang from the limb, landing on the forest floor with feline precision.

His bow, gripped by hands sheathed in leather gloves with the fingers cut off above the knuckles, remained deadly in its continued aim. Strong, taut muscles strained at the sleeves of his gambeson. His cloak was tossed over one shoulder, exposing the badge of the silver stallion on a field of blue. He was one of the English after all—one of the archers she had seen beside the wagons.

She may be a prisoner, but she was still a proud Poitevin. She lifted her chin in defiance of her captor's glare, walnut brown and just as implacable as that nut's shell. Waves of russet hair flowed over his ears and halfway down the back of his neck. A memory washed through her of a man with hair and eyes just like his, only generous, good-humored, and kind—a man who'd once shared her every thought, knew every beat of her heart, and carved their initials in a tree, interlocked as he'd promised their lives would be just as soon as he . . .

Her eyes widened.

It could not be him. He had left her a clean-shaven young man just shy of his twenty-first year. This man wore a well-trimmed beard but appeared the right age for a seven-year absence. Did that beard conceal the cleft she adored? It did not hide the square, straightforward cut of his jaw or the shape of his lips, now drawn as tight as his bowstring, lips which had once been so quick to laugh and so delicious to kiss.

"Jevon?" She took an impulsive step forward.

"Stay where you are."

His words, like water iced by a winter storm, doused her into stillness, but she knew his voice. She had thought him lost to her, perhaps dead. How could he stand there, glowering as though he had never seen her?

"Do you not know me?" she asked. Had she changed so much? She had been a seventeen-year-old girl when they kissed in these woods. Now she was four-and-twenty.

"I know you perfectly well *now*, Constantia," he replied in that same voice that cut like the lash. "The question is how I was ever so blind to think I loved you."

Jevon steeled himself against the shock on Constantia's sun-tinged face. The loose braid he'd glimpsed as she fled had come riotously undone. The day he'd kissed her, her rippling hair had scattered around her shoulders like a thousand rebellious serpents—just as they did now— serpents that tumbled docilely around his hands as he'd cupped her cheeks to raise her mouth to his. He dreamed of those sinuous locks almost as often as he reluctantly dreamed of that kiss through the years. But those dreams had not softened his heart against her betrayal. Nor would they prevent him from doing his duty.

"Walk. That way." He indicated the direction with his arrow's broadhead, keeping his voice flat and his bowstring taut.

She stared at him. Dirt smudged her cheeks, and so much gray-brown dust filmed the front of her gown that he could no longer tell its color. But although the sun had begun to sink behind the trees, there was still enough light to set a seductive glitter to the gilt flecks in her forest-green eyes.

"Where are you taking me?" She sounded breathless. From their head-long race through the woods? Or from astonishment that he confronted her coldly rather than falling like a besotted slave at her feet?

"Back to Vere Castle."

Her gaze fell to the badge sewn to his shoulder. "You serve the English earl? How? Why? Jevon, where have you been all these years?"

Her gaze swept back to his face. His chest inexplicably constricted at the sudden tears that sheened her eyes like woodland leaves after a summer's rain.

He forced the painful memories to stiffen his resistance. "Surprised I eluded capture by our neighbors for the price the baron placed on my head?"

Constantia's fist curled into her dirt-stained bodice as though his still-poised arrow had just pierced it. "How can you ask me that? I have done nothing but pray for your safety and weep for fear that some lord would see the mark of guilt on your hand."

"You mean this?" Jevon risked lowering his bow. He kept two fingers wrapped around the arrow's shaft and his fist on the grip while he used his teeth to pull the glove off his freed left hand. He turned the back of his hand to her.

Her cheeks blanched. "What did you do?"

He laughed, a harsh crack of anger and irony against the forest air. She feigned shock well, but he was no longer a moonstruck boy. He tucked the glove into his belt, repositioned the arrow so that it pointed straight at her brow, and said, "Move."

She stared at the stiff, waxy pink scars on his bared left hand. The added level of disfigurement had come at an almost unbearable cost, but it had kept him alive.

She pretended to shake off her distress and straightened with that proud lift of her head that defied her humble position as a forgotten and dowerless daughter. Or had that changed too? He glanced at her finger for a wedding ring, but she had tucked her left hand into the folds of her skirts.

"I am sorry for what Lord Laurant did to you," she said. "Had I known what would happen, I would never have spoken regardless of your guilt. But I saw what your devil lord did to Vere. He is coming after Pennault next, isn't he? You must let me warn the baron so he can prepare to repulse the attack before he ends up like poor Sir Damien."

"I cannot let you do that, Stantia." The once-affectionate diminutive of her name rolled off his tongue before he could catch it.

The slip lit a spark of hope in her eyes. "I do not blame you for hating Laurant for—that." She jutted her chin toward the scars on his hand. "If it were only him, I would not ask this of you. But his family does not deserve to suffer this terror with him. Let me go. Please."

"No."

Her chin tilted up another defiant notch. "Then you will have to loose that arrow at my heart, for that is the only way you will stop me."

She started to turn so she could round the oak tree. Jevon lowered his aim and loosed the arrow. It landed an inch from her toe, its shaft quivering in warning.

"The next one goes straight through your foot. I do not have to kill you, Stantia. But I would not test my willingness to disable you."

She stared at him as though *she* were the one betrayed by *him*.

He nocked another arrow. "Pick up the sword." Even if she knew how to wield that blade, his arrow would strike her before she could reach him.

She chewed her lower lip for a pensive moment before obeying.

"Now, hand it to me hilt first." He lowered his bow just long enough to tuck the sword into his belt. "Let's go."

They trudged through the trees in silence for some time. Jevon did not have to bark directions. She knew the path to Vere and she knew that *he* knew the path, so it would be useless to try to mislead him as she had her other pursuers. Neither the English troops nor the mercenaries the earl hired in Normandy knew their way about these woods. But Jevon, like Constantia, had passed his childhood and youth at Pennault. He had easily followed her flight through the trees, spurred by the promise of a royal pardon for past offenses if he proved worthy and loyal on this royal-commissioned campaign through Poitou. Jevon dreamed of restoring his good name—even if it was the false one he had given the English earl—almost as often as he had dreamed of Constantia through the years.

He walked a few steps behind her, trusting her memory of his drawn bow to work on her mind while he let his bowstring go lax and lowered the weapon to his side. He could whip it and its arrow back into position in an instant if needed. As a mercenary archer, the lords of Normandy, Brittany, and France paid him handsomely for his falcon-like vision and the speed and precision of his arrows. But he had never loosed his shafts at a woman. He hoped Constantia would not force him to choose between the chivalry of his youth and the ruthless demands survival exacted on him.

Gradually the shadows lengthened and the warm summer air began to cool.

"Is it your intent to march me through the night?" Her voice grated, as though spoken through clenched teeth.

She had led him far afield through the woods before he caught her. She was right. They would not reach Vere Castle before the last rays of daylight snuffed out.

"Start gathering wood," he said. "The clearing is not far. We can build a fire and pass the night there."

She paused to grab up a dry tree branch from the forest floor. "So now I am your servant as well as your prisoner?" She tossed the words over her shoulder with a distinctive sting.

"You brought this on yourself."

A small qualm chided him for his spite. She may well deserve his contempt, but no matter how much Lady Gwenllian had treated Constantia like a drudge, she was as nobly born as her mistress. He should be the one gathering wood, not she. He forced the chivalrous thought away. Constantia was far too clever not to take advantage of such misguided gallantry. She would fly from him like a loosed arrow while his arms were full, and it would not be so easy to follow her in the dusk. She proved herself faithless seven years ago. He doubted her nature had changed, though her charms had certainly blossomed in the interval. A glowing, curvaceous woman had replaced the winsome girl he'd left behind.

He crushed temptation beneath a ruthless heel in his mind. "Include some twigs for kindling."

She fumbled with her growing bundle of disparately sized sticks. "If my hands are full of twigs, I cannot pick up any more wood." She sounded huffy and exasperated.

"If the nights no longer grow cold this time of year, then by all means, ignore my advice."

A mutter followed by a *hmph* floated back to him. She squatted to balance the wood on one knee as she scrabbled around for twigs. She almost lost her balance when she tried to stand, wobbling precariously to one side. Instinctively, he scooped his palm beneath her elbow to steady her. Her gasp and the befuddling charge the innocuous touch chased through him made him pull her up more sharply than planned. She lurched straight back into him, burying his face in what felt like a mass of coarse, knotted ropes that smelled an odd jumble of acrid smoke, musty earth, and invigorating greenwood.

The latter scent, fresher than the others, washed him in sensations that almost drew his lips to the smooth skin where her neck lay exposed through her tangled hair.

He released her and stepped back, grinding the lure to dust under his imaginary but determined boot. He raised his bow as she turned to face him, her lips softly parted like during that hopeful, terrifying moment after he'd declared his love for her.

Love. What a cruel jest fate played on men who duped themselves into thinking that word meant anything to women.

He nudged the air with his re-nocked arrow, indicating for her to resume their path. "We're almost there."

His voice sounded thick in his ears. Did she hear it?

She hefted her bundle to rearrange the weight, then turned and walked ahead without a word.

It was almost fully dark by the time they reached the clearing. Jevon had been too intent on catching Constantia to take stock of his surroundings when he chased her through here earlier. Now the light was too dim to see much beyond the shadow of a tree stump at the center. Was it still covered with soft, spongy moss? If he listened closely, would he still hear the echo of children's laughter?

A clatter startled him back to the present. Constantia had dropped the sticks and kindling next to the stump. She planted her hands on her hips. He was certain she glared at him.

"I suppose you expect me to set the fire too?"

She may be a faithless wench, but she was as audacious as ever. "Do you have a tinderbox?"

"Why would I have a tinderbox when I expected to be back at Pennault in time for supper?"

"Fortunately for us, I always carry one since I rarely know what sort of shelter I will find, if any, when the sun falls."

Jevon had spent months evading capture and death in these woods. From the first, men had hunted him for the bounty the baron placed on his head, one hundred livres if Jevon were caught within the borders of Poitou. Men he knew, brave knights he'd hoped to one day emulate, stalked him for the silver. Yet Jevon had lingered here because, despite Constantia's duplicity, like a fool, he'd still loved her. It had been the mysterious Brown Hoods who finally drove him over the border of Brittany. The umber-cloaked and hooded men had pursued Jevon with a stealth and tenacity that still raised the hairs on his arms.

Even though he'd escaped the threat, the mark on his hand still carried danger. No matter how many lies he told to try to conceal his identity, his constantly gloved hands eventually drew suspicion. Safer to sleep in woods or fields or alleys than accept an invitation of hospitality even to a peasant's hut. All because of her.

Mustering those memories made it easier to make another unchivalrous though practical demand. "Turn around."

"Why?" she said.

"So I can tie your hands."

Her fists fell to her sides. "Jevon!"

"I have to set down my bow to light the fire, and I cannot trust you not to bolt. Turn around, Stantia."

She resisted for a moment, then, perhaps recalling the arrow shaft near her toe, turned around.

A tinder box was not the only thing Jevon carried with him. In addition to his arrow bag, money pouch, and flask, a second pouch at his belt held such useful items as a needle and thread; dried meat, fruit, beans and nuts, a few useful herbs, including sage to soothe the itching from his gloves, and a length of rope.

He pulled her wrists behind her back before wrapping the cord around them and felt her flinch when he inadvertently jerked the knot too tight. He ran his thumb over her tender skin in apology, throttling the same hum of pleasure that charged through him when he'd been so near her hair. He retied the knot, then once again cupped her elbow to balance her as he seated her on the tree stump.

Once she was settled, he placed the sword beside his bow on the ground, then scuffed his boots across the earth to form a safe patch for a fire, clearing the leaves and other debris mantling the well-trampled grass. Fortunately for his arrowshots today, yesterday's wind had died down.

"What has happened to you, Jevon?" she asked as he knelt to pile some of the sticks together and tucked kindling between them. "How can you treat me like this?"

"How could I—?" She had the gall to ask him that question? "*You* happened to me, Stantia. If you are shocked by what I have become, look in one of Lady Gwenllian's mirrors."

"Me?" She sounded genuinely shocked. The trickster.

He curled his lip. "Who told Lady Gwenllian I stole her brooch?"

"I never said you stole it. Never!"

"But you told Lady Gwenllian I took it without her permission, which was the same thing."

"She was so angry when she found it gone. You remember how she is. Someone always suffers when she loses her temper. She threatened to switch all three of us, me and Guia and Beatris, because she thought we were the only ones who knew where she kept the key to her jewelry casket. Poor Guia had already been switched twice that week, so I told Lady Gwenllian I saw you with her brooch in the yard, but I told her you only took it to repair the clasp. It never occurred to me you were lying and meant to sell the brooch."

Jevon's neck surged with heat even before he set fire to the kindling. "It was not a lie, and I did not sell it. My only sin was stopping to show it to you before I took it to the smithy."

"But, Jevon"—Constantia's voice quavered—"I saw the silver when they poured it out of your purse. You never had so much money in all the years I knew you! Where did it come from, if not the brooch?"

Laurant had not believed Jevon's reply when the baron asked him the same question. Nor had Lady Gwenllian. Nor the baron's council when he summoned them to judge Jevon's crime. The only man who could corroborate Jevon's story had left the castle before the brooch went missing. Jevon could not prove his innocence then or now. Unfortunately, everyone had taken Constantia's word as evidence of his guilt.

"They never found it?" he asked. He began working the flint and steel over the tinder in its rough wooden box.

"The brooch? Of course not."

Would she tell him the truth if they had? He had misjudged her from the day they met—her responsive smiles, the camaraderie between them, the way their thoughts seemed as reflective as an image in a lake.

He rubbed the back of his hand across his mouth, trying once again to erase the sweet kiss that, in spite of all the years, stubbornly lingered there. He had been a fool to believe her. He'd thought her true affection his alone despite the kind way she treated all the squires, even Lady Gwenllian's churlish cousin. But that day in the woods, she had given him good cause to believe her friendship, like his, had turned to love.

Why mock him so when he had never seen her mock anyone? But perhaps she'd derided them all when alone with Beatris and Guia. More than one beauty had betrayed Jevon during his mercenary years. Those provocatively enticing women were eager to heal his wounded heart until they saw the scars on his hand. Then they accused him of seduction or worse and agitated their menfolk into driving him off like a wolf caught ravaging the sheepfold. Only the protection of his mercenary band allowed him to escape a bloody fate until he learned his lesson: attempting to forget Constantia by dallying with equally shallow, manipulative wenches was not worth risking life and limb.

"So," he turned the subject—there was not much point in continuing their cross-accusations—"you and Raimon are now . . . ?"

He trailed off, giving her space to finish the phrase.

"Are what?" she asked.

He hesitated, then shrugged. "I overheard you both on your way to Vere. He asked you to go tourneying with him."

Jevon had considered Raimon and Franco, the two squires he'd shared a bedchamber with, closer than his own brothers. He could not ignore a stab of envy that Raimon was on the brink of fulfilling the dream the three had shared.

"You heard us?" Constantia said. "How?"

"I was sent to spy out Vere Castle before our army attacked. I watched you from the trees as you rode past yesterday. Raimon said, 'Our love will resound through the ages.'" Jevon forced the words out past the distaste in his mouth, trying to sound as neutral as he could.

The tinder caught during her pause.

Her voice sounded smaller when she answered. "I do not love Raimon, Jevon. I have never loved anyone but you."

Her lie should have curled his lip in scorn, but something about its quality curled it between his teeth instead. *Fool. I do not know what she wanted from me then, but I know what she wants from me now. To free her. Do not be taken in by her poignant tone.*

He touched a twig of kindling to the smoldering piece of hemp in the tinder box. "You must be married or betrothed by now. Love has little enough to do with that."

He felt her hesitation as he used the twig to light a series of small flames amongst the kindling in his assembled woodpile.

"Lady Gwenllian wants Llygad to marry me," she finally confessed. "But there can be nothing formal until my father agrees."

Jevon glanced up in surprise. "You said your father would never dower you."

Her face remained in shadow. "I never thought he would. I thought certain Lady Gwenllian would force me to marry some fat old widower or let me languish as a singlewoman. But my brother died last year, and my stepmother is too old to bear my father another heir. Lady Gwenllian has taken it into her head that she, or rather Llygad, can convince my father to bequeath his lands and fortune to me instead of my eldest sister. But Father is dragging his feet with his decision. He told Lord Laurant when the baron agreed to foster me that I should have no more than my mother's fifth-best necklace and fifth-best ring as a dowry. I showed them to you, remember? They were nothing more than chrysolite set in brass."

Constantia had been at Pennault a year, ten-years-old to his thirteen, when she showed him the jewelry and told him of her father's humiliating words. Her pitiful endowment was exactly what had lured Jevon into selling the only valuable item he ever possessed to try to win her hand.

"But now Lady Gwenllian views me as a prospective bride for Llygad if he can convince my father that marrying a baron's kin-by-marriage is worth declaring me his new heir before my sisters."

Jevon remembered her father, a hulking man in a fur-trimmed hat and thick, bristling beard that appeared to flow into one another like the pelt of a bear. Jevon had just knocked down the baroness's arrogant but clumsy cousin, Llygad ap Dafydd, on the training field when Sir Enguerran de Ormande rode into the yard on a huge bay, accompanied by his nine-year-old daughter on a diminutive pony. Laurant called Jevon to help the Lady Constantia dismount while her father conducted his business with the baron.

Constantia had looked frightened, lost, and fragile in a pretty, green gown designed more to impress the baron and his wife than fit her slender figure. The grown-ups talked over her head as though she were simply a package being delivered. Recalling his own first day at the castle, Jevon had impulsively given her an encouraging smile. Her grateful grin cemented their friendship before he even knew her name.

"I should think your father eager to ally his house with the baron's." Jevon poked the fire with the sword to encourage the flames.

"That is what Lady Gwenllian says. She is always sending Llygad to negotiate with my father, but Father only sends Llygad back, promising to think about it. I presume he does not want to offend the baron, but I am only his fifth daughter, and he has never held any great affection for me."

"You presume? You have not spoken to your father?"

"I have not laid eyes on my father since the day he washed his hands of me by giving me to Lady Gwenllian to raise."

"Still? Even now that Lady Gwenllian has offered her cousin in marriage to you?"

Constantia shook her head and shuddered. At first Jevon thought her as repulsed by the thought of marrying Llygad as he. The cloddish, sullen Welsh boy had been particularly loutish to Constantia.

Not until she shivered again did he notice the nip in the air. She was not repulsed. She was cold. The days cooled quickly after dark. He was long used to gritting his teeth through chilly nights, but she had lost her cloak. He puffed on the struggling flames, coaxing them to catch the larger branches.

"Here," he said, "take my cloak until I persuade the fire to cooperate." He stood, loosening the ties at his neck as he crossed to her shadowed form.

"Jevon—"

Her voice trembled. He cursed himself for not thinking of her discomfort sooner.

"I'm sorry."

A little late for apologies. But he bit back the sarcastic reply.

As he bent to drape his cloak around her shoulders, she drove her head into his chest like a battering ram. The blow threw him off balance long enough for her to spring to her feet and shake the ropes off her wrists.

The sneaking little minx! She had tricked him into softening the knot, and now she intended to escape. If she thought him too chivalrous to grapple a woman into submission—

She angled to one side as though trying to evade his attempt to grab her. By the time he saw her swipe a sturdy branch from the woodpile next to the tree stump and swing it at his head, it was too late to block her. The *crack* in his ears echoed the explosive pain through his head. He saw a sickening flash of sparks as the blow hurled him into a sprawl across the forest floor.

NOVEMBER 1166
PENNAULT CASTLE

Jevon reached down a hand to Llygad, but he gave his fallen opponent a hard jerk as he "helped" him to his feet. The Welshman slammed into Jevon's chest before bouncing back like a leather ball off a stone wall.

"If you call her *merkawit* one more time," Jevon growled, "I don't care who's watching. I'll hit you so hard your head spins all the way around."

He released Llygad's hand on the last snap of the Welshman's recoiling body. Llygad flew several feet before landing in the mud again. Franco and Raimon doubled over with laughter, and even some of the younger knights smirked.

Lady Gwenllian, watching the swordplay from the top of the wooden stairs that led to the door of the keep, frowned. Fortunately for Jevon, her displeasure lighted on her young cousin sprawled in the mire of the training field rather than on him.

Constantia stood with Lady Gwenllian, holding the hem of the baroness's fur-lined mantle so that it would not drag along the mud-spattered stairs. Jevon knew Constantia's frown betokened as much displeasure at Llygad's fall as that of her mistress, although for entirely different reasons. If Constantia only knew the vile things Llygad said of her, she would not pity the oaf.

Llygad glared at Jevon as he sat up, his blue eyes almost feral with rage. "It's *merch y gwynt,* you idiot. And if you saw the way she flits around your so-called friends when you're with my cousin, you would know it perfectly suits her flighty heart."

Constantia was kind to everyone, and everyone respected her in return, including Franco and Raimon. Jevon saw nothing "flighty" about that. And he could not care less about how to pronounce the guttural Welsh insult any more than the other foul things Llygad called her in his native tongue. Jevon knew the epithets Llygad flung at Constantia were nasty by the slur in the Welshman's voice.

"Get up," Lady Gwenllian called to Llygad from the stairs. "Pick up your sword and try again. And this time, watch where you put your big feet."

Llygad's slightly flared ears reddened to match the rest of his face. He ran a sludge-grimed hand through his short gold hair, the only feature that remotely linked him to the beautiful baroness and her two eldest children, then clambered up and retrieved his sword. Some of the mud he briskly shook from his blade spattered Jevon's face and tunic. Deliberately, no doubt.

"Again." Their sword master, Sir Guilhem, echoed the baroness.

Jevon wiped the mud from his face with a sweat-dampened sleeve. With their knighthood soon approaching, Sir Guilhem drilled the squires harder than ever and in every kind of weather. The vigorous exercise quickly quelled the chill left behind by the recent rain and the dark, lowering clouds overhead.

Llygad repositioned himself in front of Jevon and raised his blunted training sword, a near exact replica of Jevon's. Once Jevon was knighted, he would buy himself a more distinguished blade, but for now, all the squires and most of the knights had to make do with the plain, unsharpened, utilitarian weapons the baron doled out. "Killing edges," the baron said, "should only be used in war." Some, like Franco and Sir Milo, had scratched their initials into one of the unadorned pommels so they could quickly find their favored weapons, but Jevon never had trouble adjusting to the slight variations in each sword's heft.

He eased into readiness now, softening his knees, weighting himself just so on the balls of his feet as he angled his sword deep and steady. As always, Llygad's attempt to mimic Jevon's posture was so obvious that Raimon snickered loudly. Much as Jevon wanted to snort, he was too disciplined to make any sound or expression that might warn his opponent to correct his flaws. The Welshman's tall, gangly body slumped rather than relaxed for quick, fluent maneuvering as Jevon's did. Llygad shuffled his feet to try to match Jevon's but planted them too far apart. The too-sharp angle of his sword forced Llygad's elbow into an awkward crook. This would be all too easy.

Jevon shifted to the right. Llygad followed. Jevon flowed to the left. Llygad lurched the same direction, like a lumbering image in a mirror. Jevon spun, then thrust. Llygad was only halfway through his imitation when Jevon, fueled by Llygad's slurs at Constantia, slammed his sword into Llygad's unprotected side. Llygad stumbled, flung sideways by the force of the blow. He struggled once, twice, to right his balance, then dropped his sword, arms spinning. Ultimately, he tumbled anew into the mud, this time flat on his face.

The squires and knights roared, and even Sir Guilhem gave a boisterous guffaw. Jevon somehow managed to choke his laughter down, but he knew Llygad saw his contemptuous smile.

The swish of threadbare skirts and toss of long, ripply curls caught Jevon's eye. Lady Gwenllian had returned to the keep, no doubt in disgust. But in spite of years of the Welshman's insolence and rudeness, Constantia extended her hands to Llygad to help him up.

As always, Llygad rejected her offer and sloshed out of the mud on his own.

"Go buzz around your manly roses, *gwenynen fach,*" he said when she used her sleeve to try to wipe the mud off his cheeks. "He thinks your nectar is all for him . . ."

Of course Llygad mangles his own analogy. And he calls me *an idiot.*

". . . but I saw how tenderly you cleaned Franco's lip when he cracked it on the hilt of Jevon's sword and the soothing way you bathed Raimon's black eye when it landed on Jevon's elbow while they were wrestling. You pretend you care about me, too, but I'm not fooled. Your father abandoned you without a dowry. I'm the only one with fortune enough not to care, but neither am I stupid enough to fall for your tricks. My wife must be a beauty, not a sly, beggarly, pie-faced wanton."

That word Jevon understood. He flew across the yard, but Constantia blocked him from swiveling Llygad's head with a punch he'd not soon forget.

"Stop it," Constantia said. "If you would be kinder to him, he would not taunt you so."

"It's not me he's taunting. You're the one he calls *merkawit* and *hilpun* and *jawdahn*. I should think you'd *want* me to defend you."

She tossed her head. The gilt flecks in her green eyes twinkled. "Perhaps they are compliments."

Only someone as good-natured as Constantia would think so. Or pretend to.

"They're not compliments, and you know it," Jevon growled. "Get out of the way, Stantia. I'm going to teach this lout how to speak to a lady."

"De Cazalet!" Sir Guilhem called. "Get back to your place. You're up against him next, Tirell."

"Go." Constantia shooed Jevon with her hands. "If you get in trouble, Lady Gwenllian may change her mind about not needing you this afternoon."

The baron had sweetened his wife's temper with a new jewel-studded chain so she would go riding alone with him. Jevon had never seen a man so smitten with his wife after nearly fourteen years of marriage. Of course, he had also never seen a man with such a gloriously beautiful wife as the Lady Gwenllian de Laurant.

Jevon glanced over his shoulder and saw Raimon waiting for him to return to the training area.

"Can you stay and watch?" Jevon asked Constantia.

"I have to help Lady Gwenllian change for the ride, but after that, I will be free until she returns. I will be back in time to watch you trounce Raimon and Franco on the archery field again."

Jevon could do that with his eyes closed. Franco and Raimon barely bothered to try to beat him with the war bow anymore. Like all the other men at Pennault, they preferred the crossbow. Only Llygad spent hours practicing with the war bow as well as his sword, with equally negligible results. Jevon held a grudging respect for his doggedness. Did Llygad feel the same empowering thrill in the pull of his muscles when the hemp string flexed the strong but supple wood? The odd clarity that filled his mind when he leveled his arrow at a target? The exhilarating hum of the shaft as it twanged free, the pride when it *thwacked* into its mark, the joy when one achieved a fluid, entrancing rhythm in release after release after release in that moment when man and bow became one?

Jevon grunted. Of course not. Llygad was merely too stubbornly Welsh to forfeit a weapon that held such pride for his people.

A hand slapped Jevon's shoulder. Franco had crossed the yard to join them. "Go on," he said, "before Sir Guilhem penalizes you like he did the last time you lingered too long talking to Constantia instead of expeditiously obeying his orders. I will keep her entertained while you drub Franco like you did Llygad."

"Not this time," Raimon called. His brown-and-blond locks bounced jauntily around his face on a gust of wind. "I knocked you down with my new trick, didn't I, Franco? And Sir Milo and Sir Baudri and even Sir Eudes and Sir Guilhem. When I am through with Jevon, he and Llygad will be scrubbing the mud off together."

Llygad had skulked off to the edge of the training field, where he tried to wipe the mire from his tunic, but he only made the smear worse.

"Yes, go," Franco urged. "I heard the drollest story from one of the arbalists this morning. Constantia will giggle when I tell her. She has the most elfish laugh."

She did, indeed. Franco's grin at Constantia seemed a little too ardent, but Jevon reminded himself that her smiles for Franco or Raimon or Llygad were never as warm as those she gave him. Not that Llygad's smiles at her were ever anything but snide.

Jevon's pulse skipped. *Will she smile as warmly after I open my heart to her? What if I ruin the fellowship between us?*

If she cut him out of his life because she feared encouraging emotions she did not share, how would he live without her?

"Now, de Cazalet!" Sir Guilhem's voice rang with impatience. "You are altogether too cocksure in your ability because the others train thrice as much and you still best them with ease."

Because of Lady Gwenllian's demands on Jevon's time. Did Sir Guilhem not think Jevon would rather drill a thousand extra hours than read one more extravagant paean to some beauty in a book she liked to interpret as praise for herself?

"Well, not every blow in battle comes from a duel between two men," Sir Guilhem continued. "Get over here. You, too, de Marché. Let's see if you and Tirell can take de Cazalet down together."

Raimon and Franco both scowled. Franco clearly did not want to leave Constantia, and the glory of defeating Jevon would be no glory for Raimon at all if he had to share it. Jevon regretted only that Constantia could not linger to watch him best both his friends as easily as he did individually. But she excused herself to go help Lady Gwenllian change her gown, and he and Franco took up their positions with Raimon.

"Well?" Constantia asked. "Did Raimon and Franco humble you?"

Some delay with Lady Gwenllian had prevented her from returning to watch them on the archery field. Jevon had taken advantage of her absence after training to wash away the mud, change his tunic, and, with Beatris's help, sneak a little clove powder from the kitchen to rub on the back of his neck. Thankfully, the baroness had excused Constantia from attending the children or helping in the kitchen or laundry while Lady Gwenllian rode out with her husband. Jevon seized their dual escape from the baroness's demands to invite Constantia to walk with him in the woods.

He tried to keep his expression self-effacing, but he could not lie. "Franco is too impulsive. He—"

"—strikes from reckless positions. Even I can see that." Constantia dallied near the training field as often as possible between chores to watch the squires at drills. "So when he—"

"—drops his shoulder, I simply—"

"—dip under his blade and—"

"—flip it out of his grip."

How did she always know *exactly* what he was going to say before he said it?

"And Raimon?" she asked as though she had not noticed the nearly precise harmony of their thoughts.

The air felt heavier here amidst the throng of rain-soaked trees than on the open castle grounds. The musky scent of oak bark was so thick that Jevon found it hard to breathe. And the smoky, steamy fragrance released from the carpet of fallen leaves he and Constantia trekked through nearly smothered him.

Or perhaps it was not the storm's muggy aftermath that made it difficult to fill his lungs. Perhaps it was nervousness that clamped his chest and dampened the clothes against his skin.

"Raimon is quicker than Franco," Jevon owned, hoping his voice was not as husky as it sounded to his ears, "so he withstood me longer than Franco, even though—"

"—his eyes still shift toward his intended target before he strikes?"

"Yes. But his reflexes are getting faster, so it's becoming harder to react in time."

"But you still disarmed him?"

Jevon nodded.

"How quickly?"

He hesitated, then admitted, "Fifth strike."

"But you could have done it in four?"

He hesitated again.

"Three?" Constantia's voice rose in awe.

He gave a rueful nod.

"How can you anticipate him so exactly?" she asked. "When I watch you and Raimon fight, his movements are a blur to me. I see what you mean about the shift of his eyes, but there is scarcely a breath between his glance and attack. No one else blocks him as consistently as you."

Jevon shrugged. He could not explain it. The squires' and knights' lightning strikes laid against him swung with perfect clarity to him.

But this was not what he wished to talk about. He had not been able to contrive a moment alone with her since Beatris interrupted them a month ago. If Lady Gwenllian returned early, she would undoubtedly find some reason to call him or Constantia or both back to the castle.

Jevon stopped. "Stantia, I—I need to ask you something."

She appeared to hesitate midstep before turning toward him. "Yes?"

Her eyes, green and gold like a spring laden tree kissed by flecks of sunlight, stared so deeply into his, he wondered how she could not simply see what he wanted to say. She nearly always seemed to know what he was thinking and what he meant to do or say. *My heart's twin.* 'Twas a playful term he'd devised for her when he realized they mirrored one another's words and laughter and gestures so often they might have been raised as brother and sister.

Only there was nothing brotherly about the way his chest had pounded for the last few months or the way it drubbed now.

He saw her eyes drop a fraction of an instant before his awkwardly did the same, then lift a mere a moment after he raised his gaze again.

"Yes, Jevon?" she repeated.

They concurrently moved their hands behind their backs—he to avoid the temptation of sweeping up her slender fingers, which he so desperately wished to hold.

He tried to clear his throat. "Stantia."

They both brought their hands back out and linked them in front. Did she notice their echoing movements as keenly as he did?

"Stantia," he began again. He pushed through the lump in his throat. "Sometimes things change."

Her eyes widened as though his statement alarmed her.

"In a *good* way, I mean," he said quickly. "We have been friends a long time, but not like me and Franco and Raimon. Our friendship has always been—well, special."

Oh, saints, could he sound any more doltish? Comparing her to Franco and Raimon? He'd had nearly a month to better prepare his speech, but now that they were at the moment again, his words still came out scattered.

Constantia twisted her hands slightly. "It has always felt special to me too."

Did her voice sound odd, or was it just because there seemed to be a faint ringing in his ears?

"Stantia."

He kept repeating her name like an idiot, but he could not seem to stop himself. He was wasting too much time stammering around. He had to just say it. However she reacted, he needed her to know.

"Remember at dinner a few months ago when Sir Damien and Lady Aline dined with us? Beatris and I waited on Lady Gwenllian that day while you sat at the side table between Sir Baudri and Sir Eudes. Their prattling irked you more than usual, and you threw me one of those looks when you're bored beyond bearing but trying not to show it, so I crossed my eyes to make you laugh, and you sparkled at me with such merry annoyance that I—well . . ." Once committed to his goal, he could not slow his words. "You have always been pretty, but that night, I had never seen anything more beautiful. And ever since, I haven't been able to think of you quite the same way. I ache to be with you during the day and I dream of you every time I close my eyes, and I-I-I want so very much to kiss you. May I?"

He was not quite sure when her hands stilled, but the silence that followed his request was the longest of his life. If she shrank from him or kindly but firmly said no—or worse, if she thought he jested and laughed . . .

She lowered her eyes, then took a small step closer. "Yes." Her voice sounded breathy. "If you really want to, then yes, you may kiss me."

He had not thought beyond this moment. He had not dared. Had she really just said yes? She stood waiting. Not shrinking, not laughing, just . . . waiting. He thought his heart might burst clean out of his ribs.

He gulped. How exactly did one kiss a woman? Raimon and Franco had teased some of the serving girls with kisses, but Jevon had never been tempted—until he looked across the tables at Constantia that day. He awkwardly placed a hand beneath her chin. Could she feel the way his fingers trembled? To his relief, she willingly tilted her face up to his. He lowered his head, surprised by how easily his lips found hers.

Llygad had intended to mock her, likening her to a bee and nectar, but Jevon never tasted anything more heady in his life than the soft, ambrosial nest of her mouth. Marveling, he let his lips simply linger for a moment. Then he slipped his hands inside the riotous ripples of her hair to cup her cheeks, savoring the soft, smooth skin he had never had the courage to caress. Her curls coiled around his fingers as though to trap the pleasure of his touch and bind it there.

In the next heartbeat, they melted into each other. When her arms slipped around his neck, he deepened the kiss and felt her lips return his pressure. Her fingertips moved up the back of his neck, tickling the fringe of his hair, before jerking somewhat timidly away to settle on his shoulder. A tempering caution sought to restrain the startling rush of heat that coursed through his body. He clung to the fragile thread before the waves of desire overpowered him. He had not finished saying all he meant to. The high bar of chivalry demanded that he do so before he let this newly discovered passion carry him beyond the bounds of honor.

He pulled away. "Stantia."

"Yes?"

The glow in her eyes and the bemused, blissful smile on her lips nearly sent the rest of his determined speech from his head. The quicker he asked, the sooner he could kiss her again.

"Stantia, I know you thought you must remain a singlewoman all your life, but if . . . if . . ." *This is not the time to falter, Jevon. This is not the time to doubt yourself.* "If I could raise enough money to provide you a dowry so that my father would let us marry, would you—?"

To his horror, she shrank out of his arms just as in his worst visions.

Her entranced expression vanished, replaced with a stricken pallor. "Jevon, your father will never let you marry me. You are the son of a wealthy baron, and I am only the fifth daughter of a churlish knight.

"And I am only a fifth son," he reminded her. "Hardly worth my father's notice."

"Except for once a year when he reminds you of what you owe the de Cazalet name. He will expect you to wed a woman with a respectable dowry, and all I have is my mother's chrysolite necklace and ring."

Thoughts of his father's patronizing lectures every Easter supplanted Jevon's misgivings with an obstinate resolve. "Didn't you hear me? I will make such a dowry for you that Father will have to let me marry you."

He and Constantia both planted their fists on their hips, he in frustration, she looking exasperated at his reply.

"How?" she demanded.

"On the tournament field. Just as soon as Raimon and Franco and I are knighted, we are leaving for Flanders. We will make our fortune there, and once I have mine, I will return and give it to you. My father need never know where your dowry came from, but I promise it will be enough to satisfy him."

She shook her head. "That is nonsense, and you know it."

"Why? Do you think I can't knock other knights out of their saddles as easily as I can the knights of Pennault?"

"Of course you can. But—"

"'But, but, but.' Yes or no, Stantia. If I can win you the money, will you marry me?"

So many expressions whipped across her face that he did not know whether to hold his breath or exhale. Then, faster than anything Raimon had ever challenged him with, her arms were around his neck again, and she laughed in her happiest, most elfish way.

"Yes, yes, yes! Oh, Jevon, yes!"

He spun her around in the air. But the ring of her happiness barely chimed against the barren branches overhead before panic replaced his triumphant joy. Sir Guilhem called him cocky. What if he could not fulfill his ambitious boasting for the tournament? Jevon had never fought in a single real battle. He would face knights with years of experience.

But I am nimble and quick and clever. Sir Guilhem says so.

But some of them would be the same. And if he lost his horse and armor to them . . .

Horse and armor. Where would Jevon get a horse and armor? His father would change his mind. Or Laurant would. Once he received the accolade, one or both would agree that Jevon's knightly skills would serve them best in the tournament, where he could bring fame to the man who sired him and the man who fostered and trained him.

He set Constantia down but dared not kiss her again lest she sense his flagging confidence. He masked his internal scrimmage with a brash grin, then pulled his dagger out of its sheath and turned toward the oak tree.

"See?" He dragged the dagger's tip through the deep, gnarled ridges of the gray-brown bark, carving a C, then an interlocking J. "We will be like these letters—forever inseparable."

And they would. The intensity of his love for her could only drive him to victory after victory no matter how seasoned his challengers. He could not fail to win because he could not fail her. Fate wanted them together. He knew it from the crown of his head to the soles of his feet. He would win her a dowry. He would marry her. And he would cherish and adore her forever.

AUGUST 1174
THE WOODS BETWEEN VERE AND PENNAULT CASTLES

Constantia sprang across the clearing, the crown of her head still tingling from her collision with the flinty muscles of Jevon's chest. She seized his bow, snagged the sword, and dove into the darkness of the woods to the sounds of his groaning on the forest floor.

He will hate me forever. He will hate me forever.

She sped as fast as she could, but the tears in her eyes so blurred her vision that she nearly collided with three separate trees. She had taken advantage of his gentleness when he softened the knot binding her hands. The tender caress of his thumb still lingered along the skin of her wrist. In that brief touch, she had known, beneath his bitterness, that he still cared for her. And how had she responded? She had used the shadows of the clearing to work her wrists free of his considerate knot, done her best to knock him unconscious, and escaped, undoubtedly robbing him of some reward from his English earl for her capture.

Bad enough that he had joined the enemy to terrorize his own people. More painful the revelation that he blamed *her* for his unjust fate. The first she might reluctantly understand. But the latter was incomprehensible. How could he believe she would ever deliberately betray him so, even to protect Guia and Beatris? Yet now that she had struck him and fled, he would never believe anything else.

He will hate me forever.

She'd had no choice. But the heart she thought completely broken proved it retained one last uncracked fragment, because she felt it shatter as she ran.

Without the pebbles in her shoes, she sailed faster than before until once again her toe caught on something—a root? a stone?—and tumbled her forward. She gave a startled cry, but the springy branches of a large bush caught her. She was grateful to be spared a fall, but its branches tangled in her already snarled hair. She had to release the sword and bow to its greedy grasp to work her hair free.

Once liberated, she took a moment to assess her surroundings. Trees that stood as familiar friends in the daylight became mysterious strangers in the dark. She had no idea which way Pennault Castle lay. Would Jevon find himself as lost as she?

She strained to hear a rustle, scrunch, or snap that might betray his footsteps. The broken shards of her heart jumped at a long *hoooo*, followed by a trilling *hoo-hoo-hoo-hoooo* of a nearby owl. After she'd agreed to marry him, Jevon had mimicked the call from below her chamber's window at night, inviting Constantia to meet him in Lady Gwenllian's rose garden while Guia and Beatris slept. Did he try to trick her now?

Insects chittered. Some animal issued a series of sharp, shrill barks. A fox, perhaps. Thankfully not a wolf. Wolves hunted here when she was a girl, but Laurant, Sir Damien, and their neighbors had gradually driven the predators north to maintain the deer for their own hunting.

The owl called again, this time from farther away. Something skimmed her wrist so lightly that she flicked it without glancing down.

Her finger brushed against cold, human flesh.

"Do not be afraid, my lady. I am a friend."

A set of blanched knuckles protruding from the back of a skeletally thin hand moved from her wrist to her sleeve. Constantia screamed, but the sound barely escaped her lips before the hand smothered it with lightning speed.

The stranger shoved her against a nearby tree, his palm crushing her into silence. She could not see his features in the dark, but no "friend" would hold her with such bruising strength.

"I saw you at Vere," he murmured. "Tell me, is Sir Damien dead?"

Long hair fell about his shoulders. She could not tell its color, but she guessed it to be pale. Surely this was the quicksilver stranger she mistook for Llygad earlier? This man was taller than Jevon and more slender, but cruelly strong. The rough way he held her bespoke a lack of any grain of Jevon's innate gallantry.

She gestured, equal parts frightened and angry, at his stifling hand.

He eased it away with a caution. "Keep your voice down. One of Gunthar's men hunts you."

Gunthar? The English earl? If so, he must mean Jevon.

"Who are you?" she demanded, instinctively sensing it wiser not to show fear.

"A friend," he repeated. "I need to know what happened at Vere."

"If you saw me there, then you should know."

"I saw Gunthar's mangons shatter the curtain wall," he said. "I saw his troops pour through them into the bailey. I saw Sir Damien's fight with Gunthar and his fall from the ramparts. And then I saw you bolt across the rubble-filled moat. You must be very important for Gunthar to call out an order to stop you. Sir Damien's daughter?"

If he thought that, he could not be familiar with the residents of Vere, for Sir Damien had no daughters. That meant he must have witnessed the events from some hiding place in the woods.

If he did not know her, then he could not expect her to know him. Then he should not be surprised if she asked a simple question. "What do you want from me?"

"I want the same as you—revenge on Gunthar. Sir Damien could not have survived the fall. Do you not wish to avenge him? Help me punish Gunthar for both our wrongs."

She grieved for Sir Damien's sons, Triston and Etienne, but they were not her kin. It was not her place to seek revenge for their father's death. Her mind raced for a way to escape this villain.

"Or perhaps you are not Sir Damien's daughter. Perhaps you are his comely widow, eh? Happy to be freed of your wifely duties to a man old enough to be your father?"

The scoundrel groped Constantia's womanly curves. She gasped and tried to shove him away but failed. "Let go or I will scream."

She had left Jevon groaning. Surely he had recovered and followed by now?

"Will you?" The scoundrel's arm snaked around her waist. "What makes you think Gunthar's henchman will be any gentler with you than I will be?"

"Because he is a gallant, honorable, chivalrous knight who will run you through like the dastard you are—"

"So the rumors are true," the villain broke in. "I heard Sir Damien's new wife had a wanton eye, but betraying your husband with the English enemy? All the better, then. Scream away. Bring your lover down upon us. It will give me pleasure to kill one of Gunthar's gallant, honorable, chivalrous knights and leave his body on the road for Gunthar to find."

He reached out his free hand and pulled the sword loose from the bush.

Kill Jevon? Horror jolted her. She had taken his only weapons—the sword from Vere Castle, which this villain now held, and Jevon's bow, which still hung in the bush. She clamped her teeth, determined to do the opposite of what she had previously threatened.

"Stubborn, are we?" The villain mocked her silence. "Well, I have all night to change your mind. I may even enjoy it, although I doubt you will. Whether you scream from pleasure or pain makes no difference so long as Gunthar receives my message."

He ran a bold hand over her hip. Constantia shuddered but tried to use his weakened grasp on her to twist herself loose. He slammed her against the tree with a vicious laugh. She sensed his mouth swooping toward hers. She flung up a clawing hand to block him and raked her nails over his eyes and nose.

The scoundrel howled, then hurled her sideways. The sudden blow to her hips and back knocked the air from her. Then the monster was atop her. She twisted and flailed, trying to wrench his grip from the neck of her bodice, all the while choking back the urge to scream. If Jevon came upon them now, he would have no defense.

The scoundrel's hands. Both wrestled with hers. Where was the sword? He must have dropped the weapon when he threw her down.

"Stantia? Constantia!"

Jevon. He must have heard the scoundrel shout when she scratched him. She clamped her terror down so hard her jaw ached. *No! Go back, go back!*

"Stantia!"

"She's over here!" the scoundrel called.

Jevon's footsteps crashed through the still night air.

The scoundrel's weight lifted. He was going for the sword. Constantia rolled after him, scrabbling to reach it first. Her fingers curled around the leather-wrapped grip just below the cold metal pommel. She jerked the weapon toward her, but a brutal blow to her face hurled her onto her back again. Stars swirled in the sable canopy that arced above the trees.

After what felt like an eternity of befuddled numbness, her mouth began to burn. A burst of light appeared over her so bright she squeezed her eyes shut. When a pair of strong arms scooped her against a broad chest, she somehow knew this embrace betokened safety.

"He's gone." Jevon's tones, soft and gentle, vibrated against her ear. "You're safe. He's gone."

She clung to him until her bounding pulse slowed. When she finally leaned away to look at him, the blinding light had receded, its glow vacillating across Jevon's handsome features from someplace over her shoulder.

"He—" She winced at the fire on her lips. "He wanted you to find us so he could . . . could"—renewed horror choked her—"k-kill you."

"Kill me?" Jevon exclaimed. "Why? Did he know me? Did you know him?"

She shook her head. "I glimpsed him as I ran through the trees today, but he disappeared before I could see him clearly. I thought perhaps he was an outlaw . . ." She trailed off, immediately regretting the word.

"You mean like me." Jevon's tone hardened.

"No," she said fiercely, "not like you. You are not a ravisher and murderer."

"No, I am only a thief," he said coldly. "Or I was. You do not know what I am anymore, Stantia."

She did know. He'd bound her too solicitously, embraced her too tenderly, to have lost the chivalrous nature she loved.

But the eyes that bore into hers were not chivalrous now. They shone dark as jet and hard as iron in the flamelight that washed their brown warmth to a thin ring around his pupils. A purpling knot swelled near the curls along his temple. He might think she no longer knew him, but she saw his conviction that he knew her—the woman who repaid him in the generous act of lending her his cloak against a chilling mist by bludgeoning him with a tree branch.

She had spontaneously called Jevon "knight" to the scoundrel despite his never having received the title. What unflattering terms must Jevon be calling *her* behind his flinty gaze?

She looked over his shoulder to evade his scrutiny. A stout branch— perhaps the same one she hit him with—held a crackling flame at one end while its other had been driven into the ground an arm's length from where they sat. Jevon must have improvised a torch to find her in the dark.

"My attacker knew you served the English." She carefully watched the flame rather than Jevon. "He said he would leave your body"—she shuddered at the hideous vision and curled her hands into fists to avoid clutching Jevon again—"in the road for Gunthar to find when he rides to Pennault. Is that your earl's name?"

"Aye. He attacked you to draw me out because I serve Gunthar? What quarrel does he have with the earl?

"He did not say. Only that he wanted to send Gunthar a message with your murder. He hates your earl. I heard it in his voice. He wants revenge for something your earl did, but he never said what."

"If I find him, I will ask him after I beat him to a bloody pulp."

Jevon sounded so savage that she stared at him.

"You should have screamed so I could find you faster," he said, his voice rough with anger. "Why the blazes didn't you? What if he had ravished you?"

She had planted that fear in Jevon's head with her description of the scoundrel. "You had no weapon. He would have driven that sword through you before you reached him."

Jevon pulled her to her feet. Without thinking, she skimmed her thumb across the scars that bubbled the back of his skin. It should have traced the clear, raised outline of an *R*, but the maze of raised and twisted flesh obscured it.

"That was foolish, Stantia. I had a weapon. I had this." He walked over to the torch and plucked it from the ground. "This is how I followed your footprints in the dark. Blazes! He hit you?"

This time Jevon looked as ferocious as he sounded. She had been angled away from the light while he held her, so he must not have noticed the swelling around her mouth.

"He struck me with his fist . . . I think. It all happened so fast as we grappled for the sword. It is only a bruise."

"It is more than a bruise. Your mouth is bleeding. Devil take it, I've half a mind to tie you to a tree while I find that villain and thrash him."

Before she could object, Jevon gently tilted her chin up and dabbed the cut with the edge of his cloak.

"How did you drive him off?" she asked to distract herself from the tiny stabs of pain his careful blotting caused her cracked lip.

"I waved my torch in his face to blind him, then kicked the sword out of his hand. He must have feared I meant to set him alight, for as soon as I disarmed him, he scuttled off into the trees. Did you give him those bloody stripes on his face?"

"I scratched him."

"No wonder he shouted so. What a wildcat you've become. Here, hold this." He handed her the makeshift torch. She heard a faint *thunk*. The next dab of his cloak tanged with wine. "The woman I remember was unfailingly meek and cheerful, however meanly Lady Gwenllian treated her. Did you finally snap and scratch her eyes out? I would hardly blame you."

"No, I am the same docile drudge you knew when you left." She resisted the urge to smile, knowing her cut would hurt even worse.

If she'd endured the baroness's meanness meekly, it was because Constantia felt so completely content with Jevon's friendship. Her submissive indifference of the last few years had come from a broken heart. But just being with him again almost, *almost*, mended the fractured pieces.

He moved back a step, closing the lid of the flask. The torchlight revealed a crimson smear across the silver stallion on his gambeson's shoulder, just where she had pressed her face against his breast when he rescued her from the pale-haired stranger.

The emblem reminded her of their divided allegiances. "I've ruined your badge," she said.

Jevon glanced at the stallion. "The earl will forgive the stain when he sees I have caught the castle crier who meant to alert the countryside of his arrival in Poitou."

"Not all the countryside." Though if she could, she would. "Jevon, just let me warn Pennault."

"I cannot," he said so firmly her fragile hope plummeted.

"Why? Out of revenge for what Lord Laurant did to you?"

"It is not revenge to want my life back, Stantia. Lord Gunthar has promised a royal pardon for any crime short of murder to the mercenaries who joined his campaign to humble the Poitevin barons and force Duke Richard to accept the king's terms for peace."

"You cannot trust promises from a devil like your earl. He murdered Sir Damien. As soon as he finishes using you to humiliate your own countrymen, he will cast you aside or, worse, turn you over to Lord Laurant and demand the bounty on your head for returning to Poitou."

"Gunthar is not a devil, and whatever happened to Sir Damien, he brought on himself when he refused to surrender Vere. A pardon means everything to me, Stantia. No more skulking about in the woods, fearing for my life. No more wearing gloves day and night to hide the shameful brand of thief I had not the courage to eradicate at the inn. No more sitting by whatever fire I can find, trying to screw up my courage to thrust the whole of my hand into the flames and this time hold it there until all my flesh melts away."

A frost of dread dropped over her. "What do you mean 'this time'? Jevon, how did you come by those new scars?"

He reattached the flask to his belt alongside his purse of jingling coins and his leather pouch. "I spent years hiding in forests, dodging every voice and footstep. Laurant's banishment had no authority to follow me beyond these borders, but there was no place I could go to escape the repercussions of his brand." Jevon picked up the abandoned sword and slid it back into his belt. "It is simply presumed that an *R* burned into a man's hand or neck or cheek means he is guilty of robbery. And if a man steals once, he has likely stolen twice and will undoubtedly steal again, so it is simple good sense to eradicate him as one would any other vermin that preys on the community, whatever county or duchy or kingdom he is found in."

Constantia untangled his bow from the bush with her free hand and gave it to him. It seemed an inadequate gesture for the sickening guilt in her belly, but at the moment, it was all she could do besides listen and hate herself for the part she had unintentionally played in his tragedy.

"I skulked from the woods of Poitou to the woods of Brittany, crossed to Anjou, then Maine, and finally Normandy. Along the way, I discovered that people lose all sorts of things in the woods—arrows, tinderboxes, hats, coins. I even found a small dining knife, one sharp enough to carve a rudimentary bow for the arrows I gathered." He bent to pick up his arrow bag, which she had not noticed he'd dropped on the ground. "Berries were abundant but not very filling, and it was always a risk to venture onto the open banks of a river to fish. I was grateful when I could trap an occasional hare, but after the bow, I ate much better."

There was nothing "rudimentary" about his current bow. As she'd passed him the weapon, the torchlight revealed burnished nocks of polished horn.

Once his bow was on his shoulder and his arrow bag retied to his waist, he took Constantia's arm and pulled her along beside him. She knew he was taking her back to the clearing.

"Eventually, some careless hunter or traveler left a glove behind in the trees. Only then did I screw up the courage to venture into a town. With my brand hidden inside the glove, I purchased a meager meal with the coins I'd found, along with a bed for the night. The innkeeper cast wary looks at the glove, likely because my right hand remained bare, but he asked no questions.

"My bedmates were more curious, pressing me about it. I finally claimed an unsightly but harmless rash. That alarmed them and they insisted I sleep in the far corner on the floor, but they let me take the single candle afforded to the chamber. After they fell asleep, I stripped off the glove and held the flame to the back of my hand. I placed my one remaining coin between my teeth to help me bear the pain, but the agony grew worse than I'd remembered."

Constantia froze, forcing him to stop. "Jevon! Had you lost your mind?"

"Nearly so," he said, though he sounded flippant. "I had not dared let another human look me in the face for over two years. The loneliness grew unbearable. I thought if I could conceal the *R* beneath a deep, fresh scar that I could live in the world of men again. But I'd forgotten the agony that comes with fire. I bore the pain as long as I could, but in the end, I gave a shout and dropped the candle. I stamped out the flame, and my commotion woke the others. I swore it was an accident, that I knocked over the candle while I slept. They plunged my hand into a basin of water. In the dimly lit room, no one could see the brand through the blisters, and by the time I left the inn the next morning, my entire hand was well bandaged."

The fool! "How could you be so witless! You might have set the whole inn on fire. You might have died!"

"Would you have cared, Constantia?"

"Of course I would have! You have no *idea* how many tears I have wept, wishing I had lied to Lady Gwenllian when she asked about the brooch. Had they given me the choice when the baron banished you, I would have left Pennault at your side."

His hand gripped her arm tighter. "I would give anything for those words to be true."

She could not blame him for his doubt after the way she had clubbed him and run away. He may have rescued her from the scoundrel, but he had not forgiven her for tonight or for seven years ago.

The torchlight illuminated the series of squiggling marks carved into an oak tree as they walked past it. C-J. She had been so near Pennault without knowing it.

Did Jevon see the entwined initials too? He gave no indication, but she thought his jawline clenched.

He will hate me forever.

Constantia's stomach rumbled. Jevon could not tell whether she blushed, for the torch she carried bathed her cheeks in a ruddy glow.

He dug a piece of dried pork from his pouch and held it out to her. She bit off a corner. A rather *large* corner. From the speed with which the pork disappeared, she must be famished. He gave her another chunk, then took a bite himself. He, too, had not eaten since this morning.

Between chews, she mumbled, "Lady Gwenllian would ban me from the table if she saw me guzzling my food like this."

"You always had elegant table manners," he recalled, "never picking at the bones or wiping your fingers on the tablecloth and *never* talking with your mouth full."

She gave a muddled giggle. The elfish sound kindled a painful pulse of loss in him. He rubbed the tender knot on his temple, trying to replace one ache with another.

"Do you remember when we served Lady Gwenllian together on the dais?" Constantia asked. "The games we played behind her back?"

From the age of twelve, Constantia had taken turns with Beatris and Guia every third day to attend the baroness at mealtime, bringing a bowl of rose-scented water for Lady Gwenllian to rinse her elegant fingers between courses and a blue-bordered towel to dry them. When Jevon overheard Llygad trying to bribe Raimon to take his place serving Lady Gwenllian at dinner, Jevon accepted Llygad's offer. Carving the baroness's meat and keeping her goblet filled with wine felt like a gift, if it allowed him to spend more time with Constantia.

"We hid our hands behind her chair and used the signals you translated from the silent monk who visited Pennault to guess which dish the knights would choose from the servers," she continued. "Whenever Sir Guilhem was offered a platter of fruit, he chose—" She pressed her thumb and the tip of her little finger together.

"Cherries," Jevon said, reluctant to relive the game yet unable to resist.

"Sir Eudes was partial to . . ." She stretched her hand flat, holding it vertical to the ground, and wove it through the air like a . . .

"Fish." That one was too easy. Would she remember this sign? "Laurant was always partial to any dish with . . ." Jevon drove his forefinger straight down into the palm of his hand, then moved his open hand to his nose.

"Leeks," Constantia said promptly. "We always had to wait until we were certain no one was watching to make that sign."

Along with the twohanded motions for cheese, honey, pears, plumbs, and wine. Foods signified with one hand, like cherries, eggs, and beans, were easily concealed by Lady Gwenllian's high-backed chair.

Recalling the rapport with Constantia that he had never shared with anyone else, frayed the harsh edges of her betrayal. Was that her intention? He turned the subject away from the past.

"What were you doing at Vere yesterday?" he asked.

The makeshift torch she carried gave off a faint popping sound. "Lady Gwenllian sent me to deliver a welcome gift to Sir Damien's new wife."

Her answer startled him out of his intended follow-up question about Raimon's whereabouts. "Lady Aline has died?"

"Three years ago."

The news saddened Jevon. Sir Damien's late wife had been a kind, generous woman. She once overheard Lady Gwenllian ordering Jevon to stay away from their chaplain's books, scolding that she did not give him enough to do if he had time to dawdle about and read. After that, Lady Aline snuck her little prayer books, no bigger than her palm, into Jevon's hand whenever she and Sir Damien dined at Pennault. Jevon read them late at night by the light of a sputtering candle, then passed them on to Constantia, who read and returned them to Lady Aline when Lady Gwenllian sent her on errands to Vere.

"Triston has been to the Holy Land and back," Constantia said. "He went there to pray for Lady Aline's soul. It broke his heart when his mother died."

Jevon had envied the closeness between Sir Damien's elder son and his mother. Jevon loved his mother, too, but he had not seen her for years, even before his banishment, although she frequently wrote to him. And the one token of affection she had sent him, he had squandered on—

He broke off the thought, but not before he glanced again at Constantia's lovely, traitorous face.

"What is she like?" he asked. "Sir Damien's new wife?

"You mean his widow."

Jevon had seen Sir Damien's horrific fall from the damaged wall where he and Gunthar battled. But Jevon's defensiveness rose at Constantia's accusatory tone.

"Gunthar is not the monster you think. His herald called out three requests to let our knights ride peaceably through the gates of Vere. Sir Damien not only refused, he stood atop the gatehouse and cursed the king to Gunthar's face. It was only after that the earl ordered his mangon to release its volley at the walls."

Jevon looked up through the black army of trees around them to the cluster of stars twinkling through the branches. Perhaps that was yesterday by now.

"While the king fights a double war in Normandy and England," he continued, "against his grasping heir, young Henry, and Louis of France, he has charged Gunthar with convincing the allies of his equally scheming son Duke Richard to abandon their allegiance to the prince and accept the king's authority in Poitou. Gunthar believes stealth his best weapon. As soon as a castle yields to his siege, he leaves a force of men to seal it off so word of his arrival in Poitou will not give the other rebels time to prepare a defense against him."

The planes of Constantia's cheeks tightened in the fluctuating flamelight. *So that is why you have chased me down like a defenseless hare,* he imagined her thinking. If she believed his pursuit ruthless, so much the better. She would consider twice before trying to escape again.

The affinity they had shared was dead. She would never understand the choices he had been forced to make.

Rather than marching along in brittle silence, he asked again, "Tell me about"—what had she called her?—"Lady Osanne."

"They say she is graceful and young." All warmth had fled, replaced by a snappish clip in Constantia's voice. "Dark of hair and eye, with a sultry beauty that, had her husband lived, would likely make him guard her jealously."

Jevon ignored the dig about Sir Damien. "More beautiful than Lady Gwenllian?" He could not conceive it.

"No. No one is more beautiful than the baroness except for Clothilde."

Lady Gwenllian's elder daughter, an enchanting twelve-year-old when Jevon left.

"Clothilde is married now, too, two years past to a man more than thrice her age. It broke my heart to see her in such listless despair at her wedding, but he was very rich, and one simply does not tell Lady Gwenllian no."

Indeed. When cross, Lady Gwenllian slapped the page boys and subjected them to the old harridan Sybil's switchings just as freely as she had her daughters and the young girls entrusted to her care. The beatings ceased once the pages became squires. Jevon might have forgotten about them had Lady Gwenllian not humiliated him on the threshold of his anticipated knighthood with two sharp slaps across his face after Constantia told her he took her brooch.

Constantia repositioned the torch when the heat grew too intense on her hand. "Heléne is still at Pennault. And Therri. Remember how you used to guard them with me, along with Clothilde and Etienne, when they played knights and ladies in the clearing?"

Sir Damien's younger son would be seventeen now, like Therri. That would make Heléne and Clothilde sixteen and nineteen, respectively.

Jevon tried to imagine them all grown up, but he could not. Constantia had been the girls' near-constant companion, charged by their mother with keeping them safely entertained and out of trouble so that Lady Gwenllian need not be bothered more than necessary. And Jevon had volunteered to "guard" them all so he could spend time with Constantia.

"Sir Raimon and Sir Franco are knights now, but they continue to serve Lord Laurant. Remember how you all used to dream of making your fortunes on the tournament field one day?"

"Woolgathering fancies," Jevon replied.

"That is not what you thought when you were twenty."

"I was a fool when I was twenty."

He'd known it the moment Constantia accepted his impulsive offer to marry her. The panic in his stomach had tried to warn him that his cocky ambitions were impossible no matter how skilled he was with sword and lance. But he had loved Constantia too much to heed it, clinging to his brash overconfidence until his mother unexpectedly gave him a faster, surer way to win her hand, one that did not depend on some future, unlikely turn of fortune.

"Fate or his father appears to have smiled on Raimon if he plans to win you glory in the tournament." Jevon tried not to let envy show in his voice as he kept pace with her brisk stride. She instinctively knew the way from years of accompanying the children to and from the clearing.

"Franco still dreams of it but has resigned himself to the baron's service for now. But the tournament is still all Raimon talks about," Constantia said. "Like you, he is a younger son without expectations of inheritance, and I do not think his father is any more generous than yours or mine, so I am not sure how he intends to come by the horse and armor he needs. But he seems confident." She swept on a few more steps before asking, "Do you not miss them, Jevon? Raimon and Franco and even Llygad?"

Jevon snorted.

"Raimon and Franco, then. They were your chamber mates and friends. The three of you were well-nigh inseparable. Remember how—?"

"'Remember, remember.'" Jevon saw what she was doing. "You are trying to manipulate my emotions so I will let you go and 'save them all' from my wicked earl. It is not happening, Stantia."

"Jevon, they were your friends. Will your conscience truly allow you to abandon them? Heléne, Therri, all of them to your earl's"—he sensed her choosing her next word carefully—"rebuke?"

Smoke from the torch blew into her face, and she coughed. Jevon took the branch from her. Carrying it left him with less maneuverability should she decide to bolt, but they were almost to the clearing, and he trusted she had more sense than to risk encountering that brutish stranger again.

"Gunthar won't harm the castle or anyone in it if Laurant surrenders."

"He won't do that." She wiped some soot from her eyes. "Laurant has sworn allegiance to Duke Richard, and unless the duke commands him, he won't lay down his arms."

Jevon was not sure the Poitevin barons would obey Duke Richard even if he ordered them to. Jevon knew the barons' recalcitrant natures. After all, he was Poitevin too.

"Then what will come, will come," he said.

Except for a few more coughs, Constantia fell silent.

Gunthar had hired Jevon not only for his skill with the bow but for his knowledge of Poitou and its barons. Jevon found the earl uncompromising but fair, implacable in his devotion to the king, relentless toward those who betrayed his royal master, but generous to those who proved themselves loyal to his trust. Jevon had responded to the earl's call for mercenary soldiers in Normandy. He recalled the terrified lump in his throat when Gunthar studied the scars on his hand. Jevon had feared by the lift of the earl's eyebrow that, under the bright noonday sun, Gunthar saw the deep *R* beneath the scars. But Gunthar accepted Jevon's service and promised him a royal pardon "for whatever crime" he stood accused of if Jevon proved faithful.

Over the last six months, Jevon grew confident he'd been employed by a man of honor—until he had watched, aghast, as Sir Damien plummeted from the wall.

You do not know what happened on the rampart. Perhaps it was an accident.

Jevon prayed it was true.

The fire had grown in strength while they had been gone from the clearing, but, thankfully, no sparks had spread to the tall bushes that concealed their retreat. Jevon tossed his makeshift torch into the flames.

"Are you still hungry?" he asked. Constantia shook her head. "Tired, then? You have been awake a long while today."

"Where do you propose I sleep? On the ground like some wild beast?"

Just as he thought. He may have saved her from the skulking stranger, but she remained indignant at Jevon's capturing her in the first place.

He hesitated, then lowered himself cross-legged into the grass, his back against the tree stump. He untied his arrow bag and placed it, the sword, and his bow beside him. Then he patted his knee. "Rest your head here. It may prove a bony bolster, but you will not awaken with your hair full of twigs."

The firelight threw her features into a storm of emotions. Confusion. Hesitation. Doubt. Temptation? While she stood irresolute, he told himself this was the most practical solution. Any movement would awaken him should he fall asleep as well. His night-long march with Gunthar, fighting their way into Vere, and two breakneck chases after this infuriating minx had left him exhausted. She must be just as weary.

He turned his invitation into a command before his eyes fell shut and he lost her for a third time. "Come." He firmly slapped his knee. "It is either this, or I tie you up again. And this time, I promise my knot will hold till morning."

From the way she stiffened, he knew his ultimatum irked her, but after a moment, she curled up beside him. She laid her head gingerly against his knee. The heat from her cheek penetrated his hose and set his blood afire.

His body flared into vibrant wakefulness. He slid his arm over her shoulder and wove his fingers into hers. "If you try to slip away from me, I'll know it," he growled through a smothering surge of longing.

He felt her curt nod, followed by a rebuffing silence. As the quiet stretched, her body relaxed, her breaths lengthened, and the weight of her head on his leg increased. Her slumbering vulnerability held him vigilantly alert. He watched the sheltering bushes for any unnatural stirring. His ears strained for furtive footsteps. Who had Constantia's attacker been? And what quarrel did he have with Gunthar? Would the villain try to harm them again, or would he remain cloaked in the darkness, unwilling to reveal his face?

When no fresh threat challenged Jevon's vigil, fatigue crept over him once more. He tilted his head and gazed at the shimmering infinity that stretched above the clearing. How many hours till daylight? He pressed Constantia's fingers gently and fancied a faint, responsive squeeze.

He moved his free hand to caress the hair that meandered over her shoulders in dozens of sinuous tendrils. Her hectic chases through the woods had snarled and knotted them. The boy who had courted her had been smitten with her hair's rippling sleekness. But the man who held her prisoner could have been content to stroke these coarsened gnarls for the rest of his life.

If only her heart had beat as true for him as his still beat for her. For through his bitterness and her betrayal, he still loved her. He had known it from the overwhelming rush of yearning he felt when they walked past the initials he'd carved in the tree the day she promised to marry him.

But that longing would not stop him from doing his duty and delivering her to Gunthar. Whatever he continued to feel for her, the hopes he had built around her lay in ruins. If ever he were tempted to forget that, he had only to look at the scars on his hand. And yet . . .

He closed his eyes. *Oh, kind heaven, if I could have just one wish, it would be that morning never come. Let me remember her laughing and kind, merry with the children, protective of anyone she thought less fortunate than herself, generous and forgiving even to louts like Llygad, the gamesome girl who could complete my every thought, my confidant, my soul's reflection, my heart's twin. Let us sit like this forever, just her and me, in one eternal night of stillness. No hurt. No betrayal. No bitterness. Just a quiet, loving peace.*

DECEMBER 1166
PENNAULT CASTLE

"Are you listening to me, boy?"

A brisk buffet to the back of Jevon's head brought his attention to his father's droning voice. Lord Vidal's swipes never hurt, but their vigor always effectively snapped Jevon out of his woolgathering. It was not as though he had not heard the same lecture for the past twelve years.

"Yes, sir," Jevon said, careful not to let resentment show in his voice. He had let his thoughts wander to a much more pleasant place: his tryst with Constantia last night in Lady Gwenllian's rose garden.

"Then what did I just say?"

Jevon had long since mastered the ability to follow the dull thrum of his father's speech while drifting off into other thoughts.

"'Be humble. Remember your place,'" he recited. "'Train hard. Fight honorably and be true to the oath of chivalry you will one day swear. Show Laurant by your valor, skill, and strength that it is worth his while to foster you so he will one day promote you to the forefront of his knights.'"

His father resumed where he'd left off. "Do not waste time gathering wool over vain and impractical dreams of tourneying. More men lose fortunes there than win them."

Jevon scoffed under his breath.

"Be content to serve the baron. Should it please Laurant to someday find you a wife, be grateful for his beneficence and content with his selection."

His father never explicitly added that Laurant's choice would require Lord Vidal's approval, but Jevon knew his father would have the final say on his bride. And that would never be Constantia unless Jevon could dower her with something better than her mother's fifth-best necklace and ring of chrysolite and brass.

Jevon had dreamed of the glorious mêlée as long as he could remember, fired by the tales the troubadours and jongleurs sang of them in his father's hall. It was why, at the age of seven, he had chosen the path of knighthood when his father asked him whether he wished to inherit his father's lands with Jevon's two older brothers, join the church like his two middle ones, or be fostered by his father's friend, Lord Aumary de Laurant. But every Easter, his father made the same statement about the tourney. Jevon gave up asking Lord Vidal to sponsor him after his wheedling attempts to change his father's mind received a crushing retort, followed by an unusually sharp slap on the head, when Jevon turned fourteen.

Only desperation to win Constantia made him consider raising the issue again when his father surprised him by arriving to spend Christmas with the baron instead of Easter. Well, then, Jevon would have to change Laurant's mind instead. Lord Vidal could not object if Laurant wished his best knight to represent him on the tournament field.

"I have trained hard," Jevon said. "Very hard. Laurant praised me to you just last night—"

"Boasting ill becomes you, Jevon," his father cut him off. "I see you weren't listening after all. And don't scrunch your shoulders at me in that surly way. You will crumple your mother's gift."

Jevon straightened and smoothed the breast of his new crimson-and-gold surcote. His mother rarely sent him gifts and even more rarely visited Pennault with his father, but she wrote to Jevon often, her letters full of such humor and affection that he always walked about in a warm glow after reading them. He had never owned such a handsome surcote as this one she had sent him for Christmas. He could scarcely wait for Constantia to see him in it.

"I did not mean to appear surly, sir," Jevon said, "and I did hear you. You told me to be humble, and I am. I am very careful not to swagger or smirk when I defeat the other squires"—*even Llygad, though you could not fault me for an occasional glare if you knew him*—"and I never complain when Lord

Laurant's lady asks me to sit with her and entertain her while the other squires are training with Sir Guilhem."

"And exactly how does that task still fall to you so often?" his father interrupted. "I could understand it when you were younger. Laurant says you were most gracious about taking her young cousin's place in serving her on the dais. Laurant has done naught but extol you to me ever since you were a page, calling you clever and good-natured with flawless manners, always generous and courteous. He says you fight bravely and honorably with your sword, though given the hours you spend in service to his wife and children, he wishes you would squander a little less of your training time on your bow."

Jevon resisted the urge to drum his fingers against his thigh.

His father dug his thumbs into the belt of his simple but luxuriously shiny green surcote. "You have done well here, son. I am proud of you."

Jevon almost thought his father's mouth softened a little in his gray-mottled beard, but that was probably just the blush of afternoon sunlight slanting through the window of the chamber he shared with Raimon and Franco.

"But you will be one-and-twenty next March. How is it you still wait on women and children?"

Because it was the only way he could spend more time with Constantia. But saying something so foolish would earn Jevon another cuff to the head.

"I do not mind it, sir," Jevon replied. "You have always said the true measure of a knight is how chivalrously he treats others, especially the weak and defenseless. I do listen to you, Father. And I do try to follow your advice."

Most of it.

"But as you say, I will soon be knighted, and there is no better place to test my training than on the tournament field. I am not asking you to provide me with the necessary equipment, but should Lord Laurant wish to do so—"

"He won't."

Jevon drew a deep breath before trying again. "But if he *does*—"

"I was here last Easter when he knighted that squire whose hair was already beginning to thin." Lord Vidal ran a hand over his own thick head of graying brown hair. "What was his name?"

"Sir Milo." Jevon saw clearly where his father intended to go with the memory.

"And what," his father asked, "did Laurant say to all of you after he knighted Sir Milo?"

The same thing Laurant said every time he gathered his squires just before knighting the one who came of age. Jevon had heard the speech so many times he could repeat it word for word, just as he could his father's lectures. And he knew his father would not uncross his arms and stop tapping his toe until he did.

"'In return for a modest fee from your fathers,'" Jevon quoted, "'I have poured years of training into each of you as well as providing you with bed and board. Once knighted, your pay will rise to a sol a week. If you are called to war, I will equip you with everything you need, mail, weapons, and destrier. If, however, you prefer to chase dreams of tournament glory . . .'"

Jevon held his shoulders square beneath his father's firm gaze, though he felt his spirits slump a little as he finished.

"'. . . you will be free to leave my service. But I advise you to hoard your sols very closely, for once you leave Pennault, you will not have another denier from me. You must purchase your own mail, your own sword, and your own horse. I suggest a courser over a destrier for the mêlée.'" Jevon left out the hint of sarcasm that always colored this advice. "'That will take you years, likely more years than you have on the earth, unless you can find yourself a patron who does not view the tournament as a frivolous waste of time.'"

Lord Vidal nodded approvingly and unknit his arms. "Well said. I have always thought Laurant a sensible man in all things except his wife. Follow his counsel, son, and you will bring all the honor to our name that I could ask for."

Jevon bowed his head, knowing his father would approve his show of humble submission. The gesture also hid any rebellion that lurked in his eyes. Yes, Laurant had made the same speech to his squires every year Jevon lived here. And yes, none of the knights Jevon knew had left Pennault to pursue the tournament circuit. But Laurant had never raised a squire as gifted as Jevon. It was not pride, he told himself, simply an acknowledgment of what he'd heard Laurant tell others time and again. Surely Laurant would make an exception and sponsor Jevon to bring fame to the baron's own reputation. Jevon just had to ask him one more time.

"Jevon?"

The lilting voice tripped Jevon's heartbeat even before he heard her light footstep cross the open threshold. She brought with her the warm aroma of cinnamon and cloves. She must have been helping in the kitchen to prepare the Christmas feast.

He turned to greet Constantia. "Yes?"

His chest puffed a little beneath his surcote's gold-embroidered crimson cloth. The admiration in her eyes told him how the rich cloth flattered him.

It appeared to take her a moment to shake herself from her bemusement. "Therri could use some cheering."

"What mischief has he fallen into now?" Jevon asked.

Her pretty, sun-tinged features crinkled with a mixture of amusement and sympathy. "He got bored and hid the new puppy in Clothilde and Heléne's bedchamber. When Clothilde opened the door, Gaweyne came darting at her, baying and barking and leaping all around her skirts. It sent Clothilde into a screaming fit, which made Lady Gwenllian so cross she boxed Therri's ears. Then Lord Laurant scolded him because he should have been with the other page boys listening to Peyre Mazel explain how to corner the roebuck, and now Therri thinks his mama and papa do not love him again. I gave him a bit of gingerbread, but he still looked very glum when he went off to apologize to the huntsman."

"It is Lord Laurant's son," Jevon said over his shoulder to his father. "Do you mind if I go and speak with the boy?"

He realized he had been blocking Constantia's view of Lord Vidal when he saw her dip into a curtsy.

"Forgive me, my lord," she said. "I did not mean to interrupt."

Lord Vidal gave her the casual nod he reserved for servants. Likely, with her drab-blue gown and the threadbare veil over her coily hair, he did not recognize her as one of the better-dressed women who waited on Lady Gwenllian at dinner during his annual visit to Pennault Castle.

"Father, allow me to introduce—"

Constantia touched Jevon's arm just long enough to check him. Jevon guessed she was too embarrassed by her shabby appearance to be intro-duced as a lady.

"I will take care of it," she began, but Lord Vidal cut her off.

"No, no. Go along with her, boy. You should have found a younger squire to take up your duties to the baroness and her children years ago, but since you did not, it would be boorish of you to ignore Laurant's son now. We will talk more at the feast."

"Will you be staying till Epiphany, sir?" Jevon asked.

If so, what would he and his father talk about for twelve days? Lord Vidal had finished his annual discourse of "advice." *Heaven help me if he has eleven more sermons for me!*

"No, I promised your mother I would return to Rouquard tomorrow. She was disappointed that I left her and your brothers for Christmas, but you will be knighted before next Easter. I wanted to be sure you remembered my counsel before you receive the accolade."

As though Jevon could forget a single patronizing word.

"I will be back for your knighting ceremony. And I will bring your mother along. Oh, I almost forgot. She sent a letter with me." Lord Vidal dug the sealed parchment from the pouch at his waist. "See that you answer her promptly. And do not forget to thank her for the surcote, which I suggest you take off if you mean to entertain children. You can don it again for the feast. At my request, you will sit with me at the high table instead of serving the baroness."

That would be a pleasant reprieve. It was Guia's turn to wait on Lady Gwenllian, so Jevon could watch Constantia practicing her table manners while he practiced his. He could not make faces at her to relieve the tedium of her dining partners' prattle, not with his father at his side, critically watching Jevon's every move and expression. But he could tease her over her long-suffering cheerfulness later.

When Lord Vidal excused himself for Jevon to change, Jevon held Constantia back with a look.

"I'd not have bothered you about Therri if I'd known you were with your father," she said.

"It was no bother. You spared me from the rest of his dusty lecture." Jevon crossed to his clothing chest against the wall next to Raimon's and Franco's.

Her familiar sigh trailed after him. "I would give anything for my father to come to Pennault and lecture me for just one hour."

She said it every Easter after he complained about his father's monotonous admonitions.

"No, you wouldn't." Her neglectful old bear of a father did not deserve the wistfulness in her voice. "I get so tired of Father's lectures on chivalry that sometimes I wish my ears would fall off while he's talking."

Her elfish laugh lit up his soul. He dug a serviceable tunic out of the chest, one that wouldn't mind a puppy's muddy paws or a rough-and-tumble wrestling lesson to restore a nine-year-old boy's good humor.

"What took you so long to wake up last night?" he asked as he set his mother's letter in the chest to read later. "You made me stand in the frost so long my feet grew numb even through my boots."

"Guia was mopey about something, but she would not tell me and Beatris why. We tried to cheer her up with extra-long prayers to Saint Ni—to the saints, but it took so very many I nearly fell asleep on my knees."

"You pray to the saints every night?" She had never mentioned it before.

"I think it was Beatris's idea before I came to live here. She and Guia invited me to join them when we were still small. We were all sad at leaving our families, and it was comforting at the time. Now it has become a familiar ritual. By the time we all dragged ourselves to bed, I could not hold my eyes open long enough to listen for your call." Her admiring gaze ran over his surcote again. "I don't suppose you will dare to call me again tonight?"

"Not with my father here. I've endured enough cuffs to the back of my head today. But listen for Old Sir Hoo tomorrow night. And remember to wrap yourself up in Guia's and Beatris's cloaks along with your own to stave off the cold. It's not that I minded enfolding you in my own last night, but Stantia—if we are not very careful, I will not be able to tear myself away from you to go tourneying three months from now."

He said it with a teasing grin but knew she saw the worry in his eyes.

"I know." Her gaze fell shyly from his. "It is difficult for me too. I will be more careful. It is just that I wish to be with you all the time, especially knowing that soon you will have to leave me."

The precious moments they stole together in Lady Gwenllian's garden sped by all too fast. For the last two months, after an excruciating wait for Raimon and Franco to fall asleep at night, Jevon slipped away to stand beneath Constantia's chamber window and mimic the call of an owl. Sometimes it took her a long while to open her shutters and look down on him, likely because of equally restless chamber mates. Then Jevon would gesture as if sniffing a rose to indicate where to meet him. Sometimes she could not join him for one reason or another, but whenever she could, they sat together beneath the moonlight on one of the garden benches and held hands while they talked about their days and dreamed of the future.

Jevon had been ever so careful not to kiss her again, and until last night, he'd been equally cautious not to embrace her, the fire of their kiss in the woods still so powerful it frightened him. But when she sat shivering inside her meager cloak, the only chivalrous thing had been to pull her inside his own much thicker one and warm her against him. From her stifled voice as they'd attempted their usual innocuous exchange, he knew the intimate closeness was as torturous for her as it was for him. Their twin thoughts agreed it best to cut short their tryst and return to the safety of their chambers.

Jevon loved her with an intensity that took his breath away. Too much to dishonor her with a hasty moment of selfish passion.

"I will let you change so you can go find Therri," Constantia said, the safely neutral subject giving her the composure to look at him again. She added with a mischievous quirk at the corner of her mouth, "And assure Old Sir Hoo that I will not leave him shivering long tomorrow in the cold."

She left him with a merry bounce of her ripply curls.

Jevon was not sure an extra cloak would be enough to stave off his aching for her. What if . . .

He stubbornly tried to ignore the little squirms of doubt that sometimes woke him in the middle of the night, but as she sailed from his chamber, they wormed through his brash confidence again. Even if Laurant agreed to equip him for the tournament, what if his father was right? Men did lose, as well as win, fortunes on the tournament field. The troubadours sang of that too. What if, when Jevon came breast to breast with other knights in the mêlée, he was not the best? He would lose much more than just his armor and horse to an opponent. He would lose all hope of wedding Constantia.

No. He gave himself a mental slap to the head as rigorous as anything his father dealt him. He and Constantia were fated to be together. It might take a little longer than he liked, but in the end, he would not fail—he *could* not fail—to win her.

AUGUST 1174
CLEARING BETWEEN VERE AND PENNAULT CASTLES

Jevon roused to find himself in a slump, though still propped against the tree stump. The poignant sanctuary of his mind dissipated in a vague awareness of a cool draught on the back of his neck and a dull warmth on his face. His left hand remained interlaced with Constantia's, while his right sank deep into her tangled mane.

A sudden toss of her head jerked him awake. At first he thought she fought to free herself from his intrusion in her hair.

"Forgive me," he stammered, attempting to free his fingers.

"So much silver," she muttered. "There was so much silver."

Silver? What was she talking about? The firelight had slumped almost as much as Jevon with no one to stir the flames for who knew how long. *Long enough for my legs to begin to cramp under her alluring head.* But there remained enough light for him to discern that Constantia still slumbered.

"There was . . . so . . . much . . ."

He carefully extricated his hand from her hair, then gently shook her. "Stantia, wake up. You're dreaming."

Her lashes fluttered, then lifted. She sat up, sleepy and dazed. "Where—?" She gazed around the clearing, at the waning fire, at Jevon, then looked startled as she rubbed her cheek and found a tear. She wiped it swiftly away.

The air had chilled in the deepening night. He grabbed a branch from the woodpile beside the tree stump, stood, and walked over to the fire, grateful to stretch his legs and avoid a resurgence of recrimination for the callous captivity in which he held her. He tossed the branch into the flames, then stoked them with the sword.

"You were dreaming about silver," he said. "Pining for a dowry from your father so you can marry Llygad?"

Or is it Raimon you hope to snare with your father's inheritance?

Was that how Raimon planned to equip himself for the tournament? With her dowry? If both her father and Lady Gwenllian expected Constantia to marry Llygad, she and Raimon would have to elope. Raimon had confessed as much, hadn't he?

"You mean where would *we* go?" Jevon had heard Raimon say as he and Constantia traveled the road toward Vere. "To the tournament fields, of course! Our love will resound through the ages."

What do I care who the conniving minx loves after all these years?

"I was dreaming about you."

Jevon spun to stare at her. "Me? I don't have any silver." Aside from the few deniers the earl paid him.

"You did. I saw it." Accusation leapt high in the flecks of gold the flames set glittering in her forest-green eyes. "All in a heap beside your money pouch on the great table on the dais. Llygad could never have paid you so much to serve Lady Gwenllian in his place. Where could it have come from but the sale of Lady Gwenllian's brooch?"

That silver. A wave of heat that had nothing to do with the resurging fire worked its way up Jevon's neck. "I did not steal that brooch. And you were the last person I ever thought could believe I would, much less tell Lady Gwenllian I did."

"I never told her you stole it." Constantia had the audacity to look hurt. "But what could I say when the baron dragged me in front of his knights' council and commanded me to repeat what I told his wife? It was too late to retract my words to Lady Gwenllian. And I saw no harm in telling the truth, that I had seen you with the brooch in the bailey and that you said you were taking it to the smithy to repair the latch. Had I known you were lying—"

Indignation bristled down his spine. "When did I ever lie to you, Stantia? Ever?"

Her lower lip quivered pathetically. "I-I did not believe you ever had—until I saw all those coins."

Jevon shoved both hands through his hair and paced across the clearing, too infuriated to look at her. His memory flooded with visions of that day he'd been summoned before the baron's council over the disappearance of Lady Gwenllian's brooch. It was a costly piece, an enameled dragon with a curling scarlet tongue and a thrice-looped tail, the whole of it liberally sprinkled with twinkling emeralds and rubies. More importantly, it had been a gift from Lady Gwenllian's powerful Welsh father.

Jevon had heard the baroness lamenting its broken clasp. And he knew where she hid the key to her jewelry casket from the many occasions he'd sat with her in her chamber, listening to her gossip or reading poetry to her. So he'd "borrowed" the key, hoping that by mending the brooch, she might be so pleased that she repaid him with a day free of her service. A day he'd planned to spend with Constantia and tell her he'd found a way for them to wed, not in some hazy future after he made an improbable fortune on the tournament field but the day after Laurant knighted him, less than a fortnight away.

On his way to the smithy, Jevon encountered Constantia and Guia in the bailey. Guia, her arms full of soiled linens, had gone on to the laundry hut while Constantia, carrying a pile of neatly folded clean garments, lingered with Jevon. He had not been able to resist showing her the brooch and confiding his plan for its repair.

But then disaster struck. After they parted, he lost the brooch. And before he could confess that he'd borrowed it, he had been summoned to the great hall, where he heard Constantia's sweet voice floating over the heads of a circle of Laurant's most trusted knights as they stood below their master and mistress on the dais.

"As I told your lady, I saw Jevon with it in the bailey today, just past None."

An owl hooted somewhere nearby. *Hoooo hoo-hoo-hoo-hoooo.*

"Jevon." Her husky voice pulled him from the bittersweet perfume of fragrant roses. "Where did all the silver come from if not from the brooch?"

"I did not sell it." Why bother repeating it? However many times he said it, she would not believe him.

"Then what happened to it? Because it was never found."

"I lost it during the sword fight with Llygad. If anyone did anything dishonorable with it, it was him."

"Llygad? Sell his cousin's brooch? He would not—"

She broke off as Jevon turned to glare at her. Of course she would defend her prospective bridegroom.

"What sword fight?" she asked.

"I'd knocked Llygad down at sword practice the day before, as always. After you left me in the bailey, he came out of the stables before I reached the smithy. He said he had a new trick and could disarm me in a trice. He demanded I face him with my blade then and there. You remember how obnoxious he could be. I wanted to be rid of him, so I agreed."

"Llygad saw you with Lady Gwenllian's brooch?"

"No. I knew he would blather to her that I had it and was flaunting it about and she would be too angry to listen to why I borrowed it. As soon as Llygad called my name, I slipped it into my money pouch, safely out of sight by the time he reached me."

A flurry of cold air reminded Jevon how low the fire burned. He stopped beside the woodpile. As though she'd read his mind, Constantia handed him several sturdy pieces of wood from where she sat on the ground. One by one, Jevon threw them into the blaze.

"It only took me a few pivots and strikes to prove Llygad's new 'trick' was as clumsy as his feet." Jevon could almost see their clash again in the surging flames. "I spun his sword out of his grasp before he tripped and hit the ground. Raimon and Franco and the other squires roared with laughter. They had seen us fighting and came to watch."

Constantia drew up her knees and wrapped her arms around them, but not before Jevon saw her shiver even though she still wore his cloak. It would take awhile before the fire grew warm enough to reach her. He stretched his hand to help her up and draw her closer to the flames, ignoring the charge of pleasure her slender clasp sent through his worn, cropped glove.

He positioned her within the fire's radiating glow and quickly released her. "As soon as I was done with Llygad, I returned to the smithy. But just as I reached the door, something struck my foot—a coin from my money pouch. The seam must have been weak and ripped while I fought with Llygad. I discovered the brooch had fallen out, along with several more of my coins. I ran back to the scene of our fight, gathering up coins along the way, but the brooch was nowhere in sight, and Llygad and the others had already dispersed."

"Are you saying Llygad or one of the other squires took the brooch to sell? Why would they?"

"Why would I?"

Constantia went quiet for several moments, avoiding his gaze to stare into the flames.

When the silence stretched, he finally asked, "When did you see the silver?"

She had been in the hall after testifying about Jevon and the brooch when Lady Gwenllian sailed off the dais to deal him two hard slaps, but Constantia was dismissed before one of Laurant's knights seized Jevon's purse and poured out the silver. Of course, they found no brooch. When Jevon could not prove his explanation for the silver, Lady Gwenllian called him a liar and thief, and the rest of the knights joined her.

Llygad, the snake, stood there feigning shock instead of confessing. Llygad *had* to have picked up the brooch. None of the other squires would have done something as despicable as letting one of their fellows take the blame. Only a month before, they all watched Raimon receive the accolade and stood listening while he swore the oath they each looked forward to repeating: to defend the Church, serve their liege lord with honor and faith, guard the honor of their fellow knights, and *always* tell the truth.

"I saw it after they locked you in the gatehouse," Constantia said. "Lady Gwenllian called me back to the hall with Guia and Beatris and showed us the pile of silver with your empty money pouch. Llygad had been left to stand guard over the coins until Lord Laurant and his knights returned from the gatehouse prison. By then, Lady Gwenllian guessed that I'd either given you the key to her jewelry casket or told you where she kept it. She dragged me over to the table and pointed at the coins. 'You stupid, stupid girl,' she said. 'You should have told me the instant he took it. I should have you locked up as complicit in his theft.'"

Jevon cursed Lady Gwenllian loudly at this baseless abuse. Constantia would never have shown him the key's whereabouts, and he would never have risked exposing her to the baroness's temper by asking her.

To his surprise, Constantia began to cry. "She was right. It was my fault. You did it for me, didn't you?" She wiped her cheeks with the edge of his cloak but failed to stem the sudden flood. "I should never have told you I would marry you."

Just as he'd thought. "Because you regretted it. Then why did you agree?"

Her eyes flashed at him in the firelight. "Because I loved you. *You.* I felt sorry for Llygad because you were all so unkind to him when you were pages and then became squires. But wed him? Or Raimon, or Franco, or anyone else?" She shook her head so hard her gnarled hair swung like whips. "You sold the brooch for me. To make a dowry for me. If I had realized it then, I would have lied to Lady Gwenllian and made you buy the brooch back before she could learn the truth. Jevon, how could you have thought we could build a life together based on such a crime? But I still would have lied to protect you!"

The cat. Pretending to shoulder the blame while throwing it back on him? "If you thought I would start our lives together in such a way as that, you never knew me, Stantia."

"I did not believe it at first, and I told Lady Gwenllian so. But when she pointed to the coins and said, 'Then where did he get all that silver?', I had no answer. Then the baron came back into the hall with his knights. He had questioned Hubert the smith, and Hubert said he never saw you or the brooch."

Because I allowed Llygad to distract me before I entered the smithy.

"I insisted that there must be some mistake about the silver," Constantia continued, "but Lord Laurant would not listen. He said you admitted to taking the brooch." Which Jevon had when the baron's clamorous council finally allowed him to speak. "And that you made a ridiculous excuse for the coins which you were unable to prove. Then he ordered me out of the hall, calling me frenzied and overwrought because I shouted that Lady Gwenllian was a vain, ungrateful wretch for treating you so shabbily after the patient, uncomplaining way you bore with her temper and slights when you served her."

Jevon gasped. "You did not!"

"I did. I knew she was the one egging the baron on. He never allows testimony from women in front of his knights' council. When he holds court to settle quarrels between his servants or serfs, he requires a father or brother or uncle to lay the complaint on a woman's behalf. But he listened to me because Lady Gwenllian told him to, and while he can say no to a great many people, he cannot say no to her."

"Stantia, she must have had Sybil beat you black and blue for insulting her like that!"

Constantia's eyes shone with fresh tears. "She did something worse. She made me watch from a chamber window when they branded you three days later."

Jevon had not known. He'd been dragged again in front of Laurant's knights' council after spending two miserable, sleepless nights in the gatehouse's stinking prison. The council had agreed on their judgment. Lacking any proof to the contrary and given his own admission that he had taken the brooch, Jevon was determined guilty of theft. The iron had already heated to a white-hot glow by the time he was taken out to the yard, his hand branded with the shameful *R* for *raubaire*. Jevon had tried not to scream at the pain, but he remembered a shout escaping him at the end when Laurant's marshal held the iron to his flesh for a few extra seconds.

He smothered a surge of shame at his weakness beneath a different, more bitter kind of hurt. "No matter how much I loved you, Stantia, I would never have stolen anything to marry you."

She flinched, then squared her shoulders, lifted her chin, and stared him straight in the eye. "You have protested your innocence a great many times, but you have yet to explain the silver in your pouch. Or will you say Llygad placed it there without your knowledge, just as you accuse him of taking the brooch?"

Jevon's hand might be marred, but her sarcasm bounced off his unblemished conscience. "No, the silver was mine. Legitimately mine. I did not sell Lady Gwenllian's brooch. I sold my mother's ring."

Constantia continued staring at him, but her chin dipped in surprise. "What ring? You never told me your mother sent you a ring."

No, he hadn't. He had wanted to surprise her.

Her face had grown ruddy so near the flames. Even he had begun to sweat. He guided her to what he hoped was a spot between too hot and too cold, then, sensing her tiredness—and acknowledging a renewed weariness of his own—suggested with a gesture that they sit in the grass.

"Remember my scarlet surcote?" he asked as she arranged her dust-stained skirts decorously around her ankles.

"The one with the gold flourishes? I remember you were afraid to tell your father Lord Therri's puppy dug it out of your clothing chest and mauled it to shreds when you left the lid up."

The pup had the gall to sit in the middle of the expensive rags and wag a happy tail at Jevon when he came upon the gruesome carnage.

"Whatever happened to that fiendish creature?" he asked.

"Lord Therri or the pup?" She chuckled, the same spontaneous reaction as when Jevon had shown her the ruined cloth. It was not the surcote's sad fate that made her laugh, she'd insisted, but his ridiculously woebegone expression.

After all these years, Jevon finally found he could laugh too. "Both. What a scamp Lord Therri was."

"Gaweyne has become one of Lord Laurant's best hunting hounds," she said. "Lord Therri is still impulsive and careless, but he's a goodhearted youth. He's grown as beautiful as Lady Clothilde, as we all suspected he would. Women flirt disgracefully with him, and he is now old enough to flirt back, but he does not take advantage of them however much some of them wish he would."

Therri a golden charmer? The whimsical Clothilde a listless bride? What had become of the youngest, Heléne, a kind, levelheaded, honest girl, though shockingly plain for having such a dazzlingly beautiful mother and sister? Had she grown more comely over the years?

Jevon thought he had shaken the dust of Pennault from his feet in his rage at Laurant and Lady Gwenllian, but Constantia was right. The children stirred fond memories in him. How much of their lives he had missed!

He shrugged, trying to dislodge the tug of nostalgia. "My mother heard about my surcote. I don't know how—"

"Your mother? Oh! She must have intercepted the letter."

"What letter?"

"You said your father spent all his time lecturing you when he visited Pennault. I did not want him to chastise you for something that had not been your fault, so I made Lord Therri write your father explaining what his dog had done and apologizing for letting Gaweyne dig through your clothing chest."

A kind gesture, so typical of Constantia. But—"Father would have blamed me anyway," Jevon said with a familiar glumness.

The nearer Jevon's knighthood drew, the farther away his dreams of the tournament began to slip as the full requirements for such an independent path grew increasingly elusive. Without support from his father or Laurant, it would take Jevon years to raise enough money to buy his tournament equipment, and likely years more to win enough on the tournament field to dower Constantia. The thought of waiting so long to wed her had begun to feel unendurable.

"The reason I was so dejected over my surcote's destruction was that I'd decided to sell it."

Constantia was rubbing at a stain on her skirts but abruptly stopped. "Sell your surcote? Why?"

"To start a dowry for you so Father would let us marry. The surcote wouldn't have earned enough by itself, but it would have brought more to my purse than the drip-drip-drip of Llygad's coins alone. I thought perhaps the surcote combined with Llygad's coins and the ring and necklace from your mother might make Father at least consider—but to my surprise, my mother sent me a ring with a breathtaking emerald encircled by tiny pearls and leaves etched into the gold band. Her letter said word had reached her that my scarlet surcote had met with some misfortune."

Thanks to Constantia's attempt to forestall his father's anger. But she had always done thoughtful things like that, protecting Guia and Beatris, the pages and servants, even Lady Gwenllian's own daughters from Lady Gwenllian's pique and the crone Sybil's switch whenever she could.

"Mother suggested I sell the ring to buy a new surcote, as identical as possible, before my father visited Pennault and asked me where it was."

Constantia's gaze returned to her hands as she resumed rubbing at the stain. "Your father would have been doubly angry had you sold the surcote for me."

Her voice sounded dull, sad.

"My father never knew you, Stantia. He only visited once a year and stayed at Pennault a single night. Just long enough to see if I was behaving and to give me long, stern, very boring lectures on being grateful, not squandering opportunities, and not letting him down."

Jevon's alleged theft had undoubtedly done exactly that. Had his father publicly repudiated him? He must have wished Jevon to Hades.

Jevon followed Constantia's hands as they moved across the lap of her gown. "Did he come after I was gone and grovel an apology to Laurant for my crime?"

"He came, but I only saw him from an upper window. What he and Lord Laurant discussed, no one ever confided to me. I do remember that your father's face was very white when he rode into the yard and still stark when he rode out."

Jevon tightened his jaw to defy the ball of shame in his stomach. He was glad he had not had to witness the hurt in his mother's eyes.

"Your scheme was foolish," Constantia scoffed. "Your father would never have accepted the price of a surcote as a dowry for me, even with my mother's jewelry."

She was probably right.

"But my second plan would have worked." Jevon remained confident of that. "The ring my mother sent me was worth much more than the surcote. Not enough to dower a wife for an eldest son or even for a second son, but for a fifth? *His* wife can hardly be expected to bring a fortune with her. And considering I'd agreed to forfeit inheriting his lands with my brothers, he had no right to quibble over a dowry equal to the price of a gold ring with a magnificent emerald and all those pearls cradling it."

Constantia frowned almost as sternly as his father. "Your mother did not send you that ring to dower me with."

"She wanted me to be happy. She said it in every letter she sent with my father from the time I was seven years old. How I used the ring would not matter to her. Father would have *had* to let his fifth son marry a wife with fifteen livres."

"Fifteen livres!" Constantia looked fittingly impressed with the sum before her brows knit in fresh censure. "But you earned them with her ring, a ring she explicitly did not intend you to sell for me. Did you tell her what you meant to do?"

"I did not need to."

"Not need to? Jevon! Selling it behind her back was deceitful and dishonest. Had I known, I would never have agreed to let you do such a thing."

"But it was not dishonest, Stantia."

"Of course it was! That ring belonged to your mother, so any silver you earned from its sale belonged to her too."

"I knew you would say that. That's why I did not tell you about the ring before I sold it. But Mother did not write, 'Sell this ring and buy a new surcote.' She wrote, 'I *suggest*'"—Jevon emphasized the word—"'you sell this ring for a new surcote as near to the one you lost as you can, but the ring is yours, my son, to do with as you please.' And it pleased me much more to dower you than try to avoid my father's next lecture. The ring was a gift, Stantia. My mother made that clear. And once I sold it and gave the silver to you, the silver would have become yours, not mine. A gift once given no longer belongs to the giver but to the receiver. That makes perfect, honest sense."

Constantia opened and closed her mouth three times before a fresh sound came out. When it did, it was a blubbering burst of sobbing laughter that rocked her onto her back in the grass.

12

Tears streamed from the corners of Constantia's eyes and ran into her ears. She scrubbed her palms against the crawly sensation while her breast heaved with peals of laughter.

I lost him because he feared my scolding? Because he feared me too proud to accept his gift of silver? I threw away our future because he thought me too rigid to see his devotion over my pious disapproval of his methods of dowering me? Was I that sanctimonious in my youth?

A part of her still strained against his reasoning. Selling his mother's ring to benefit Constantia simply *felt* wrong. But from however many angles she viewed his argument, it carried such logic that it left her speechless.

But not silent. She lay on her back, giggling like a madwoman then, in a shift so sudden she could not pinpoint when it changed, her laughter turned to sobs again. If only he had shown her his mother's ring. She could have vouched for its existence and sale to the baron. Instead . . .

I lost him. I doubted his honor when I saw the silver . . . and I lost him.

Her palms ground against her ears. *Scrub scrub scrub.* The tickle of water, now a flood, threatened to drive her fully over the edge of sanity, but she could not stem her broken weeping.

Jevon's face appeared above her, rippling as though she gazed at him from the bottom of a lake.

"Constantia, are you all right?"

All right? Nothing has been right since the day I saw Lady Gwenllian's brooch in your hand.

He pulled her into a sitting position and gave her a firm but measured shake. "What the blazes, Stantia?"

His handsome features rippled, smoothed, and rippled again through her water-filled eyes. She could hear the exasperation in his voice. A hundred answers clamored to her tongue and died there. What could she say? After all these years, after her repeated gibes at his integrity, after striking him on the head and fleeing from him, why would he believe anything that came out of her mouth? She felt ill with regret and grief.

A weary, leaden weight engulfed her. She had been up since yesterday dawn, eaten only a few bites of dried meat, made two hectic dashes through the woods, and could not have slept more than an hour or two in Jevon's lap. No wonder she had lost all control over her emotions.

Understanding the source of her tumultuous outbursts helped her curb them.

"Do . . ." She gulped down another sob. "Do you have anything more to eat?"

He gave her a wary side glance but rummaged through his pouch, handing her another chunk of dried meat, followed by his flask.

"You can thank my wicked English earl for that," Jevon said. "He provides generous rations for his men. Lord Fulcard d'Eveque made us scavenge our own food whenever we marched. I served d'Eveque a year with my bow as a mercenary."

"Mercenary?" She recoiled. Mercenaries were men without principles or conscience, soldiers who delighted in terrorizing the weak with wanton acts of violence as long as they were paid for their destruction. Jevon could never—!

The sardonic curve of his mouth cut off her shock.

"Did you think I survived the past seven years by poaching alone? After my debacle with the candle at the inn, I joined a mercenary band in Normandy. I found their captains less likely to look too closely at missing ears or suspicious scars. One called Serlo had assembled an elite company of archers and hired out our services to quarreling Norman lords. Serlo dubbed me le Falquet because I never missed my targets. Our reputation reached Gunthar when he was hiring soldiers to join his campaign in Poitou."

Constantia washed down a mouthful of pork with some watered-down wine. "And the earl offered you a pardon for your theft?"

She could have bitten off her tongue as soon as she said it. She should have said, "alleged theft," but from the hardened planes of Jevon's face, she knew it was too late to correct herself.

"He has seen my scar," Jevon said, "but he has not asked me for details. That was not part of the bargain he struck with us."

No, his earl asked only for loyalty. A royal pardon would nullify the bounty Laurant placed on Jevon's head. No wonder he was so determined to return her to Vere.

She rolled her head back to avoid his hard gaze and stared at the sky overhead. Was the dome above the clearing beginning to tint from charcoal to smoky gray, or was it merely obscured by the smoke from the fire? There was still time to try to find a way to escape. Doing so would rob Jevon of his earl's reward and leave him at risk of retribution by the Poitevin barons who remembered his "crime," but she could not trust his assurances that his earl would not harm the innocent at Pennault, along with its rebellious baron, not after she had watched his earl fling Sir Damien from Vere's wall.

What am I to do? she asked the dimming stars. *Is there some way to talk Jevon out of his thirst for vengeance on those who wronged him? Do I even want to try?*

She looked at the smooth, unblemished skin of her hands. Had she been cruelly branded, driven out of her home, and declared a malefactor whom anyone could kill without question or repercussion, she might have wanted revenge too.

She drank again from the flask. The wine stung the cut on her lip. She dabbed the corner of her mouth with the edge of her sleeve. Jevon kept her supply of meat replenished as she ate, eventually joining her in the modest feast. This time she made sure she consumed enough to maintain mastery of her composure.

"I meant what I said earlier," she told him. "I would have gone with you into your banishment. I would have gone with you if they'd let me."

He took her chin in his hand and tilted it toward the firelight. She quivered as his thumb feathered along her cheekbone.

Dear heaven, let there be light enough for him to see the truth in my eyes.

"What you mean," he said, "is that you would have gone with Jevon the thief."

Maybe he read *too* much truth. There remained a few holes in his story.

"The brooch has never been found," she said, "and I do not believe Llygad would take it. Why do so only to keep it concealed all this time? If he'd wished to curry Lady Gwenllian's favor, he would have returned it to her."

"Or sold it. He could have claimed his uncle sent him the money and no one would question it."

"Lady Gwenllian would. His uncle is her father, and you know he gave Llygad a generous stipend to stay at Pennault and serve her. If Llygad had more coins than usual, she and Lord Laurant would have noticed."

Jevon took a turn drinking from the flask. "Not necessarily. A few extra coins are easily hidden. You remember how Llygad clung to his Welsh ways, taunting us with slurs he knew we could not understand. Maybe he wanted money he did not have to account for to pay his way back to Wales once Laurant knighted him."

"But he has never left Pennault, and I do not think he ever wants to." Constantia swallowed the last bit of pork while she sorted through the past. "And he did not cling to Welsh ways beyond the language. Lady Gwenllian wanted someone to talk to in her native tongue, and Llygad was all she had. But remember how he cut off his long Welsh locks when he became a squire? He resented you, Jevon, because everything that came so hard for him came so easily to you, but I think he also admired you. He watched you and Raimon at training for hours, trying to learn how you so successfully wielded your swords."

Whenever she could, Constantia slipped away from her duties to watch Jevon train too. She had seen how Llygad's eyes followed Jevon's movements more than Raimon's or Franco's or any of the other squires'.

More recollections flowed back. "When Llygad turned fourteen, he started using his uncle's stipend to buy clothes in the Poitevin fashion to replace the Welsh styles Lady Gwenllian wanted him to wear. Even then I noticed he purchased styles and colors similar to yours. And Llygad favored the crossbow, which the other squires preferred, over his long Welsh war bow, until he saw how you favored the speed of the war bow. Then he suddenly became fond of his old bow again."

"So he was jealous because I trounced him in every competition? That's all the more reason for him to have blamed me for selling the brooch." Jevon dug through his pouch but his hand came out empty. "That's all the food except for some dried beans we've no time to boil. The flask is empty too. The pork and wine will have to hold you until we get to Vere."

He stood.

"We're—we're leaving now?" she stammered.

"As soon as I put the fire out."

She realized with a touch of panic that the fire had died down as they ate and the sky had grayed from smoke to pewter.

"It is still too dark to find our way," she insisted.

"While I hid in these woods, I learned how to evade men hunting me at every hour of the day or night. I only need a little light to find both Pennault and Vere."

His words appalled her. "Men hunted you?"

He shrugged as he stirred the embers with the sword. "For the bounty. One hundred livres of silver can be highly motivating. They probably thought it would be easier to catch me unawares after dark. Or maybe they thought the challenge would redound to their greater courage, like stalking and killing a wild boar on a midwinter's night."

He used the blade to churn up the damp earth beneath the grass and throw it on top of the embers.

That men would hunt one another for greed and sport sickened her. "Did you ever see their faces?" Surely no man she knew would be so vile, even for silver.

"A few knights from Belle Noir, though never Drogo or Raynor."

Drogo and Raynor de Molinet, the sons of the castle across the river from Vere. Both men were knights themselves now.

"What about Triston?" Sir Damien's eldest son and Drogo were the same age and friends.

"I never saw him or any of Sir Damien's men. Perhaps Lady Aline dissuaded her husband from joining in the hunt."

"She was a kindhearted woman," Constantia said. "Do you remember how she lent us her prayer books?"

"Aye, always with a smile and a twinkle in her eye, knowing Lady Gwenllian would chide her for it but not caring."

Constantia thought she caught an undercurrent of fondness in Jevon's voice before he gave the remaining embers a rough swish.

"What made Lady Gwenllian miss the brooch that day of all days?" he asked as he kicked another clod of dirt atop the embers and stirred the amalgam into a dark, orange-flecked mound. "She neglected to mend the clasp for months after it broke."

Constantia fiddled with the ties of his cloak, reluctant to relive that day. "After you showed it to me, I returned to the keep and went to help in the kitchen until Lady Gwenllian called me and Guia to her chamber. Lady Gwenllian was in a foul mood, berating Beatris for accidentally stepping on the baroness's hem and tearing it."

Without the fire's warmth, Constantia felt the brisk riffle of a breeze again. She pulled the cloak closer.

"Lady Gwenllian sent for Sybil to switch Beatris, and while we waited for her to come, Guia and I helped Lady Gwenllian change her gown. I was lacing up her surcote when Heléne came in to tell her mother that Therri was teasing Clothilde with his new puppy again. You remember Clothilde's fear of dogs, and as small and harmless as Gaweyne was, he liked to show his teeth and growl to make her hop about and scream. Therri thought it was funny."

"Scamp," Jevon muttered, but she could hear the amusement in his voice.

Constantia smiled too. It was wrong of Therri to let the puppy frighten his high-strung sister, but Gaweyne had been so small that everyone in the castle was hard-pressed to conceal their mirth as they calmed the terrified twelve-year-old.

"Of course, Lady Gwenllian could not chastise Therri until flawlessly dressed. To hurry things along, she told Heléne to fetch her gold chain with sapphires. Heléne discovered the brooch missing and innocently asked what became of it."

"I see." Jevon stomped the dirt on top of the embers, his humor extinguished with the fire. "So, of course, you told Lady Gwenllian I stole it."

Constantia's patience with his stubborn refrain nearly snapped. "Before I could tell her anything, she insisted Guia or Beatris or I had taken it because we were the only ones who knew where she kept the key. It never occurred to her that you might have seen her place it under the third candlestick on her hearth while you attended her in her chamber. She sent for Sybil to switch all three of us. I could not let her punish Beatris and Guia when they had nothing to do with the brooch's disappearance, you know I could not."

He said nothing, but he shook his head. She hoped in agreement. The noble squire she had fallen in love with would have been the first to protect the innocent.

"I explained why you'd taken it. I was certain that once Lady Gwenllian understood, she would be grateful for your thoughtfulness."

Jevon squatted and ran his fingers through the now-dark earthen pile to make sure the ashes were cold. His broad back looked square and solid, his posture alert. Was it too much to hope he had accepted her story?

An owl *hooo-ed* in the distance. For a moment, the breeze carried the scent of roses.

Constantia shook the fancy away. "But instead, Lady Gwenllian, took it as a betrayal of her trust. You had been in her most intimate surroundings. She had confided her most personal thoughts to you. You, more than anyone, could have humiliated her and the baron had you spread abroad her disparagements of our neighbors and guests. To have taken her key and brooch without asking her suggested, in her mind, that your intentions toward her were malicious. When she dragged me to the hall to tell Laurant, I was sure he would pacify her anger. Laurant regarded you most highly among all his squires. At most, I thought he might deal you a sharp rebuke. I *never* thought he and his knights would turn against you." Bitterness filled her mouth. "I knew he doted on Lady Gwenllian, but I did not realize how completely he sat under her thumb until I watched how he let her fan his anger against you. By then it was too late. I had already told Laurant I saw you with the brooch."

Jevon continued crouching where the fire had recently burned. Then he stood and dusted off his hands.

He slid the sword into his belt, then picked up his bow and arrow bag. "Cunning to use Guia and Beatris as a shield for your actions. Had you not confessed yourself as good as betrothed to Llygad while I saw how warmly you smiled at Raimon two days ago, I might have believed you. Get up. It's time to go."

Of course he did not believe her. The sky looked much the same as before, a dark-gray silver, but she could no longer see any stars. She reluctantly stood and shook out her skirts while she tried to decide whether to go with him or flee again.

"If you'd wanted to marry Llygad," Jevon said as she smoothed the creases in her gown, "you should have told me instead of letting me make a fool of myself over you. Though how you could even consider him after the way he treated you—! But I suppose he had more to offer than any pittance of a dowry I could raise. He'd have been a Welsh lord someday."

Jevon's sarcasm blistered the air that had rechilled with the fire doused. Nor was he finished with the grudge he still nourished.

"On the other hand, Raimon and Franco were skilled enough with lance and sword to do well in the tourney and they always treated you with respect and courtesy. I can forgive you for not knowing your mind at seventeen, Stantia. I could have forgiven you for saying you were unsure. But I cannot forgive you for deceiving all of us. You played us against each other without any of us realizing it."

Llygad had taunted Jevon with that very accusation. Hurt at being excluded from the other squires' friendship, Llygad had lashed out at them, especially Jevon, with his immature gibes of her. But young as they all were, Jevon should have known Constantia's heart.

She snapped her skirts with impatience. "I did not. I meant every word I ever said to you."

"Have you forgotten the troubadours who will immortalize your and Raimon's love?"

Had Raimon said such a foolish thing as they rode past Jevon on the road to Vere? Constantia could barely remember. Raimon constantly spouted folderol these days, trying to persuade her that he loved her.

Jevon pointed toward the murky shadows. It was useless to defend herself again. Lacking a viable plan for escape, she moved in the direction he indicated.

"I do not know what you think you heard between me and Raimon," she said as Jevon's footsteps crunched behind her, "but there is nothing but friendship between us."

"Does Raimon know that? Does Llygad? Or do you think you can marry one and take the other for your lover?"

Constantia gasped and whirled on him. "How dare you!"

"Considering how many deceitful wives have tried to lure me to their beds until this frightened them away"—Jevon flicked the back of his hand toward her even though she could not see his brand in the fledgling light—"I learned very quickly what a fool I was to think any woman could be trusted."

It took a moment for Constantia to turn around and move again. How had it not occurred to her that the handsome squire whose thick, wavy hair she had been too shy to caress as a girl, whose warm kiss had taken her to dizzying heights, would grow into a man other women coveted?

Had he let any of them seduce him? His sardonic motion demonstrated how easily the dark could mask a scar.

Her last illusions of the selfless, chivalrous youth she had known snuffed out. The harsh reality of the hardened, vengeful mercenary he'd become marched her mercilessly toward the enemy's arms. Jevon would not rest until he punished them all, Lady Gwenllian for condemning him, Laurant for branding him, and Constantia for betraying him.

They walked for some time in silence. The fresh, woodsy smells of oak, beech, wild thyme, and lavender thrummed at the edges of her thoughts with a zest she'd never experienced in the daytime.

"You are wrong," she finally said. "If I married Llygad, I would never betray him with another man. He has already been hurt too much."

"Llygad? Hurt?" Jevon snorted. "The pompous oaf was the most pampered brat at Pennault. Even Therri was not as coddled by his parents as Llygad was by Lady Gwenllian."

"And Llygad hated it because it made everyone resent him, even the baron. He did not want to be favored by his cousin. He wanted to be like the rest of you, jovial rivals who, after heatedly losing to you on the training field, passed the evenings drinking and gaming and jesting like brothers. You and Raimon and Franco never invited him to join you."

"He never wanted to. He was happy eating sweetmeats with Lady Gwenllian and playing draughts with her when the baron was too busy to entertain her."

"He hated it," Constantia repeated. "If you had not been so cocky and condescending, you would have known that."

Jevon muttered something that sounded like an indignant, "Cocky?"

Llygad had been the only thing Constantia and Jevon ever quarreled about in those days. She had only been at Pennault a short time before she saw Llygad's insecurities and frustration at being disdained by the Poitevin boys his age. She'd repeatedly tried to make peace between them, but Jevon, Raimon, and Franco refused once Llygad reacted to their initial rebuff by insulting Constantia, knowing his cousin would protect him from their retribution. Llygad's belittling abuse of Constantia cleft an unbreachable chasm between him and the other squires.

The flush on Llygad's cheeks and the way he avoided Constantia's eyes when she spoke to him told her he knew his behavior was shameful. Yet again and again he fell back to insulting her when he was with Jevon and his friends, as though doing so shielded some wounded part of him with a reflex so strong he could not resist. Until one day, after Jevon was gone and Llygad and the others had been knighted, they all seemed to grow up and forget past offenses. Or at least pretended to.

But all Jevon remembered was the churlish Welsh squire who had tormented him through Constantia seven years ago.

"If you had any idea of the slurs he called you," Jevon said, "you'd not defend him."

"I do know." She hesitated. "Well, not exactly. Do you?"

Jevon hesitated. "Not . . . exactly. He always insulted you in Welsh. But I could tell by the look on his face the slurs were nasty."

She readjusted the too-large cloak, which had begun to slip from her shoulders. "He apologized after you left for the names he'd called me."

"Easy to be sorry now when you have a fat inheritance dangling in front of him."

The urge to shake Jevon was so great she had to grip her hands tight into the cloak. "My father has not yet agreed to give me precedence over my elder sisters. And what of you?"

"What about me?"

"You have blamed everyone else for your misfortune." Such an inadequate word for what he suffered, but she could not dismiss the gaps in his story. "Me for some imaginary betrayal, Lady Gwenllian for being angry you took her brooch, Lord Laurant for punishing you for all that unexplained silver—"

"Unexplained? Are you suggesting I lied to you?"

"You mean about selling some magnificently expensive ring no one ever saw but you?"

"Every word I said to you was the truth."

Did he realize how he echoed her own protest back to her?

She stopped in her tracks and pivoted to face him. "Therri's puppy ripped your surcote just after Epiphany, and the brooch did not disappear till March. If your mother sent you a ring, why did you not show it to me? Or to Raimon or Franco? You three shared a chamber. You borrowed one another's clothes. You admitted that Franco rummaged freely through your chest whenever he wished to borrow something. How could you possibly have hidden so much money from them for two months?"

She crossed her arms and stared into his shadowed face, knowing exactly where his eyes would be if there were enough light to glare into them. She had carried the guilt of that silver in her hollowed out breast for seven years, convinced that if she had only said no when he'd asked her to marry him, or even "wait," the tragedy that befell him would not have happened. Better to have lived together forever only as friends than to endure this relentless, perpetual pain of having their love wrenched apart because she had tempted him into theft by foolishly saying yes.

The least he could do after all this time was admit to what he had done. He owed her that much. Until he did, she would not move another inch.

MARCH 1167
PENNAULT CASTLE

"Aren't you praying with us tonight, Constantia?"

She only dimly heard Guia's query. Constantia sat in the middle of her narrow, lumpy bed in her sleeping chemise, knees drawn up with her arms wrapped around them, envisioning Jevon's knighting in only ten more days. Would he wish her to be brave when he rode away in six weeks with Raimon and Franco to fulfill their dreams of tournament glory and fortune? Or would it please him to see her weep to lose him? She hoped the latter because she did not think she could conceal her tears at their parting, even if it were only long enough to win her a dowry.

At least he will have to kiss me again. No more of this vexing restraint when we sit in the garden. He cannot leave his promised bride without at least one more kiss to remember him by.

"Constantia!"

She sighed and left her bed. She did not need to pray to Saint Nicholas anymore, but it was better to go through the motions for now. She had not told Guia and Beatris about her betrothal to Jevon yet. *Betrothal.* Her body warmed at the joyous word. She knew her two chamber mates would not deliberately betray her, but she also did not trust them not to inadvertently slip in front of Lady Gwenllian.

Constantia knelt next to Guia, who knelt next to Beatris in front of their shared clothing chest, the same order they had prayed in from oldest to youngest for the last eight years.

"What happened to your old picture of Saint Nicholas?" Guia asked as Beatris placed a new drawing on a scrap of parchment atop the chest they used as an altar.

This face was just as lopsided as the one Constantia had prayed to since she was nine, still with a slash for a mouth to indicate sternness because, Beatris said, no matter how generous Saint Nicholas might be, the saints on the wooden panels in Pennault's chapel all stared sternly during mass. She had drawn the same pointy image for both the saint's miter and beard. The shoulders were crooked, his robe flying out at the sides more like floppy wings than a bishop's sober vestments. Three circles depicting coins floated between the four lines that represented his fingers.

"I accidentally dropped the old picture out the window when I closed the shutters last time," Beatris said. "That stupid old owl that keeps us awake at night scooped it up and soared off with it. This one is better anyway. I draw much better now than I did as a child."

Constantia and Guia exchanged glances in the smoky candlelight, their lips squeezed together to suppress their laughter. Amusement at Beatris's boast helped quell Constantia's guilt over how often Jevon's "call" to her woke the other women. It was his own fault if he grew impatient waiting for them to fall back to sleep so Constantia could slip out to meet him.

Beatris began her petition. "Dear Saint Nicholas, I have prayed so very faithfully all these years and have waited ever so patiently for your reply. But I am eighteen and still have no husband because I have no dowry. Lady Gwenlllian says no man will overlook my poverty because I am not lissome and willowy like she and that I'm too fluttery to make a good wife."

Constantia felt a stab of anger at Lady Gwenllian's cruelty.

"But that knight who tried to seduce me at Sir Raimon's knighting called me pretty and buxom. I told him no because I wish to remain a virtuous woman. But you know how men are. Hot and lascivious and eager to take advantage of defenseless women. I would very, very much prefer to be an honorable wife, and you, oh, glorious saint, have proven you can provide me a way."

Beatris continued to make her case to the saint, laying out her many self-perceived talents—spinning, sewing, and cooking—all of which Beatris was as "accomplished" at as drawing. But no one could deny her kind heart.

Constantia still vividly remembered her painful loneliness when she first came to Pennault. The indifference with which her father sent her off to serve in his liege lord's castle while she still grieved the death of her mother hurt and disconcerted her. The incongruity of Lady Gwenllian's soft beauty with her cold nature bewildered Constantia, while Sybil and her switch terrified her. Everyone at Pennault ordered Constantia about as though she were some drudge and not the gently born daughter of a respectable knight. She had softly cried herself to sleep every night while listening to Guia and Beatris repeat their ritual prayers.

Until Beatris had taken Constantia's hand and said, "Join us."

The three girls were too different to have become the sort of friends Constantia and Jevon were, but Constantia had not cried herself to sleep a single night since.

"Can you not show me the kindness you did the three daughters of the rich man reduced to penury by envy, whose daughters were nearly forced into harlotry because their father lost their dowries? If you could just spare one more purse to toss through our window . . ."

Constantia felt Guia stir and knew she had nudged Beatris as she always did.

"Three purses through our window," Beatris corrected, "as you did for them. Guia, you did remember to open the shutters, didn't you?"

Guia scrambled up from her knees and hurried to the shutters. She was not usually so addled, but she had seemed moody and distracted for a while now. Constantia was not sure when it had started. Ever since Jevon asked her to marry him, Constantia had been too blissfully distracted to think much about Guia's glumness.

"Amen."

Guia had barely knelt again before Beatris pronounced the word.

Guia hastily refolded her hands for her turn at prayer. "O Holy Saint Nicholas, I am plain and dull and as mousy as my hair, but I have worked very hard and uncomplainingly to serve my mistress, and I should work twice as hard to serve a husband well."

Guia always began her petition by demeaning herself. In truth, she was quite pretty in a quiet, unassuming way. Constantia envied Guia's pale, smooth skin and fine, light-brown hair, which always stayed pinned exactly where it was supposed to and fell in a well-behaved sheet when loose. But years of Lady Gwenllian's belittling had dulled Guia's once-bright spirit and subdued the self-confidence in her step.

"It would be ever so nice to be loved."

A forlorn wistfulness cradled these words. Constantia always imagined the plea cupped tenderly in Guia's hands and extended beseechingly toward the saint, though, when she looked, Guia's palms always remained piously pressed together when she spoke them.

"But if I am unworthy of love, I would most humbly take a man without it if he would deign to take me for a wife. My stitches are neat and small. I never burn the bread. I can whisk the most stubborn stain out of a soiled shirt. I would be the meekest, most obedient wife any man could ever wish for if you could only spare me one very modest purse for a dowry. Amen."

Now it was Constantia's turn. Her petition tripped a little too briskly off her tongue. "Saint Nicholas, friend of maidens and impoverished daughters, lift our hearts from longing. Send us kindness. Send us hope. Send us dowries if heaven wills it. Amen."

Guia and Beatris both stared at her. Constantia's petitions for a husband were usually longer and more eloquent. Even when she mimicked the other girls to Saint Nicholas with allusions to the grandly attired barons and knights who sometimes dined at Laurant's table, from her very first prayer, Constantia's vision included only one image: the tall, handsome squire who smiled at her on her very first day at Pennault when no one else in the whole castle had. Jevon de Cazalet had soon been teasing her with a twinkle in his eye, even as he always seemed to appear out of nowhere to help her with the menial tasks Lady Gwenllian assigned her. How could Constantia ever have thought of anyone else?

Now Saint Nicholas had answered her prayers, and Constantia was eager for her bed. There were not many more nights for Old Sir Hoo to call her to the garden.

In a glow of gratitude to the saint, she impulsively hugged Guia, then Beatris. "Saint Nicholas will be kind to all of us. I know he will. You—we must only be patient a little bit longer. Let us show our trust in him by going to sleep and dreaming of happy tomorrows."

"I lay awake all night listening for you," Constantia whispered to Jevon in the great hall the next day.

They stood a few steps behind Lady Gwenllian and the Baron de Laurant as their lady and lord welcomed a newly arrived guest to the castle. Constantia blinked at all the gilding stars woven into the man's indigo silk surcote.

"Raimon kept me and Franco up till nearly dawn."

She heard a yawn in Jevon's soft tones. Neither of them wished to elicit one of Lady Gwenllian's glares for interrupting her fulsome welcome.

"Of course, Raimon sleeps with the other knights in the garrison quarters now, but Franco and I will be knighted soon, too, and then—"

"You will all ride off to the tournament fields, and Raimon wanted to make plans." She did not know whether to be glad Jevon would not be traveling alone or worried that his two ramshackle friends would get him into trouble. Neither Franco nor Raimon had a beloved at Pennault waiting for him to return and marry her as expeditiously as possible.

"Aye. Except that . . ."

"What?" She tore her gaze away from the dazzling surcote to look at Jevon as he trailed off. "Did Lord Laurant refuse to sponsor you?"

"I have not asked him. I was waiting until Raimon and Franco and I were all knighted."

His friends seemed equally confident that Lord Laurant would help them purchase their gear when she heard the three talking at Raimon's knighting two months ago. Jevon must be nervous about it, though. Why else would he fidget so with his fingers ?

He must have seen her glance at his hands, for he suddenly balled one over the other to quiet them.

Even though part of her wished the baron would refuse just to keep Jevon near her, Constantia tried to reassure him. Without his tournament winnings, how else would his father ever agree to let Jevon marry her? "I am certain Lord Laurant will not refuse you. No one at Pennault fights as well as you."

His eyes snapped with excitement muted with a glimmer of uncertainty. The baron had not lectured his squires on leaving Pennault to follow the tournament circuit before he'd conferred the accolade on Raimon. Jevon had taken that as a hopeful sign. Unless, he'd confessed to Constantia,

Laurant was waiting until he'd dubbed Franco, the last of this year's eligible squires, so he could instruct them all together.

Jevon suddenly grinned and tilted his head toward the visitor with his bushy blond beard and balding head.

"You may simply call me Albrecht," the visitor said. "I am a humble pilgrim on my vay to pray at ze shrine of Santiago de Compostela. I stopped at your *Kloster des Heiliger Lukas*—" Albrecht must have seen the baron's puzzled expression. He paused as though searching for a translation. "Monastery *des* Saint Luc. But zeir guest quarters are quite meager, and my bones are very delicate, very delicate indeed. Ze monks suggested I vould find more comfortable lodgings viz you, *mein Herr*, if you vould be so generous as to offer me a bed for ze night."

Jevon choked down a chuckle while Constantia muffled her giggle. The pilgrim's bones had so many layers of cushioning flesh that a rough pallet should offer him as much comfort as a feather bed.

Lord Laurant affably assured Abrecht that not only was he welcome to stay the night but also join the baron and his lady on the dais for the midday meal. The servants bustled around them, setting the tables. Constantia and Jevon had been on their way to take up their serving positions behind Lady Gwenllian's chair when Lady Gwenllian and the baron met them on the stairs and bade their attendance as they welcomed their visitor.

"Your chains are most exquisite," Lady Gwenllian exclaimed after the pilgrim thanked her husband with a lavishly deep bow for one so stout.

The pilgrim puffed his husky chest, which was overlaid with seven jewel-crusted chains, and held up his portly hands to show off the seven rings that adorned them. "Zank you, *meine Dame*. Zank you. I vear zese to remind me of ze Seven Heavenly Virtues."

"He should have donned them as warnings against the Seven Deadly Sins," Jevon muttered, almost sending Constantia into giggles again.

Jevon lowered his right hand to his side so that it dangled close to Constantia's, as he always did when he intended to initiate a furtive game behind the baroness's chair while she dined. Together, they ticked off the pilgrim's sins.

"Greed," Jevon whispered. He jutted one finger from the fist he'd formed along his thigh.

She stretched out two fingers against her dark-green skirt. "Gluttony."

There could be no more doubt of that than of the pilgrim's love for gold and jewels.

They continued down the list of sins while Lady Gwenllian cooed over the pilgrim's jewels. Laurant's efforts to divert the subject to hunting had failed. Their garrulous guest gabbled on in his odd, guttural voice about his "modest" chains and rings and how earnestly he looked forward to showing his devotion to the saint by kneeling at the altar and kissing Saint James's holy tomb.

Jevon murmured, "Do you suppose he will make . . ."

". . . a donation of those chains or rings to the shrine?" Watching the way Albrecht caressed his glittering ornaments, Constantia doubted it.

Albrecht prattled so long about his arduous journey from his homeland and the manifold comforts he had given up for the saint—"Not zat I begrudge a single one, *meine Dame,* not a single one!"—that the servants finished setting the tables and other members of the castle's household began to stroll into the hall to dine.

Jevon and Constantia found themselves pushed away from the baron and his wife as Laurant's more senior knights pressed between them to welcome the pilgrim guest. Constantia finally felt free to openly smile up at Jevon. She missed the crimson surcote that had accented the tints in his russet hair and warmed the deep brown of his walnut eyes. But his squire's serving attire—a black surcote with the symbol of Laurant's house, a double-headed phoenix rising from flames, sewn to its shoulder—complemented his handsome face sufficiently to make her tingle with longing.

He returned her smile, but it held the same tempered eagerness she had seen in his eyes before the pilgrim distracted them.

"Stantia"—his hands again fretted briefly with each other before he tucked them behind his back—"if I can persuade Lady Gwenllian to free me for an hour or two tomorrow, will you stroll in the woods with me?"

Oh, how her heart leapt to answer yes! But—"Tomorrow is laundry day. Guia and I will be occupied all morning."

"I have something to do in the morning too, something I hope will please Lady Gwenllian so much she excuses us both for the afternoon. We can make an excuse to take Heléne and Therri to play in the clearing if we have to, but I'd rather have some time alone."

Twice Laurant had nearly caught Jevon and Constantia late at night when, apparently unable to sleep, the baron had relieved his restiveness by wandering about his wife's rose garden. Thankfully, they successfully slipped into the dark before he saw them.

"I would love that." Constantia's lip trembled despite her determination to be strong. "You will be leaving me so very soon."

"It is no easier for me to think of it," Jevon said. "But maybe—maybe . . ." His eyes darted to the cluster of knights surrounding Lord Laurant, Lady Gwenllian, and the pilgrim. "Well, just promise to walk with me tomorrow. It may be our only chance to say goodbye with no one else looking on—but maybe . . ."

"Constantia!" Raimon, with Franco at his heels, negotiated his way through the crowd with the confident adroitness he had cultivated since his knighting. "Did Lady Gwenllian tell you? You're to dine with me at the sideboards today."

Constantia glanced from him to the baroness in surprise. "No, she said nothing to me. I am not dressed for table dining."

"You look beautiful in everything." Raimon's gaze swept her neat but unembellished green wool gown. She did not take the admiring glance seriously. Gallant exaggeration also accompanied his elevated status. "But I knew you would think your gown too simple, so I bought you this."

He rather boldly removed her simple white veil and replaced it with a gold-banded veil that floated against her cheeks like gossamer.

"Oh, Raimon!" she exclaimed. "I cannot accept—"

"Of course you can," he said. "It is simply a gift between friends. I cannot gamble all my sols on dice, no matter how often I win."

He glanced slyly at Jevon, who watched their exchange with a stony expression. It was *not* gallant of Raimon to tease Jevon so, but men often indulged in odd pranks. And Raimon did not know she and Jevon planned to marry. Jevon would have told her had he confided their secret to anyone. As Raimon said, the veil was simply a gift from a friend.

Jevon asked, his voice somewhat stiff, "How exactly did you persuade Lady Gwenllian to excuse Constantia from her service?"

Raimon folded his arms across his surcote, a mere shade darker than the color Constantia wore but more smoothly woven, and tossed his head just jauntily enough to stir the mix of brown-blond locks that fringed his brow. "I defeated Pennault's three best knights today, Sir Guilhelm, Sir Eudes, and Sir Baudri. Lady Gwenllian happened to be passing through the bailey and saw my victories. She asked me what reward I would ask for my knightly prowess. So I replied, 'To dine at the side of the most beauteous lady of the castle. But since my lady's lord would frown on granting me so bold a boon, then bid the lady who stands nearest her on the dais holding the laver in which my lady washes her resplendent hands to sit with me in poor proxy for my lady's glorious company.'"

Jevon snorted. "I see you've become a poet as well as Pennault's best knight."

Constantia pinched her lips at Jevon. His sarcasm ill-suited him, even if Raimon *had* become boastful of usurping the title of "best" from Jevon simply because Jevon was not yet a knight.

"The point is," Raimon said, "Lady Gwenllian agreed. Now Beatris will be serving the baroness today with you. Franco has another six weeks of taking my former place on the dais with the baron."

Franco scowled. He wore the same black surcote and badge as Jevon. "It should be Llygad," Franco complained, "since he's next to be knighted after Jevon, but Laurant says the Welshman is so clumsy he's likely to slice his finger off while carving or topple Laurant's goblet into his lap."

Constantia gave them all a rebuking frown. "I wish you would not all call him that. Llygad does not like to think of himself as Welsh."

Jevon's face creased with his usual glower. "Then he should stop insulting you in his barbarous Welsh tongue."

"And eating barbarous Welsh foods," Franco said.

"And fight like a clever, agile Poitevin instead of tripping over his big Welsh feet," Raimon added.

A shadow fell across their group.

"Hush!" Constantia hissed.

Llygad had materialized from the milling crowd to stand right behind them. From the glare in his deep-blue eyes, she knew he had heard every word.

"I see your court is assembled around you, *merch y gwynt*. When they ride off to their tournament folly, which of your favors will land in the mud first? The ribbon you embroidered for Franco, the feather with the dried lavender sprig you gave Raimon, or the linen knot you tied for Jevon?"

Her gaze darted to Jevon's. Like Raimon's veil, she had made the simple gifts for his friends because she thought of them as her friends too and wished them *all* well in the tourney. Jevon, of course, would excel the most. She knew it, and he knew it, just as he knew the token she had given him held far more meaning than the others. The trinity knot he would wear on his armor as he fought symbolized the fidelity between them, the three interwoven loops reflecting the eternal nature of their love, just like the initials he had carved into the oak tree.

She had been mindful to wait until he and his friends were together to present them with her tokens so that one might not think himself more favored by her than the others.

Except for you, Jevon. You know you are the only man in my heart.

It dismayed her when his gaze dropped from hers.

Llygad continued with his gibes. "Most likely Laurant will refuse to sponsor any of them and spare you the humiliation, *gwraig ffôl.* If they knew what a *neidr bach* you were, playing with their affections under the guise of kindly goodwill—"

Jevon moved as though to hit Llygad, but Franco blocked him.

"Not here," Franco warned. "Lady Gwenllian will see you."

Constantia stared at Llygad. He lifted a defiant chin, but she glimpsed the misery in his eyes before they, too, dropped from hers and he strode off to one of the sideboards to sit beside Guia. Llygad's pain hurt Constantia's heart. If Jevon and Raimon and Franco would only be kinder to him . . .

Raimon drew Constantia's arm through his, possessively patting her hand. "Forget about him. Llygad's a surly beast and will never be anything else. He is jealous because he knows he'd be trampled in the mêlée before he even managed to draw his sword. Come, my lady. It is time to dine."

He tossed another amused glance at Jevon as he escorted Constantia to a table on the opposite side of the hall.

"Just ten more days," Jevon called after them. "Then we will see who Pennault Castle's best knight is and with whom Lady Constantia dines. And don't forget that you've promised to walk with me tomorrow, Stantia."

Raimon's veil glided against her cheeks as she shook her head. Men. Jevon could not possibly take Llygad's taunts seriously. She saw Jevon's hands fidgeting again. She would assuage his doubts with all the farewell kisses he wanted tomorrow, kisses that would leave him in no doubt of her sole and complete love.

AUGUST 1174
THE WOODS BETWEEN VERE AND PENNAULT CASTLES

Jevon felt Constantia's resistance as he laid his hand on her shoulder. He tried to turn her back onto the path to Vere, but she stood rooted like an oak. He could compel her to move. He was taller and stronger than she. But however hardened his hellish battles as a mercenary had left him, he could not bring himself to bully Constantia.

He released her. "Fine. I did not sell the ring at once because I had no one to sell it *to*. And until I found someone willing to pay enough to satisfy my father, I did not wish to raise your hopes that I'd found a way to marry you. That's why I did not show you the ring."

He did not realize he had crossed his arms, imitating her posture, until the words were out of his mouth. He dropped his arms at the exact same moment she lowered hers.

Mirrored hearts. Soul's twin.

The phrases he had boyishly embroidered in his mind to describe the bond between them rushed back before he could stop them. That naive dream had been false then, and it was false now. Their reflective actions were nothing more than coincidence.

Her arms vanished deep inside his cloak. Had she noticed too?

"If the ring was as valuable as you say," she told him, "someone at Pennault would have been eager to buy it. Lady Gwenllian would have coveted such a ring, or Laurant to give her as a gift. He loved showering her with expensive trinkets."

"If I'd tried to sell my ring to either of them or to anyone at Pennault, they'd have wanted to know how I came by it. I feared word would reach my father and he would put a stop to my plan, saying, like you, that the ring belonged to my mother and was not meant for some poor woman's dowry."

Her shoulders drooped, Jevon's cloak nearly slipping off her shoulders. "I know he never liked me."

She sounded deflated, as she always did when he mentioned his father.

He pulled the cloak back into place and secured it around her neck. "Father did not know whether he liked you or not. He did not know you, Stantia. What he would not have liked was the idea of a dowerless woman marrying his youngest son."

His father could not possibly understand how Jevon had felt. His parents' marriage had been arranged by his grandparents. Jevon's father had never experienced the heart-thumping, blood-pounding, dizzying ecstasy of youthful love.

Constantia sighed. "He would have cut you off had you married me. It was selfish of me not to think of that."

Jevon almost reached inside the cloak to press her hands. Would her fingers still fit perfectly in his? He clenched his fist to resist. She wanted him to console her, to fall under her spell again so he would let her go.

"We can stand here all night in the cold regretting the past," he said, steeling his voice, "or we can journey on to the warm hearth fires of Vere. The earl's men will provide you with a hot meal and all the privacy and security you need to bathe and sleep. But if you prefer to stand here with an empty belly, shivering until the sun comes up, that is up to you. Either way, the one thing you are not going to do is warn Pennault that Gunthar is coming for them next."

Constantia shivered under his cloak. Had he been too harsh? She cupped her hands and huffed into her palms. No, she was merely cold.

He pulled his gloves from his belt and slid them onto her hands. He hoped they would not irritate her skin as they did his. His mercenary captain said most likely the leathermaker Jevon bought them from had soaked the skins in something chafing to him. Constantia's fingertips would still be exposed to the cold, but the leather would warm her palms. The gloves gaped around her slim wrists and fingers, but it was the best he could do until they reached Vere. That, and pull his cloak more snugly around her.

"Thank you," she murmured. "But now *you* will be completely chilled."

"Then take pity on me and walk more briskly to heat up my blood."

He tried to make it sound like a jest, but standing so near her stirred his blood enough to turn his voice husky. If he were not too angry and hurt and betrayed to kiss her, he might have considered warming her with an embrace that kept them both well heated for what remained of the night.

He cleared his throat, hoping scraping out the rasp could also scrub away his desire. He checked the arrow bag at his hip, ran his fingers down his bow string to check the tension before readjusting it on his shoulder, then started moving toward Vere again. Hopefully she would be too disoriented in the slowly lifting darkness to do anything but follow him and he would not need to "urge" her forward with the weapon again.

After the smallest lull, her footsteps scrunched alongside his. "I understand you not wanting to show your ring to anyone at Pennault," she said. "But how did you keep it hidden for so long?"

"I kept it in my money pouch." Jevon counted silently as they walked, marking off the paces between the trees he'd notched when hiding in these woods. "The baron gave his squires a denier a week to gamble with. He said games like passe-dix and rafle were part of our education, but I think he meant for us to learn not to waste our precious coins on reckless games of chance. We lost most of our deniers to the knights, so I began playing less and saving more. If Raimon and Franco heard my mother's ring jingling in my pouch, they would just think it was my coins. I kept the pouch tied to my belt by day to be sure I didn't lose it and under my bolster with my hand around it when I slept."

Twenty-nine, thirty. There they were, three vertical slashes in the tree to his right. Three small slits in the bark every thirty steps meant he drew nearer to Vere. Two slashes warned he was turned about and headed for Pennault. By always keeping the desired marks to his right, Jevon could tell which direction he was headed between the two castles whether the sky was overcast, moonlit, or he traveled before or after the deepest pitch of night.

"I kept hoping Laurant or Lady Gwenllian would send me on an errand into town." He started counting afresh. *One, two, three . . .* "I knew I could fetch a high price for the ring if I sold it to a merchant who recognized its worth and would travel somewhere my father would never hear of it. But they always gave tasks in town to one of the knights. So I finally resigned myself to doing what you said." Jevon still felt the blow of the moment he'd surrendered to reality. "I donned the ring for dinner, intending to offer it to Laurant in exchange for enough silver to buy a new surcote, as my mother suggested."

Constantia sighed. "And go tourneying for us as you'd always planned."

He lightly touched the small of her back to guide her around a tree to keep her on the path. "At sixteen and eighteen and even twenty, it all seemed easy," he confessed. "All I could think of was how my mastery of sword and lance knocked the other squires down and, as I grew older and stronger, all of Pennualt's knights as well. Surely those skills would unhorse contender after contender in the mêlée. With the wealth I imagined earning when they ransomed their horses and armor from me, I could marry whomever I wished. But the closer I drew to knighthood . . ."

The cloak rustled in his trailing pause. Constantia broke it, disconcertingly reading his thoughts.

"You were afraid that no matter how skilled you were, Lord Laurant would refuse to sponsor you after he knighted you. Then you would have to supply your armor and weapons yourself."

"Not to mention a horse. Even with Laurant raising my pay to a sol a week once I was knighted, the baron was right, it would take me years to save enough to buy those things."

"I would have waited for you." The earnestness in Constantia's voice brought a lump to Jevon's throat. "I would have waited for you—for *us*— forever."

Her fingertips slid out of the cloak and brushed against his. In spite of his caution, her touch sparked memories so tender that the last seven years almost melted away. How he had loved her!

She deceived you, he grimly reminded himself. *She only seeks to manipulate you now.*

Yet, instead of shaking her fingers away when they slid into his, he closed his hand around them, trapping the leather glove against his palm. The bulky, over-large barrier failed to prevent her hand from snuggling into his like a perfectly matched note in a monks' choir.

But there was nothing monkish about the bittersweet longing that threatened to thicken his voice again. He drew a deep breath of cold air before he answered.

"It would have taken that long. No one has won more fame in tourneying than William Marshal, yet he remains a bachelor knight, even though he has won King Henry's favor. I would have been an old man by the time I won enough to marry you, if I ever did."

Constantia sighed again. "Then I would have been content to be an old bride."

For a heartbeat, he thought he felt the sweet weight of her head on his shoulder, but when he glanced down, she was staring and walking straight ahead.

"I never saw you with a new surcote."

The dreaminess was gone from her voice. Or perhaps he'd just imagined it. Perhaps he'd imagined she spoke those wistful words at all.

They glided past another trio of slashes. "That's because just as I despaired of selling the ring in town, I found a buyer for it."

The pewter fragments of sky above the trees had begun to silver. It would lighten more quickly as the hour sped toward dawn. There was enough light now for him to glimpse the surprise on her face as she swung around to look at him.

"A buyer? Who?"

"Do you remember that pilgrim who sought a night's rest at Pennault on his way to the shrine at Santiago de Compostela?"

"The fat one with the strange accent who wore a gilt-spangled surcote and complained to Lord Laurant that the hospitality offered at the monastery was too austere for his 'delicate bones'?"

Jevon nodded, unable to resist smiling at her merry grin.

Constantia paused and released his hand. "When Lady Gwenllian admired his seven jeweled chains, he bowed like this"—Constantia flung out her arms and swept an elaborate obeisance—"'I vear zese to remind me of ze Seven Heavenly Virtues.'"

Jevon laughed. She captured the pilgrim's obsequious inflection, if not his guttural intonation and manly register, perfectly.

Jevon repeated the same quip he had then. "He should have worn them as warnings against the Seven Deadly Sins."

She sportively bumped his shoulder with hers, then resumed walking.

"Greed." She lifted a finger.

It took Jevon a single stride to catch up with her. "Gluttony." He held up two.

Constantia raised a third. "Sloth. He must have been indolent to have grown so fat."

Jevon lifted a fourth. "And pride." The pilgrim's choice of clothing and jewels had made that as obvious as his greed.

At the time, they jointly agreed to excuse the pilgrim from wrath, as he seemed to be a jolly fellow. But they'd argued over lust. Constantia insisted the pilgrim had not ogled Lady Gwenllian as most men did, while Jevon contended that one could lust as much for gold and jewels as for women.

In the end, they'd agreed to disagree, but now Jevon added a fifth finger for the sin that had not become apparent until hours after the dining ended. "And envy when he saw my ring."

The faintly bluing sky with its tinge of rose lit the querying lift of Constantia's brow. "That was the day you wore the ring to dinner? But I stood right beside you while the baron and Lady Gwenllian welcomed the pilgrim. Why did I not see it on your hand?"

"Because I kept the emerald turned inward on my finger and tried to conceal the band as best I could. Raimon had come to our chamber while Franco and I were changing our clothes to serve on the dais and told us he'd seen a wealthy traveler riding into the yard just in time to dine with us. Well," Jevon said as the details of that day flowed back, "Raimon really came to tease Franco about taking his place carving meat for the baron, but he'd glimpsed the pilgrim from one of the garrison's windows and told us about the man's extravagant dress. That's when it came to me that a wealthy guest might be interested in purchasing my ring for more than the cost of a surcote and carry it far away from my father's ears when he left Pennault. But until I knew whether he would agree to buy it and for how much, I did not—"

"—want to raise my hopes," she repeated.

Not at the risk having to dash them if the pilgrim said no. Jevon remembered being so hopeful that he had trouble concealing his excitement, but he'd bitten off every overly optimistic word that had tried to slip off his tongue.

"The pilgrim dined with the baron and baroness on the dais," he continued, "and since the pilgrim sat beside Lady Gwenllian, I served them both. I turned the emerald around, hoping he would see and envy it." This time Jevon playfully bumped Constantia's shoulder. "I'd deliberately placed it on my left hand so Lady Gwenllian and Beatris might be less likely to notice it while I held the serving platters. Lady Gwenllian was too preoccupied gossiping with the pilgrim to pay me much attention anyway, but the pilgrim stared at my ring each time I set down a platter to pour my lady some wine."

"But I never saw the pilgrim speak to you," Constantia said. "After dinner, you said he asked Lord Laurant for a place to nap. He was sleepy because he'd consumed three times as much wine as anyone else at dinner."

She broke into a full-fledged grin but winced when it stretched the cut at the corner of her mouth. It had been too dark for most of their journey for Jevon to remember the stranger's vicious blow. He wished the brute might materialize in their pathway so Jevon could throttle him.

"It is nothing," Constantia said when Jevon frowned. "If I hold my mouth thus"—she still smiled, just not as wide—"I can barely feel it. Tell me the rest." The gold flecks in her green eyes flickered, and her smile vanished. "That was the day before you took Lady Gwenllian's brooch."

Jevon forced his anger at her assaulter down to finish his story. "I thought mending the brooch would please her. I needed Lady Gwenllian to be in a generous temper before I asked for an afternoon free so that you and I could walk in the woods. I wanted to be alone with you to either confess my fears that it might take longer than we'd hoped for me to buy equipment for the tournament or hand you a bag filled with silver enough to dower you so we could marry as soon as I was knighted."

His chest ached at the memory of the too-brief night of elation that followed the successful sale of his mother's emerald.

"The pilgrim found me after he woke from his nap and asked if I would sell him my ring. He said he wanted it as an offering to the saint, but his eyes glittered with so much lust"—despite Jevon's bleak memories, he could not resist cocking an I-told-you-so brow at Constantia, prompting a chuckle from her—"that I knew he intended to keep it. So I drove a hard bargain for it. I expected him to haggle, but he agreed without a quibble and counted out the coins. That's why there was so much silver in my money pouch the next day. After the brooch and a few of the coins fell out, one of the remaining coins lodged itself in the tear in such a way that it prevented the rest of the silver from pouring out too."

Constantia's eyebrows knitted. "Why did you not tell the baron about the pilgrim?"

"I did, but not until they dragged me to the gatehouse prison. I could not get a word in between Lady Gwenllian's vociferous accusations in the hall." Not to mention Jevon being too taken aback by the strength of her vigorous slaps. Some women grew grotesque when enraged, but Lady Gwenllian's enchanting face shone like a glorious, ferocious sun. "While Laurant returned to the hall to consult with his knights, I told Sir Eudes about my ring and the pilgrim. The fellow had left at dawn, but I begged Sir Eudes to ask the baron to send someone to find him to prove my story was true."

Sir Eudes had grunted but made no promises before the key clanged in the prison lock. Jevon had been left in a stygian darkness with a coarse, flea-bitten blanket, a basin of stale water, and a pot of cold gruel to await he knew not what judgment. As the interminable hours stretched, as his teeth began to chatter with cold and his ears grew numb with silence, the weight of the darkness began to play havoc with his mind. Constantia's shocking "accusation" rang through his frame. Flashes of insecure memories gradually overwhelmed him. Her encouraging smiles at Franco every time Jevon beat him at horsemanship or swordplay or archery. The good-natured way she listened to Raimon boast of his grand ambitions for the tournament field once knighted. The tournament tokens she made for them all. The veil Raimon had given her. Worst of all, her kindness to Llygad despite his Welsh taunts.

A torment bordering on madness seized Jevon during his long, black hours in prison. He thought his bond with Constantia unique from all the others, but had it been? When he was not watching her, had she professed her love as easily to each of the other squires? Had love been a game to her, as Llygad always said?

For the first time in seven years, a wink of uncertainty flicked through Jevon as they walked hand in hand. When had her fingers nestled back into his? He held them a little tighter. Was her hand's embrace another manipulation or was her clasp as honest as his? Would he ever know?

She leaned forward to look around his body. "I think we have strayed near the river."

He glanced in surprise at the sprawling willow tree they passed. Caught up in his memories, he had lost track of his markings. No matter. In the growing light, he would easily rediscover the path. He led her away from the sound of the gurgling river in search of a trunk with three slashes.

"Did Sir Eudes not tell the baron?" she asked.

Nothing in the clasp of her fingers in his suggested she intended to attempt another escape, but he held them firmly just in case.

"He did, though I did not know it for three wretched days. When Laurant finally summoned me back before his council, he said he'd sent messengers to look for the pilgrim on the road to Santiago de Compostela but they found no sign of him. Likely, he turned for home, taking my ring with him."

Constantia's expression grew reflective. "He was not from these lands. His voice carried an inflection I had never heard."

Neither had Jevon before he'd become a mercenary. "It was the way men speak who hail from Barbarossa's lands, men from Saxony and Swabia and Bavaria. He only introduced himself as Albrecht to the baron." A twig snapped crisply under Jevon's boot, breaking the stillness of the morning air. "Since no one else had seen my ring but all had seen my silver, the baron and his council decided there could be no other verdict than my guilt."

"I should never have spoken." Her profile went stiff, her words suddenly thick and stifled. "I wish I had bitten my tongue off when Lady Gwenllian found the brooch missing!"

Jevon surprised himself with a shake of his head. "I would not have loved a woman who allowed others to be abused, even to protect me."

Constantia stopped and turned to stare him full in the face. The first filaments of dawn softened her gnarled mane and painted a dusky hue around her eyes, shading them into huge, glistening pools of green. "The verdict was Lady Gwenllian doing, I know it was. But it was my fault too. I should never have called her a shrew. That made her vengeful. I warned her I would follow you if the baron sent you away. She said, 'Try it, you shameless cat, and I will see his hand lopped off as well.'"

Constantia's body shook as tears poured out of her lustrous eyes. Jevon reached inside the cloak to stroke her arms, trying to quiet her trembling.

A sob broke from her. "I could not understand at the time why Lady Gwenllian cared what I did. She never treated me as anything but a drudge. But she said it would cause a breach between my father and Lord Laurant if she let me run off with a felon like you. I thought she would have Sybil switch me for being pert, but she punished me with something worse." Constantia's palms ground the wet hollows beneath her cheekbones. "She made me and Guia and Beatris watch from a window when Lord Laurant's knights marched you out to the yard. I nearly fainted with relief when I saw the marshal draw the iron from the coals and only brand you." Constantia's hand flew to her lips. "Oh! I did not mean 'only.'"

She caught Jevon's hand and showered his scar with kisses and tears.

Ashamed for her beautiful lips to caress the hard, raised cords of his disfigurement, he pulled his hand away and placed it behind his back.

"Stop it, Stantia," he said gruffly. "You were not to blame for my brand. Some of the knights argued that Laurant should cut off my hand, saying the theft of his lady's brooch was as bad or worse than a serf who poached a deer. But Laurant refused to maim me, replying the brand would be enough to prevent any honest man from giving me shelter for the rest of my life."

The baron had been right, until Jevon met Gunthar.

He wiped Constantia's tears away with his unblemished hand. She leaned her cheek against his palm. He let it rest there, stroking her cheekbone with his thumb each time she hiccuped between subsiding sobs. Thrice now, she had insisted her love for him remained true.

"I swore I would follow you if the baron sent you away. . . . Had they given me the choice, I would have left Pennault at your side. . . . I meant every word I ever said to you."

Had she, though? Perhaps he should test her. "Stantia, if I asked you—"

A lump formed in his throat. What was he afraid of? That she would say no or prevaricate, trying to make a "no" sound like a "yes" to concurrently beguile and deceive him? He shifted his feet apart to brace for either, then began again.

"Stantia, if I asked you to come with me to Vere, not as my prisoner but of your own accord, as my affianced bride—would you?"

She gave a tiny gasp. He heard her draw a breath to reply. Terrified of what she might say, he kissed her. Gently and a little lopsidedly to avoid causing pain but also with a sudden, aching hunger. Saints! Had she tasted this sweet seven years ago? The memory of her ambrosial lips had felt so vivid, but this nectar weakened his knees. He swept her into his arms and felt her melt against his chest.

He was mad to speak of marriage. The best he could ever hope for with this brand on his hand was the royal pardon the Earl of Gunthar said he could win him. A pardon would not absolve Jevon's "guilt," only free him from spending the rest of his life running from the consequences of his alleged crime. It galled him to know men would still mutter "thief" when they saw his scar, but that was a shame he had no choice but to endure.

But if Ned was right that Gunthar might keep Jevon le Falquet's bow and falcon-eyed aim among his household archers after the earl returned to England . . . Gunthar paid an astonishingly generous wage to his archers, one that had enabled Ned to marry. In another pair of years, Jevon might well earn enough to marry too. Even a lady without a dowry.

Constantia's mouth warmed quickly to his, as though she were as parched for him as he was for her. She wrapped her arms around his neck, melding into him. The void in his soul began to teem with incredulous hope. Had he misconstrued everything about this night?

The plaintive warbling of a robin startled them both. He allowed her to ease away as they glanced up through the trees at a string of wispy, deep-pink clouds that heralded the arrival of dawn.

Desperate not to lose the moment, he tilted her face back to his. "You will receive safe and honorable shelter at Vere, I swear it on my life. Once Gunthar wins me a pardon, I can serve him honorably in England. You said you would have followed me seven years ago. Come with me now."

He kissed her with all the persuasive power he could muster.

Once again she returned the kiss with fervor. Then he felt her mouth tremble, her fervor ebb. Slowly, she pulled away.

Fresh tears welled in her eyes. "Stop." She slid a hand over his mouth when he tried to recapture hers. "Oh, Jevon, stop. You know I cannot go with you—unless you force me to."

He flinched inwardly. Her answer confirmed his deepest fear. But he stood stalwart and still, searching her shiny, gold-flecked eyes until she finally lowered her hand.

He challenged the excuse she had used to evade him all night. "What if I swore to you that Gunthar will not harm Pennault or anyone within its walls? All Laurant needs to do is open his gates and let the earl ride through in peace. You can ride with us as proof that Gunthar comes in friendship, escorting you safely back to your home."

The shake of her tangled locks stung. "Lord Laurant will see me for what I am, a hostage, and a poor one at that. He will not bargain his entire castle for me, even to appease my father. He will never open his gates without a command from Duke Richard. Your earl will have to force his way in as he did at Vere."

She cupped her hand against Jevon's cheek as he had cradled hers earlier.

He wanted to jerk angrily away, but her caress churned too strong a thrill through him.

Her eyes pleaded. "After the way Lord Laurant treated you, you have no reason to care if my lord suffers Sir Damien's fate. But what if it is *not* Lord Laurant who tries to withstand your earl when the English pour through the walls? What if it is Raimon or Franco or even Therri? Could you bear to see any of them harmed?"

"Therri is too young to stand in any danger." *And Raimon and Franco are knights. They understand the risks of war as much as a mercenary archer.*

"Therri is seventeen, headstrong, and eager to prove himself to his father. I know him. He will find a way to take part in the battle no matter what the baron says. I cannot let that happen. I *must* warn them all."

Once again it startled Jevon to envision the ten-year-old he'd guarded now so near manhood. But he had seen Raimon with his own eyes. His friend's chest had grown broad and his arms thick with muscles, as Jevon's had. Raimon rode with the confidence and swagger of a knight rather than the cocky eagerness of a squire. Of course, the years would have changed the children and everyone else at Pennault.

Everyone except Constantia. The longer Jevon stared into her eyes in the growing light, the more clearly he saw the woman he'd loved. She would have abandoned Pennault to accompany an outlawed thief into the woods, but she would not abandon the castle to the earl's assault because there were people she still loved there. Lady Heléne, Lord Therri, Guia, Beatris—did it matter if Llygad and Raimon and Franco were among them? Reminiscences tonight had filled Jevon with fond memories of the children who were no longer children and of once-loyal friendships. Even his bitter rivalry with Llygad carried a strange allure of happier times.

Jevon had no right to be hurt by her choice. After all, this was why he had loved her. Not for her sparkling green eyes or sun-tinged cheeks or her sinuous, spirited hair. Not for the mirrored mischief in the glances they'd shared or even for the way his pulse raced when he was near her. It was the way she thrived on kindness, not only to Llygad and the children, Guia, and Beatris, but to all the servants harassed by Lady Gwenllian's querulous nature as well as the frightened, lonely page boys who arrived at the castle less eager and ambitious than Jevon had been at their age.

From the time they met, he'd been awed by Constantia's capacity to care for everyone drawn into her orbit. Of course she could not desert them now.

A fluttering sound drew his attention to two tiny brown, red-breasted robins darting up from the ground, each with a wiggling worm in its beak. As the birds soared into the branches of a nearby oak to enjoy their morning meal, Jevon's gaze slid down the rough bark to the white marks dug into its trunk. An interlocked C and J. When in the course of his determined march to Vere had his heart double-crossed his ambition and turned him back toward Pennault?

What was he to do? Surrender his pardon by letting her go? The earl would turn Jevon off before he loosed a single arrow at the castle for allowing her to warn the rebel fortress. Jevon would have nowhere to go but back to his mercenary band, still a thief, still an outcast, still loathed by the very lords who hired him and his fellow "reprobate soldiers" to fight in their petty wars. And until he crossed the border of Poitou, still with a price on his head.

Such a future felt unendurable when the pardon lay so near his grasp.

He lowered his lips to hers again with a gentle fierceness, as though their kiss could provide some miraculous answer that simultaneously satisfied his dilemma and hers. Of course, there was none. But for a few more moments, with her hand curling into the hair at the back of his head, he blotted out his torturous decision in another flood of pleasure.

A sharp jab against his back wrenched his mouth from hers. He recognized instantly the threatening prod of a blade. A chill voice kept him frozen in place, with Constantia still in his arms.

"Do not move if you and your hellcat want to live. For a few more heartbeats, anyway."

Constantia stared over Jevon's shoulder into the malignant eyes of the quicksilver stranger. Two bright-red stripes gashed the flesh just below one of the stranger's eyes, and a third and fourth scored the center and side of his nose where she had raked her nails down his face. Retribution burned in the pale-blue glare that latched onto hers.

She felt Jevon's muscles go rigid beneath her hands, but he stood perfectly still. Did the villain hold a weapon at his back?

"You." The stranger jerked his chin at Constantia. "Remove his bow and arrow bag."

Jevon's face was drawn as tight as one of his bowstrings. He nodded for her to obey. With shaking fingers, she slid the bow from his shoulder, untied the bag from his waist, and let them fall at his feet.

The stranger funneled his words into Jevon's ear loudly enough for her to hear. "She called her pursuer a gallant, honorable, chivalrous knight, but she must have eluded him, for you look like a middling archer at best. Or maybe she made it up to frighten me. I mistook her for a lady in the dark, but Sir Damien's wife or daughter would never be clothed in such filthy rags."

She must look completely bedraggled after being thrown to the ground by the collapse of Vere's tower, then sprinting twice through shrubbery and tree limbs that snagged and tattered her gown.

The stranger sneered. "Still, you wear Gunthar's badge, so you are clearly one of his men."

Jevon tipped his head aside with a look of disgust, as though the stranger's breath were foul. Beyond that, he remained completely motionless. Some threat must hold him so.

"Such passionate kisses you two have been sharing." The stranger's gaze lingered so lewdly on Constantia's mouth that her stomach convulsed. "She was begging your mercy quite vigorously. Perhaps I was simply not as convincing a captor as you. I should try again. Do you think this time she will return my embraces as lustily as yours while she begs forgiveness for these stripes on my face?"

Jevon growled, "If you touch her—"

"Touch her?" The stranger's laughter rang grotesquely amidst the trees. "I am going to thoroughly debauch her at my leisure in a snug little spot in these woods where no one will hear her screams. What happens to her after that depends on whether I decide she serves my purposes better dead or alive. Unfortunately, there is no question at all about you."

Over Jevon's shoulder, she saw the stranger's body shift. Jevon's face went blank as a stone except for the barest twitch at the corner of his eye. Constantia knew the villain had underscored his threat with some painful action Jevon did not want her to guess.

"Even a middling archer can be useful if he serves the right man," the villain said. "I would have preferred to leave the corpse of one of Gunthar's knights in the road, but one must make do with what fate delivers into his hands."

Corpse. The horror came rushing back. This fiend had wanted Jevon to find him "debauching" her earlier so the villain could kill him! She leaned toward Jevon, laying her hand protectively over his heart. Her motion brought their bodies close together again. Her other hand brushed against something cold and metallic tucked into his belt—the hilt of the sword she had taken from Vere.

Jevon caught her eye and gave a tiny shake of his head.

She ignored him and shuddered, hoping the stranger would think she shrank from his filthy taunts as she gave a small tug to the hilt.

"We have done nothing to you." She assumed a whimper. "Why do you want to harm us?"

"You were nothing more than a pawn to draw this one in." The villain tilted his head at Jevon. "If you had been more cooperative, we would have shared a quick, entertaining romp, and after I finished with him, I'd have let you go."

He lied. She saw it in his eyes. He would have used her just as despicably if she had helped him murder Jevon and never scratched his face. She slid the sword up another notch.

Jevon sucked in a sharp breath. She knew from his glare that he was angry at her attempt to retrieve the sword, worried what the stranger might do if he caught her. But Jevon could not move to stop her without the stranger seeing.

She needed to distract the villain. "What is your grudge with this man?" She maintained the pretense that she and Jevon had never met before this night. "What harm has he done you?"

"Him? I never laid eyes on him before I saw him chasing you. My grudge is with the badge he wears."

The silver stallion prancing on a field of blue sewn to the shoulder of Jevon's gambeson identified him as one of Gunthar's men.

"Then what grudge do you have with the earl?" She eased the sword up a little farther.

"If I tell you that, I will have to slit your throat, and that would be a shame before I sampled your charms." He curled his lip like a wolf baring its teeth for a kill. "Enough of this slippery banter."

His arm snaked around Jevon's body, locking a hand over Constantia's. The villain pried the hilt from her, then yanked the sword from Jevon's belt.

Jevon must have hoped the angle of the villain's body would throw the villain off balance. Jevon lurched forward, pushing Constantia out of the way, then spun with a fist aimed at the stranger's face.

The quicksilver stranger dodged backward far enough to plant the tip of the sword against Jevon's breast. "I wouldn't."

Jevon's fist froze midair, then dropped to his side.

"Did you think I have not been watching the pair of you as you circled back around toward Pennault?" the stranger jeered. "I saw this in your belt at the first gray light of morn. It will be much easier to carve you up with a sword than with this paltry dagger of mine."

The ruddy dawn light revealed the weapon he'd held at Jevon's back. Above the stranger's grip, Constantia saw on the dagger's coin-flat pommel the image of a woman with flowing hair and sinister, winking ruby eyes. The sanguine blush of sunrise made the dagger's blade glimmer red. But the tip shone a slick, wet crimson. Oh, saints. Blood?

He slid the dagger into the sheath at his hip too quickly for her to be sure, then swiveled the sword tip against Jevon's breast. Constantia's knees swayed. If the thick-quilted garment could not prevent a dagger's piercing, it would not deflect a sword thrust.

The villain sneered at Jevon now. "Gunthar's troops have left Vere. I will leave you strewn bit by bit along their path to Pennault. Gunthar will know you were one of his men when he sees the badge. He can find your head last of all. Now, take the rope you carry in that pouch of yours and tie her to that tree so we can get on with it."

Jevon glared defiance at him, hands clamped at his side.

"You can tie her up," the stranger said, "or I can kill her here and now. I would regret forfeiting our romp, but I will do it, and you will die anyway."

Jevon refused to move. Constantia knew exactly how the stranger would deal with his intransigence. He would simply thrust that sword the rest of the way through Jevon's heart, tie her up, and proceed with his grisly deed right in front of her.

A sudden idea flashed into her mind. Jevon had not been the only soldier who tried to chase her down. Surely the English earl would be angry—and anxious?—that Jevon had not returned her to Vere. With the breaking of dawn, might the earl not send men to look for them, hoping it might not be too late to find and prevent Constantia from warning Pennault of the impending attack?

Constantia gasped loudly, stared straight over the stranger's shoulder, and screamed at the trees behind him, "Loose your arrow! Loose it now, and I will submit myself to the Earl of Gunthar!"

Doubt slashed through her as soon as the shout left her lips. Would her bluff make the stranger dive out of the way and give Jevon the advantage, or would it provoke the villain into plunging the sword through Jevon as he ducked?

The stranger flinched and dodged to one side, the sword swooping away from Jevon. Jevon's foot flew up, kicking the sword out of his hand with a loud crack.

"Run!" Jevon shouted at her.

Leave him alone with this monster who wanted to carve him up like a Christmas goose? Never! Constantia scooped up Jevon's bow and arrow bag as the stranger lunged to reclaim the sword. Once he reached it, they could hold him at bay with these.

Jevon must not have seen her, for he shoved himself into the stranger, knocking him down before he reached the sword, then dove for the sword himself. The stranger writhed on the ground like a worm, then swiveled himself up and flung himself on top of Jevon. In their joint scrabble for the weapon, they knocked it along the forest floor, out of reach.

Jevon got off a blow at the stranger, disentangling from their scuffle long enough to wave an urgent hand at Constantia. "Go!"

"I can't leave you! Jevon—"

The stranger threw Jevon onto his back, straddled him, and slammed a fist into Jevon's face. Jevon appeared stunned. But the stranger's triumph again left his own back unprotected, this time primed for a real arrow.

Constantia whipped an iron-tipped shaft from the arrow bag, but she had never nocked an arrow before, and her nervous, fumbling hands took more heartbeats than she liked to position the notch on the string. She had spent hours watching Jevon at archery practice, but she had squandered all her time admiring his broad shoulders, the strapping muscles that flexed through his sleeves, and how breathlessly handsome he looked as he intently measured the distance between him and the butts before the bowstring thwanged and his arrow sailed cleanly into the target's heart.

He'd made it look so easy. She wrapped her fingers around the grip as she had seen him do. Something was etched at eye level into the curved wood that faced her, but there was no time to wonder what it meant. Jevon had recovered from his blow and struggled to free himself from his opponent's weight. If she did not shoot now, she might lose her target. Fastening her gaze on the stranger's exposed back, she pulled back the string and loosed the arrow.

It sailed a good foot wide of the tussling men.

Jevon blocked the stranger's fist from landing a second strike but failed to dislodge the villain. Constantia nocked a second arrow, more quickly this time, tried to aim more carefully, and again let the arrow fly. It landed just as far off her mark as before. She should have paid more attention to Jevon's technique than to the provocative way her heart beat when she'd watched him train.

She looked around for a more dependable weapon, a branch or a rock. Before she found one, Jevon hurled the stranger off him.

"Blazes, Stantia!" The stranger's fist grazed Jevon's chin as he tumbled off, forcing a punctuating pause to Jevon's shout before he recovered. "Go! I've got this . . . knave . . . under control."

Jevon scrambled to his feet, dragging the stranger with him. He pushed the villain against a nearby tree and locked his arm against the stranger's throat. She scanned Jevon's back, remembering the stain she thought she'd glimpsed on the dagger. The quilted gambeson he wore looked unmarred. Or did she see a small slit in the cloth? The branches above their heads cast too much shadow. Surely if he were wounded, he would not have strength to hold his captive so firmly pinned.

"Stantia!" Jevon snapped her name impatiently.

"Come with me," she pleaded as the stranger grappled ineffectually against Jevon's armlock. Once the villain passed out for lack of air, he would be no threat to either of them.

"I can't. You know I cannot go to Pennault. I would return to its walls a thief. If Laurant did not hang me for my brazenness, he would take my hand for sure."

Pennault? Only now did the stranger's earlier words register with her. *I watched the pair of you as you circled back around.*

While the stranger clawed at Jevon's arm, she searched the nearby trees for something familiar to confirm their location. Her gaze froze on the oak tree with the interlocked C and J. It was true. At some point during their trek through the night, Jevon had circled them back to this cherished spot where they had sealed their pledge to marry with a kiss.

"Go!" Jevon barked. "I will wager you are closer to the castle than Gunthar is. Warn them while I drag this miscreant to the road and deliver him to the earl. The delay will buy you time."

The stranger sagged against Jevon's chokehold. She finally dared move to his side and pointed at the carving. "Why?"

His gaze lingered on the initials before returning to her. "My head did not mean to bring you here, but my heart chose otherwise. You were right. I would gladly see Laurant and Lady Gwenllian groveling before the earl, but risk Therri's or Heléne's safety from the volley of the magnon's stones or a section of crumbling wall?" Jevon shook his head. "Gunthar will take the castle. There is no stopping him. But you can get the children somewhere safe."

The children. No matter how many times she told him how they had grown, Jevon still thought of them as children. And he had not forgotten how he'd loved them, along with her. No wonder she loved *him* so!

She set the bow and arrow bag on the ground beside his boots so he would not be without defense should the stranger escape.

"Take the sword with you," he said.

She obediently picked up the blade, then set her hand to his shoulder. He tightened his arm across the stranger's throat, warning him not to take advantage of Constantia's nearness.

She stretched onto her toes and kissed Jevon's cheek. "I am yours forever," she whispered. It took all the strength she possessed to wrench her hand away from him. Then she turned and ran.

Jevon kept his knees locked until Constantia fled, but once he and the villain were alone, his knees began to tremble. The fiend's dagger had punched through Jevon's gambeson and into his flesh. Jevon had forced his face as blank as he could so as not to alarm Constantia, but when a few moments later the stranger gave the dagger a small, cruel twist, Jevon had been unable to fully stifle his gasp.

The wound had not disabled him immediately, but as he and the stranger struggled, he'd felt the growing wetness at his back. His gambeson's thick padding must have prevented Constantia from seeing the blood. But if he did not dispose of the stranger quickly, the unstaunched wound would weaken him to the point where the stranger could break free. If that happened—well, the villain had made his intent clear in both word and steel. He could easily have killed Jevon with a quick, clean thrust but had, instead, taken pleasure in torturing his victim. This man would not hesitate to carve Jevon up, just as he had sworn, and if he then went after Constantia . . .

The villain's eyes closed as his body slumped against Jevon's hold. Though a golden tinge to the sky attested to a fully risen sun, a hazy shade of gray hovered at the edge of Jevon's vision. Their brawl had no doubt accelerated the tearing of his wound.

With a massive effort, he steadied his knees. The road between Vere and Pennault was not far from here. Once Jevon dragged his prisoner there, he should not have to wait long before Gunthar and his army joined them and took this villain off his hands.

Then Gunthar can do with me what he will.

Jevon pulled the dagger from the stranger's sheath, then eased his arm's pressure across the stranger's throat. He shook the man's shoulder to rouse him.

"Come. You were so eager to send a warning to Gunthar. Let us see if you are as keen to tell him why to his face."

The stranger erupted in a whirlwind of spinning limbs. Jevon thrust his arm forward, trying to regain his hold across the man's neck, but a fist clouted him in the ribs, forcing the air from his lungs. The stranger tried to wrestle his dagger back. Jevon clung doggedly to the hilt as his watery knees made him stagger. He swung a fist at the stranger's blurring features. His knuckles connected with something that gave a loud crunch before the stranger's hand splayed over Jevon's face and shoved him sideways. The stranger wrenched the dagger from Jevon's hand as Jevon's knees crumpled, pitching him into a dizzy tumble. His palms slapped the ground to break his fall, one into a pile of leaves and twigs, the other against a curve of slender, polished wood.

His bow. A wave of calm flowed through him, his senses heightening, his vision clearing. Training and a reflexive burst of vigor swiveled him onto one knee. He wrapped his left hand around the bow's grip, while his right flicked an arrow from his bag, notched it, and drew back the string.

Blood oozed like a beckoning target from the stranger's nose where Jevon's fist must have landed. He could shoot clean through the fiend's skull, a killing hit so that he could never threaten Constantia again.

As a mercenary, Jevon had showered arrows into enemy forces and sometimes struck down men with a sword in self-defense when pressed into close-quarter fighting, but he had never deliberately aimed his arrows to kill. Even when his mercenary captain wanted to use the advantage of his falcon-sharp eyes to assassinate an enemy, Jevon chose only to wound. Murdering a man at a distance felt dishonorable.

A light flashed above his head. Jevon honed his focus on the blade raised to strike him before he could loose his arrow. The same sunlight that illuminated the dagger accentuated the bulging sinews that stretched beneath the stranger's fist and up his arm where it extended from his sleeve.

Jevon's bowstring twanged. The arrow hissed, the stranger screamed, the dagger thumped against the ground. Jevon whipped a second arrow into his bow, but the stranger turned and plunged into the trees, howling in pain.

Jevon's vision briefly blurred, then cleared again. He looked about for some sign of his arrow, but it was gone. The stranger must have taken it with him, lodged in his arm.

As Jevon's racing pulse slowed, he sat back on his haunches to regather the wits that too quickly scrambled after their few instants of clarity. His wound burned and throbbed. He could not go after the villain like this. He had lost too much blood. But he could show this to Gunthar. Jevon scooped up the abandoned dagger, then drew a slow, determined breath and pushed himself to his feet. Perhaps the earl would recognize the odd insignia on the weapon's pommel and through it, the unnamed enemy who stalked him.

Jevon fished a square of linen from his traveling pouch. He wrapped the cloth around the dagger, slid it into his arrow bag, positioning it carefully so as not to harm the arrows, then slung the bag over his shoulder.

Before starting for the road, he crossed to the oak and leaned against it to rest a moment. He traced his finger along the white lines of the scars he had carved so long ago. J C.

Jevon and Constantia.

"I am yours forever," she had whispered, her soft lips pressed to his cheek.

"And I am yours," he said into the air. Whatever had really happened seven years ago, it was true. "But so are the children, and Gui and Beatris and Raimon and Franco, and even Llygad. You love them all, and I would never desire it otherwise." Well, maybe Llygad.

Jevon would not change a gnarled lock of Constantia's head or a beat of her loving heart. Yet some selfish part of him could not help but wish she had chosen him over all the others when he asked her to come with him to Vere.

He sighed and turned to start for the road. Her decision extinguished his sliver-brief hope of reclaiming a future with her. However much she might love him, he knew now she would never leave Pennault and he could never return as anything but an enemy to everyone in the castle. But at least they had had this night together. He cherished the few moments when they had bantered instead of quarreled and walked hand in hand with wistful long-ing, as they had before Jevon's world shattered.

And he had a second kiss to remember her by. One he would hold in his heart like a blessed, sacred ember to his dying day.

Jevon had not trudged far before he heard the crackling of shrubbery and pounding of boots in the dry leaf fall. He stopped and readied his bow, expecting the stranger, perhaps too maddened with pain and revenge for stealth, to charge out of the trees like a bloodied boar intent on rending out Jevon's bowels before Jevon could fire off another shaft.

The man who burst from the trees threw up his hands and skidded through the crumbling leaves to slow his advance as he stared, alarmed, at the tip of Jevon's arrow.

"Hold!" the man cried.

Jevon instantly lowered his bow, recognizing the man's stolid face and the badge he wore on his tunic. Sir Thomas Enslye, one of the earl's knights.

"We heard a scream from the road," Sir Thomas said. "Gunthar sent me and Julian to see if someone was in need of help."

A squire with gracefully flowing red-gold curls stood a pace behind and to the side of Sir Thomas. The earl's party must have heard the stranger's howl when Jevon's arrow pierced his arm.

Jevon felt himself sway a little. "To be honest, *I* could use a bit of aid to the road. Has Gunthar ridden on?"

Sir Thomas shook his head. "He'll not wait long for us, though. He wanted to surround Pennault before dawn, but Sir Damien's injuries forced Gunthar to linger at Vere longer than planned."

"Injuries?" Jevon motioned to the squire who, at a nod from Sir Thomas, moved closer so Jevon could lean a hand on his shoulder. "I thought Sir Damien dead."

"His body was badly broken in his fall from the wall," Sir Thomas said, "but he still breathed when we left Vere."

The squire craned his neck to stare at Jevon's back. "Sir Thomas, he's bleeding!"

Jevon's blood must have finally leaked through his gambeson.

Sir Thomas rounded behind them. "Saints, le Falquet! Was it you who screamed?"

Jevon fought a temptation to sag against the squire's shoulder and forced himself to stand a little straighter. "Nay. The wench Gunthar sent us to capture"—there was no point in betraying Constantia's name—"was attacked by some madman hiding in these woods. I drove him off with my bow, but he took one of my arrows with him."

"Not before he did you some harm, I see." Sir Thomas sounded grim.

"A flesh wound only, I think," Jevon said. "A few bandages and a chance to catch my breath, and I will be fine."

As though to contradict his cockiness, his knees buckled, but he pulled himself upright with the help of the squire's strong shoulder.

Sir Thomas's face crinkled with worry. "Can you make it to the road?"

"With a little help." Jevon's voice sounded more stout than his knees. He was grateful when the squire pulled Jevon's arm around his neck to lend him support.

"What of the wench?" Sir Thomas glanced at the conspicuously empty space around them. "The others came back before dark, saying they lost her. Sir John muttered some distrust in your loyalty when you did not return as well, but Gunthar said he would wait till daybreak to pass judgment on whether you held by the oath you swore to him when he took you into his service or if you were as faithless as your Poitevin brethren. You had the wench in your custody?"

Jevon gritted his teeth against the dig at his honor. "Through the night until we were attacked."

"I presume she escaped in the confusion." Sir Thomas stated it as a conclusion. "Gunthar will not be pleased, but I suppose, like the others, you did your best. Well, let us get you up to the road. You can ride in one of the wagons until someone can attend to you."

Jevon's vision had begun to blur again by the time they reached the road. They stopped in front of a waiting column of knights, squires, archers, foot soldiers, and the rest of the martial company the Earl of Gunthar had mustered from among his English forces and Norman mercenaries. Horses snuffled, restless to resume their journey to the battle ahead. Chain mail chinked against voices rumbling from the earl's knights. Idled wagons creaked. Never one to waste time, the earl was undoubtedly using this lull to have his engineers check the soundness of the disassembled parts of his mangon. Gunthar had done the same before the attacks on Blancaval and Vere, determined that no flaw affect the siege engine's accuracy once he ordered an assault.

Jevon blinked and gave his head two quick, tight jerks. As his vision cleared, he met the Earl of Gunthar's probing, critical stare. Though only a few years older than Jevon, the earl's firm air of command reflected Gunthar's proven skill as a military leader. Gunthar sat astride a stamping black destrier at the head of his men. The same silver stallion sewn to the shoulder of Jevon's gambeson pranced proudly across the breast of the vibrant blue tunic that overlaid the earl's mail hauberk. Jevon was intently aware not only of Gunthar's aggressive scrutiny but of the sudden silence that fell over the previously garrulous company. Jevon especially felt the weight of Sir John Lee's glare from his mount at Gunthar's side. As the earl's closest friend, the lanky knight spoke with a freedom few would dare, and ever since Gunthar hired Jevon and his bow, Sir John dared very freely and loudly to express his doubt that a Poitevin like Jevon could be anything but a doublehearted traitor in their midst.

Gunthar sat at first in silence while his destrier pawed the road and snorted demonic puffs of steam in the morning air. Sunlight glanced off the bright sheen of the earl's helmet where he carried it under one arm. The light flashed into Jevon's eyes and made him blink again.

When the earl spoke, his soft, even question did not quite mask the anger in his voice. "Where is she?"

Jevon forced himself not to look away from Gunthar's intimidating gaze. Men who did so earned a derisive quirk from the earl's haughty mouth. But remaining firm also carried risk. The last time Gunthar subjected Jevon to so penetrating a stare, the earl had discerned the half-truths Jevon told him about his scarred hand. Gunthar had not yet demanded the full story, but Jevon knew he would in time. How much about the events of this night with Constantia would the earl perceive as well?

"We were attacked," Jevon said.

He weighed his words, simultaneously trying to decide how to phrase the rest of his answer while worrying Gunthar could see straight through his head into the furious workings of his mind.

Before he could continue, Sir Thomas spoke up. "He's been wounded by a forest bandit, my lord. The wench got away in the confusion."

The squire shifted Jevon around so the earl could see the bloodstained gambeson.

Jevon's throat clutched momentarily, sorely tempted to seize upon Sir Thomas's defense. But he glanced at the disfigured brand on his hand, fully bared now that he'd given his gloves to Constantia. One half-truth the earl had chosen to overlook for now. Two would brand Jevon's character as deceitful as the skin he'd held to the candle's flame to try to obscure the condemning *R*. Gunthar would see through this falsehood as he had the first, but Jevon knew this time, the earl would not so quickly suspend his judgment.

He tugged himself back around, still leaning on the squire, until he faced the earl again. "No. She did not escape. I let her go."

Gunthar's mouth tightened into a hard line. His heavy brown brows plunged ominously over his piercing grey eyes. "You let her go . . . where?"

Jevon suppressed a shudder at the dangerous calm in Gunthar's voice. "To warn Pennault. It won't save the castle from your chastisement, my lord. There is not time for them to raise a serious defense."

He managed not to recoil from the springing fire in Gunthar's eyes.

"So your oath to me was a sham."

"No! My lord, I swear that I am your man. Give me any command you will, and I will obey it."

"I commanded you to stop the wench and return her to Vere. If your faith to me is true, why did you release her when you had her in your custody?"

Jevon wished there were not so many eager, listening ears. Only the full truth, with all its shameful connotations, had any hope of salvaging his position with the earl and the promised royal pardon.

"Because Pennault was once my home. I was driven out by false accusations."

"Of theft?" the earl interrupted.

Jevon felt the knights staring at the rarely exposed mark of his shame. He'd feared Gunthar had long ago discerned the outline of the R beneath his more recent scars, but to confess it before the earl's entire army, many of whom already doubted Jevon's honor, scorched his cheeks as ferociously as the branding iron had his hand.

But he had committed himself to the truth. "Yes. But falsely," he repeated.

"Yet you chose to aid to your false accusers rather than keep your oath to me. That makes you a liar, sirrah. Worse than that, you are a despicable oath-breaker."

"No, my lord. I swear! My bow remains yours to command and yours alone."

"Then why do you not want revenge on the men who 'unjustly' did *that* to you"—the earl gave a curt, angry nod toward Jevon's scar—"and thus made you an outcast among all honest men?"

"Because those who shamed me will not be the only ones to suffer in your assault on the castle. Not everyone at Pennault is guilty of the baron's maltreatment of me. There are women there who did me no harm, and children—"

"You think me a butcher of children?"

Oddly, the thunderclap of Gunthar's outrage made it easier for Jevon to withstand his furious glare. "I have seen you in battle only twice, my lord. Though you overcame both castles fairly and treated the vanquished at Blancaval with honor, at Vere, your sword flung a man from the walls."

"An accident," Gunthar snapped. "And Sir Damien was no child. If he had surrendered when I commanded him to, he would be hale and safe in his own hall this day instead of lying broken in his bed."

Constantia's earnest arguments echoed in Jevon's ears. "But accidents do not discriminate in their victims. Sir Damien defied you, as did Lord Merval at Blancaval before his heart gave out during the terror of your siege, but others were injured, too, some fairly, others . . ."

Jevon paused, once again choosing his words carefully. He had not been among the men left behind to secure the defeated castles. On the earl's orders, he'd marched swiftly with the earl's forces to their next target, preventing him from witnessing the damage they'd left behind. The aftermath of the attacks had not troubled him until he'd passed the night with Constantia.

"An errant arrow, a falling shard from a wall shattered by your mangon, the toppling of a tower from your miners, can kill or injure anyone, the blameless, the young, and the guilty alike. The woman I released will have time only to gather the children and women to some protected part of the castle, safe from the worst of our assault and our storming of the walls."

Was it petty of Jevon to wish Lady Gwenllian were a man?

Sir John Lee's plain, amiable features carried an unusually severe frown. He said brusquely, "It sounds like a ploy to make us delay our attack. While they claim to be 'protecting' their women, they will be strengthening their fortifications, perhaps laying traps for us when we break into their ward. They may view the woman's warning as weakness on our part, judging us too careless or feeble to stop her." He turned his glower back to Jevon. "If your treacherous countrymen try to shield themselves behind their wives and daughters, thinking we will not cut our way through them all—"

"They are not my countrymen. Not anymore." Jevon spoke hotly, repudiating the land that had driven him out.

In the same moment, Gunthar sent Sir John an admonishing glance. "John."

Sir John fell silent, but his scowl held no repentance.

"The men of Pennault are not craven cowards," Jevon told the earl. "They will fight with courage and hide behind no one. My lord, I swore to you my loyalty, and I will stand beside you in this conflict." His knees gave an ironic wobble, but he swiftly stiffened them again. "I will prove it at the walls of Pennault. If I fail, you can slay me with your own sword as a liar, thief, and traitor."

Gunthar gave an ambiguous snort through his hawkish nose. "Sir Thomas, find someone to stitch up le Falquet's wound. Fortify him with wine, but do not make him drunk, and let him rest. We will leave one of the carts behind for your use. Once he is steady on his feet, bring him along to Pennault. And then"—Gunthar turned his narrowed, razor gaze back to Jevon—"then we will see."

Constantia ran across the lowered drawbridge and sprinted beneath the iron-tipped spikes of the raised portcullis before doubling over inside the gatehouse entrance hall. Hands on thighs, she sucked breath after dry, scraping breath into her burning lungs.

"What the blazes?" a man's voice exclaimed.

"Close . . ." she gasped, "the . . ." *gasp* ". . . gate!"

"Lady Constantia?"

As the drub of her heart in her ears slowed, she recognized the gatekeeper's voice. She straightened, shoving her snarled hair out of her face. "Quickly, Sir Eudes, close . . ." *gasp* ". . . the gate! The English are about to lay siege to our walls!"

Sir Eudes dubiously surveyed her disheveled state. "Beg pardon, my lady, but you look a fright. Lady Gwenllian expected you back yesterday. Where have you been all night?"

He did not believe her, the slackwit! "Take me to Lord Laurant," she commanded, *"now!"*

Footsteps scuffled down the recessed stairs to her left. Her heart lurched at the bounce of the long golden curls around the shoulders of the man who joined them. For an instant, she was trapped again in the woods with the quicksilver stranger.

"Constantia!" Llygad's voice pulled her back to the gatehouse. "I have been worried sick about you." He caught her hands and held them wide, taking in her frazzled hair, filthy, crumpled gown, and, with a raise of his brows, Jevon's finger-cropped gloves.

Her terrified vision of the stranger dissipated. Llygad had grown his hair long six months ago and his new look still felt odd to her, but the dazzling blue eyes were Llygad's through and through. He shared their deep jeweled color, along with his lush, blond hair, with his cousin the baroness, but the family similarities ended there. Llygad's face was too narrow to be angelic, and his ears flared slightly from the sides of his head, a "flaw" Lady Gwenllian had bemoaned for as long as Constantia remembered. The baroness might have forgiven the imperfection had Llygad not embarrassed her with his clumsiness on the training field all these years. His tall, angular body simply defied coordination, which made him a frequent target of mockery, only reinforcing the baroness's scorn for her favorite uncle's son.

Constantia squeezed Llygad's hands, engulfed by the sympathy that always flooded her when she thought of everyone's unkindness to him.

"What happened here?" Llygad asked.

She had not remembered the cut on her lip until Llygad's frown settled on her mouth.

Her breaths grew more composed. "It is nothing. I am fine. But you are all in danger. Pennault has stood with Duke Richard in defiance of the king's authority, but now the king is at our doors. Or his English devil is. The king has sent the Earl of Gunthar to chastise us. He and his men are already on the road." She whirled again on Sir Eudes. "Why is the gate open? Why is no one watching from the walls?"

She knew why. Because the baron had been at peace with his neighbors for too long. There had been minor clashes over boundaries between the lords of Pennault, Vere, and Belle Noir, but they'd not drawn swords in years. They had all been fools, herself included, to place their faith in the king's seventeen-year-old son, however martial Duke Richard's spirit.

"I was on the wall only a short time ago, looking for you." Llygad sounded defensive. "I saw no one on the road, not even you."

"I kept to the trees for as long as I could so the earl's men would not stop me. I tried to enter by the postern gate but it was locked." Thank goodness for that, at least. "But the earl will not be far behind me. Laurant must prepare the defenses. The earl has already devasted Vere. I was there when he launched his attack. His siege engine crumbled the walls like they were made of almond cakes."

Llygad and the graying gatekeeper both looked shocked.

"Sir Damien surrendered?" Llygad said. They all knew the quarrelsome Sir Damien never yielded to anyone.

"Sir Damien is *dead*. He resisted, the earl pursued him onto one of the walls, and Sir Damien fell." Bile mingled with her panic at the memory of Sir Damien's flailing limbs just before he struck the ground. "I barely escaped. The earl's men chased me all night." Should she tell them about Jevon? No. She could not bear to hear Llygad and the others call him traitor for siding with the English earl against them. "They tried to stop me from warning you, but I managed to elude them. Pull up the drawbridge. Close the gate!"

"Do it," Llygad snapped at the gatekeeper. "I will take her to the baron."

"Yes, Sir Llygad." Sir Eudes trotted up the stairs. The machinery that controlled the drawbridge and gate resided in the third level of the gatehouse.

Llygad drew Constantia's arm through his and escorted her through the long gatehouse passageway. She glanced at the slits in the walls where archers, concealed behind them, could fire arrows at an invading army, and upward at the holes in the ceiling where rocks or boiling water could be poured to slow the enemy's advance. Before she and Llygad emerged into the castle's bailey, they passed beneath a second portcullis that could be lowered with its outer twin to trap the enemy in the narrow space behind them, helpless to retreat from the lethal defenses. That should prove a daunting deterrent to an army brazen enough to try to break into the castle through the gatehouse.

But the English earl had not come through the gatehouse at Vere. With the help of his mangon and miners, he burst through a side wall and the castle's rear. Constantia could still feel the horrific quaking of the ground.

She slipped out of Llygad's hold and began to run toward the group of knights and squires with Laurant near the stables. Therri, his pale-gold hair shimmering in the sun, stood on one side of his father, the seventeen-year-old now as tall as the baron. Though Raimon's back was to her, she recognized him on Laurant's right by the chaotic mix of brown and blond hair.

That's where Jevon would have stood once he was knighted, in the place of trust and honor at Laurant's right hand. She had never thought of Raimon as a supplanter, but with Jevon so newly heavy on her mind and heart, the unfairness spasmed in her breast.

Then she registered the green-clad men holding hounds on leashes. Of all the times to be planning a hunt!

"My lord!" she shouted.

The men around the baron turned. The parting circle exposed the baron's diminutive wife at its center, previously hidden by the knights' tall frames. Lady Gwenllian never joined her husband's hunts, but from the purposeful frown on her enchanting face, Constantia guessed Lady Heléne had determined to and Lady Gwenllian wanted the baron to turn their younger daughter away if she asked. Lady Heléne loved the excuse to ride at the speed of thunder and practice shooting her hunting bow. As she never came home with a blood prize, Constantia suspected she always deliberately chose harmless targets.

While the men gaped at Constantia, the wheedling in Lady Gwenllian's bewitching face turned to irritation. Her sapphire gaze appraised Contantia's bruised mouth before sweeping over her disordered appearance.

The baron initially looked relieved at the interruption. "What is it, Constantia?" Then he, too, frowned at her tangled hair and rumpled gown. "We expected you yesterday. Where have you been? If you meant to be late, you should have sent word. My lady fretted for your safety all night."

Oh, I am sure it was for my "safety." She is merely afraid I have dallied away the night with some man and if my father learns of it, he will refuse to choose me as his heir and Llygad will lose a fortune.

Llygad's long strides brought him to Constantia's side. "She says there are armed men on the road, sent by the king."

Laurant lifted his dark-blond brows, his expression skeptical. "How can she know this? She looks addled." He turned to his wife and said in the brash tone he always used when he wished to portray himself as the firm master of the castle and not a henpecked husband, "Take her to her chamber, wife. I will listen to her story when we return from the hunt, after you have restored her wits."

Constantia laced her fingers together in frustration, though the baron might view her stance as a plea. "My lord, I beg you to listen. I speak the truth!"

She poured out an account of the surprise attack on Vere, telling them of Sir Damien's refusal to surrender, the earl's launch of missiles from his siege engine, the shattering of one wall and the collapse of the other. Shuddering, she recounted the earl's battle with Sir Damien, Sir Damien's fall, and how she had used the distraction to escape. Then she briefly described her hectic chase through the woods, her capture by one of the earl's men, once again careful not to mention Jevon by name, and how she slipped away once more but not before learning the earl and his men were headed for Pennault. No time to mention the stranger. He had nothing to do with their imminent danger, anyway.

She spoke in such a breathless rush that her words repeatedly squeezed out Therri's multiple attempts to break in. Not until she stopped to draw air into her exhausted lungs did she notice how pale his face had gone.

"Is Sir Damien dead?" he asked. "What happened to Etienne?"

At least she could reassure him of his friend's safety. "Etienne was not at Vere. Triston was, but Sir Damien sent Etienne to escort his new wife to visit Poitiers before I arrived. But I am afraid Sir Damien could not have survived a fall from such a height."

Perhaps she should not have mentioned Sir Damien's fall. Crimson anger burned away Therri's pallor as the sapphire eyes he shared with his mother, elder sister, and cousin blazed. Etienne and Therri were like brothers. Therri would want revenge for Sir Damien's death on Etienne's behalf. When battle with the English came, Therri would try to be in the thick of it, but at least the baron now had time to find a way to protect his son from the worst. Bless Jevon for letting her warn them!

Lady Gwenllian's delicate lips curled in derision. "It is nonsense." She turned to the baron. "Lord Merval has assured us that so long as we all hold firm, the king will be forced to abandon this purported 'peace' he tries to force on his sons. He will tire of the conflict and go back to England, leaving us to manage our own affairs as we have always done."

Contradicting the baroness would only enflame her, but there was too much at stake for Constantia to do anything else.

"My lord, your son-in-law undoubtedly means well"—Constantia smothered the disgust that threatened to tinge her tone when she spoke of the lustful old man the baron had wed his eldest daughter to—"but his castle is miles from here. He can know nothing of the present risk to Pennault."

"Any English forces would have to pass Blancaval before they reached Vere," Lady Gwenllian pointed out. "Merval would have seen them and sent word. I tell you, Constantia has concocted the whole thing to conceal her wanton behavior with some man last night."

A sudden possibility flashed into Constantia's mind. "Unless he could *not* send you word. I was there at Vere, my lord. No one was prepared for the speed with which the English surrounded the walls. No one saw them coming until it was too late to do more than slam the gate shut. And the earl did everything he could to prevent me from reaching Pennault to warn you. Perhaps Blancaval has already fallen."

While the baron bit his lip indecisively, Llygad said, "I have ordered the gate raised as a precaution."

Laurant nodded. "I suppose that is wise until we are sure. Sir Raimon, set some men on the walls to watch the road."

Constantia heard the disappointment in Llygad's sigh. *He* had the good sense to close the gate, yet the baron asked Raimon to organize the guard. No matter how hard Llygad tried to win the baron's respect, Laurant treated the young Welsh knight with thinly veiled contempt, kin by marriage or not.

Raimon called out several men among the knights of Laurant's preempted hunting party. He included curly-haired Franco but not Llygad. Though the younger knights were never rude to Llygad anymore, they rarely included him in their tasks or amusements.

As the men passed Constantia, Raimon maneuvered close enough to brush her fingertips with his. "I thank heaven you are safe," he murmured.

She caught the worry and relief in his eyes and gave him a smile before he moved on.

Therri gave an eager bounce. "Let me join them."

Constantia almost blurted out, "No!," but it was not her place. The baron hesitated, then nodded, and his son loped off with the other men to the gatehouse. Llygad followed despite the lack of invitation. There could be no harm for Therri to watch, she told herself. The knights would send the boy to the keep when the English appeared.

Laurant ordered the horses restabled, the hounds returned to the kennels, then went with the rest of his knights to take counsel in the hall.

"To my chamber." Lady Gwenllian said to Constantia when all the men were gone.

Guia, red-eyed and tear-stained, came out of the baron and baroness's great chamber as Constantia and Lady Gwenllian reached the door. Lady Gwenllian sailed inside, but Constantia paused to touch Guia's arm.

"Have a care," Guia whispered. "Sybil is inside with her switch. Lady Gwenllian caught Llygad kissing me."

Constantia clapped her hand over her mouth to smother a gasp. "Llygad *what?*"

Guia wrung her fingers, chapped and red from the laundry chores Lady Gwenllian assigned her. "I am sorry, Constantia, but he kissed me. He does not want to marry you at all. Do you mind? I—I thought you did not want to marry him either."

"I don't," Constantia whispered back. "Do you want to marry him, Guia?"

Guia rubbed her wet, ruddy nose with her knuckles. "Ever and ever so much."

Unlike Lady Gwenllian, Guia's mild prettiness deserted her when she cried. The red blotches on her cheeks deepened to purple as more tears streamed down her face. "I have loved him as long as I can remember, but I thought he only had eyes for you. But he says he has loved me for years as well. Lady Gwenllian would not let him marry me because I have no dowry and she's been hoping to marry him to you, so he never told me what was in his heart. Until last night."

"What happened last night?"

Guia snuffled inelegantly. "Llygad came back from his latest visit to your father yesterday while you were still at Vere. He rode into the yard, grinning ear to ear—you know how endearing he looks when he smiles."

Endearing was not the word Constantia used for Llygad's smiles, though they were certainly pleasant enough. But she was not in love with Llygad.

"Of course," Guia continued, "Lady Gwenllian thought his grin meant he had finally won your fortune and your hand. I was standing with her in the yard, but he did not see us until Lady Gwenllian called his name. It was too late for him to affect a mournful demeanor, although I saw him try. He told her your father settled his inheritance on your eldest sister and has married her to an Aquitanian lord who will assume your father's lands when he dies. So now you are a pauper again, like me and Beatris."

Constantia blew out a breath of relief, the weight of the threat that hovered over her these last many months soaring from her soul.

Guia gave a forlorn sniffle. "Llygad asked me to meet him in the garden last night. That's when he told me he loved me and kissed me, only Lady Gwenllian heard me leaving our chamber and followed me to the garden. She heard everything Llygad said to me, then blamed me for seducing him."

A shadow fell across them. The sunlight from the chamber window elongated the dusky outline of Lady Gwenllian's petite figure.

"When you are finished gossiping about me," she said, her voice as sweet as poisoned honey, "would you be ever so kind, Constantia, as to join me in my chamber for a word?"

Guia scurried away like a terrified mouse. Constantia stepped across the threshold.

As she passed Lady Gwenllian, the baroness said, "If Guia told you I was surprised that your father cut you off, I assure you I was not. If he'd intended to dower you, he would have done so a year ago."

Constantia longed to retort, *Then why did you waste both our time by making Llygad woo my father with praises of me all year?*

She wisely held her tongue. The old crone, Sybil, stood beside the great chamber's large, curtained bed, lovingly caressing the supple, stinging rod in her age-blotched hand.

Lady Gwenllian closed the door behind them with an ominous click. "I feared your father would repudiate you in the end. That is why I urged Llygad to grow his hair out again. Returning to Wales looking like a Welshman rather than some crop-haired stranger will make it easier for him to win a pure-blood, well-dowered Welsh wife."

Urged? Browbeat, you mean. But Lady Gwenllian's words surprised Constantia. "Llygad is going to Wales?" Did Guia know?

"I sent a messenger to my father this morning, bidding him to find Llygad a meek, obedient bride. Once they wed, he will bring her back Pennault to keep me company. I have had my fill of pert Poitevin women."

Constantia barely suppressed a snort. Lady Gwenllian calling Poitevin women "pert" was like old wine calling vinegar sour.

"When your sires entrusted you, Guia, and Beatris to my care," Lady Gwenllian said, "I hoped I could arrange respectful marriages for each of you. If I'd asked him, the baron would have dowered you each with at least a few linens and silver spoons that lonely widowers eager for young wives might have been content with. But the three of you have sorely disappointed me. Beatris insisted on growing fat."

Poor Beatris. She had not begun eating double portions at dinner until she passed the age of four-and-twenty without any sign of a husband on Lady Gwenllian's horizon.

"Guia's glum face would dampen any man's desire."

Because you told her again and again that a man would have to be old and nearly blind to consider a woman as poor and dull as she.

"And you, Constantia, have proven yourself the wanton I always knew you would become. Smiling boldly at every man in our household, thinking if you could spin one of their heads far enough, as you did poor Jevon's, that my husband might allow one of his knights to marry a wench without a denier to her name. But I assure you he never would. Even if you spent an entire night rioting with one of them in the woods."

How dare Lady Gwenllian say "Poor Jevon" as though she'd played no part in his disgrace! Constantia almost blurted out an angry, impulsive retort, but a voice from the doorway stopped her.

"Who has been rioting, Mama? Constantia? That is ridiculous!"

Lady Gwenllian gazed coldly at the pale-complexioned girl with a thick flaxen braid who entered the chamber. "Go away, Heléne. This is none of your affair."

"But—"

Lady Gwenllian silenced her younger daughter with an upraised hand, the flat of her palm stopping just short of Heléne's willful little nose. Sybil clucked what might have been a chuckle. It was hard to make out any expression in the wrinkled old face aside from the spite that snapped in the crone's eyes. Sybil had once been in charge of the castle's nursery, but with the children grown, Lady Gwenllian now employed her to discipline the pages and younger squires when they "misbehaved," along with the castle servants. And still, when she considered them deserving, Constantia, Guia, and Beatris.

Lady Gwenllian crossed her arms. The elegant cuffs of her surcote dangled halfway to the floor. "Tell me who your lover is, and I will halve your number of switches."

"I have no lover, my lady," Constantia insisted. "Everything that happened last night, I told your husband in the bailey."

Everything except that Jevon had returned. She did not dare add that. After besmirching Constantia's virtue and accusing her of "spinning Jevon's head" years ago, Lady Gwenllian would accuse her of conspiring with the enemy to take the castle.

The baroness again scrutinized Constantia's snarled hair and mussed gown, lingering on Jevon's cropped gloves. Constantia should have pulled them off and hidden them while she whispered with Guia.

"I will not tolerate these impertinent lies. Kneel by the bed." Lady Gwenllian whipped back the curtains, revealing the rumpled coverlet against which Guia must have knelt.

Constantia's position in the castle gave her no choice. She reluctantly moved toward the bed.

"You are going to switch Constantia?" Heléne exclaimed. "Why, Mama?"

"Because she has played the harlot and must be reprimanded."

Heléne recklessly inserted herself between Constantia and the bed. The sixteen-year-old stood at least two inches taller than Constantia, but that would not stop Lady Gwenllian from "reprimanding" her daughter with Sybil's switch as well. Constantia shook a warning head at Heléne, but the girl gazed stubbornly at her mother.

"I have known Constantia all my life. She would never do anything wanton."

"I told you to go, Heléne." Defiance of the chill in the baroness's voice could only end one way for Heléne. She would feel Sybil's rod next.

"Please," Constantia whispered, "do as your mother says."

Heléne chewed her lip while Lady Gwenllian's eyes sparked at her daughter. Heléne glanced at Sybil's rod, then her silvery gaze lingered just an instant on Constantia before returning to her mother.

"Yes, Mama," Heléne finally said. "Only tell me first what Papa means about war coming to our gates."

"War?" Lady Gwenllian's dismissive laugh chimed like a delicate bell. "Nonsense. Wherever did you hear such a thing?"

"From Papa. I was hurrying downstairs to join the hunt but found him in the hall with his knights. They were all talking of war. Papa saw me and ordered me away, so I came to ask you. What do they mean?"

Lady Gwenllian's rosebud lips pinched. "It is all rubbish. Constantia returned from a night of cavorting with a man she refuses to name, bearing a preposterous story she hopes will save her from chastisement. It is nothing for you to worry about. Go back to your chamber. And you, Constantia, kneel beside the bed. Now."

Constantia knelt, bracing her hands against the bunched bedding where her fists, like Guia's, would ball into the cloth when the blows fell. Sybil shuffled her girth behind Constantia.

But Heléne stretched her arm above Constantia's back to block the switch.

"Heléne, no," Constantia hissed, too frightened for the girl to remember to use her title. "Your mother will punish you too."

Heléne's slightly too-wide mouth pressed together. Red patches rose in her sallow cheeks, and her pointed chin jutted into the air. "If Constantia brought us news of war, we should listen to her."

Constantia tugged on the skirt of the dull green gown that hung like a sack on Heléne's thin frame and whispered more urgently. "Do not provoke your mother. But gather the women and pages together and take them to the cellar."

"Don't you dare," Lady Gwenllian snapped. "We are under no threat. If the king sends men, your father will stand firmly against them."

Heléne looked startled. "The king—?"

The blare of a trumpet cut her off.

"To the walls!" The shout, though distant, rang clearly through the open window. "Every man to the walls! Arm yourselves but hold your positions until Lord Laurant gives his command!"

Constantia sprang up, following Heléne to the window. The great chamber looked out over the bailey at the rear of the castle. Knights, squires, and men-at-arms ran pell-mell below them, some toward stairs that led up to the battlements, others toward the keep, where weapons and armor were stored in tower chambers.

Constantia spun toward Lady Gwenllian. "Now do you believe me? I have seen what the earl's war engines can do. We should take the women and children to the cellars for protection."

Lady Gwenllian paled a bit but shook her head. "My husband will make short shrift of the English bullies. Close the shutters, Heléne."

Heléne pulled the wooden shutters inward, pausing to watch another moment through their still-open crack before fully closing them. The shouts from outside grew muffled.

Heléne turned to her mother. "Should we not prepare some bandages and salves just in case any of our knights are injured before Papa drives the English from our walls?" Heléne knew more about healing than anyone save Sybil.

Lady Gwenllian hesitated, then agreed. "Take Sybil with you."

The young girl grabbed Constantia's hand and dragged her to the door. "Constantia can help me tear bandages and mix the herbs we have in the kitchen. Sybil can go to the infirmary garden and gather us some more."

Heléne pulled Constantia out of the chamber before her mother could protest.

Constantia squeezed Heléne's fingers, grateful for the reprieve from Sybil's rod. "Thank you."

Heléne's smile lit up her plain, pointed features to the edge of prettiness. "I know it is nonsense what Mama said about you. But where were you last night?" They swept along toward the stairs. "Therri and I were so worried when you did not come back from Vere. So were cousin Llygad and Sir Franco and Sir Raimon. Especially Sir Raimon."

Heléne slid an inquisitive glance at Constantia. Constantia guessed she meant to be sly but she lacked the guile to succeed. The girl's next words confirmed her artlessness.

"Will you consider Sir Raimon's suit now that your father has ruined Llygad's chance to marry you?"

"You know of that?"

"Everyone knows. Mama was not at all quiet about how unhappy she was over the news, nor about finding Llygad and Guia together last night in the garden. Poor Guia."

If Heléne's smile prettied her, the compassion in her silvery eyes radiated the inner beauty of her soul. Truly, she had the kindest heart of anyone at Pennault. If only some honest man could see her worth beyond her unremarkable face and figure.

Heléne released Constantia's hand to lift her skirts as they started down the stairs. "I heard Sir Raimon tell Sir Franco he is going tourneying next spring. If he wins a fortune, will you marry him? You would never have to listen to another one of Mama's lectures or worry anymore about Sybil's switch."

"Marriage is about more than escape, my lady."

Heléne's fair brows furrowed. "I know. It was the very opposite for Clothilde. Lord Merval is a horrid old man, but Clothilde wed him without complaint. I do not care if Mama has Sybil beat me bloody, I will *never* agree to a marriage so vile. Although Mama says I am so plain I can never hope for a love match like her and Papa's."

Constantia doubted love had anything to do with the baron and baroness's marriage. More likely lust for Lady Gwenllian's beauty on his part and lust for Laurant's wealth on hers.

"But Sir Raimon loves you," Heléne said as they followed the curve in the stairs. "You do not love him, though, do you?"

"Sir Raimon and I are only friends."

"But if he wins a fortune, perhaps marrying a friend would not be so bad. Even if you do not love him enough to cry."

Constantia sent a puzzled glance at Heléne. "What do you mean, my lady?"

They reached the foot of the stairs, but the great hall was empty. The baron and his knights must be in the bailey, marshaling the castle defenses. Constantia followed Heléne as she started toward the door tucked into the wall behind the dais that led to the kitchen.

"You cried after Jevon left. I asked Clothilde why, and she said it was because you loved him. Even though you still smile at everyone as you did before, your smiles have been different since then. Is that why you do not want to marry Sir Raimon? Because he cannot make you smile like Jevon did?"

Heléne was only nine when Laurant banished Jevon. Constantia had no idea she and Clothilde had been perceptive enough to discern her broken heart. Constantia opened the door, relieved that the din echoing from the kitchen preempted her reply.

Heléne helped keep the castle stocked with remedies, so Cook asked no questions when the girl prepared a salve to soothe Constantia's cut lip, then began gathering ingredients to make more. The servants bustled around her, preparing the midday meal, ignorant of the threat to the castle.

Constantia gathered some linen cloths and sat quietly in a corner. She stripped off Jevon's gloves and breathed in the woodsy scent of smoke and greenery that clung to them, memories bitter and sweet of their night rushing back to her. Then she tucked the gloves into her girdle. As she rent the cloth into strips, she wondered . . . would she smile to see him if he burst through their walls with his earl, even though they brought destruction? Or would another devastation like the one she lived through at Vere forever shatter their love?

Jevon stood behind the supply wagons, their precious cargo stationed a safe distance from any fire arrows Pennault's arbalists might let fly from the castle walls. A fortnight of stalemate had passed, thanks to a crack in the frame of the mangon. After its heavy use in vanquishing both Blancaval and Vere, Jevon was not surprised the wood had become exhausted. The ruts in the road between Vere and Pennault had not helped. According to the red-ringleted squire who came to check the supply wagons twice a day—and to see whether Jevon was still there or had run off to join his Poitevin countrymen—the Baron de Laurant was refusing to open his gates to the earl. Jevon hoped, now that the engineers had finished the mangon's repairs, that Laurant would change his mind. Jevon wanted to see Laurant defeated, humbled, humiliated, even. But he had no desire to see him share Sir Damien's fate.

The field that stretched beneath Pennault Castle's motte had been cleared generations ago. The leveled, open ground left attackers vulnerable to castle defenses, but here, where the wagons stood, the forest still thrived close to the road. Jevon paced out the distance from the ale wagon to an elm tree set a little deeper into the woods than the oak he had chosen yesterday. He carved three X's of different sizes into the gray-furrowed trunk, then returned to the wagon. Removing his bow from the wagon bed, he tested his weapon, pulling the string until he felt the tug in his wound. The stitches had been removed a few days ago. The incision, though healing, was still sore, but he would have made a poor mercenary had he not learned how to push through the unavoidable damages that came with war.

He pulled his bowstring deeper. A crossbow would cause less strain, but Gunthar had hired Jevon as an archer, not an arbalist. Any of his men could use a crossbow, Gunthar said. They were powerful and lethal but it was a slower weapon to use. What he wanted from Jevon was the speed and accuracy of his war bow.

Jevon alternately stretched and relaxed the string, gradually easing the tender skin around his wound to its greatest flexibility. Then he drew one of three arrows from his belt and nocked it in the costly bow he had bought with his mercenary earnings. Hywel ap Ioan had positioned his epigram and bowyer's mark exactly where an archer would be forced to see it every time he aimed, though the epigram would only be meaningful to a man who could read. Jevon took a moment to study the words before releasing his shaft, followed by the other two in quick succession. They landed with a satisfying shiver in the center of each X, from the largest to the smallest.

"Admirably done." A man's voice sounded from behind him. "What is that, twenty-five paces from where you stand?"

Jevon turned, surprised to see the Earl of Gunthar watching him from near the head of the ale wagon.

"Roughly," Jevon replied.

"Then I presume you are ready to join your company?"

Jevon had begun to doubt the earl ever intended to call him to rejoin his other bowmen as they attempted to soften the resistance from the castle battlements. Still, he hesitated. The malicious stranger's dagger had drawn a not inconsiderable amount of Jevon's blood. He certainly felt stronger and steadier now than a fortnight ago, but . . .

"I believe so," he answered cautiously, "but I have not fully tested the extent of my stamina."

"I will take precision like that for an hour"—Gunthar nodded at the three arrows in the tree—"over a day's worth of volleys from my other archers, as skilled as they are." He crossed to the elm, pulled out the arrows, ran his thumb over the three notches they left in the bark, then rejoined Jevon and handed him the arrows. "The real question is, can I trust you to aim where I tell you to?"

"I will stand by my oath to you, my lord. And when I do, I trust you will stand by yours to ask my pardon from the king."

Gunthar crossed his arms and leaned against the wagon, weighing Jevon with his grey, hawkish gaze. "What did Laurant accuse you of stealing?"

"A costly brooch that belonged to his wife." Jevon inspected the arrows to be sure the shafts had not splintered and the iron heads had not been mangled by the tree.

"And they found the brooch where? Amongst your things? On your person?"

Jevon slid the arrows into his arrow bag where it rested in the back of the ale wagon. "They never found it. As far as I know, it remains lost to this day." According to Constantia, anyway.

"Then what evidence did they bring against you? Laurant must have believed you guilty to have branded you like that."

Was Gunthar trying to find a loophole in the promise he made to Jevon? Hoping Jevon's "crime" had been so dark it would not stain the earl's honor to break his word? Jevon supposed Gunthar had every right to seethe at Jevon's decision to let Constantia warn the very castle the king had ordered Gunthar to defeat.

Since Jevon had given his gloves to Constantia, his hands remained bared to the earls' army. He held up his brand so Gunthar could clearly view his scars in the morning sunlight. "This was a compromise. Laurant's wife wanted the baron to take off my hand, but Laurant said this would be punishment enough."

Careful to hold the earl's gaze, knowing that a single flicker to the left or right would be interpreted as equivocation, Jevon told Gunthar how he had borrowed the brooch to repair it for the baroness and lost it, how Laurant had misconstrued the silver Jevon received for his mother's ring, and the disappearance of the pilgrim with the guttural accent who could have proven Jevon's story.

"A lady of the castle saw me earlier that day with the brooch. In Laurant's mind, that was all the 'evidence' he needed to condemn me."

Gunthar cocked one of his heavy eyebrows. "On the testimony of a single woman? Were there no men who witnessed against you? Had you a questionable reputation among them that no one spoke on your behalf?"

"My reputation was perfectly honorable. You can ask any man of Pennault." Jevon knew that sounded self-serving, but it was true.

"Laurant judged you guilty on so little?" To Jevon's surprise, Gunthar's mouth tightened as though in distaste. "This would not have happened in England, not anymore. King Henry has reordered the courts to stop such abuses among his barons. Twelve free men would have been required to make inquiries into the question of theft and determine on oath whether Laurant's accusation was warranted. In a criminal case like theft, only one of the king's justices, not your baron, could have sanctioned a punishment like that."

Gunthar indicated Jevon's brand with his chin. The flash of heat in his eyes surprised Jevon.

Jevon had never questioned the arrogance of his Poitevin countrymen in what he, too, had once proudly called their "ancient liberty." Each baron settled quarrels with his neighbors and judged his own household however it suited him. Once Jevon left his father's house, he'd looked to Laurant as the one and only arbiter of his fate. Judged by twelve men under oath? Punishment dispensed not by barons but by an officer of the king? What Gunthar described sounded like a fantasy.

Jevon gazed at the castle in the distance. Had he been knighted by Laurant, he would be standing atop Pennault's walls like the tiny figures of his former friends. He would have sworn the same oath as they to spill his blood to defend Laurant's right to brand a squire or cut an offender's hand clean off with no rebuke from anyone, even their own duke. The seventeen-year-old Richard could not control the powerful, headstrong barons of Poitou. Jevon knew that was why they had sworn allegiance to the young prince in this war with the king, so they could continue to brand and maim and terrorize their households and neighbors without interference.

Jevon had never given two thoughts about any other way to live. Now, at Gunthar's words, Jevon questioned everything about his homeland.

"Ned Woodville said if I prove my faith to you and win a pardon, you might take me with you to England as one of your household archers after you have humbled our barons and restored their loyalty to the king."

The island across the Breton Sea could not be as glorious as Gunthar professed, but Jevon had a sudden, fervent urge to visit it.

"We will see," Gunthar said with less anger and more deliberation than he had a fortnight ago. "What can you tell me about Pennault's defenses? You must be familiar with them if you grew up at the castle."

Jevon told Gunthar all he remembered: the double portcullises of the gatehouse, one at the entry, the other at the rear of the passageway, which could be lowered to trap attackers in between; the number and location of the murder holes in the ceiling; the arrow slits in the walls archers could use to pick off intruders in the passage.

He paused, wondering if he were betraying Constantia by sharing such detailed information. But having witnessed the earl's successful subjugation of Blancaval and Vere, Jevon knew Gunthar would defeat Pennault just as completely with or without Jevon's help. The more Gunthar knew about Pennault, the more targeted his attack and perhaps the less haphazard the destruction.

So Jevon continued. Should Gunthar's men successfully break through the gatehouse, he told the earl the location of the well, the storehouses in the bailey, the stables, the postern gate, and the layout of the chambers inside the keep, along with the stairways, storage chambers, kitchen, and every nook and cranny he could recall of the great central fortress. He recited which rooms in which towers held caches of weapons when he lived there and which housed Laurant's treasury. He even told Gunthar the location of the garden and dovecot and of the oubliette deep in the earth of the South Tower.

Gunthar listened, injecting an occasional question for clarification, then gave what Jevon hoped was an approving nod when he finished.

"Take your bow and arrow bag," Gunthar said, "and ride up to the front to join the rest of the archers. You may use my horse so you do not grow weary."

The earl's black destrier, one of the finest Jevon had ever seen, stood loosely tethered near the grain wagon.

"What about you, my lord?"

"The stroll will not hurt me. It will give me time to consider your information and decide what course to take next."

Jevon picked up his arrow bag and caught sight of the cloth-wrapped bundle beside it in the wagon. He'd removed the bundle from his bag so he could whip out the arrows to practice his launching speed. Now he unwrapped the cloth and held the dagger out to Gunthar.

"You have been occupied with the siege, my lord, so I have not had a chance to show you this. It belonged to the stranger I fought with in the woods."

Gunthar glanced somewhat indifferently at the blade. "I see you have wiped your blood from it. Why would that or this stranger mean anything to me?"

"Because he threatened you to my face."

"Which of your Poitevin brethren have *not* breathed out threatenings against me? I am in your lands as the king's agent in the middle of a rebellion."

"But this grudge was something more. Something personal, I think. He threatened to carve me up and leave me strewn along the road for you to find. He said you would know me as one of your servants by the badge I wear. My lord, my Poitevin brethren are quarrelsome and headstrong and they delight to war among themselves. They are fiercely jealous of the freedoms they have enjoyed under the lax hand of our counts and dukes. They would cut you down in battle without a blink, and they will hold their castles ferociously against you while they breathe fire and perdition upon your head. But not one would be called coward for driving a sword—or a knife—into your back or show themselves so vile as to sunder one man with cold calculation to taunt another. Unless that 'other' had dealt him some grievous affront in return?"

Jevon tried not to voice the last statement as a question, but an upward lilt at the end escaped nonetheless. Despite Gunthar's promises and Jevon's hope in them, he once again reminded himself that he knew next to nothing about this English earl, and, accordingly, his doubts leaked out.

"I can assure you I have never 'sundered' anyone, either in heat or in cold calculation." Gunthar sounded annoyed at Jevon's unintentional inference. "Have men fallen by my sword in battle? Regrettably, yes, but only those engaged in blatant insurrection against the king. Death is a risk all men take in war."

Jevon knew that truth too well.

Gunthar straightened from where he leaned against the wagon, his formidable height just as daunting as when he glared down from his destrier. "I find no pleasure in warmongering for the sake of war alone. If I did not believe as I do in Henry and his desire to bring order to his kingdom by good and sensible laws, I would never have set foot on your shores. The day his subjects are willing to petition the king with their grievances rather than take up arms against him and bring misery to everyone around them, I will lay down my sword and happily return to England." He thrust out a commanding hand. "Let me see the dagger."

Jevon handed it to him. It was true that the queen and princes, egged on by the king of France and unhappy barons begrudging a loss of their power, had begun this series of wars.

Not until he watched Gunthar studying the pommel did Jevon realize the etching had been hidden in his fist when he retrieved the dagger from the ale cart. Gunthar's brows plunged. His mouth flattened until his lips nearly disappeared. When he finally spoke, his bark made Jevon jump.

"You know this." Gunthar thrust the pommel toward Jevon.

Jevon shook his head emphatically. "I have never seen that dagger."

"I mean the design on the pommel. You are Poitevin. Your countrymen have sworn their oaths to Richard. You must know it."

"*I* have not sworn my oath to Richard. I left Poitou seven years ago, before King Henry proclaimed Prince Richard duke. You found me and hired my bow in Normandy, remember? I have never seen that emblem in my life." Jevon waited until the sharpness in Gunthar's gaze blunted a little before he asked, "What does the emblem mean?"

The corner of Gunthar's mouth gave a grim quirk. "It is a conceit Duke Richard has adopted since the beginning of this rebellion against his father." Gunthar traced the image with one of his long, tapered fingers. "See the woman, how her lower half coils into a serpent? It is a representation of his ancestress, the demoness Melusine. Richard takes delight in repeating the legend as though his 'fiendish blood' absolves his reprehensible behavior. The knights of his household have begun wearing this figure on their badges, and he has given a few of these daggers to his friends." Gunthar lifted his gaze back to Jevon. "What did your attacker look like?"

"Our struggle took place in the graying light before dawn. Much of the time, he stood behind me, the rest we flung one another to and fro. In sum, I did not get a good look at him except that his hair was pale and he wore it to his shoulders. He was tall and slender and nimble and fast." Jevon racked his brain for a fuller description, but it remained too blurred by the pain of his wound. "I regret that I cannot tell you more."

"Tall? Pale haired, with locks that fell to his shoulders? There is such a man who stands each day with the baron atop the gatehouse. One of Laurant's knights. Might it be him?"

Laurant, in league with the villain who threatened to ravish Constantia? Jevon's blood seethed. "I cannot tell until I see him, my lord."

Gunthar startled Jevon with a clap to his shoulder. "Hold on to that heat in your eyes. It will secure your arrow's aim."

Constantia should have remembered that Laurant was a very different man from Sir Damien. Where Sir Damien railed at Gunthar with blasphemous defiance, Laurant had spent the last fortnight alternately blustering that he would bury the English in Poitevin soil and bluffing a willingness to consider surrender while plotting another way to avoid the devastation of Gunthar's siege engine. But yesterday, while Laurant had been in the hall with his knights, deliberating the latest ultimatum from the earl, Lady Gwenllian had taken matters into her own hands, behind her husband's back.

"It is my fault," Guia sobbed.

Constantia sat on the edge of Guia's narrow bed in the draughty chamber they shared with Beatris, patting Guia's back while Beatris stood near them, wringing her plump, dimpled hands.

"That is nonsense," Constantia said. "You had nothing to do with what happened."

Guia's fine, light-brown hair clung to the tears on her blotched cheeks. "Llygad would never have done it had Lady Gwenllian not told him she would have Sybil beat me again. And she could never have threatened him with me had she not caught me letting him kiss me."

Beatris sniffled woefully. "We are destined to be miserable singlewomen all our lives." She reached inside the pouch tied to the painted leather girdle looped around her buxom hips and pulled out a fistful of honeyed nuts. The more dejected she became at her marriage prospects, the more sweets she sneaked from the kitchen.

The sparse light admitted by the slit of a window in the chamber's thick stone wall weighted Constantia's spirits with a despondent fear that Beatris was right about them all. Constantia's reunion with Jevon, careening between joy and anguish, left her emotionally wrung out. It did not help that she had hidden his gloves under her bolster and woke every morning with her hand curled into the supple leather that had hugged his palms. Having experienced afresh the exhilaration of his embrace and the fervent glow of his kiss, she did not think she could ever bear to marry anyone else, even to escape the drudgery of her life at Pennault.

Her heart ached anew as she rubbed little swirls of inadequate comfort between Guia's shoulders.

"It is nobody's fault but Lady Gwenllian's." Thoughts of the baroness flowed bitterly through Constantia. "If she had not made poor Clothilde marry that loathsome old bear Merval, none of this might have happened. Remember how the baron snorted and said, 'I am not such a fool,' when Lady Gwenllian urged him to throw his support to Duke Richard seventeen months ago? He changed his mind after Merval questioned his courage in front of his knights."

Beatris gave a snort of her own. "The only thing the baron fears more than his wife is being humiliated in the eyes of his men." She scooped more nuts into her mouth.

Constantia silently agreed. The baron had a reputation for bravery and daring in battle. 'Twas a pity he was too beguiled by Lady Gwenllian's beauty to see through her manipulations. Constantia had watched with dismay the way Lady Gwenllian persuaded the baron to allow their son, Therri, to stand alongside him atop the gatehouse, defying the dangers of the English siege. Lady Gwenllian despised weakness and tolerated it no more in her son than in her husband. When Laurant balked over risking Therri's safety, she reminded him with a sirenic sweetness—in front of his more senior knights—that her father fought with the ferocity of a maddened boar alongside Owain ap Gwynedd when he'd been no older than Therri.

And, of course, the baron capitulated because he could not let his knights think his son more cowardly than his father-in-law.

"I do not understand," Guia hiccupped between her sobs, "why Lady Gwenllian made Llygad do such a dishonorable thing."

Beatris dug more nuts out of her pouch. "That's because you were helping the scullery maid scrub the cooking pots yesterday when Sir Franco brought the news to Lady Gwenllian, but we were with her in her chamber. Sir Franco said the English earl, in a burst of anger, warned the baron not to risk the sort of misfortunes that befell Lord Merval and Sir Damien by continuing to defy the king. The baron had known about Sir Damien's death because Constantia told him, but he'd had no idea that Lord Merval also died while under the earl's siege."

"Lord Merval is dead?" Guia exclaimed. "How?"

"Apparently some sort of rage-filled fit in the middle of the earl's attack on Blancaval." Beatris poured the nuts into her mouth, then mumbled through her chewing, "Lady Gwenllian feared the news would convince Laurant to finally accept the earl's terms and open our gates. She wanted to stop him, so she made Llygad break the earl's truce."

Why had Jevon not mentioned Merval's death? Constantia could have assured him the news would likely convince Laurant to capitulate to his earl's demands. She had told Jevon of Clothilde's marriage, but had she ever spoken Merval's name? She combed through her memory and feared she had not.

Guia folded her arms tightly against herself at the news of Merval. "I am glad the Lady Clothilde is free of him. Merval was a dreadful old man! But it is not fair that because Lady Gwenllian is piqued by his death, Llygad must suffer for it." Guia began to rock on the bed. "Oh, I shall never, never forgive myself for letting him kiss me! He told me years ago he would rather die a knight in Laurant's service than ever return to Wales."

Constantia tried to calm her. "No one has said anything about Llygad returning to Wales."

"Llygad must fear it, though," Beatris mumbled unhelpfully. "The baron has never liked him. Llygad's face went white when Lady Gwenllian told him to order our archers to launch their arrows on Gunthar's men while still under the truce he'd granted us."

"He protested vigorously," Constantia added in Llygad's defense. He may have sunk to some vindictive depths as a bullied, insecure boy, but he had grown into an honorable knight.

"But he did it," Guia said, "for me."

Constantia had wanted to shield Guia from the whole ugly business. She warned Beatris not to tell Guia any of it. But their small chamber lay close to the baron and baroness's so that the three of them could respond quickly if Lady Gwenllian called during the night. They had all been awakened by shouting in the great chamber, and when Guia sat up in bed, wondering what was going on, Beatris thoughtlessly blurted out, "They must be arguing over Llygad."

Of course, Guia had nagged to know what she meant until Beatris admitted everything. Guia flew from her bed with her blanket clutched around her to listen outside the chamber door, and Constantia and Beatris followed. They could not catch every word bellowed through the thick timber door, but they managed to glean that Llygad's command to the archers resulted in two deaths among the earl's men, an affront they guessed, as Laurant must have, the English earl would want to avenge.

When news of the debacle reached the baron, Laurant did the only thing he could. If he laid the blame on Lady Gwenllian, his men would view him as an emasculated husband, too weak to control his wife. So the baron shouldered responsibility for the attack and resumed his defiant stance atop the gatehouse. The English might call him a truce breaker, but at least his men would call him bold.

But once darkness forced both sides to halt hostilities for the day, the baron, for the first time in Constantia's recollection, had retreated with his wife to their bedchamber and blasted her with a force that made their chamber door rattle.

Guia chafed her wet cheeks so hard her fair skin purpled. "I have never heard the baron so angry. He may pretend the archers' attack was his idea to save face in front of his men, but he is going to punish Llygad horribly."

"We do not know that," Constantia said, though it was probably true.

Guia's shoulders slumped. "*I* know it. Why else did he shout Llygad's name so many times as he roared at Lady Gwenllian?"

Names—Llygad, Merval, and, shockingly, Dunawd—had rung more clearly through the timber than the other details of Laurant's tirade.

Guia gave a fresh sob. "He is going to send Lady Gwenllian back to her father and make Llygad go with her."

"Just because we thought we heard her father's name—" Constantia began, but Beatris interrupted.

"I heard the name quite distinctly. He shouted Dunawd at least seven times. The baron almost never speaks of his father-in-law. I overheard him tell Sir Rolf once, when his brother visited, that he was seduced into the marriage and that all the Welsh are crafty tricksters."

Constantia sought to distract Beatris before she distressed Guia further. "The glare of the sun is in my eyes. Will you close the shutter, please? But light some candles first."

Constantia braced herself for the reek of tallow. Laurant, mindful, if somewhat absently, of the girls' noble births, provided their draughty chamber with a brazier to ward off the cold at night and a tapestry, howbeit a faded one, to cheer the wall, but drew the line at costly beeswax candles for anyone but himself, the baroness, and his children.

Beatris fished around in her pouch for more nuts as she moved to oblige Constantia's request. From the sigh that trailed after her, her search came up empty.

"Laurant also shouted Merval's name," Constantia reminded Guia. "It is Merval who convinced him to support the princes' revolt, and it is Merval he will blame in the end. You will see. However angry he might be at Lady Gwenllian now, her beauty holds him too enamored to ever part from her."

Guia snuffled. "But not from Llygad. Beatris is right. Lord Laurant has never liked him. *Never.*"

Beatris doused the chamber in darkness by closing the shutter before she lit a candle. Her voice floated through the gloom. "Llygad reminds Lord Laurant of his weakness in falling in love with a Welsh shrew."

While Beatris clattered about for a tinderbox, Guia began weeping again.

"I do not want to live without Llygad. I would rather the English burn us all to the ground."

Beatris squeaked and dropped the sparking tinderbox.

"You do not mean that," Constantia said as she left the bed to find a candle, helped by the murky light seeping through the shutter's cracks. "My heart broke when I lost Jevon, but I have continued living"—as difficult as it still was to breathe when crushed by the emptiness of her life without him—"and you will, too, if you need to. Besides—"

She found the tinderbox and lit the candle.

"I do not think Lady Gwenllian would allow Llygad to go back to Wales, even should the baron wish him to. Llygad is her kinsman. She likes to bully him, but he is also the only one at Pennault she can bemoan with over the lack of *bara lawr* and *cregyn gleision* at our table"—no matter how many times Llygad tried to teach Constantia Welsh, her tongue still mangled the pronunciations—"or reminisce with over the *ei-stedd-fod.*"

She had to divide the last word as she stumbled through it, which always made Llygad grin.

"You will see," Constantia said. "The baron's quarrel with his wife will blow over, and Llygad will be forgiven."

A shallow, shaky exhale drifted from Guia's bed. "Not if the English knock down our walls because of what Llygad did. What do you think they are waiting for? You said they leveled Vere in a single day."

Beatris shuddered in the candle's dim light. "Will the English knights ravish us, do you think?"

"Of course not," Constantia said sharply when Guia whimpered and tightened her arms around herself in a protective hug.

"How do you know?" Beatris challenged.

Because Jevon would not serve a man who loosed his knights to abuse helpless women.

But a nagging doubt festered in Constantia. The garrison floor of the castle had been turned into an infirmary for the wounded. Each time she helped Heléne and Sybil bandage a man injured by an English arrow, Constantia wondered if the shaft had come from Jevon's bow. Surely she would have heard someone cursing his name by now had he been recognized amongst the earl's troops. Perhaps he had changed too much since his banishment from Pennault. He had not worn a beard when he left. Constantia had known him in a heartbeat, but he had been her love and her life.

She tried to reassure herself, along with Guia and Beatris. "I saw the earl's knights as they poured through the broken walls of Vere. They battled the men who resisted them, but there was no slaughter, and knights who do not butcher do not violate innocent women."

She forced conviction into her voice to calm the other women, but once Constantia made her escape from Vere, she had no idea what had happened there.

"Still," Guia moaned, "I wish it were over with."

Constantia could endure their chamber's doleful atmosphere no longer. She needed to know what was going on, not stand here trying to placate Guia's fears and beat back Beatris's dire speculations.

"I will go see if there is any news." Constantia lit a second candle, set it next to the first, then gave the tinderbox to Beatris, whispering, "Do not say anything more to upset Guia, and I will bring you a chicken pasty from the kitchen."

Beatris harrumphed at the suggestion that she had said or done anything amiss but muttered, "Bring me two, and I will divert her with a game of three in a row."

Jevon dismounted from the earl's destrier near the engineers who sanded the mangon's sturdy new frame. A pile of large stones were heaped nearby. The mangon sat at the rear of Gunthar's army, but the castle's defenders would be able to view the siege engine from the height of the castle wall. Whether the defenders realized it or not, the earl's engineers knew exactly how to angle the mangon's arm to hurl its missiles with breathtaking precision to batter and break through those walls. Jevon witnessed its devastating success at both Blancaval and Vere.

The red-ringleted squire ran up to take the destrier's reins and ask the earl's whereabouts.

"Lord Gunthar lent me his mount," Jevon said. "He desired time to think, so he is walking back."

As the squire led the destrier away, Jevon surveyed the changes to his old home. Whereas Sir Damien sought to strengthen his defenses by building outward, Laurant had built upward. Unable to increase the height of the motte that sustained his castle's heavy stone weight, Laurant had raised the walls instead. Jevon could see exactly where the new portion of stonework began by the paler beige of the blocks against the darker, timeworn ones. The twenty-five-foot walls he remembered now stood thirty-five, perhaps thirty-seven, feet high. It took at least a year of labor to raise a castle wall twelve feet.

Some of the merlons on the east still looked unfinished. The baron had clearly prioritized the fortifications on the front of the wall. Pennault's four towers—West, South, Southeast, and East—had risen along with the walls between them, but the great square keep on the mound at the center of the bailey appeared unchanged from seven years ago.

The gatehouse was higher too. That must be Laurant standing between its two center merlons. Though a conical helmet with a nose guard obscured the man's face, a double-headed bird with outstretched wings splashed brightly across the front of his black surcote. The strips of red and orange beneath the creature's feet represented tongues of fire. Jevon had worn the image of the double-headed phoenix when he'd served Laurant as page and squire.

"Le Falquet!"

Jevon turned. Ginger-bearded Ned loped out of the crowd of knights who rattled swords and spears against their shields while bellowing fiery threats and insults at the men on the castle walls. Ned's conical helmet concealed his short blond hair.

The archer sergeant shouted over the din. "The earl has given you leave to join us? Thank the saints! We have sorely missed your falcon's eye this past fortnight." He waved. "Come, we are over here."

Jevon had seen his fellow archers as he'd ridden in, popping up from behind their mantlets to shower arrows over the walls, then darting behind the wicker barriers to dodge the reciprocating hail from the baron's arbalists. Jevon itched to join them. But—

"The earl told me to wait for him here."

Ned looked disappointed. "As soon as you can, then," he called before running back to join their company.

Jevon fidgeted and paced and counted and recounted his arrows a dozen times while he waited for Gunthar, even though he knew the earl provided a nearly infinite supply for his bowmen. Jevon tossed occasional glances at the gatehouse and adjacent walls, but the number of men there never changed. Four mailed knights stood with Laurant, along with three men-at-arms and three arbalists clad in padded gambesons, like Jevon. More knights and men-at-arms were sprinkled along the walls between the towers. They raised their shields each time the English launched a volley of arrows. Their arbalists retaliated with bolts sent through arrow slits in the merlons or by ducking up and down behind the crenels atop the wall.

The sun reached midheaven before Gunthar's tall frame came striding toward Jevon. As soon as Gunthar came abreast of him, he clapped Jevon on the shoulder. Gunthar guided Jevon into the middle of his clattering army, then swiveled him toward the gatehouse.

"That man beside Laurant," Gunthar said. "He and the baron speak frequently, but I have no firm identification for him. Do you know him?"

The mail-clad man stood slightly taller than the baron. A double-headed phoenix blazed across his surcote's breast, but unlike Laurant, the man held his helmet under his arm. Jevon's sharp vision examined the man's bared face. A martial obstinacy prevented features that hovered on the verge of beauty from appearing effeminate, but combined with his short-cropped, pale-gold hair, there could be no question he was kin to Lady Gwenllian. Too handsome to be Llygad and too young as well. Jevon judged him little more than a youth. Therri?

But Jevon could not be sure. Last he saw the baron's son, the boy had been only ten years old.

Jevon answered honestly. "Related to Laurant, undoubtedly, but I do not recognize him."

Gunthar gave an impatient grunt, then wove with Jevon through his army. When Gunthar stopped to point, knights near him moved in and hid his gesture.

"Him, then. Pale hair to his shoulders. Is that the man you fought with in the woods?"

Jevon scanned the wall until he found the only man with flowing hair. He stood at the far corner of the crenellated wall that extended west from the gatehouse just before the wall crooked rearward toward a tower. He, too, wore a black surcote over his mail with the badge of the double-headed phoenix sewn to the shoulder, but a helmet hid his features.

A rising steam hissed in Jevon's blood. Nothing would give him greater pleasure than to send an arrow through the heart of the villain who had threatened to ravish Constantia. But—would Laurant have allied himself with such a devil?

"Without seeing his face clearly," Jevon said, "I cannot be sure he is the same man."

Gunthar clicked his tongue. "You are right, of course. But let us assume it is no coincidence that a pale-haired stranger attacks you with one of Duke Richard's daggers, then shortly after appears atop the wall of a rebel lord who has sworn his loyalty to the duke. Are your falcon eyes keen enough to strike him from this distance?"

"To kill?" Jevon had hesitated in the woods, but Constantia was no longer in danger then. But if Constantia were at Pennault, and this villain were at Pennault, and if this villain had so much as touched her—

"Can you hit his heart from here?" Gunthar asked.

Jevon had avoided playing the assassin all these years, but if it meant defending someone who stood in danger—and who knew how many innocents within the castle the miscreant might have abused or intend to—then Jevon's conscience would lie quiet.

He whipped several arrows from his bag and tucked them in his belt for quick retrieval, then nocked one in his bow.

"Wait," Gunthar said. "What about Laurant?"

"What about him?"

Jevon drew back his string, aiming upward. Gunthar's well-trained men parted enough to allow him a clear shot, but not enough to draw attention to their movement. The breeze might carry Jevon's first arrow astray, but he would know exactly how to correct the second.

"Can you hit him too?"

"Hit"—Jevon lowered his bow—"Laurant?"

"Or that man at his side. Perhaps that would frighten the baron even more to see his own kin fall beside him. Can you do it?"

"You want me to kill the boy?" Horror curled Jevon's stomach.

"You know him to be a boy?"

Jevon bit his lip, angry at his careless slip. He could not *know* the man at Laurant's side was Therri, but he did not want to risk it. Putting down a vicious viper like the felon who tried to kill him and ravish Constantia was one thing. But a boy or man, rebel or not, who simply sought to defend his home?

"Laurant has a son," Gunthar said while Jevon tried to gather his response. "You think that is him. If he stands to fight at his father's side, he cannot be one of the children you wish to protect from my wrath."

"He is little more. Seventeen. I cannot tell if that is him, but if it is . . . My lord, you said you were not a butcher."

"I am not," Gunthar snapped. "And I have not asked you to kill anyone, only if you could. I wanted to know how accurate you really are. My archers' arrows have had little effect on Laurant's nerves, as little as

Laurant's arbalists have had on mine. What my archers *can* do is keep Laurant's arbalists distracted while a single bowman enjoying complete freedom of movement can aim and hit where I tell him to. If you can kill from this distance, I presume you can also disable?"

Jevon found the new question only slightly less worrisome than the first. Arrow wounds could quickly fester. "You—you want me to disable the man beside Laurant?"

"I have exhausted my patience with the baron. One day Laurant breaths out insolent resistance, the next he attempts to haggle terms of a potential surrender. Yesterday I thought we'd established a truce, but now two of my men are dead. I do not know whether Laurant gave the order or if *he*"— Gunthar indicated the long-haired man—"provoked the attack on his own. Either way, I am done negotiating. Before I resort to the mangon or mining, I want you to frighten the wits out of Laurant and see if that brings him to heel. However you can best accomplish that, I will leave for you to decide. But that one"—Gunthar pointed again at the long-haired man—"that one I want brought down."

That command, Jevon was perfectly willing to obey.

"Not killed." Gunthar must have seen the fire in Jevon's eyes. "I want him alive to interrogate. Cripple him only, if you can. But first let me create a diversion to draw their attention away from you. Wait for my signal."

"Yes, my lord."

While he waited, Jevon weighed the strength of the breeze, the position of the sun, everything that could affect the precision of his hit. 'Twas harder to strike an arm or a leg from this distance than a man's torso, but the right shoulder should be doable, provided the man made no sudden movements. As for Laurant and his companion . . .

Jevon sorted through the arrows in his bag, studying his options. The shapes of the heads, the lengths of the points, the strength of iron versus steel—all played a vital role in the success of piercing mail and gambesons when combined with the strength of his draw and the precision of his aim.

Men shifted around him while he decided on his strategy, but the din of swords and shields clashing never ceased. He looked up periodically to check for Gunthar's signal. The earl had remounted his destrier so he could clearly be seen by his men. He gave orders to some of his knights, who then dissolved into the crowd to carry them out. When the knights nearest Jevon quietly melted away, he glanced around to see where they went and finally understood Gunthar's subterfuge.

Jevon turned back toward the castle. A woman appeared beside the long-haired knight. Constantia! Someone inside the castle must have forced her to bear him some message.

Who is he allied with, and what has the fiend done to you, Stantia? Whatever it is, I will make him pay this day in blood.

Ever since an English arrow had soared over the wall and set the roof of the stables on fire, Laurant had ordered everyone on the castle grounds to take refuge inside the keep. Everyone except the handful of squires Constantia discovered in the bailey stirring coals in iron braziers and tossing in bits of wood to build up the flames.

"Is that for Lord Laurant's arbalists?" she asked the youths.

"Yes, my lady," one answered. "Sir Raimon came down awhile ago saying the baron wants more fire. That is a good sign, don't you think, that our archers are wreaking havoc on the enemy?"

"Perhaps." Or Laurant feared the English were about to wreak worse havoc in the bailey. "Have any of you seen Sir Llygad?"

The squire pointed at the farthest corner of the wall that stretched from the top of the gatehouse off to the west before kinking rearward to connect with the tower. That was not a good sign for Llygad. Previously he had stood with the baron and Therri, flanked by Sir Eudes and Sir Raimon atop the gatehouse. If Llygad had been exiled such a distance away, the baron must still be furious with him.

The muted clatter she heard from the bailey burst into a cacophonous clamor as she emerged through the West Tower onto the curtain wall. She moved along the wall-walk, past several knights, men-at-arms, and arbalists, before she paused to gaze between two of the soaring merlons at the enemy knights. They shouted up at Pennault's defenders, rattling swords and spears against their shields.

Llygad abruptly appeared beside her. "What the blazes are you doing here? Go back inside before one of their devilish arrows hits you."

"We have arbalists." She nodded at the men with crossbows stationed behind some of the merlons carved with arrow slits. "I trust they have harassed the earl's knights as ably as his archers have harassed ours?"

She lied. If one of their crossbolts should strike Jevon . . .

"We have fire," Llygad said, "but so do they, and we do not have any of those." He pointed over the field of men spread beneath the walls.

She had been searching that field for Jevon's face but paused to follow the direction of Llygad's finger to a series of wicker squares with slots cut across the tops. "What are they?"

"Mantlets. Wicker shields for their archers to hide behind. They can move those mantlets wherever they wish, while our arrow slits force our arbalists to remain in one position."

Some of their arbalists' crossbolts stuck in the wicker. Was Jevon behind one of those mantlets? Was that why she could not find him?

"We lit a few of those up with fire arrows a few days ago," Llygad said, "but they built new ones and covered them with wet skins that are quenching our darts. They have access to the river, while we only have the well. We will need that water for drinking if the siege goes on too long."

"How long can we hold out if the baron refuses to surrender?" The size of the English force dismayed her. She recalled that archers were not the only mercenaries Jevon told her the English earl hired in Normandy. Pennault did not have half so many men.

Llygad had not drawn his mail coif up beneath his cone-shaped helmet, and the breeze blew a strand of his long hair across his mouth. He brushed it away. "Weeks, perhaps months, until our food supply runs out or the well runs dry."

She presumed the baron had abandoned any further thought of surrender since he'd accepted responsibility for breaking the truce.

"But our arrows have had a few lucky strikes," Llygad added. "We've nicked a few of their men-at-arms, as they have notched a few of ours."

He did not mention the *unlucky* crossbolts that killed some of the earl's men, but from the slight sag of his shoulders, she guessed the baron had excoriated him for it.

She looked at the mantlets again, willing Jevon to step out from behind his wicker shield so she could see him. Surely he could grant her that much of a boon before his earl knocked down their walls and Jevon left with the rest of the army to humble the next rebel castle, abandoning her to desolating loneliness once more?

A few moments of silence passed between her and Llygad before he asked, "How is Guia?"

"She has not been switched again, but she is anxious for you." A great deal of movement was going on below. Mailed men periodically came to the forefront to relieve the knights engaged in their clamoring intimidation, while the noisemakers melted into the surrounding troops. "She is afraid the baron might send you home to Wales for what you did."

"Wales is not my home. I have not seen the land since I was seven years old. Cousin Gwen has kept the language alive in me so she has someone to converse with in her native tongue, but I am as Poitevin as the rest of you now. Look at me!"

His exclamation turned her gaze back to him. He flung his arms wide, resentment flashing in his eyes.

"I am not standing here waiting and willing to spill my blood in defense of Wales but to uphold our Poitevin rights along with the baron and the rest of his knights. But will Cousin Gwen let me marry a Poitevin lady? No! Now that marriage to you has fallen through, she wants another Welsh woman to keep her company. She told her father he must find me a bride from Wales. As though I have no choice in the matter."

Constantia gave up her empty search for Jevon and leaned against the merlon to give Llygad her full attention. "You are a knight now," she reminded him. "You do not have to obey her."

Llygad pulled off his helmet and rubbed the sweat from the back of his heated neck. He scrunched his face in a rueful grimace. "I know that. I defied her for over a year with you and your father."

"What do you mean?" Constantia had never seen him do anything but trot away on his horse to her father's castle every time Lady Gwenllian told him to.

Llygad seemed to struggle with how to answer, but he finally shrugged. "I never actually asked your father for your hand."

"Never asked him?"

"No. And if Cousin Gwen learns how I disobeyed her, she will loose a worse hellfire on me than Laurant. But I did not think you wanted to marry me, and as generous and kind as you have always been to me, I did not want to marry you either."

His fair brows lifted in question when surprise left her too startled to answer. She gave a small laugh, smoothing the worry from his face.

"You are right," she said. "As well as we suit as friends, we should *not* suit as husband and wife. But then, what have you been doing at my father's castle all these years? He must have wondered why you visited so often?"

Llygad gave a half-relieved, half-guilty grin. "He was flattered at first. Before I left Pennault each time, I paid one of our serfs to poach me a deer or a boar—because, as you know, I am as inept a hunter as I am a swordsman." His grin crooked with a wry recognition of his shortcomings. "I presented the beast to your father as a gift from Laurant to explain my arrival. Such generosity from his liege lord puffed your father up no end. I encroached upon his hospitality in the most deplorable way for weeks at a time without ever discussing you until I thought it safe to come back to Pennault." Llygad's grin faded. "I couldn't tell you, Constantia. If Cousin Gwen knew that you knew what I was doing, she would have accused you of putting me up to the deception and punished you."

Llygad might not be an adept swordsman or a talented hunter, but since becoming a knight, no one had a quicker eye to observe an injustice in the castle and try to avert it than he. Numerous times, he had distracted Lady Gwenllian into forgetting her grudges against Constantia. Had he fallen in love with Guia while finding ways to protect her too?

His surprising confession raised a wistful question in Constantia. "Did my father ever ask about me?"

Llygad's hesitation told her all she needed to know.

"No. I am sorry, Constantia. He always intended to make your eldest sister his heir if your brother died. Cousin Gwen would only have told me to try harder if she'd known, so I just let her keep hoping."

Constantia nodded and tamped down her hurt.

Llygad gave a despondent sigh. "I have done everything I can think of to court Cousin Gwen's favor. I let her jabber to me in Welsh for hours on end. I eat foods the other knights make fun of just because they have Welsh names. I even grew my hair out"—he jerked one of his long locks so hard his eyes watered—"just to please her, knowing it would make everyone call me 'the Welshman' again, as they did when I was a boy until I bribed Jevon to take my place waiting on Cousin Gwen so I could finally cut these cursed things off. After that, they mostly mocked me for being clumsy."

He released his hair but rubbed the tingle his yank left behind in his scalp. He turned to look at the field below, so she did the same. The English troops continued milling and clacking and shouting. There was still no sign of Jevon.

"Raimon and Franco do not mock you anymore," she said.

"Not in word, but I see the looks they exchange and hear their snorts of laughter, and I know full well what they think. Not only am I still clumsy, I am now my cousin's pampered, privileged kin again. Fah!" Llygad's vexation burst out on the word. "I hate it all. I feel Poitevin to the very core of my bones. Why can they not see I am one of them?" He thumped his fist against the waist-high crenelation between the merlons.

Constantia rubbed his hand, worried that he'd bruised it on the stone.

Llygad appeared oblivious to her touch. "When I brought the baron word that your eldest sister had wed"—along, Constantia learned, with a liberal chest of silver from her father to appease Laurant for not asking his liege lord's permission before marrying her sister off—"I thought, 'This is my chance. There is no further reason for Cousin Gwen to object to me marrying Guia.' I just had to catch my cousin in one moment of generous feeling and persuade her to petition the baron for me. Guia's birth is perfectly noble, marriage would have pleased one of Laurant's vassals, and it could only have vaunted Guia's father's pride to marry her to the baron's kin by marriage, especially since I was willing to take her without so much as a copper trinket to her name."

"I do not think Lady Gwenllian would ever have agreed to that," Constantia said. "Like my father, she is too ambitious and, as her kin, you are too valuable a husband to squander on a dowerless bride."

"To blazes with her! Before I could even try, Cousin Gwen sped off that letter to my uncle. I panicked."

Constantia watched the emotions on Llygad's face. It was no wonder the other knights knew exactly how to needle him when his expressions betrayed his every thought.

Anger flashed. "I had some wild idea of running away with Guia even though I knew I would have no means to support her with my abysmal swordsmanship." Self-disgust. "All I could think of was how long I had waited to be with her." Agonized yearning. "Then I realized I did not know whether Guia loved me in return. So I asked her to meet me in the garden after everyone went to bed to tell her how I felt. Only Cousin Gwen followed her and saw me kiss her, and it has been one disaster after another since then. If Laurant sends me to Wales, I will never see Guia again."

Pain squeezed Constantia's chest. For him. For herself. "I am sorry, Llygad. I fear it is the fate of all dowerless ladies, like me and Guia and Beatris, to remain singlewomen."

Bitterness flushed his face. "It isn't fair. A shrew like my cousin weds a baron because she is rich and beautiful, while women who are kind, like you and Guia—"

A great shout went up, drawing their attention to their right. Laurant gestured wildly at the knights who guarded the wall on the opposite side of the gatehouse where it folded around to link with a tower on the east. Sir Raimon raced along the wall where Constantia and Llygad stood.

"The English have launched a barrage of arrows at the east wall!" he shouted. "We need all our arbalists there *now*."

The arbalists immediately flew off with their crossbows.

Archers at the east wall? Franco commanded that quarter. A dark smear stained the sky—enemy arrows, so many Constantia could no more count them than a swarm of locusts. Surely that's where Jevon was? Would he make sure Franco stayed safe?

"How did they take our men unaware?" Llygad asked.

Raimon's mailed fist clenched the hilt of his sword. "It was a fiendish trick. Their archers traded surcotes and cloaks with their knights and strutted around to deceive us so that when the 'knights' gathered to the east, our men thought they merely intended to taunt a new quarter of the wall with the annoying clatter. Instead, they whipped bows from their cloaks and rained arrows upon our men. Our arbalists cannot reload their crossbows quickly enough to mount an effective defense to their war bows. Laurant wants you to bring your shields to help repel their arrows while our arbalists reload. Sir Baudri, Sir Milo, Sir Guilhem"—Raimon pointed at most of the nearby knights, as well as the men-at-arms—"all of you, come with me." Llygad started to follow, but Raimon blocked him. "You are to stay here, Sir Llygad."

Llygad looked startled. "Stay? Why?"

"Because the baron says so, that's why. But we can use your shield." Raimon's expression remained impassive, but his voice conveyed his, and no doubt the baron's, scorn.

Llygad surrendered his shield, as did the few other knights left to guard this stretch of wall.

Raimon turned to Constantia. "Do me a favor and call down to the squires in the bailey. Tell them to bring those braziers up to the eastern wall for our arbalists."

That he made the request to her was another slap of the baron's distrust of Llygad. As Raimon ran off after the others, the remaining knights dispersed to their former points of watch duty. The gaps between them widened with the arbalists, men-at-arms, and other knights gone.

The wall-walk was open on this side but wide enough to avoid inadvertently stepping over the edge. Constantia heard Llygad grumbling as she yelled down to the boys and watched them scramble to don their padded gloves to protect their hands from burning on the braziers' hot iron handles.

"Laurant is right," Llygad muttered. "I am nothing but a stupid, cloddish boor. Guia is better off without me." Constantia began to chide him as she started to turn around, but Llygad's exclamation cut her off. "What the devil?"

Constantia saw the blur of the missile that pitched Llygad backward from the crenellation he gazed through. She caught his arm and tugged him sideways. Llygad staggered with her, then dropped to his knees on the stone walkway, an arrow lodged in his right shoulder.

Once assured he was safe from further assaults, she leaned cautiously around the merlon to peer at the field below. A lone archer stood at the base of the motte. He slowly lowered his war bow. Jevon stared straight back at her, his expression as keen and satisfied as a falcon whose talons had just hit its prey.

"Constantia," Llygad panted on a ragged breath, "get down!"

He pulled urgently on her skirts, but her gaze remained riveted on Jevon. What was he doing here? Why was he not with the other archers at the east wall? Had Llygad recognized his attacker? And why—*why*—had Jevon tried to kill Llygad?

She remembered on a sudden wave of horror how Jevon said he suspected Llygad of stealing Lady Gwenllian's brooch and letting him take the blame. Was this vengeance, then? Thank the saints for whatever waft of air had carried his aim off-center!

Jevon turned and walked away, leaving her frozen in shock.

"Constantia, *down*."

"He is gone now." Her voice cracked with revulsion. Whatever Jevon thought Llygad had done, to try to kill with no more proof than mere conjecture! Had Jevon's soul grown as scarred as his hand? How had she not seen so dark a change in him during the night they spent together?

She heard the chink of chainmail as the knights still stationed on the wall hurried to their side.

"Get Sir Llygad to the keep," she told them, her gaze trailing after Jevon, "and call for Lady Heléne. Her touch will be gentler than Sybil's."

Constantia had not thought the shards of her heart could cut more cruelly than on the day Laurant branded and banished Jevon. To have the bittersweet joy of his return shattered by this malicious act of a stranger who bore her beloved's face! Yet, despite her abhorrence, she could not tear her eyes from him.

He stopped at the foot of the motte in front of the gatehouse and tilted his head to look up, the lethal war bow still in his hands. The hairs on her arms soared as her gaze swung to Laurant and Therri, the only two men still standing on the gatehouse tower. Neither saw Jevon as they watched the commotion to the east. And neither held a shield. Laurant, renowned for his courage in battle if not for equal pluck with his wife, must have volunteered his to protect his arbalists, and Therri had done the same. Now father and son stood defenseless.

If Jevon blamed Llygad for the theft, how much must he want revenge on the baron for the shame of his brand and exile?

Constantia screamed, but Jevon's arrow flew faster than her warning. So fast she barely saw him nock and aim before his shafts flew straight for Laurant's head. One, two, three, four, five—she stopped counting the shafts. Jevon's arm whirred, releasing the shower of missiles from his arrow bag.

Laurant appeared initially flustered by the hail of arrows, then he shoved Therri down behind the wall and dove down with him. It was impossible for Constantia to tell whether either of them had been hit, but with such a violent volley—! She shuddered.

Jevon continued the torrent of shafts until his arrow bag was empty. Then, once again, he lowered his bow and coolly strolled away.

T he wind picked up with the darkness, ruffling Jevon's hair. He waited in the inky shadows just beneath the castle wall. The moon, drifting in and out of wispy clouds, provided sporadic light. But an earlier scouting mission for Gunthar confirmed Jevon's suspicion that this portion of the battlements stood, at least temporarily, abandoned. Gunthar's bowmen had picked off a number of Laurant's arbalists, several of his men-at-arms, and a few of the mailed knights with their volley at the east wall, forcing Laurant to reorder his remaining men. The baron withdrew his guards from the west side of the castle to defend the north, east, and especially south walls, where Gunthar had moved his mangon late in the day. Jevon advised the earl that Laurant would be most complacent about the western stretch of his defenses because, although the motte's slope was gentler here than the other three sides, the forest abutted the mound closely on the west, making a direct large-scale attack by an enemy force difficult to launch.

No crossbolts or shouts of alarm met Jevon as he'd climbed the path worn into the motte's slope by generations of the baron's forebears coming and going through the postern gate tucked into the western wall. The hidden door provided a source of quick retreat for members of the castle to flee a siege for the safety of the woods. Tonight, Jevon would be ready for whoever slipped through that gate. The lack of torchlight overhead suggested Laurant did not want anyone to know his plans, not even his own men. Still, it was wise to remain in the shadows of the wall. A single guard could raise a loud enough hue to draw one of the baron's remaining arbalists to this quarter.

Twice as the moon crawled higher, Jevon stilled his hand when it began fidgeting with the hilt of the sword he had strapped on. If his gamble tonight succeeded, the earl would have to swallow all lingering doubts of Jevon's loyalty. A royal pardon would be assured.

Jevon squelched the small qualm that skirmished against his intent. *The earl will not harm him. He will be too valuable an asset. And I will make sure he is honorably treated.*

The postern's hinges finally sighed.

"Let me go first," a woman's voice murmured through the crack of the slowly opening gate. "Wait here until I signal. There will be no harm done if they capture me."

Jevon stiffened. He had not expected Constantia. Had he guessed wrong? Was it Lady Gwenllian and her ladies the baron meant to send away?

A faint beam of light appeared. She used a lantern to cautiously survey the space in front of her. Jevon pressed himself against the base of the castle and pulled his cloak's hood over his head. He supposed Lady Gwenllian would be just as useful a prize. As for Constantia—the jolt of seeing her only hours ago conversing easily with the long-haired stranger, laughing with him, caressing his fist when he thumped it against the hard stones of the wall, made Jevon feel a fool. She had tricked him—again. The sooner he could win his pardon, the sooner he could shake the dust of Poitou from his feet and strike her from his heart once and for all.

The yellow shaft of light swung his way, stopped just short of his nose, suspended for a moment, then moved to cast its light in front of the gate again. Jevon slid a few feet farther away from the beam. The glowing ball of light silhouetted Constantia's outstretched arm and the billowy outline of her cloak on the wind. Elegant and graceful even as a rippling shade. Alas for him that her substance was as empty as the apparition she appeared. Seven years of women whispering love to him one moment, calling the law down upon his head the next should have steeled him against Constantia's duplicity. She had lied straight to his face, convincing him she still loved him, all the while in connivance with the fair-haired villain who sought only a few weeks ago to kill him.

Who is he really, Constantia? Do you know who stole the brooch as well?

She turned the lantern the other direction to allow its beam to penetrate the black void between the castle and the woods. Then she took a few steps into the open, perhaps testing whether anyone waited to intercept her. Apparently satisfied that the way was clear, she motioned to the gate.

Two dark shapes also shrouded in cloaks emerged from the postern, both men, from their height and breadth. Jevon waited to see if a diminutive woman followed, but no such figure appeared.

One of the men threw back his hood. "I feel like a coward. Why can I not stay and fight alongside Papa?"

Lord Therri. I guessed aright after all.

Constantia pressed her free hand to the young man's arm. "Pray, keep your voice down, my lord. You and your father made a lucky escape today. He wants you someplace safe."

Jevon smirked. This was not exactly what Gunthar had expected when he ordered Jevon's attack on the baron and his son, but it was close enough. Judging by the baron's disappearance from the gatehouse for the rest of the day, Jevon's arrows had badly shaken Laurant. Gunthar hoped Jevon's barrage would frighten Laurant into surrendering, but Jevon knew it would not be that easy. Laurant would feel compelled to consult with his knights' council first, and Jevon had learned just how much weight their opinion of the baron's courage carried. They might well convince Laurant to hold out for pride's sake, and the baron would listen . . . so long as he thought his only son and heir was safe.

"Here, my lord, take the lantern." Constantia held it out to Therri.

Anxiety frayed the edges of her rigidly controlled voice. Had it shocked her to watch Jevon's volley at Therri and Laurant? *No more than your solicitude for the villain surprised me.*

Jevon knew she had recognized him when she looked down from the wall as the stranger fell with Jevon's shaft in his shoulder. Jevon hoped the wound festered. He hoped the villain who had viciously driven a dagger into his back suffered a lingering, painful torment before he crossed to hell.

"But—" Therri began a protest without accepting the lantern.

The second man cut him off. "The castle is about to fall, young lording. You must live to avenge your father if the earl cuts him down."

Raimon. Jevon felt a twinge of jealousy. His former friend had risen high in Laurant's confidence if the baron had entrusted his son's protection to him as he had once trusted his children to Jevon and Constantia.

"But—" Therri said again.

Raimon spoke across him, this time to Constantia. "I wish you would come with us. There is no telling what these English devils will do to you if they break through the walls."

Constantia lowered the lantern. "I do not think the English will harm us. It is said they treat women honorably."

Jevon had assured her of that.

Raimon moved past Therri to put his arm around her shoulders. "I can guard you both. There is no reason for you to risk yourself here. Once Lord Therri is with his uncle, neither of us need return to Pennault. You and I can ride for the tournament fields of Flanders."

"Tournaments are fought in the spring." Constantia eased herself out of Raimon's embrace. Because she had pledged herself to the fair-haired stranger?

"Then we will join the Young King in Normandy. He is passionate about the tournament and will gladly accept a swordsman as skilled as I am in his fight against his father. This rebellion will be over by spring, and Young Henry will likely be full king in his father's place. He will reward me richly for my support and my success in the tournament will redound to our new king's honor. I have most of what I require for the mêlée, and soon I will have the rest. But there is no need for us to wait until then to be married."

Jevon saw Therri's head snap up. "You and Constantia are going to marry?"

The lanternlight caught Raimon's annoyance, as though he'd forgotten Therri was there. "That is not your concern, young lording. Let us be off before the English cut you down too."

Raimon reached for Constantia's hand, but she pushed the lantern into his hold and stepped around him toward the postern gate. "The baron told me only to be sure the way was clear before you and Lord Therri ventured outside the walls. I would slow you down if I came along. Go quickly. The longer you linger, the greater your risk should the earl send a patrol to check this side of the castle."

Raimon huffed. "I suppose you are right. We should be on our way. But I will be back for you."

"But—" Therri objected a third time.

"Come along, young lording." Raimon's nudge of Therri looked more like a push, and a none-too-patient one.

Raimon's rudeness raised Jevon's hackles, as did the patronizing way he called Therri "young lording", as though he dealt with a child. When had his friend grown so pompous? Therri was clearly no longer the boy Jevon left behind. He might not be a man yet, but he had shown a man's courage facing down the English at his father's side.

Despite the near shove, Therri refused to move. "I need to show Papa something before I go. In case—well, I just need to tell him something first."

"There is no time for that, young lording."

"There has been no time ever since that archer sent that volley of arrows at us." Therri sounded angry now. "I tried to tell Papa then, but he just said, 'Hush!' and 'Do as I say,' and 'Later, Therri!' Well, it's later now, and all he's done is shut me out of the hall while he confers with his knights, then send you and Sir Eudes to order me about. And now he wants me to run like a coward when I don't even think—"

"Forgive me, young lording, but you are too young to be thinking at all at a time like this."

Therri gave a sputter of frustration, followed by an expletive hurled at Raimon, then a muttered apology to Constantia.

Constantia quickly interceded. "All your father wants is your safety, my lord. And you, Sir Raimon"—her voice grew more stern—"should speak more respectfully to Lord Therri."

Raimon sighed again. "Your pardon, young master. Tell me what you wish your father to know, and I will inform him of your wishes when I return from your uncle's."

Therri said nothing, but Jevon could fairly feel the youth's brimming resentment. Jevon grinned. He wondered if Therri looked as mulish as he had as a boy when his sunny, mischievous temper turned cross.

Jevon felt the broad spread of his mouth and swiftly pursed his lips. He had nearly forgotten why he lurked here, to take that willful young man prisoner and end this siege before anyone else could be wounded or killed when Gunthar unleashed the stones of his mangon in the morning. Gunthar's archers, who outnumbered Laurant's arbalists now, would be employed to pin the defenders down to slow their attempts at countermeasures. As rigorously as Ned had trained the earl's bowmen, none were as precise as Jevon. Had Gunthar asked one of his other archers to loose his arrows at the gatehouse today, Laurant might be lying wounded or dead and Therri alongside him.

Therri would view Jevon's act as a personal betrayal, but that could not be helped. And hopefully Therri's capture would avert the destruction of Pennault's walls and any further harm to the castle's inhabitants. Once Therri was in Gunthar's custody, Jevon felt sure Laurant would throw open his gates without condition to get his son back. Capturing the baron's heir would secure Gunthar's faith in Jevon's allegiance and win him a permanent position among his archers.

Jevon brushed his thumb along the scars on the back of his hand. Then why did he have to quell another uncomfortable twitch in his stomach as he quietly slid his sword from its sheath?

"Tell *me* what you wish your father to know," Constantia coaxed.

"No," Therri said. "I must tell Papa first myself."

The lantern swung in Raimon's fist as he crossed his arms. "We cannot stand here arguing all night. This is not a game, young lord—my lord. This is war. Remember that the English earl killed Sir Damien at Vere, and heaven knows what fate Sir Triston suffered at the hands of the English. All the more reason to take refuge with your uncle. Etienne will need your help to avenge his father's death, and if your father falls, you will need Etienne's help to avenge yours. Together you can rally an army to make the English earl pay. But not if you fall at your father's side."

Therri seemed to hesitate. Jevon knew the rage he must feel on Etienne's behalf. Jevon wished he might reassure the youth that Sir Damien still lived, but he dared not reveal himself until . . .

Therri cursed again but started moving toward the woods. Jevon launched himself past the Raimon and Constantia, whipped his arm around Therri's chest, and spun him toward the wall.

Constantia cried out. Jevon was startled to feel Therri's arms locked across his breast beneath his cloak, making Jevon's grip on the youth awkward. He clutched Therri more securely and pressed the edge of his sword across Therri's throat—close enough to frighten but with sufficient space to avoid an undesired casualty should Therri attempt to break free.

"Hold still."

Jevon growled the command at Therri to disguise his voice. If anyone had been stationed on the wall, Raimon would have called to them, warning them not to discharge their crossbolts. Since he had not, his old friend's weapon must be Jevon's only threat.

He shook his hood forward to keep his face hidden, then threw a gravelly order at Raimon. "You, drop your sword, then kick it over here by my feet."

Raimon swore and raised the lantern. Jevon lowered his head farther but held the blade steady, nudging Therri's chin up with his knuckles to be sure the light caught the gleam of his blade.

"Do as I say," Jevon warned.

Raimon tossed his sword at Jevon's feet and a string of blasphemies at his head.

"Let him go," Constantia pleaded. "He is only a boy."

Jevon forced himself to ignore the panic in her voice. "He is his father's heir," he rumbled, "and he will prove a fine bargaining chip to persuade your lord to open his castle's gates to mine. Sir Knight," he said to Raimon, "take the lady back to the safety of your keep. No harm will come to the youth if he does what he is told."

"If you take me to your earl," Therri swore, his voice thick with fury, "I will bash in his brains the way he bashed in Sir Damien's."

"Sir Damien was an accident." Gunthar had sworn it to Jevon. "It is regrettable, but such hazards are risked by all men in war." Jevon's necessity to keep his voice gruff prevented him from injecting the sympathy he wished to impart to Therri.

Therri snorted like a fuming young bull. "Accident? You come ravaging through our lands, butchering our barons, and expect us not to defend ourselves? We will return your atrocities with Poitevin fire and death."

"Therri!" Constantia rebuked him. She must fear him provoking the enemy knight who held him.

Therri scoffed. "I am not afraid of these English dogs. You may as well cut me down here, for if you drag me to your camp as a hostage, I vow, the first chance I get, I will send you all to the same purgatory you sent Sir Damien to. And so help me, if you kill my father—"

Some instinct warned Jevon to move his foot as he felt Therri's leg jerk. Therri's stomp grazed the toe of Jevon's boot, the near miss sending a shiver through his foot.

Jevon shook the youth, trying to rattle some sense into his head. "Stop thrashing about. No one wants to kill your father. We only want him to lay down his arms and open his gate."

"He won't do it, not even to save me. King Henry is a usurper in our lands, abducting and imprisoning our queen and former duchess. Papa has sworn an oath to her son, Duke Richard, to uphold his rule over our lands, and Papa is not a perjurer."

That's exactly what he is, though Jevon chose to reword his retort.

"Your father swore an oath to King Henry first, as did all our barons when our former duchess surrendered her rule of these lands to him at their marriage. Now she has stirred their sons to rebellion and dragged us all into their feud. Our barons have broken their oaths of fealty to their king. It is they who are in the wrong."

Therri squirmed in Jevon's hold, ignoring the hovering blade. "The king has broken his oath to *us* by scorning our rights and traditions. It would be a shame to our ancestors not to defend our ancient liberties."

Jevon had heard such Poitevin rubbish spouted all his life and never questioned it until he felt the sear of the branding iron. If only he could open Therri's eyes.

"Maybe our traditions are wrong. Our barons never obeyed our duchess before she became our queen, any more than they intend to obey her son the duke. And those 'ancient liberties' they fight to defend are simply the right to do as they please. Our barons make war on their neighbors without rebuke, burn each other's fields, rule as petty kings on their own fiefs and the fiefs they steal from their enemies or weak-willed friends. Our women are not safe from their envy and lust, while our youth of noble lineage are falsely accused and condemned at a whim. To whom can they appeal for justice? Our dukes, who should be protectors of the innocent, are weaker than the barons who swear false fealty to them."

A sharp gasp came from Constantia. "Jevon?"

He bit off his impassioned tirade. Had his bitterness betrayed him? But he knew she could not be sure with his hood draped over his face.

"I do not know that name," he said on a gruff rumble.

"But you are Poitevin. You keep saying 'our' when you speak of our people. Then you must know Jevon de Cazalet, for he serves in your earl's camp. He is Poitevin too."

"There are many Poitevin mercenaries in his camp," Jevon lied, "driven from their homeland by their cruel, oppressive lords. I do not know the man you speak of." He roughened his voice so coarsely it hurt his throat.

"But she is right," Raimon said. "You speak with a Poitevin accent. Yet you cast such slurs as these against the land that bore you? Against our duchess and her son, against our fearless barons? For shame, Sir Knight! Or should I call you Sir Traitor?"

Of course. Jevon's use of a sword instead of his bow would make Raimon think he bore the accolade.

"Show us your face," Raimon demanded, "if you are not a coward."

He swung up the lantern at the same instant Therri lunged to break free. The lurch brought the sword dangerously close to Therri's throat, but Jevon managed to evade a disastrous slash. They wrestled for a moment, then he cinched his arm more tightly around Therri's chest, jerking the youth against him. He let the edge of his blade rest against Therri's skin just long enough to frighten him into quieting down.

Not until Therri stilled did Jevon realize their tussle had dislodged his hood. The light of the lantern flowed into his face. More than that, the beam also bathed the scars on his hand.

Raimon uttered an incredulous oath. "Jevon? It really *is* you!"

"Stay where you are." Jevon dropped any further attempt to mask his voice. "Go back to the keep with Constantia. I swear no harm will befall Lord Therri, but he is coming with me."

With the light in his eyes, Jevon could not see Raimon's expression, but he heard the contempt in his voice. "Thief was not enough for you, but you return to our land a servant of the vile English? What did they promise you for slaughtering your Poitevin brothers? The baron's head as revenge for the just punishment he dealt you?"

Jevon had never known whether Raimon and Franco believed the charges against him. They had not been allowed to speak to one another before the baron banished him. Jevon had clung to a hope that friendship would supersede doubt. But, like Constantia's love, that hope crumbled to dust. His last tenuous ties to Pennault Castle were dead, then.

No, one more fragile thread remained to be burned.

"Last chance." Jevon laced his warning with all the coldness seven years of hurt and anger had welled inside him. "Go back to the keep with Constantia and tell the baron to open his gates if he wants his son returned." So what if Therri hated him too? The youth probably barely remembered him. "Do it, or I will shout to the earl's men and they can take all three of you prisoner."

Therri began to wriggle in Jevon's hold again. Blazes! The youth's foolish thrashing would have slit his throat by now if a less conscientious captor had caught him. If Jevon could make Therri lower the arms he'd crossed over his chest, he could establish a firmer grip. He tried pulling one of the youth's wrists downward, but he had to tilt the sword farther away to protect Therri from his own impulsive squirming.

"Raimon, no!"

Constantia's scream alerted Jevon as Raimon dropped the lantern and dove for his surrendered sword. Jevon shoved Therri out of the way, barely repositioning his weapon in time to deflect Raimon's strike to Jevon's exposed side.

"You fool!" Jevon thrust Raimon's blade away with a force that spun Raimon around. "You could have struck Lord Therri!"

Raimon snarled as he regained his balance. "Don't pretend you'd care. You will finally have your revenge on Laurant when your earl strings the baron's dead heir up in front of the gate. I'll deliver your head to Laurant instead. Raimon Redblade, men will call me after they hear how I bathed my sword in your blood. The fields of Flanders will tremble when the heralds announce my name in the tourney."

The force of Raimon's steel against Jevon's quickly quelled his temptation to laugh at Raimon's extravagant boast. The strength of his former friend's muscles well matched the vigor of his imagination. Sparks ignited the darkness around them as their blades flashed together in a flurry of clashes. Jevon could not fully fault Raimon for his confidence. Raimon undoubtedly thought seven years as a banished thief would degrade Jevon's former proficiency with the sword, but Jevon had used his mercenary years to maintain his skills. Some battles pressed too close, even on archers. A skillfully wielded blade against the enemy could mean the difference between life and death for oneself and one's mercenary companions.

Raimon's blows were cunning, his deftness clearly improved since Jevon last fought him. Since the lantern still lay on the ground, Jevon had only the murky glow of the moon to guide him, and even his falcon's vision was not enough in the dark to see whether the shift of Raimon's eyes still gave his old friend's strategies away. But patience was always Jevon's best ally in any battle. Counteracting Raimon with defensive parries gave Jevon time to sense a rhythm to Raimon's assault until Jevon finally felt an opening. He struck Raimon's sword down so sharply that Jevon felt the tip skim the ground. In a heartbeat, Jevon bounced forward and hurled his free fist into the shadowed spot where Raimon's nose should be.

Constantia saw something fall from Therri's cloak as he moved toward Raimon, who lay sprawled on the ground. A series of dark, thin shapes clattered against some rocks in the grass. Therri stepped over them and knelt next to the knight.

"Is—is he dead?" The youth's voice shook. He looked up at Jevon. "He's hit his head on a stone here."

Constantia retrieved the lantern and knelt beside them. She saw what had alarmed Therri. Blood stained the grass under Raimon's head. She lightly pressed her fingers at the angle beneath his jaw where Heléne had once shown her to feel for a pulse of life. A steady throb met her fingertips.

Relief eased some of the tension in her chest. "No, but he is hurt. We must get him to the keep and attend to him. Jevon, help Therri lift him."

Jevon had taken a few steps toward them but stopped several paces away.

"No." The lantern light lapped over the taut planes of his face. He sounded like himself again, only grim. And obdurate. Unforgiving. Like when he captured her in the woods. "You can fetch help for him as soon as Lord Therri accompanies me to the earl's camp."

Therri stood. "What if I refuse? Will you threaten to cut my throat again?"

Jevon pointed his sword at the youth. "I will do whatever I have to, to make your father honor his oath of fealty to the king."

Constantia felt as though some malicious fae had snatched her beloved and replaced him with a stonehearted apparition. Surely only that could explain the cold-eyed man who tried to murder Llygad, Laurant, and, heaven help him, Therri, where they stood on the wall today?

Or had Laurant's cruelty broken Jevon so completely it had fractured his soul in ways she could not comprehend?

Therri took a step toward Jevon and his leveled blade. "I don't think you will."

Constantia jumped up and tried to pull him away from the sword. "Go back inside the castle, my lord. Tell Sybil that Sir Raimon has been injured and we need help to carry him to the keep.

"That is bad advice, Lady Constantia," Jevon said as her tugs failed to move the stubborn youth. "Do not make me do something to Lord Therri that I will regret."

"Like send a volley of arrows at his head?" Constantia retorted.

"None of you would be at risk if Laurant ended his rebellion and simply opened his gates to Gunthar."

Acrid disappointment swelled inside her. "If you were not so bitter about what Lord Laurant did to you, you would see how your desire for vengeance has warped the kind, generous man you once were. It is not only Lord Laurant and Lady Gwenllian who will suffer at your earl's hand. It is Therri and Heléne, Guia and Beatris—and me. Jevon, *please.*"

"Are you really Jevon?" Therri broke into her plea. "I was trying to twist around to look at you when Sir Raimon lunged for his sword." Therri took the lantern from Constantia and held it up to study Jevon's face. "You look different."

"It has been seven years," Constantia reminded him. "You were only ten when he left."

Therri nodded. "He didn't have a beard."

A reluctant smile tugged at her mouth. As though the beard accounted for more than a child's murky memories. Just for an instant, she thought Jevon's mouth quirked up too.

One blink proved her wrong. His lips remained a hard, uncompromising line. "I am not asking you, Lord Therri. You must come with me to the earl's camp."

Therri slipped from Constantia's hand and took another step toward

Jevon. This time his long legs carried him beyond her attempts to restrain him.

"I meant what I said about bashing in your earl's brains. You had better let me go."

"What happened to Sir Damien was an accident," Jevon told him.

"I believe Lady Constantia. She was there and saw it all."

She clenched her hands at Therri's brazenness. It was not too late for him to make a run for the postern. "My lord, go back inside the castle."

"No. Sir Raimon was right. If Papa falls, too, I will need Etienne's help to avenge him."

Did Jevon hear the vulnerable tremor in the youth's voice? Did he care?

"I cannot allow that, Lord Therri," Jevon said, his voice flat, implacable. "But Lady Constantia is free to go and inform your father that you are the earl's hostage. And if he wants to see you safe again, he will lay down his arms and let the earl ride through his gate."

Constantia's frustration erupted like the tongues of fire spewing from Lady Gwenllian's lost dragon brooch. "Why did you let me return to Pennault if you intended this all along?"

"I made you no promises, Stantia. I never said Laurant would not have to pay for his sins against the king."

You mean against you.

"I only agreed to give you time to warn them and persuade Laurant to submit or, failing that, to get the children someplace safe from the repercussions of his defiance."

He was right. Constantia had failed to convince the baron of the gravity of the earl's menace, and now Jevon meant to inflict his thirst for vengeance on the son who was no longer a boy.

"This is the last time I will ask, Lord Therri," Jevon said. "Do not make me drag you there, kicking and screaming like a squalling babe."

Therri took another step. He stopped just short of Jevon's sword. Oh, heavens! If she screamed for help, would anyone in the castle hear her?

Therri cocked his chin. "I don't believe you."

"I assure you, my lord, I will do whatever it takes to win a reprieve from your father's false judgment of me."

"I don't know if you are a thief or not," Therri said. "But I know you are not a murderer. However much you hate my father, you still showed him mercy today."

"As Lady Constantia said, your father was lucky."

Therri shook his head. "You can try to drag me to your earl's camp, but you won't hurt me, and once I am there, I swear I will wreak so much havoc that your earl will wish he had never crossed our borders."

Jevon's mouth quirked up again. This time she thought the lantern caught humor in his eyes, but it had to be mockery of the youth's naïve, if impassioned, challenge. Jevon lowered the sword Therri continued to ignore and fisted his hand on the front of the youth's surcote. He gave a jerk that made Therri stumble forward. Jevon meant his threat. He intended to physically drag Therri to his earl's camp. Constantia sucked air into her lungs for a shriek she prayed would bring Therri aid from the castle faster than it brought the earl's men upon them.

Before she could scream, Therri somehow wrenched himself out of Jevon's grip. He ducked down as Jevon made a second swipe to grab him. When Therri bounced back up, he'd left the lantern on the ground and replaced it with two hands full of objects that seemed to make Jevon freeze.

"Then why these?" Therri said.

The sudden stilling of Jevon's body suspended Constantia too. When he stood silent to Therri's question, she edged forward to view the objects.

They looked like shadowy sticks. "What are those?" she asked.

Therri glanced at her. "The blunted arrows he loosed at me and Papa today. I gathered them up after the volley ceased and tried to show them to Papa, but Papa was too frantic to look or listen to me." He turned back to Jevon. "You only wanted to frighten us. Now I know why. Because it was *you.*"

Jevon shook his head, but when Constantia picked up the lantern, she saw what Therri must—the momentary indecision that passed over Jevon's stony features.

"You think I was too young to remember," Therri said, "but I was not. You gave me my first fishing rod and taught me how to fish. When Sir Guilhem declared me hopelessly inept at archery, you showed me how to aim my crossbow until I could hit the mark with such exactness he had to confess he was wrong to Papa. You drilled hours with me with my wooden sword until I learned how to best Etienne seven times out of eight in the clearing. I wanted to be just like you, my father's best swordsman and one day his best knight. I was terrified after Gaweyne destroyed your expensive surcote that you would never speak to me again. You must have thought me nothing but an annoying brat, but you continued to grin and jest with me as though you still counted me among your friends. Oh, Jevon, you have no idea how much I've missed you!"

Therri threw his arms around Jevon's neck, the arrows still clutched in his fists—and Jevon dropped his sword.

Constantia had never seen either of Therri's parents embrace him, even as a boy, but Jevon returned the youth's hug so swiftly she guessed the memories that must be flooding through him. How many times had she found him and Therri in some corner of the bailey or castle and overheard the six-, seven-, eight-year-old boy pouring out his worries to Jevon? How his mama was angry with him again for putting a mouse in his sisters' bed or sneaking extra pepper into some knight's dish to make him sneeze and snort. Or how Papa was so disappointed with reports of his son's failure to master this skill or that as quickly as the other boys his age that the baron had to draft Jevon to practice with him. Therri was cleverer than all of them, Jevon told Constantia. It was just that the boy's attention wandered when the knights explained things to the other, slower pages, and his boredom gave him too much time to plan mischief about the castle. Therri, Jevon promised, would someday surpass all of them as a knight.

Therri always turned cheerful and roguish again after talking to Jevon. No wonder he'd dogged Jevon's heels whenever he was not engaged in some escapade with Etienne. She had seen the boy's eyes shine with admiration of everything Jevon did, even if Jevon seemed oblivious to the depths of the boy's love for him. But Jevon did not look oblivious now. When she stepped near enough to lift the lantern's light to his face, she saw tears on his cheeks.

With a lump in her throat, she gave the man and youth another moment of reunion, then gently pulled one of the arrows from Therri's fist. He was right. The head had been filed down to a blunt tip designed to rebound harmlessly off its target. As had the other arrows, she discovered, when Therri finally released Jevon and allowed her to pluck them from his hand and study them one by one.

"You used these on Lord Laurant and Therri?" she said. "Then why did you send a sharpened arrow into Llygad? You might have killed him!"

Jevon glanced away and swiped his palms across his cheeks, embarrassed by the tears. "Llygad? I didn't. I shot the stranger who stalked us—me—in the woods." His voice hardened on the accusation.

"The stranger? At Pennault? Why would you think him here?"

"I did not 'think him.' I saw him, Stantia, plain as day, standing next to you on the wall."

How could Jevon have possibly confused the two men? He must have stared too long into the sun! "Jevon, that was Llygad."

Jevon looked at her, his cheeks dry, his face flinty. "With hair flowing down to his shoulders? Llygad cut off his long locks the day he became a squire."

Of course! Jevon could not know. "He grew it out again to please Lady Gwenllian. He wishes to marry Guia, but he knows Lord Laurant will not consent unless Lady Gwenllian does so first."

"You said Lady Gwenllian wanted Llygad to marry you."

"She did. But when I got back to Pennault, I learned that my father had declared my sister his heir and married her off before Lady Gwenllian could do anything to interfere. So now I have no dowry again, and Lady Gwenllian wants Llygad to marry a Welsh heiress so she will have one of her own countrywomen to bully along with the rest of us."

Jevon's eyes widened, then narrowed. "Is that really what Llygad said?"

"No. Llygad said 'to keep her company,' but we both know he meant bully."

She tried not to chuckle. The levity felt ill-matched to the tension of Jevon's suspicions, but her soft laughter bubbled out anyway.

Jevon's chuckle blended with hers. But he sobered quickly, this time with his cheeks paling beneath the lantern's golden glow.

"I did not know. I swear I could not tell it was Llygad on the wall. Gunthar and I both thought it was the stranger conspiring with Laurant against the king." Mortification thickened the rush of Jevon's words. "I never saw the stranger's face clearly, and with the helmet Llygad wore, I could not see his either. I just assumed from his long blond hair—Oh, saints! I wanted to kill the man I saw today for what he did to me and threatened to do to you. I would have sent my arrow straight into his heart if Gunthar had not ordered me to only wound him."

No wonder Jevon had gazed up at her and Llygad with such anger.

"Is he badly hurt?" Jevon sounded anxious.

"No," she assured him. "It is only a flesh wound, a clean one which Sybil and Lady Heléne will keep that way, as they almost always do." Thank heaven for the earl's order not to kill! "Did your earl also command you to assault Lord Laurant and Lord Therri with blunted arrows, or did you defy him by doing so?" She glanced at the youth, then whirled toward the space where Therri had stood but a moment ago. "Where is he?" She scanned the empty darkness, then dropped the arrows and spun around again, combing the shadows a second time on a wave of panic. "Jevon, where is he?"

Jevon swore softly under his breath. She thought he cursed Therri until he said on a mutter, "Someone is coming. Quick, Stantia, go back inside the castle."

"But Therri!"

"I will find him, but I will not let you become a prisoner too. Go back inside." He grabbed her arm, dragged her to the postern gate, pushed it open and shoved her through. "Bar it shut. Unless you want the earl's troops surging in behind you, do it! I will find the boy."

"But—"

"I will find him," Jevon said again, his promise as firm as the *thunk* of the door he shut in her face.

Therri! Where could he have gone? Voices thrummed on the other side. Had he returned? Or was it the earl's men? Raimon still lay outside the gate. What would they do when they found him?

She forced herself to draw in a deep, quelling breath. Jevon was right. If the enemy, she could not risk the rest of the castle. She tried to lift the wooden crossbar to slide it into its metal braces but found it too heavy. Raimon had lifted it down.

"Constantia? What are you doing?"

She turned, surprised to see Llygad. He had a torch in his left hand. His right arm hung in a sling. "You should be in bed," she said through teeth that chattered with the horror of this disaster. "You lost a lot of blood today."

"I do not want Laurant to think me more useless than he already does, so I decided to patrol the grounds. What's happening?" His eyes flicked to the unbarred postern. "Have you been outside the castle?"

"I-I've lost Therri."

"What do you mean you've lost him?"

"I've lost him! He slipped away while I was talking to Jevon. The earl's men must have heard us. I have to bar the gate before they find it and try to force their way in!" She pulled one end of the crossbar up from the ground where it lay.

Llygad secured the torch in a bracket to the right of the gate, then pulled his right arm out of his sling and hefted the crossbar by himself. Its weight must have jarred his injured shoulder, for his face went white in the glow of the flame, but he slammed the bar into place.

"Now tell me what happened." He gripped his arm as though trying to squeeze back the pain. "What is this nonsense about Therri? And who is this Jev—" He broke off, his eyes widening. "You mean Jevon de Cazalet? Are you telling me he's back? And he's abducted Therri?"

"No! I mean, yes, he is back, but . . ." *But what, Constantia? Jevon promised he would find Therri, but he did not promise he would restore him to Pennault.*

Surely after that frank embrace she witnessed, Jevon would not give Therri to his earl?

"Constantia, tell me what is going on. What were you and Therri doing outside the walls in the middle of a siege? And what has Jevon to do with all this?" When her reply lay tangled in confusion about Jevon's intentions, Llygad said, "He's come back to take revenge on us, hasn't he?"

Jevon showed mercy to the baron today. But had he done so by his own choice or by his earl's command? Therri's disappearance had prevented Jevon from answering.

"I don't know. I only know Jevon has come back to Poitou with the English." There was no point in concealing Jevon's presence after she had carelessly blurted out his name. The entire castle would know he'd returned if the earl presented Therri at the gate as a hostage in the morning. "The baron was trying to send Therri to safety in case Pennault falls, but Jevon was waiting outside the postern, and Therri slipped away while we were talking."

If any harm befell the youth, she would never forgive herself or Jevon! She wanted to charge back into the night and join Jevon's search, but it would not help Therri or anyone if all she did was stumble into the arms of the English.

Constantia had never felt so helpless in her life.

"I—I must tell the baron. And Lady Gwenllian." Constantia shuddered. "She will have Sybil switch the flesh from my back for this, and rightly so. But first"—she tucked Llygad's arm back into his sling—"we must ask Lady Heléne to check your wound in case you have pulled the stitches free."

"The devil take my wound! The only one who will lose his skin tonight is that treacherous thief when I find him."

Constantia reluctantly placed herself in front of the postern before

Llygad could lift the crossbar back down. "No. The English will only take you hostage, too, and how would that aid Therri?"

She had to trust Jevon. To find Therri, to keep him safe, even if he became a prisoner.

Safe? Where would Therri have gone but in search of Etienne? Poitiers was days from Pennault, and if Therri had any chance of evading the English, he would have to keep to the woods, where a monster still lurked. The vicious stranger whom Jevon had mistaken Llygad for remained at large. He had threatened to ravish Constantia, to murder Jevon and subject his dead body to unspeakable horrors. If the fiend came across Therri . . . !

The full weight of this night's calamity suddenly collapsed her knees. She dropped to the ground, her back against the postern gate, and rolled her head into her hands.

Jevon barely had time to reclaim his sword and stride over to Raimon before the shadow climbing up the slope of the motte came near enough for the torchlight to bathe Jevon in its glow.

"Sir Roger just finished a headcount of the camp, and yours came up missing," a dry voice said. "Woodville told him you'd insisted on checking the rear of the castle before retiring for the night."

Was it that late? The moon had slid too high behind the clouds for Jevon to keep track of it. Why could the marshal or Ned not have come looking for him instead of Gunthar?

"It seemed wise to survey this area," Jevon said, "since Laurant's men were working so hard to keep ours occupied along the other walls. And as you see, I found trouble brewing." He motioned to Raimon, who groaned but had not yet opened his eyes.

"Except for a token guard, Laurant's men have retired too." Gunthar carried the torch to the prone man's side. "Who is he?"

"One of Laurant's knights." Like Therri's, Raimon's surcote bore no insignia to link him to Pennault, but Gunthar might expect Jevon to know him. There was no reason not to admit it. "His name is Raimon Tirell. He resisted when I tried to take him into custody. We scuffled, he fell and hit his head." Surely that was near enough to the truth to content the earl.

"Hmm." The fluctuating torchlight permitted Jevon to view the harsh V of Gunthar's brows drawn down over the bridge of his nose. The earl turned slowly, lowering the flame to survey the ground. "Footprints."

Jevon saw them, too, freshly pressed in the soil where frequent foot traffic had worn away the grass.

"At least three sets," Gunthar observed, "including one the size of a woman's. What has occurred here tonight, do you think? An escape by some from the castle? Were they attempting to save their skins from royal retribution or hoping to obtain aid before I knock down their walls?" The torchlight splashed over Jevon's face again. "Did this fellow reveal anything useful to you while you struggled? Did you see anyone else?"

A direct query and an equally direct look from the earl. Jevon could not avoid answering.

"He knew me." Jevon nodded at Raimon. "He called me a thief and a traitor. He was angry to learn that I fought for you, and his anger made him rash."

A gust of wind swirled Jevon's cloak behind him. Gunthar glanced at the weapon in Jevon's hand. "So, your sword is as deft as your arrows?"

"I have spent more time with the latter in recent years, but I was still competent enough to disarm him."

Did Gunthar notice that Jevon had not fully answered his questions?

Gunthar waited a heartbeat, then turned toward the wall and swept his torchlight in a slow arc over the stones. "This wall faces west. You told me there was a postern gate here. That must have been how they left the castle. Show me the gate."

Jevon should have known Gunthar would remember his description of the castle's defenses. Thankfully, the castle's builders had done their best to obscure the postern by painting the wood in a pattern of stones to match its flanking walls, a detail Jevon had not thought to include at the time. Telling Gunthar the gate existed was one thing. Showing him exactly where it was, knowing Constantia no doubt hovered on the other side, worrying about Therri, was another.

"I have been absent a long while, my lord. My memory is imprecise."

"Perhaps we can find it together." Gunthar's voice sounded a little too cool.

Jevon moved to the right of the gate and pretended to examine the wall. Torchlight appeared over his shoulder to aid him. He led their hunt away from the postern until, at some point, he realized the light behind him had withdrawn and traced a path back the way they had come. His pulse quickened. Raimon moaned again, more loudly this time. Surely he would have the good wits to keep his mouth shut about the gate's location when he awakened?

Gunthar moved his free hand along the wall just about waist level, for sometimes doors were built lower than his uncommon height. "Here," he said abruptly.

Gunthar slid his nails into a vertical crack. The cunning paintwork could not conceal the change in texture from stone to wood. There was no further point in feigning ignorance. Jevon joined Gunthar as the earl searched for some means to open the gate. Jevon showed him the dent carved into the wood that served as a hidden, inverted handle to lever the gate when it wasn't barred shut. Which, thankfully, it was.

Gunthar stepped back. "No matter. The mangon is repaired, and we've gathered enough stones for a full day's assault. The south wall will come down tomorrow unless Laurant yields the castle unconditionally to me in the morning. I had hoped to hear from him by now. I saw his panic when you loosed your volley at him and his son. It was noble of them to send their shields to the aid of Laurant's men under my archers' assault. Noble but foolish."

Gunthar made a half turn toward Jevon. Jevon kept his gaze on the postern, hoping his profile revealed less than the full sum of his features.

"I watched how easily you took down the fair-haired man at the corner of the gatehouse wall," Gunthar remarked. "I presume it required more skill to aim near enough to make Laurant fear he was staring at his final moments on earth than it would have taken to hit him?"

Jevon simply nodded.

"You did well. But just to be safe, you used blunted arrows with the baron."

Gunthar must have seen the arrows Therri left behind along with the footprints.

"You said you did not want Laurant dead." Jevon spoke more sharply than he meant to.

"You needn't snap. I know what I told you. I said I was pleased."

Gunthar's voice was mild, but Jevon felt the earl watching him and remembered the doubt in Gunthar's heavy, plunging brows. Jevon prayed Constantia was secure somewhere in the keep by now, where she and the other innocents of the castle would be safe when the mangon finished its work on the morrow and Gunthar's troops poured through the broken wall to battle Pennault's knights.

"You executed my orders perfectly," Gunthar repeated. "It is not your fault if Laurant would rather drag himself and his son to ruin than swallow his pride and submit to the king. And your fair-haired villain from the woods—we will have his story when we take Pennault too."

Llygad. Oh, saints, Jevon had nearly killed him. The thought made him sick. Would Gunthar believe him if he said he'd mistaken Llygad for the stranger, or would Gunthar grill the Welshman like a felon already headed for the hangman's noose?

"Come back to the camp. Get some rest." Gunthar gestured at Raimon, who was beginning to stir, but weakly. "I will send some men to carry him and attend to his broken head."

"He is just a household knight. Laurant won't bargain the castle for his release."

"No, but the fellow might be able to tell us who left the castle tonight and why."

Jevon turned to face the earl. Gunthar's brows were straight slashes above his eyes now, but even in the flicker of the torchlight, it felt as though his gaze raked Jevon's soul.

Jevon felt the moisture in his mouth withering beneath Gunthar's piercing stare. Gunthar suspected him of lying, Jevon was certain of it, or at least equivocating about what he'd witnessed tonight. Jevon might still salvage a pardon if he told Gunthar the truth. Gunthar might even let him go in search of Therri—as long as Jevon promised to return with the young hostage. But after Therri's embrace nearly burst Jevon's heart, how could he betray the youth's trust by delivering him into his enemy hands?

Jevon licked his dry lips with a tongue that felt as thick as wool. "My lord, if Laurant fails to yield to you in the morning, what will you do?"

"You know perfectly well—"

"No, I mean after the mangon, when your men ride into the yard. If Laurant and his knights still try to resist."

The torchlight flapped in the wind, tossing forbidding shadows over the hard, uncompromising planes of Gunthar's cheeks. "If he refuses to renew his oath of fealty to the king, I will drag him in chains to England to face the judgment of the king himself. Henry knows how to be merciful to those willing to repent of offenses against him, but to those who remain defiant—well, there is a reason King Henry is known as the Castle Breaker in England."

"The Castle Breaker?"

Gunthar hooked the thumb of his free hand in the leather girdle that belted the deep-blue surcote over his mail hauberk. "During the anarchy of King Stephen's reign, greedy barons too powerful for the king to control built hundreds of illegal castles throughout England and set themselves up to rule as tyrants of their own little fiefdoms. They robbed and pillaged and raped the countryside without restraint."

Like the barons of Poitou.

"When Henry succeeded to the throne, he restored order to the kingdom by demolishing those castles and forcing those same barons to submit themselves to his authority. Henry humbled them to a man and reestablished peace in England. He will do the same here."

"Through you," Jevon said.

"I have participated in his siege strategies for years. His success can be reduced to four words: do not waste time. Seeking to frighten the enemy into surrender by harrying his lands in advance of a siege only allows the enemy opportunity to seal his up gates and organize his defenses before the siege can begin. No, when Henry doubles his forces with mercenaries, he pays them, clothes them, and arms and feeds them from his own treasury. Relieved of the necessity of providing for those needs themselves, those mercenaries are left with a single aim: to obey with complete exactness the king's commands."

Gunthar did the same. Not once had Jevon had to forage for a meal or provide a single arrow for his bow.

"With his forces marshaled and focused, Henry then goes for the lightning strike—a swift investment of his enemy's walls followed by a shattering assault with his siege engines before the castle defenders can gather their wits, much less effectively prepare their garrison to repel him."

As Gunthar had done at Blancaval and Vere.

Gunthar slid his thumb out of his belt, passing the wind-tossed torch from his right hand to his left. "Had the mangon not required repairs, Pennault would have been brought low by now. That will change tomorrow. While the king brings his son Richard to heel, he has entrusted me to subdue your fractious barons. I will not fail him."

From the square set of Gunthar's shoulders, Jevon did not doubt him.

"Did he humble your father, too, when he broke the castles of England?" It was a bold question, but Jevon was curious. Gunthar could not have been much more than a boy when Henry came to the throne. It seemed an odd way for the king to have gained Gunthar's loyalty. Therri swore he would bash in the earl's brains to protect his father.

"I was only eleven, but I was old enough to be aware of the chaos around me. My father abhorred the lawlessness and hoped to combat it by throwing his allegiance to the Empress Mathilda in her struggle to take the throne from Stephen. She failed, but in the end, it was not the empress's fierce pride that England needed. It was her son, Henry. Henry has an astuteness and vision that neither the empress nor King Stephen possessed."

Somewhere in the darkness, an owl hooo-ed, whisking Jevon away from this moment to one perfumed with roses and a smile more enchanting than a sky bedazzled with stars. The dreamlike reminiscence, so dissonant against Gunthar's words, came with a prick of pain. He pulled his attention back to the earl's voice, grateful for the way Gunthar's firm but reflective tones helped disperse the fragments of loss.

"O'er the last twenty years, Henry has brought peace through law to England. By a multitude of actions great and small, the king has won my admiration, respect, and love. I serve him because I believe in his cause. It is true he is jealous of his royal prerogatives and his rights to rule, and he will thwart any man who challenges him. But he is also determined to establish law throughout the rest of his domains. Law protects the weak as well as the strong. It might have protected you."

Jevon felt it again, an almost overwhelming hunger to see England, only this time it was not merely a nebulous vision of a golden, glorious land that flooded his mind. This time he imagined a golden king ruling benevolently at its heart. Surely in such an exalted land as that, he could finally forget Constantia?

The dream crumbled almost as soon as it rose. There was nothing benevolent about razing castles and dragging rebels before a king in chains. If Laurant insisted on following Sir Damien's example—

"What will happen to Laurant's son?" Jevon asked.

"How old is the boy?"

"Seventeen."

"Is he as obstinate as his father?"

Jevon paused to select his words. "Lord Therri was a high-spirited but cheery-tempered boy when last I saw him, but he was only ten years old."

A movement from Raimon provided Jevon an excuse to look away before Gunthar's probing gaze could discern the less-than-fully honest reply. The knight pushed himself halfway up, then rolled prone again, one hand draped over his eyes.

Gunthar's torchlight fell over the knight as he answered Jevon's question. "Depending on how deeply Laurant's son has been influenced by his father, the king may place the youth in the custody of a man he trusts to teach the boy loyalty to the crown, then confirm his father's lands to him when Laurant dies. If he judges the son's Poitevin loyalties too intractable, he might give Laurant's lands to a trusted vassal instead and disinherit the boy completely." The earl tilted his head at Jevon. "Why do you care what happens to the boy? I thought you wanted vengeance on his father."

"I do. That is . . . not vengeance. Justice." The thought of Laurant in chains for his recalcitrant breaking of his sworn homage to the king did not trouble Jevon's conscience at all.

"But?" There was an almost gentle prodding in the earl's voice.

"I was fond of the boy," Jevon admitted. "My grudge is with the baron, not his son. I do not wish to play a part in any harm befalling Lord Therri."

"Ah." The earl's soft exclamation carried a note of comprehension. "Hence the blunted arrows because he stood next to his father."

Jevon tried to resist the commanding pull of the earl's quiet waiting by keeping his gaze fixed on Raimon, but the potency of Gunthar's silence compelled him to turn and meet the earl's eyes.

"Yes," Jevon said.

Gunthar studied him a moment. This time Jevon could detect no hint of the earl's thoughts in the turn of his mouth or the position of his brows.

"You have repeatedly sworn yourself loyal to me," Gunthar said. "I had high hopes for you and your expert arrows. You did not flinch at subduing Blancaval or Vere, both ruled by men you had no personal quarrel with. But now that we stand on the threshold of crushing a man who has given you every reason to hate him, you hesitate."

"Hesitate?" Jevon bristled. "No! I sent my arrows exactly where you asked me to today. You said yourself that I executed your commands perfectly."

"Because I asked you to frighten, not to kill." Gunthar's fingers tightened around the torch. Like his grip, his voice hardened too. "Do not misunderstand me. I take no pleasure in killing any man, but in war, death cannot always be avoided. And make no mistake, this is war, one of the princes' making fired by their discontented mother, funded by the troublemaker Louis of France, and fueled by the perverse support of ambitious barons hoping to throw off King Henry's yoke. But the princes' revolt against their father will fail. Henry will not rest until every last rebel bows to him, which means that *I* will not rest until I have brought every last Poitevin rebel to heel. There is no place in my camp for a man willing to follow me this far but no farther."

Jevon's jaw clenched at the implication. "This is not my first battle, my lord. Men have fallen to both my arrows and my sword. You may be assured that I will stand firm in the heat of tomorrow's conflict."

"Will you? Unlike Blancaval or Vere, Pennault was once your home. Will you aim your arrows, razor sharp, wherever I bid you? Will you thrust your sword at my command, knowing that behind each man's helmet might stand a former friend? Or even Laurant's son?"

None of those "former friends" defended Jevon when Laurant condemned and branded him. If Raimon viewed him as a thief and traitor, the others must as well. Raimon had attempted to kill Jevon tonight. When the others saw Jevon fighting for the English, would they not be just as eager to cut him down? He owed no fidelity to any of them.

Therri would not stand at risk if he were not at the castle. If Jevon simply let the youth find his way to the protection of his uncle . . . but danger lay in the woods. That malignant, skulking stranger. The villain's arm had as much time to heal from Jevon's arrow as Jevon's back to heal from the miscreant's dagger. And Jevon had promised Constantia he would find Therri and bring him safely back to Pennault. If Therri returned and again insisted on fighting by his father's side—would Jevon send his arrows at the baron's knights or at Gunthar's if one raised his sword to strike the helmeted youth?

Jevon did exactly what Gunthar had charged him with. He hesitated.

"I cannot go into combat with a man unsure of his loyalties." Gunthar's voice, expression, and stance, from the proud upward tilt of his head to the staunch placement of his feet, were as adamant as stone. "I free you from your oath to me, Jevon le Falquet. Examine your heart thoroughly. If you are certain—unequivocally certain—that you can follow my every command tomorrow, come to my tent before morning, and I will accept your oath anew. Otherwise, go and serve whom you will. But know this—if I see your face among Laurant's men when the battle comes, my sword will not show you mercy."

Gunthar leaned down and, with a strength Jevon had not fathomed the earl possessed, hefted Raimon with one hand while his other still held the torch. Raimon, clearly disoriented, slid his arm across Gunthar's broad shoulders and accepted the earl's arm around his waist before he allowed himself to be hauled half dragged, half stumbling, away.

The silence left in their wake almost suffocated Jevon. He saw his future shriveling before his eyes. All because Therri had inconsiderately grown up while Jevon was gone and been glad to see him.

With feet that felt like lead, Jevon worked his way down the side of the motte to the forest's edge. His worry for Therri with the lurking stranger thrummed in his head alongside his words to Constantia.

I promised to find Therri and return him. I promised to find Therri and . . .

Jevon stopped. "But I did not," he said abruptly to the tree in front of him. "I told her I would find him, but I did not say I would bring him back to Pennault. At least, not through the postern gate."

Jevon's former arguments to himself rushed back with greater force. Therri would be far safer in Gunthar's camp than with the forest stranger or fighting beside his father. If Jevon returned to Gunthar's camp with the youth, Gunthar would have to believe the sincerity of his loyalty.

"I know Therri will hate me," he said to the tree. "But he is young. He will be hot and angry today, but in time I will convince him of the arbitrary abuses of his Poitevin heritage. Once his eyes are opened, he will be permitted to inherit Pennault with his father's other lands, administering them all more justly than his father has done. I am doing him a service by delivering him to Gunthar, not betraying him."

Jevon was certain he could make Therri listen to him . . . eventually. Constantia was another matter. She would never understand or agree with Jevon's actions.

She will hate me forever.

He trusted the tree to keep silent about his plans for Therri, but it had no business eavesdropping on his misery over his lost love. There was no future for him and Stantia. She said she would have gone with him into banishment. But when he'd asked her to return with him to the vanquished Vere Castle on a vow to marry her as soon as Gunthar won Jevon a royal pardon, she chose Pennault instead.

Something shoved against the small of his back. Something with a point. Memory flashed through Jevon of a slow, deliberate, digging pain.

Not again.

This time he whirled before the blade could puncture his flesh. He kicked the sword aside and hurled his fist into the face of the man who stood behind him. The man went down with a swish of long, pale hair.

"Traitorous dog," the man snarled from his sprawl on the ground. "In spite of what Constantia said, I knew you could not have changed your thieving ways. Taking your mistress's brooch was bad enough, but if you think I am going to let you steal the baron's son and give him to the English to abuse—"

"Who are you?" Jevon interrupted. He would never forget the ruthless voice of the man who'd pivoted a dagger into his back—and this was not him. The wind cleft a break in the clouds, allowing a shaft of moonlight to fall across a strip of white cloth cradling the man's right arm. Jevon had aimed his arrow to the right to avoid the heart—Oh, saints. "Llygad?"

"You should not have come back, Jevon," Llygad growled. "We are going to route the English and their Angevin king from our lands, but *you* I will skin with my own sword."

Llygad groped for his weapon but, hampered by his sling, only succeeded in knocking it farther out of reach.

Jevon picked up the sword and stabbed it, point down, into the ground next to one of his blunted arrows. He sheathed his own sword, then reached down a hand to Llygad. "Here, let me help you up."

Llygad cursed him. At least, Jevon presumed it was a curse. The words sounded Welsh.

Llygad ignored Jevon's proffered hand and tossed off his sling. With a good deal of wincing and groaning, he swiveled, wriggled, and scrabbled while trying to leverage himself up.

Jevon left him to his pride but said through a guilt-thickened throat, "I did not know it was you. The last time I saw you, you'd cut your hair. If I'd realized you were still under Lady Gwenllian's thumb enough to let her make you grow it out again, I'd have thought twice before I loosed my arrow. There is a villain with long, pale hair like yours slinking about in the trees."

Llygad froze, having risen only as far as one knee. His left hand clamped his injured shoulder. "*You* shot me?"

"Constantia did not tell you?"

Llygad howled and lunged at him, but Jevon easily sidestepped him. He caught the flying folds of Llygad's cloak and jerked him upright before he could sprawl on his face.

"You're not going to win a fight against me with only one good arm." The clodpate could not win a fight against Jevon with *two* good arms unless Llygad's coordination had improved by bounds since Jevon left. He picked up the discarded sling and tossed it to Llygad as the Welshman turned back around. "What are you doing outside the walls?"

"I am going to find Therri. And if I have to break your neck to stop you from—"

"Yes, yes, giving him to the English to abuse." Llygad must have heard Jevon talking to the tree. A knot of disappointment cinched in his belly. "Constantia asked *you* to find Therri?"

She did not trust Jevon to keep his promise.

And why should she when you are plotting to betray her exactly the way Llygad says?

Llygad held the sling slack, refusing to redon it even though the returning moonlight revealed the pain in his face. "She does not know I've left the castle. I waited until Cousin Gwen sent a page to summon her to the keep. But she told me how the boy ran off by himself. If I can find him and get him safely to his uncle, Laurant might forgive me for ordering the attack that killed some of the earl's men."

"That happened on your order?"

Llygad rubbed his arm. He'd no doubt jarred it when he hit the ground and aggravated it further while struggling to get up. It must hurt terribly.

"It was Cousin Gwen's idea." Llygad's voice sounded a little squeezed.

"She made me command the men behind her husband's back. It was either that or . . ."

"Or what?"

"She said she'd send me back to Wales if I refused. So I did it. And now Laurant is so angry he swears *he* will send me to Wales just as soon as this business with your earl is over. The only way I can think to change his mind is to finish the job Sir Raimon began." Llygad glanced around in the dark. "Where is he?"

"Gunthar took him to the camp to interrogate him as soon as he regains his senses. So . . ." Jevon tried to sound disinterested in the answer—"Constantia did *not* send you after Therri?"

"She told me you would find him, but she did not know how despicably you intended to use him if you did."

Jevon squirmed a little at the word *despicable*. If he gave Therri to Gunthar, he would destroy whatever vestige of affection and trust Constantia still held for him. But without *Gunthar's* trust, Jevon had no future to offer her. And no future for himself.

Llygad might be clumsy and obnoxious, but he had also been incredibly stubborn as a squire, and from the shadowed set of his jaw, that had not changed. If Jevon tried to find Therri without him, he suspected Llygad would only dog his heels. Jevon sighed, then plucked up Llygad's sword and returned it to him. Llygad took the hilt with his left hand, looking startled.

"The longer we stand here arguing," Jevon said, "the more time Therri has to fall into trouble. We need to find him before the villain who stalked me and Stantia does. Then we will decide what to do with the boy. If you and I do not agree, we will settle the question with our swords. Fair enough?"

It was not at all fair with Llygad's injury, and Jevon knew it. Even if he were not as inept as Jevon remembered, Llygad's wound prevented him from defending himself with his dominant sword hand. But a lesser offer would insult him. Jevon saw it in the proud way Llygad accepted the terms with a nod.

"Give me your sling," Jevon said, "and I will use it to bind up your wound. You cannot save Therri from me if you bleed to death along the way."

Llygad snorted but let Jevon wind the linen strip until it lay snugly against his shoulder. Llygad wore no mail beneath his surcote. He would have had to remove it to attend to his wound. That should allow the bandage-sling greater direct pressure and, Jevon hoped, ease some of Llygad's pain.

Before they entered the woods, Jevon broke off a low-hanging tree branch, then used his dagger to shave the leaves from the top where the branch divided into smaller shoots. Positioning himself so that Llygad's body broke some of the wind, Jevon lit the shoots with his tinderbox to create a makeshift torch. To his relief, the flames revealed no blood seeping through Llygad's bandage. Hopefully that meant his stitches had withstood Jevon's rough handling of him.

Once the flames grew strong enough to withstand the turbulent air, Jevon swooped the fire above the ground as Gunthar had done with his torch.

"There." He pointed to some footprints that disappeared into the trees. "Those must be Therri's."

Jevon and Llygad followed them into the woods, where the sturdy trunks of oak and elm blocked most of the wind. With the help of his fire branch, Jevon traced the broken twigs, crushed leaves, and fresh footprints that appeared in spaces of bare earth, keeping his hopes alive that they were headed in the right direction. But the longer Therri eluded them, the greater Jevon's apprehension grew. He had lingered too long with Gunthar and then with Llygad. Who knew what danger the boy had met with by now? The vile stranger's sneering voice rang louder and louder in Jevon's ears while the scar on his back twinged in terrifying memory.

Jevon paused to study the forest floor.

"How did you learn to do that?" Llygad asked.

"Do what?"

"Track. And how can you be sure those marks belong to Therri?"

"I can't," Jevon admitted, "but they're fresh, and the clearest ones are the same size as the ones that led into the trees. If they're not Therri's, they belong to someone else prowling through the woods tonight. A man's, by the size of them."

"Like your stalker's?"

Llygad sounded as worried as Jevon felt.

"Possibly. But the direction has been fairly consistent since we left Pennault, and I have not seen any additional prints that indicate anyone has been following these besides us."

Llygad allowed Jevon to lead the way. "But how did you learn to track like that?" he asked again. "I don't recall you spending much time with Laurant's huntsman when you were at Pennault."

"I wanted to. I thought Peyre Mazel the cleverest man alive to know how to lay out a trail for us to follow the hart or the boar. Most of the time, Lady Gwenllian made me stay behind at the castle and read poetry to her while the rest of you were off enjoying the sport, but sometimes Laurant insisted on taking me along for the sake of my bow."

"Cousin Gwen made me do that after you left," Llygad said on a grumble. "Stay behind to keep her company. I did not get to hunt again until after I was knighted, and only because Laurant was embarrassed to leave one of his knights behind when he hunted with Sir Damien."

Jevon almost felt sorry for Llygad. Almost.

Jevon pointed at a fresh mark among some leaves. "I learned this after I left Pennault. I hid in these woods for months, afraid to venture near a castle or town for fear of what men might do if they saw the brand of a thief on my hand. But there were wolves here then, and the boars grew angry if I stumbled too close to their piglets. I learned how to read their tracks so I could keep my distance." Another print appeared in a patch of open earth, still unobscured by a second set. At least Therri had made it this far unscathed. "Sometimes there were men to avoid too, hunters or travelers on foot who, for one reason or another, preferred the anonymity of the trees to the open road."

He had never dared an encounter to find out if any were outlaws like himself. He'd experienced too many narrow escapes from the men who hunted him for the bounty Laurant set on his head, like the men in the brown hoods who pursued Jevon's tracks as relentlessly as a lymer pursued a stag.

He tried to shake away the unsettling memory as he and Llygad walked in silence. Occasionally, Jevon crouched and surveyed the ground more closely to confirm he remained on Therri's—he prayed it was Therri's—trail.

"I never thought of that," Llygad said after a while when Jevon paused to examine a boot-sized imprint in some flattened grass.

"Thought of what?"

"What your life would be like after Laurant branded you. I was just angry that you got caught and left me to be ordered about by Cousin Gwen again. I could not bribe anyone to take your place with her, and it wasn't because I didn't try. I suppose none of the other squires had your incentive to try to get close to Constantia. Without a dowry, they said she could never hope to become anything more than some man's mistress."

Jevon whirled on Llygad, his hand fisting.

Llygad fell back a step. "*I* never said it. Well, not after you left." His face reddened deeper in the ruddy glow the makeshift torch cast over his cheeks. "And I have apologized to her a hundred times for the stupid slurs I cast at her when we were young."

Jevon reined in his anger and resumed his search for Therri. "Stantia had too much self-respect to be any man's mistress."

"I know. Some men tried to seduce her when you were gone, but she froze so many of them to death they finally stopped."

The thought of Constantia being so insulted infuriated Jevon. "Were you one of them?" He could not stop the angry—and jealous—question from slipping out.

"No. I swear it, Jevon, not even after her brother died and Cousin Gwen wanted me to try. Raimon, though, and some of the older knights—but nothing ever came of it."

Jevon stopped again. "Raimon tried to seduce Stantia?"

"Not so obviously that she froze him, too, but Franco said Raimon wanted her. Like you and Franco, Raimon could not afford a wife. But now he's taken it into his head again that he can win a fortune on the tournament circuit and marry her whether she has a dowry or not."

So Jevon had heard his old friend tell her. Jevon had misjudged her intentions when he'd confused Llygad with the vicious stranger. Was it Raimon she wanted after all? Was he why she had been so determined to return to Pennault?

"It takes a fortune to win a fortune." Jevon moved forward again. Why should he care if she and Raimon wed? For whatever reason, she chose Pennault over Jevon. It made perfect sense that she wanted to marry one of Laurant's knights.

Llygad's boots crunched behind him. "I don't know how Raimon expects to pay for his equipment. Laurant refused to sponsor him when Raimon asked him after you left. The baron still thinks tournaments are frivolous. Raimon's become the baron's best swordsman and horseman, though, so perhaps he hopes to catch the eye of some other lord who views the mêlée differently than Laurant."

Jevon had shared that dream. He might have sympathized with Raimon's continued hope for fame and even forgiven his desire for Constantia's hand had his former friend not tried to kill him tonight.

The fire branch illuminated another footstep, and Jevon swerved to follow it.

"All those things I said about Constantia," Llygad muttered, "it was never really about her at all. I only said them to provoke you because you were so insufferably proficient at everything."

Insufferable? I was not insufferable.

"All those hours you spent with Cousin Gwen, and you were still the best at everything. The sword, the lance, the bow, horsemanship—Laurant even held you up as the epitome of courtesy for the rest of us to emulate because you waited on his wife with such cheerful patience. I wanted to knock you down a peg—all of us did."

The skills of knighthood had always come easily to Jevon. He'd been careful not to let pride puff him up to swagger when he bested his fellow squires at every skill the baron set them to learn. Displaying arrogance would have been unchivalrous, and Llygad was right—Jevon had wanted to be the best at everything, including chivalry.

He felt an uncomfortable twinge of conscience. Llygad had not deserved his respect, and Jevon rarely gave it to him. But might he not have been a little more genuinely humble in his friendly rivalries with Raimon and Franco?

A twig cracked beneath Llygad's foot. "But mostly, I desperately wanted some woman to look at me the way Constantia looked at you, as though she felt the heavens spin every time you smiled at her. I just did not know then that the woman I wanted the heavens to spin for was Guia, not Constantia."

A pain more acute than any twisting dagger pulsed in Jevon's chest as he recalled how Constantia's smiles had made the heavens spin for *him*.

He probed Llygad's confession to distract himself. "You and Guia . . . ?"

Jevon would never have guessed it. He could not remember a single time Llygad spared timid little Guia a thought. Jevon swished his fire branch along the forest floor, then followed some markings in the leaf fall around another turn.

"I would give anything to find a way to marry her," Llygad said. "I understand now why you stole the brooch to try to win Constantia. If I thought—"

"I did not steal the brooch." Jevon's old suspicion resurfaced. "I took the brooch to mend it. It fell through a hole in my pouch when you challenged me to that sword fight outside the stables. How do I know *you* did not pick it up and sell it?"

"Me? The only time I ever saw it was pinned to Cousin Gwen's mantle. If I'd sold it, do you think I wouldn't have flown out from under her thumb by now and used it to run off with Guia?"

Jevon grudgingly admitted that Llygad's defense made sense.

"Besides," Llygad added, "they found the silver in your pouch. I saw it myself."

"Everyone saw my silver, but it wasn't from the brooch. It was from the sale of my mother's ring."

"I never saw you with a ring fine enough to be worth that much money, Jevon."

That was the problem. No one had seen him with the ring.

"Jevon?" a voice called out from the trees to the left. "Llygad?" Therri burst out like an overexcited puppy reunited with a master who had lost him. "Thank the saints it's you! That fellow almost tricked me, looking a bit like Llygad in the dark, but something about him made my skin twitch all over."

The fair-haired stranger. Jevon's heart jumped. He caught Therri's shoulder with his free hand and spun him about, searching in the torchlight for any signs of harm—bruises, blood. He saw none, but . . .

"Did he hurt you?" Jevon demanded.

"What? Oh, he never saw me. I don't think. I ran—I mean, I doubled back before he knew I was there." Therri removed Jevon's grip but held his hand for a moment. "I'm sorry for sneaking away from you and Constantia. I was not running from *you*, Jevon. Once I knew it was you, I knew you would not really give me to your earl."

Jevon tried not to squirm again.

"But I did not want you to get in trouble," Therri said, "and I thought if I could find my way to my uncle's on my own, you could tell your earl honestly that I escaped." He dropped Jevon's hand. "I've had time to think while I've been walking. I know you cannot return to Pennault with my father's brand." Therri's gaze fell from Jevon's in the branch's flamelight. "I do not blame you for joining the English earl. You must hate my father. I—I understand if you wanted revenge on him by capturing me, but the moment you embraced me, I knew you would let me go."

Therri had embraced Jevon first, but the same responsive emotion that had welled in Jevon's breast did so again at the youth's frank faith in him.

Therri rubbed his nose with his sleeve but still avoided Jevon's eyes. "I meant what I said. I've missed you like the devil. I know from the blunted arrows you shot at us that you won't hurt my father, however much you may want to, so I'd tell you to go back to your earl and do whatever you must to the castle if I weren't so stumped as to how to get to my uncle's."

From the corner of his eye, Jevon saw Llygad flex his sword, waiting for Jevon's response to Therri's words.

"I thought you knew these woods nearly as well as I do," Jevon said, playing for time to think.

"I know the way to the clearing and to Vere and Belle Noir," Therri replied, "but I've only traveled to my uncle's along the road. What if your earl's men are guarding the way between Pennault and Vere?"

Which they are.

"Besides, it will take me days to reach my uncle's on foot, which only gives me more time to get caught. I need a horse, but I can't get one at Vere, and Belle Noir is on the other side of the river. I'd have to swim, but what if I find the earl's men there as well?"

Quite likely that Gunthar has sent men to surround Belle Noir and keep its garrison penned in until he can subdue it next.

"And ever since my skin twitched when I saw that fellow like Llygad, I'm afraid—I'm not sure it's safe to sleep in the woods.

Definitely not!

"I-I don't know what to do."

Jevon chewed his lip, then rolled his head back to stare at the sky. The wind had blown away the thin cover of clouds. A brilliant banner of stars now strung across the patch of ebony between the trees. Had the heavens truly spun when he smiled at her? As dizzily as the world had for him when her eyes twinkled like those impossibly exquisite lights overhead?

"Well, Jevon?" Llygad's voice ground out. "My blade is at the ready. Do you want me to tell the boy what you said outside the postern gate?"

Once again, Jevon's resolve sputtered and died. "No."

Ever since he'd reencountered Constantia, he'd become a pathetic excuse for a soldier. His weakness disgusted him. It did not matter whether Constantia loved him or not. He still loved her, along with the children he had guarded with her, Therri and Heléne. The plain but clever girl, the mischievous, headstrong boy, the woman whose face still floated against his lids every time he closed his eyes, whose laughter and kindness still warmed his heart—he could not betray any of them.

But how to get this reckless youth to safety?

Jevon gave the makeshift torch to Llygad, then unlaced his gambeson, stripped it off, and handed it to Therri. "Here, put this on."

Therri stared blankly at the thick, quilted garment.

"It bears Gunthar's badge." Jevon pointed to the silver stallion sewn to the shoulder. "No one should challenge you on the road when they see you wearing this. Especially if you tell them you've captured a prisoner from Pennault."

"You mean you?" Therri asked. "But won't they know your face?"

"He means me," Llygad said. He returned the branch to Jevon after Jevon smoothed down his undertunic. "Don't you?"

Unlike Therri and Raimon, who had donned plain, inconspicuous clothing for their escape from the castle, Llygad's black surcote still bore the badge of the double-headed phoenix.

A pair of tiny, reflective torchlights danced in Llygad's sapphire-rimmed pupils as Jevon replied. "From what you've told me of Laurant's anger over you breaking his truce with Gunthar, the baron may refuse to pay your ransom. Are you willing to bear that risk?"

Llygad signaled Therri to put on the gambeson. "If it means getting this young scamp to safety, yes. My father will ransom me—back to Wales. It would be a shame to his name to refuse his own son."

So Llygad had changed. He, too, would sacrifice himself for Therri, even if it meant never seeing the woman he loved again. Whatever rancor once stood between them, Jevon now saw a man he respected—and understood, from his aching heart to the soles of his feet.

"Where will you go?" Llygad asked.

Jevon could not return to the earl's camp and lie to Gunthar's face about where he had been and what he had been doing.

"I'll join the force Gunthar left behind to maintain control over Sir Damien's castle. Perhaps I can regain the earl's confidence by proving myself faithful there." At Vere, where there was no one Jevon felt bound to by past emotion. "If you are stopped," he told Therri, "show them Llygad's wound and tell them Gunthar gave you leave to take the prisoner to Saint Luc's for the monks to attend him."

A group of monks seeking to follow the healing path of their namesake, Saint Luke the Physician, had founded the small monastery that lay to the south of Pennault when Jevon was a boy.

Jevon gave Therri his improvised torch. "My hope is you will be allowed to pass through the lines without question. If you reach Saint Luc's without challenge or escort, you can borrow some horses from the monks. Gunthar plans to loose his mangon on Pennault's walls at dawn. While he is preoccupied with the attack, you and Llygad ride like the devil for your uncle's."

Therri nodded.

Llygad rubbed his wounded arm. "We won't see you again, will we?" he said to Jevon.

"Most likely not."

Llygad held out his hand. After a brief hesitation, Jevon grasped Llygad's forearm. Whatever the truth about the brooch, he had earned this gesture of conciliation by his determination to guard Therri—even from Jevon himself.

Llygad gripped Jevon's arm as firmly as his injured shoulder allowed, then released him and locked their left hands. He raised Jevon's hand toward the torchlight, throwing Jevon's brand into stark, condemning relief. Jevon tried to pull away, his cheeks hot with shame despite his innocence, but Llygad held his hand fast.

"Whatever you may have done in the past," Llygad said, "you have absolved your sin to me this night. If you ever need a place of refuge, join me in Wales. Poitevin law does not reach there, and neither does English despite King Henry's attempts to enthrall my birthland. If any of my countrymen dares to challenge this"—he stretched his fingers toward the scar as his grip tightened around Jevon's palm—"he will have to go through me."

Jevon gulped down the lump in his throat at the unexpected offer. Disconcerted by Llygad's magnanimity, he defaulted to a jest. "I hope your fighting ability has improved since I saw you last."

"It is still middling," Llygad admitted with a wry grin. "But with your bow and sword to back me up, all men will think twice before quarreling with us." He released Jevon with a hearty slap to his shoulder. "Come to Wales. Together we will grow old and jaded over our lost loves." His grin sagged into a mournful slant at the corner.

Wales. Where English law did not reach. So close to the golden land and yet never to cross its borders? Would that be better or worse than returning to Normandy?

"I will think on it," Jevon said.

"Do," Llygad urged, an almost eager note in his voice.

Jevon guessed why. Wales was no longer Llygad's home. Jevon would be a familiar face and a reminder to Llygad of memories they shared of better times before each had suffered banishment for different reasons.

Llygad turned to Therri. "Come, my lord. We had better be on our way."

Therri nodded, then flung his arms around Jevon in a fierce hug. "If you go to Wales, I'll come and visit you. I promise. If your earl does not snatch me up."

Therri's growl on the final words rumbled on the air as he and Llygad strode off into the night.

Jevon prayed his gambeson's badge would be enough to protect the youth and Llygad. It had been the only scheme he could think of. He believed it would, though. Gunthar had too many soldiers for all of them to know each other by sight. The earl distributed badges to all the men who joined him, Norman as well as English, squires as well as knights, so they could identify each other in the heat of battle. The only exceptions were the knights and men-at-arms who wore the badges of other lords who supported Gunthar and his English king, like Lord Challons and Sir John Lee, but they would acknowledge Gunthar's badge as superior to their own.

Jevon forfeited the prancing stallion's protection for himself, hoping someone at Vere would recognize and vouch for him. He would blame the loss of his gambeson on the fair-haired stranger who still lurked in the trees. A fierce skirmish with the fiend's dagger had left his gambeson ripped and slashed to such ineffectiveness that he had cast it off. Wherever the villain really hid, he should be too afraid of being caught by Gunthar's knights to follow Therri and Llygad once they reached the road, which they should quickly do. Jevon made sure he had his sword drawn as he began his journey to Vere through the woods, but he met with no resistance as he trudged through the night.

Dawn broke by the time he reached the vanquished castle. After enduring a little rough interrogation by some of Gunthar's men-at-arms, a knight was found who remembered seeing Jevon among the earl's archers. By the time the knight sat Jevon down in Vere's bailey and handed him some bread and watered wine to break his fast and refresh him from his scuffle with the stranger, the sun hung like a honey globe above the horizon. The assault on Pennault would be well underway by now. Jevon hoped he had saved Therri, but he had not been able to do the same for Constantia and Heléne. Constantia was sensible and clever, though. She would have taken the young girl someplace safe from the shattering stones of Gunthar's mangons. But the bread clogged Jevon's mouth like wool, and the weak wine burned his belly as he gazed around at the rubble of Vere's devastated walls.

Constantia looked up when a lantern's glow dispersed the murky darkness. Lady Heléne sat down in the straw beside her, setting the lantern between them.

"How much longer do you think it will go on?" Heléne asked.

Constantia sent a glance at the dainty woman snoring delicately in a corner of the cellar. "You will sully your gown, my lady. Your mother told you to restrict your sitting to the barrels Guia and Beatris I wiped off for you, or, if you grew tired, to sleep on the furs."

Heléne chafed her hands together. The August days were still warm outside, but the air inside the dank cellar was chilly.

"Mama is asleep in the furs," Heléne said, "and I am bored of sitting on the barrels. All Mama does is scold me when I grow restless and drub my heels against the side. But she cannot scold me while she is asleep, so I can sit with you on the floor if I want to."

Heléne's mischievous smile lit her sixteen-year-old face almost to prettiness before her features resettled into their normal, unremarkable curtness, though somewhat tighter than usual with worry.

"How much longer, Constantia?" she repeated. "I cannot tell the time anymore in the dark, but it feels like we have been here for months!"

"It has not been months or we'd all have grown fat on surfeits of cheese by now." Constantia smiled when Heléne giggled. "It has only been a few days, judging from the number of times we have eaten."

Constantia was impressed by the baron's stores. No wonder Laurant sought to manipulate a delay in surrender. There was food and wine enough to sustain the castle for more than a few of the months of Heléne's frustrated imagination. However, the rations had not been equally distributed among those who took refuge from the English siege engine in this bleak, chilly vault. Lady Gwenllian barely stopped eating at all when she was awake, although for lack of a cooking fire, she had to satisfy herself with hard cheese, dried vegetables and fruits, and oats soaked and softened in wine from the wine barrels, then sweetened with honey.

Constantia guessed that nerves fed Lady Gwenllian's hunger. The baroness constantly flitted about in the dark, berating anyone who annoyed her, which in these close quarters was practically everyone. She shared the food generously with her daughter and Sybil. The rest of the cellar's occupants—women, pages, those knights and men-at-arms injured by English arrows before the mangon's assault began, and anyone too sick or weak to defend the castle, like the older menservants—had been allowed to consume far less.

"In case this siege drags on, my family must be cared for first," the baroness said, though whenever Lady Gwenllian fell asleep, Heléne slipped extra food to the rest.

It did feel as though they had huddled in the darkness much longer than just days, the gloom relieved only by a few low-burning lanterns. Constantia was unsure how long it had really been since they'd all awakened to claps of thunder. Still befuddled with sleep, she had stumbled out of bed to stare out the window at the clear blue sky above the wall where just the night before she had slid through the postern gate and argued with Jevon over Therri's fate before they lost him. There had been just enough time for her stomach to clutch with memory of the "storm" at Vere before another crack, so loud it hurt her ears, made Guia and Beatris shriek in their beds. A moment later, one of Laurant's knights slammed open their chamber door, shouting that the walls were falling and ordering the women to retreat to the cellars.

Heléne slid her cold hand into Constantia's, as she had when they met one another in the tumult hurrying down the stairs. Like then, Constantia felt the tremor in Heléne's fingers.

"What do you think has happened to Papa? What if he—what if he is—is d-de—"

Constantia squeezed the girl's fingers, cutting off her anxious stammer. "If any misfortune had befallen your father, the earl's men would have found us by now. Your father and our knights must still be holding them at bay."

Guia stirred from the other side of her. Guia had barely left Constantia's side, as though she somehow thought Constantia would defend her and Beatris if the earl's men stormed into the cellar to ravish them. Constantia pinched Guia's arm before she could reiterate her persistent refrain within Heléne's hearing. No matter how many times Constantia, relying on Jevon's assurance, assured Guia the women would be treated honorably if the English took the castle, Guia could not shake her doubts. Perhaps because Beatris, huddled on Guia's other side, kept muttering her own dread in Guia's ear.

"How long does it take to knock down a wall?" Guia whispered. "Shouldn't the earl have mowed down all our knights by now? What if Llygad is lying dead in the bailey?" She gave a woeful sniffle.

"Llygad cannot wield a sword well with his left hand," Constantia reminded her. "The baron will not have let him join in the defense. If they are trying to hold a line against the English, Llygad would be too easily disarmed and the line broken through."

"If he is so useless to the baron, should he not be here with us?"

Constantia had not thought of that. Guia was right. With Llygad wounded, he should have been sent to the cellar, like Sir Guilhem and Sir Milo and the others.

Heléne let go of Constantia's hand and fiddled with something in the dark. Constantia leaned over to ask her, "Has your mother said anything to you about Sir Llygad?"

Heléne turned the object over twice. "No, and I have been worried about him because his wound was still fresh. I am afraid if he insists on fighting alongside Papa, he will pull the wound open and end up fainting and letting one of the English knights run him through."

"Oh!" Guia gurgled on a strangled sob. "Oh!"

Heléne, quickly repentant, leaned across Constantia, her thick, heavy braid falling into Constantia's lap. "I am sorry, Guia. I am sure Llygad will not be so foolish. I told him he must keep his arm in his sling for at least a fortnight."

Constantia knew Llygad would do no such thing if battle erupted in the bailey. Guia knew it, too, and burst into weeping.

Beatris lamented, "Poor lamb. You will not even have a wedding night to remember him by."

"Hush!" Constantia scolded, exasperated with Beatris's baleful predictions. "Do not listen to her, Guia. I am certain Llygad—"

"What if he is dead?" Guia sobbed. "What if he is dead?"

Constantia embraced her and murmured what reassurances she could, but she worried over Llygad's absence from their company. She had last seen him by the postern gate where, in her panic over Therri, she had poured out the story of his disappearance. Distraught for Therri's safety, she had babbled like an idiot, remembering little now of what she said before Lady Gwenllian called her to the keep to deal with some trivial complaint. Constantia had not dared tell the baroness her son was missing. Laurant had pledged her and Raimon to silence in the matter. And she had not seen Llygad since.

Sick with guilt for losing Therri, Constantia had lain awake till dawn. Jevon would keep his promise to find the youth, she repeated to herself over and over. But anything could have happened after they parted. He and Therri might have met with an accident. Or fallen victim to the villain in the woods. She shuddered.

Exhaustion had finally pulled Constantia into sleep until the crack of the English mangon jarred her awake again.

"I hate him!"

Heléne's vehement exclamation jerked Constantia back to their dour surroundings. "Who?"

"That wretched English earl. Why must he come here to torment us all? Oh, how I wish I could stand and fight beside Papa and Therri. Why must I sit here and wait and wonder just because I am a woman, when I can handle a bow as well as any of our archers?"

Did Heléne remember how often as a child she'd begged Jevon's advice with her aim when she'd stolen down to the butts in the early morning hours to practice with Therri's hunting bow between the lessons Jevon encouraged Etienne to give her? Even at the risk of Lady Gwenllian's rebuke, Jevon always gave in to Heléne's pleas. His clear enjoyment in making the little girl happy had only made Constantia love him more.

"If anything happens to Therri or Papa, I swear I will make the earl sorry he ever set foot in Poitou!"

Heléne spoke so ferociously that Constantia almost believed her. She prayed Therri was safe with his uncle by now, but his destination was not her secret to share, even with his sister.

And what of Jevon? They would have known by now if he had given Therri to his earl. Laurant would have immediately surrendered the castle if he'd seen Therri in the enemy's camp.

But Constantia understood the price Jevon would pay if his earl learned of his choice. He would lose his royal pardon. And what would Laurant's brother do if—*when*, Constantia determinedly corrected herself—Jevon arrived with Therri? Without a pardon, Jevon remained a thief. Would Laurant's brother overlook Jevon's brand for Therri's sake, or would he throw Jevon into his dungeon and hold him for the baron's judgment for defying his banishment and returning to Poitou?

Heléne fidgeted beside her.

"What is that you are playing with?" Constantia asked to divert her apprehensions.

Heléne flipped the object over again. She seemed to hesitate before saying, "I found this after Mama fell asleep. I was uncertain whether to show you or not."

Constantia picked up the lantern and lifted the shade. The flame licked alive flecks of red and green encrusting a sinuous, shimmering body.

She gasped so loudly Guia stopped her sniffling. Constantia scooped the object out of Heléne's hands. Despite its cold, metallic base, it scorched Constantia's palm.

"What is that?" Guia asked, then gasped even louder than Constantia.

Beatris scuttled around her to look. Her eyes flew wide as dinner trenchers. "Constantia, *you* were the thief?"

Her exclamation drew a crowd around them. A clamor of voices, some shocked, some confused, drowned out Constantia's denials and woke Lady Gwenllian. It did not take more than a few sharp commands from the baroness to let her sweep, accompanied by Sybil, to the forefront carrying a lantern of her own.

"My brooch!"

A sudden, deathly silence allowed Lady Gwenllian's cry to bounce shrilly against the beams of the ceiling. Sybil grabbed Constantia and dragged her to her feet with a strength startling for a crone so old. Sibyl plucked the switch from her girdle.

"I did *not* take it!" Constantia insisted.

Lady Gwenllian quivered with fury, her pristine white veil barely mussed from her bed of furs, her glorious face resplendent—and dangerous—in its wrath. Constantia would have retreated, but the crowd pressed her against one of the cellar's walls.

Lady Gwenllian's nails bit against Constantia's palm as she scraped the ruby-and-emerald-studded brooch out of Constantia's hand. "You lying, sneaking little thief. All these years you let me blame Jevon when it was you. I will make my husband brand *both* your hands for this."

Constantia's hands recoiled behind her back at Lady Gwenllian's threat. *Coward. Jevon bore his unjust punishment bravely.*

"Mama!" Heléne pushed herself between Constantia and her mother. The sixteen-year-old girl stood a full head taller than Lady Gwenllian. "Constantia would never steal from anyone. *I* found it. Why would she take your brooch and hide it in the cellar? It is ridiculous!"

"To spite me. She hoped if she smiled sweetly enough and pretended to obey me meekly enough and behaved as though she enjoyed watching over you and Clothilde and Therri that I might provide her a dowry." Lady Gwenllian glared at Constantia. "As though it was my fault your father had too many daughters and rid himself of you in *my* castle. You should have been honored to serve a baroness and grateful to enjoy the benefit of our bread and board. But you and Guia became vindictive instead, blaming me for your fathers' neglect, always seeking for ways to vex me for not finding you husbands and for my perfectly reasonable requests on your time."

Guia gave a tiny squeak at being included in Lady Gwenllian's diatribe and tried to hide behind Beatris.

"Lady Heléne"—Constantia's breath came out shakily—"where did you find the brooch?" Perhaps its location would somehow exonerate her.

"Over here."

At an imperious gesture from Lady Gwenllian, the crowd dispersed enough to allow her and Constantia to follow Heléne to the wall behind three barrels with the words *beans, peas,* and *oats* scratched into the lids. Her slender, girlish figure was thin enough to slide behind the barrels. Constantia held up the lantern to give more light.

"There is a crack here, in the mortar." Heléne's slim fingers slipped into the crevice. "The brooch was tucked inside."

"It must be filthy back there," Lady Gwenllian exclaimed. "Come out and turn around. All the way."

Heléne's wide mouth scrunched, but she obeyed. Constantia, Guia, and Beatris had wiped layers of dust from the barrels for Heléne and her mother to sit on, but the barrels had been too heavy to move and clean behind. Splotches of dirt smeared Heléne's bodice and skirts. The baroness moaned. She might dress her younger daughter in gowns of the dullest colors, too loose for Heléne's slight frame, but the cloth was still costly, as befitting a baron's daughter.

"Heavens, Heléne," Lady Gwenllian chided, "if the earl and his men find us down here, they will think you a scullery maid."

Guia ventured somewhat quaveringly, "Constantia could never have fit behind those barrels to hide your brooch, my lady. She is much too buxom."

Constantia's face warmed. Raimon sometimes said admiringly that she had blossomed "eloquently" through the years, but she was definitely *not* plump.

Beatris, on the other hand, wrung her dimpled fingers. "Seven years ago, when Jevon was accused, we were finishing off the winter stores. These barrels would have been nearly empty and easy for anyone to move, even Constantia."

Or you or Guia. Constantia pressed her lips together to stop her irritation from spilling out. She would not throw suspicion on others to defend her innocence.

Lady Gwenllian clicked her tongue, then stared long and hard at Constantia. "Tell me truthfully, Heléne. Did you find the brooch in the wall, or were you hiding it there for Constantia?"

"I found it, Mama. I could not stop worrying about Papa and Therri while you were asleep and wondering what will happen to us if—if they are h-hurt and the earl and his men take us prisoner."

Heléne glanced at Beatris. Had the young girl overheard her incessant mumblings of ravishment by the earl's men?

Heléne continued. "I was using the lantern to make shadows on the wall behind the barrels to try to help me think of something else when I saw something glitter. I slipped behind the barrels to see what it was. It turned out to be that crack between the stones with a brooch wedged inside. You were asleep, so I took it to show Constantia."

Lady Gwenllian's gaze remained fastened on Constantia's face.

She wants me to be guilty. Why did I not hurl the brooch into a corner before a crowd of witnesses surrounded me?

"Heléne"—Lady Gwenllian's warning tone prompted Sybil to smack her switch against her thigh with a hopeful grimace—"if you are lying . . ."

"I am not, Mama! I swear."

A sudden pounding on the door at the top of the stairs made everyone jump and half of the women screech. A mass of panicked bodies again shoved Constantia against an empty portion of the wall, cramming her so tightly they nearly suffocated her.

"The castle has yielded," a man shouted through the timbers. "Stand back. We are entering, and we are armed."

The screeches turned into wails, keens, and howling pleas for heaven's defense as a key clanged in the lock. Constantia kept her own fear clamped in the pit of her churning stomach. Jevon had promised safety to the women. Laurant must have relinquished the key. Either that, or he was dead and the earl's men had taken it off his body.

Over Beatris's shoulder, Constantia saw the pinch of terror on Heléne's young face. Constantia tried to wiggle herself free to reach the frightened girl, but the door burst open, silhouetting a man at the top of the stairs, sword drawn. The throng of women and page boys, the youngest of whom mewled as loudly as the women, squashed her into the wall again.

"Quiet!" the man roared. "There is no need to bleat like a flock of sheep. My name is Sir John Lee. Your lord has yielded the castle, and the Earl of Gunthar has sent me to bring you all out safely."

His shout subdued the cacophony to whimpers. Though some remained dubious—"Don't trust him, don't trust him," Beatris jabbered—most seemed to join in Constantia's relief.

The baroness moved to the foot of the stairs with a crisp, elegant gait. "I am Lady Gwenllian. Is my husband alive?"

Her small stature radiated a plucky courage, but her voice, iridescent as a pearl, carried a thread of strain Constantia had never heard in it.

A man bearing a torch appeared alongside Sir John in the doorway. Neither spoke for several moments. As the crowd of frightened bodies eased away from Constantia, she could finally see the men's faces. They goggled at the baroness like smitten squires.

"Yes, my lady," Sir John called down. "He is humbled but unharmed. It would be my honor to escort you to his side."

Lady Gwenllian paused to whisper something to Sybil, then mounted the stairs with measured, dignified steps. Everyone knew to allow Heléne to follow her mother before leaving the cellar themselves. Heléne bounced impatiently each time her mother's gait forced her to wait on a step.

Sir John remained at the doorway, sword still in hand, no doubt as a precautionary measure, as the rest filed out behind them. Some of the servants had brought "weapons" to defend themselves if the enemy found them here. Now, in their eagerness to escape their dismal prison, most of these items—kitchen skewers, knives, iron pots for cracking heads—lay abandoned in the straw.

Having been pressed so far to the rear, Constantia was among the last to climb the cellar stairs. By the time she reached the doorway, Sir John and his sword were gone, but a figure more ominous than an enemy knight blocked her way.

Sybil and her switch.

"My lady will deal with you later," the crone said and slammed the door in Constantia's face.

A key clanked in the lock. Startled, Constantia rattled the latch, but the door was sealed shut. Laurant had given Sir John his key, but as chatelaine of the castle, Lady Gwenllian had her own keys to all the doors, including the cellar. Constantia's knees suddenly turned to water, crumpling her onto the top stair. If she had only feared it before, she now knew despite Heléne's protests that Lady Gwenllian was determined to blame Constantia for the brooch's theft. She pressed the backs of her hands against the steps cold stone, praying they might turn to ice before she felt the sting of the branding iron.

Jevon searched the face of each woman who emerged from the cellar into the tower stairwell. Lady Gwenllian, at the forefront, had not aged a day. Still breathtakingly beautiful. Still defiantly proud, even with enemy knights standing by, alert for any unexpected threats Laurant might have hidden among his womenfolk. Jevon had been summoned back to Pennault from Vere during the final assault of the castle. Once the fortress surrendered, he and his bow were no longer needed. Urgent to know if Constantia was safe, he trailed behind Sir John Lee and Sir Thomas Enslye as they fulfilled Gunthar's command to escort the women from their cellar refuge.

Lady Gwenllian walked right past Jevon, not deigning to glance at him in the simple gambeson he had replaced at Vere. Would she have recognized him if she had? A young woman in her midteens with plain, curt features but a luxuriously thick braid of pale gold did pause to gaze curiously at him before following the baroness. Heléne? If so, she gave no indication that she remembered him. Neither did any of the other women who bustled past, not even Beatris and Guia. But that could have been because the first was too busy staring with terror at Gunthar's knights and the second had her head down, sniveling into her sleeve.

Jevon knew the woman who lingered at the cellar door, too, locking it once all the women, boys, and old men were out. Sybil, the crone who'd switched him and the other pages for infractions small, great, and imagined when they first came to the castle. He stepped in front of her before she could follow the others up the stairs. He had not seen Constantia anywhere.

He met Sybil's surly glare squarely. "Is there anyone else in the cellar?"

Her malignant eyes lit, lingering on the badge of the stallion on his shoulder. "No. Come back to dare the hangman's rope, have you?"

It did not matter if she knew him. The only man with authority to punish him for his sins now was Gunthar.

"Take care how you use that impertinent tongue in the earl's hearing," he warned the old harpy. "He takes pleasure in beating impudent servants."

Too bad it wasn't true. To see the switcher switched would give Jevon considerable satisfaction. Sybil could not know that he bluffed, though. From her look of uncertainty, he knew she would think twice before behaving saucily if Gunthar turned one of his hawk-eyed stares on her.

Jevon studied the cellar door as Sybil shuffled off. Should he rebuke her for locking it? No. Sir John had the baron's key and could open it at a command from Gunthar when they needed access to the cellar's supplies.

If not with the other women, where was Constantia? Of course. Helping to care for the wounded. The injured would most likely have been taken to the garrison quarters on the ground level of the keep. He retraced the circular steps in the mural tower, this time exiting through the first arched opening rather than the one on the floor above where he had entered the keep.

He emerged into a wide hall, thick with the rank scent of sweat. For a moment, he was an ambitious young squire again, counting the years until he could join these malodorous knights who wore this smell like a badge of honor after laboring long and hard at a day's martial training to keep their muscles and reflexes honed for war. How Jevon had dreamed of one day joining this musty brotherhood, glutting and guzzling after being relieved of their duties for the day, dicing, quarreling, and finally sleeping on the pallets scattered across the floor.

But today, the pungent cloud carried the whiff of defeat. Gray-faced men sat or lay on those pallets with bloodied heads, legs wrapped in bandages, and arms in slings. One, with a broken arrow shaft lodged in his shoulder, gave a muffled scream as one of Gunthar's barber-surgeons pulled it out and seared the wound with a hot iron. The piece of wood clenched in the man's teeth fell out of his mouth as he fainted. Jevon recognized Franco, pallid and older but still with a brash look to his face, even when unconscious.

Ned Woodville saw Jevon and picked his way through the injured men to join him.

"More than a few of these fellows are here thanks to you," Ned said, scratching his ruddy beard. "None of their wounds appear to be mortal as long as none of them fester. I could see that Gunthar was pleased with both your accuracy and restraint."

"I want as little death as possible," Gunthar had told Jevon before giving him command of his archers.

While Jevon had been vigorously helping reinforce the victory over Sir Damien's castle, Laurant's remaining arbalists sent a successful launch of crossbolts to harry the men manning Gunthar's siege engine, sending Gunthar's men scurrying for protection and delaying the attack after the first few volleys of stones. The arbalists maintained a standoff with Gunthar's men for several days, during which time the knight who recognized Jevon at Vere sent Gunthar word of Jevon's presence, puzzled that the earl had dispensed with his best archer in the midst of a siege. Gunthar responded by immediately demanding Jevon's return to Pennault. Hopeful of a new chance to prove his loyalty, Jevon successfully repositioned Gunthar's archers and directed a counterattack that swiftly ended the barrage of crossbolts. Once unimpeded, the mangon resumed its battery of the curtain wall, along with other unlucky locations inside the walls where the not-always-accurate wooden bucket flung its heavy stones.

"I understand some of these men were once your friends," Ned said, following Jevon's gaze to Franco. To his credit, the archer sergeant had displayed no resentment of Jevon usurping his position. "Try not to worry for them overmuch. Our surgeons are skilled at healing. Gunthar does not like to leave a trail of dead in his wake. He says it is an ineffective way to win hearts to the king. Of course"—Ned nodded at three bodies laid out with cloaks over their faces—"death cannot always be avoided in war."

So Gunthar had reminded Jevon.

"I laid a wager with Hamo," Ned continued, "that Laurant would retreat to the keep with his men once his walls began to fall. The baron did not seem arrogant enough to stand in the yard and try to repel us with force the way de Brielle did"—

Jevon had been relieved to discover that Sir Damien still breathed, though confined to his bed, at Vere.

—"but Laurant could have resisted us here for weeks, months even, if he had enough food and wine laid up."

Jevon studied the strong stone walls that enclosed the garrison floor of the castle keep. After the gatehouse, the keep was the strongest and most fortified part of the castle.

Ned's face scrunched. "I might have won the wager had de Grimoult not appeared with that news from Blancaval. Who would have guessed that fat wretch Merval was wed to Laurant's daughter?" Ned slanted a subtly weighing look at Jevon. "Did you know it? You said you once served the baron."

"The Lady Clothilde was still a child when I left Pennault. I had no more idea she'd wed old Merval than Gunthar had."

Constantia had not given Jevon the name of the man Clothilde had been "listless" to marry. But then, Jevon had not told Constantia that Gunthar laid siege to Merval's castle of Blancaval and that Merval died in a red-faced fit while shouting a hate-filled tirade at the earl from the top of his wall.

Jevon searched the garrison hall for some sign of Constantia as he added, "I was as surprised as anyone when de Grimoult rode from Blancaval with news that the baron's daughter was in the custody of Gunthar's men."

De Grimoult had been one of the knights Gunthar left behind to seal off Blancaval from leaking news that Gunthar and his army advanced through Poitou.

Ned rubbed the red bristles along his jaw. "John FitzGilbert, marshal to our first King Henry, swore he would let the usurper Stephen hang his young son William rather than surrender Newbury Castle during the wars with the Empress Mathilda. John said he could forge other sons with his wife in William's place. Fortunately for William, Stephen spared him. You would know him as William Marshal now."

Every knight—or formerly aspiring knight—knew William Marshal. His reputation for both success and chivalry on the tournament field had stirred Jevon's, Raimon's, and Franco's blood and enthusiasm to one day emulate the famous champion.

"John FitzGilbert refused to open his gates for his own son. Why would Laurant surrender and open them for a mere daughter?"

"Laurant was fond of his children." It irked Jevon to speak generously of the baron, but it was true. "I cannot say that I ever saw him pay them over-much attention, save for Therri's training, but he was always patient with his daughters, if somewhat absentmindedly so. He listened too much to his wife, though. It was undoubtedly she who promoted Clothilde's marriage to Merval. The baroness can be a veritable"—he bit off the word *witch* and substituted—"sorceress in her beauty. Laurant is completely enchanted with her and does everything she asks of him."

Jevon resisted the urge to glance at the scars on his hand.

His hunt for Constantia met with nothing but frustration. He finally asked Ned, "Have you seen any women assisting the surgeons here?"

"None. Are you looking for one in particular?"

"Just someone I used to know here. Perhaps she is in the great hall."

Ned's forehead creased. "We're just archers, Jevon. I do not think Gunthar would welcome any of us sticking our noses into whatever is taking place between him and the baron."

Jevon gave Ned a grin. "Then I will have to take care he does not see me."

Lady Gwenllian looked cross as she glided over the threshold, fluttering her hands in a shooing motion to hurry the young woman with the braid from the great hall. Jevon stepped into a shadow inside the entrance chamber to avoid being seen, but he caught snatches of the baroness's hissing rebuke.

" . . . unacceptably bold of you . . . no business spying . . . do not *dare* leave your chamber until I give you leave or I will have Sybil . . ."

The young woman looked more rebellious than chastened, but if she made a reply, it escaped Jevon's ears as she and Lady Gwenllian vanished into the mural tower with the stairs he knew continued upward to the bedchambers on the next floor.

Once alone, Jevon moved to one side of the arched entryway and peered cautiously into the great hall. He only wished to confirm whether Constantia was there before either waiting for her to withdraw or going to search elsewhere. Gunthar and Laurant stood on the dais, each flanked by a squire and a few of their knights. The men still wore full battle armor, Gunthar's overlaid with his blue, stallion-emblazoned surcote. Gunthar pulled his helmet, crested with the same proudly prancing emblem, from his mail-coiffed head, then swiveled his gaze toward Jevon. Was it some uncanny instinct that made the earl glance away from Laurant just then? Or the fact that Gunthar looked equal parts grim, exasperated, and bored by the baron's stream of bitter prattle.

"I take full responsibility for my actions, my lord," Laurant groveled, "and beg your deepest pardon for my transgressions."

The baron did not seem to notice the turn of Gunthar's head. Laurant wore a black surcote over his mail, embroidered with the double-headed phoenix rising from the flames. He'd surrendered his helmet to a squire who tried to look invisible and deaf to his lord's obsequious capitulation.

"If Merval had not misled me . . . Of course, I should never have listened to him, I know that now. But he was my daughter's husband, and I never thought he would endanger her by supporting a fight he knew we could not win. Well, of course, he thought we could win, or he'd not have sided with the young duke. And my wife said—not that my wife rules my decisions, mind you. The blame is mine, all of it. I will pay whatever recompense you demand. These are heated times, my lord, heated times, and I lost my way— may Merval burn in Purgatory forever!"

Laurant uttered the last on a mutter, as though intended only to shrivel his deceased son-in-law's ears, but his vexation vibrated all the way to Jevon.

"I submit fully to the king," Laurant resumed, urgency replacing his aggravation. "You will tell him that, will you not, when you see him? That I am once again his loyal servant?"

"That depends." Gunthar drew out the words, his gaze still on Jevon. "The king will no doubt want guarantees of your sincerity."

The earl's frowning brows made clear his displeasure at his archer's inquisitiveness. Jevon bowed a swift apology. He saw no sign of Constantia or any women in the hall.

He backed away from Gunthar's censuring stare and collided with someone behind him.

"*Oomph!*" a lilting voice huffed. "Clumsy oaf!"

He turned, this time with a verbal apology on his lips, and met the frosty sapphire glare of Lady Gwenllian. The girl with the braid no longer trailed her. The baroness must have accompanied her to the stairs and sent her up alone.

Lady Gwenllian tried to sweep past Jevon into the hall, but he blocked her. She would find herself no more welcome during Gunthar's reprimand of her husband than Jevon was. Lady Gwenllian glowered but still gave no sign that she recognized him.

"Your pardon, my lady," Gunthar said, observing their exchange. "My archer appears to be lost. Perhaps you can accompany him back to your bailey?"

Jevon's face heated. The way to the bailey was through the entrance chamber, back into the mural tower, through the door beside the stairs, and down the outside steps, as it was in nearly every castle. Even had he not lived at Pennault from the age of seven, a fool could have found the bailey on his own.

Rather than taking Gunthar's unmistakable hint to both of them, Lady Gwenllian swept around Jevon and sailed gracefully into the hall. "May I have a word with my husband first, my lord? I have something of import to relay to him."

Jevon recognized the falsely sweet chirp she used whenever she sought to charm a man.

"Can it not wait?"

Gunthar's impatience clearly startled her, but she recovered swiftly.

"You are right," she purred. "This matter should be brought before you as well, as I see my husband is conceding to your very proper authority over our castle. One of our servants has committed an egregious crime against us and requires punishment. I am certain you will agree that my husband is within his rights to pass judgment on her as soon as it is convenient?"

Jevon's ears pricked on the word *her*. A luckless servant or—? He slid a step sideways, removing himself from the earl's line of vision but where he could continue to listen. He knew how the earl dealt with men, haughty, peremptory, crushing, but he had never seen how he dealt with women. Would Lady Gwenllian's beauty dazzle him?

"It is not convenient now, my lady. If someone has committed a crime, have one of your knights lock him up until it is."

There was a moment of silence. Had Gunthar's brusque response nonplussed the baroness as much as it surprised Jevon?

"But, my lord, if you please . . ."

Jevon envisioned her seductively fluttering her eyes or perhaps allowing the corners of her mouth to droop in mournful allure.

"It is a personal affront of the worst sort to my husband's honor. I should be ever so grateful if you would permit him to deal with it now."

She'd chosen seduction, Jevon was certain of it. Her confidence sounded altogether too smug.

"I regret I cannot oblige you now," Gunthar said, civil but adamant in his dismissal. "Your husband and I have weightier matters to discuss than some insult by one of your servants."

"Whatever it is can wait, wife." Laurant sounded harried and stressed. "Go see to the kitchen. I am certain the earl and his men will welcome a meal after their—er, exertions today."

"A meal would be welcome in an hour or two," Gunthar agreed, perhaps hopeful of smoothing any of Lady Gwenllian's offended feathers. "Thank you, my lady."

Another dismissal. Another pause. Lady Gwenllian must be stunned to find her will so heartily ignored.

"From our stores?" she asked.

An odd question. The faint hesitance in her honeyed tones tweaked Jevon's curiosity and almost prompted him to peek into the hall again.

"Of course from our stores," Laurant said. "You do not expect the earl to feed us from his rations, do you?"

The poor man was truly beset if he castigated his dazzling wife.

"No, of course not, husband. It is only—"

"Ah," Gunthar said. "We have your keys to the cellar. Did Sir John lock the door after he let you out? Julian, find Sir John and have him open the cellar for Lady Gwenllian. The two of you can help carry up any supplies necessary to feed our men. Thank you for your courtesy, my lady. We have not eaten satisfying fare from a well-equipped kitchen for months."

"Oh, that will not be necessary. Your key, I mean." Lady Gwenllian spoke so quickly it further roused Jevon's suspicion that something was amiss. "I have a key of my own. I will attend to your request at once. My husband's knights can assist me."

She smiled enchantingly as she floated ethereally into the entrance chamber, but the moment she left the men behind, her flawless lips parted to reveal tightly gritted teeth of pearl. Her delicate steps across the floor turned into an angry strut. She appeared so intent on some resolve that she did not see Jevon as she swished past him.

He waited just long enough for her to disappear into the mural tower, then followed. Her footsteps, light though they were, whisked against the stone steps down, not up. Jevon trailed behind her with the careful, muted steps he had mastered against a crackly forest floor. He allowed her to remain just beyond his sight on the spiral stairs. She passed the exit to the garrison. Her target really *was* the cellar.

Jevon paused at the final curve that would deposit him into the recessed area in front of the cellar door when he heard Sybil's surly tones mingling with Lady Gwenllian's. They could not see him here, but he could hear them both.

"If we leave the door unlocked," Sybil said, "she is sure to flee."

"And if I underestimate the amount of wine the earl's men require," Lady Gwenllian replied, tartness grating her lyrical tones, "that wretched knight with my husband's key will come down here to fetch more, and who knows what lies she will tell him about why she is locked up here? We must put her elsewhere until I have made my case to my husband and the earl."

Did they speak of Constantia or some other hapless female servant who'd offended the baroness?

"The gatehouse prison?" Sybil suggested.

"Goose brain! We'd have to march her across the bailey for everyone to see."

"The oubliette, then."

"We would have the same problem. The earl's men are walking freely about the castle. I caught one of them nosing about right outside the hall. They are likely prying in all our towers too."

"No, my lady. I went to view the damage done by the earl's war engine. The south tower is in rubble. None of the earl's men were there."

"Rubble?"

Lady Gwenllian sounded so shocked that Jevon could not resist. He peered around the curve in the steps. In the light of the torch bracketed beside the cellar door, he saw the baroness press a hand to her heart as though the news shattered her as thoroughly as the tower Jevon had watched collapse in the earl's attack.

"Our—our defeat is as absolute as that?" Her voice quavered.

Sybil looked even more grim than usual. "For now, my lady. But the earl's men will not be here forever. Once he is gone, your lord husband will rebuild our towers and walls. Our castle and Poitou will rise again."

Despite the crone's stout words, Lady Gwenllian looked shaken. Had she thought that defeat could be as simple as her husband swearing false oaths he could immediately renege on when Gunthar moved on?

Sybil held out one of her clawlike hands. "Give me your key, my lady. I will take care of the wench for you."

Lady Gwenllian roused herself from her dismay. "How?"

"I will beat her until she goes mutely where I bid her. She will go into the oubliette as meekly as a lamb."

"But the tower must be filled with debris."

"I will order Garic to clear the oubliette's door for me. I will make sure he remains mum too."

Garic? The pretty little stableboy? He must be a handsome, strapping youth by now, though as a lower servant still subject to Sybil's rod.

Lady Gwenllian's keys jangled as she detached one from the iron ring that hung from her girdle and held it out to Sybil. Jevon could not endure any more. Locking any woman in the cellar for unknown reasons was questionable, but at least she had access to food and drink there. But forcing her into the oubliette, a prison pit that by its very name—*forgotten*—conjured terror in even brave men's breasts? Only the worst of criminals should live out their days in a living grave such as that!

Anger drove him to the foot of the stairs. Until Gunthar made up his mind about Jevon's future, he was still one of Gunthar's men. If the earl could order the baroness out of the hall, Jevon could make her forfeit her key and order her away from the cellar door.

Constantia jerked awake, befuddled for a few moments by the clammy darkness. Her body lay at an odd, cramped angle, and something hard dug into her side. Why was her cheek pressed against cold stone instead of the prickly straw she had dozed on for days? Her joints cracked painfully as she sat up and realized she was slumped on the two steps at the top of some stairs. The cellar. Sybil had locked her inside. Only now Constantia was alone and bereft of the comfort and modicum of warmth from a crowd of bodies.

She had not believed herself capable of falling asleep in a darkness so pitch she could not see her hand in front of her face. But the days of tension hiding from the earl's attack had overwhelmed her with weariness. She had only meant to rest before trying to pick her way back down the stairs to the hay-covered floor but instead had slipped fully into slumber.

"Give it to me," a man's voice ordered so loudly it vibrated through the thick wooden door. "If you make me ask again, I will drag you before the earl to explain your refusal to obey a direct command from one of his men."

Ask again? Had it been this voice that awakened her?

Whatever the reply by whomever he addressed, Constantia could not hear it through the door. She scrambled to her feet, her knees popping in protest. She was about to pound on the door to draw the man's attention when a woman's voice shrilled.

"I do not care who he is! Give him the key! If we anger the earl, it will ruin everything!"

Constantia froze, holding her breath until her lungs burned while a key clanked in the lock for what felt like an eternity. She was desperate to be freed from this chilling prison, but he'd said he was one of the earl's men. What would he do when he found her? What had the English done with the other women? Beatris's fears had only been overwrought figments, hadn't they?

The door groaned on its hinges, flooding her face with blinding torchlight.

"Stantia!"

With the barrier of the door removed, she recognized the resonance of Jevon's beloved tones. She stumbled into his arms, still too dazzled with light to see his face. His embrace engulfed her with all the comfort, tenderness, and strength of the chivalrous champion she had never stopped loving.

"You should not have come back, Jevon de Cazalet."

The bite in Lady Gwenllian's voice drew Constantia's head from the snug safety of Jevon's broad chest. As her vision adjusted to the torchlight, she saw the blue fire spitting from Lady Gwenllian's jeweled eyes.

"Yes, I know you now." The baroness's eyes flicked to the scars on Jevon's hand. "I presume you told your earl all the secrets of our castle? You may gloat all you like in your revenge on us, but my husband will wipe that smugness from your face."

Constantia saw no gloating or smugness on Jevon's features, but there was a simmer of anger as he challenged Lady Gwenllian.

"I heard the earl command Sir John to deliver the women of the castle to honorable safety. Why was Constantia locked up?" Jevon's head snapped suddenly from glaring at the baroness to stare over Constantia's shoulder. "Ho! What are you doing, you old crone?"

Constantia turned in his arms to see Sybil at the top of the cellar stairs. The crone gave a ghastly, croaking screech and tumbled into the cellar's darkness.

Jevon swore and released Constantia. He sprang down the stairs after Sybil while Lady Gwenllian screamed, "Help! Help! Oh, pray, someone help us!"

Who was she shrilling to? No one could hear them all the way down here unless . . . ?

Unless there are men in the garrison hall.

Constantia could not tell the time of day in this windowless recess in front of the cellar door any more than she could in the cellar itself. If it were night, if the garrison knights were sleeping . . .

Footsteps clattered in the mural stairway. The men who surged into the recess were not clad in sleeping smocks but in mail overlaid with blue surcotes bearing the same badge that Jevon wore.

"This knave is trying to kill us!" Lady Gwenllian's voice trilled with panic. "He pushed my servant down the stairs. You swore we would be treated honorably, but you have brought a devil in your camp!"

One of the knights grabbed the torch from its sconce beside the door, looked down into the cellar, and cursed. As he disappeared inside, Constantia moved to the top of the stairs to gaze after him. Jevon crouched next to Sybil, who lay crumpled at the foot.

As soon as the torchlight reached her, the old servant issued a pitiful howl. "Help! Help, before he chokes the life from me!"

Jevon's hands were nowhere near Sybil's neck, but the knight drew his sword and swung it across Jevon's throat so swiftly that Constantia screamed.

"What the devil, le Falquet?" the knight exclaimed. "The earl will have your head for this!"

Jevon rose and backed away from the sword. Constantia whirled to block a second knight who tried to follow his companion.

"No one pushed her," Constantia told the knight. "Sybil fell on her own. I saw it myself."

Or had that been as contrived as Lady Gwenllian's distress? Constantia would not put it past the old crone to shuffle down the stairs, lie down in the straw, and contort herself in pain.

"Do not listen to the wench," Lady Gwenllian said. "She is a thief and a liar who will say anything to protect her lover."

Constantia's indignation brimmed over. "*You* are the liar. If you ever spoke the truth, it would curdle your tongue."

Lady Gwenllian slapped her, then as Constantia pressed her hand to the sting, the baroness stared at her palm as though appalled by what she'd done.

"It was wrong of me to strike her," Lady Gwenllian said, winsomely repentant to the knight, "but I have showered her with nothing but kindness since she was a child, yet you see how she insults me. She calls herself a lady, but despite all my instructions in modesty, she has the morals of a harlot. She and Jevon de Cazalet are lovers and confederates in a crime against me and my husband."

"De Cazalet?" The knight looked bewildered until Lady Gwenllian sent a glance down the cellar steps. "You mean le Falquet? You lied about your name too?" he called to Jevon.

The knight's surliness alarmed Constantia. It suggested some hostility toward Jevon that might encourage the knight to believe whatever story Lady Gwenllian chose to tell.

"If you do not believe me, examine his hand," Lady Gwenllian urged. "It bears the brand of his guilt."

"I have seen it," the knight grumbled. "He said he gained the scars from the fire of a toppled candle. The earl believes him. Or pretends to."

"Then he has hoodwinked your earl, as this ungrateful woman has for too long deceived me. Let your lord question them before my husband. I can prove his judgment on Jevon de Cazalet was just and that she was complicit in de Cazalet's crime."

With the recovered brooch Lady Gwenllian had caught Constantia holding.

The knight thrust Constantia aside with a roughness that suggested he had made up his mind about her, then ran down the cellar stairs. While the first knight held his sword at Jevon's breast, the second relieved Jevon of his sword and dagger, then took his companion's place beside the whimpering old woman. He explored her injuries with a deferential touch. When he reached her stout ankle, Sybil emitted a pitiful bleat.

"Shoving an old woman down the stairs!" the knight spat at Jevon.

With his companion's sword still leveled at him, Jevon kept his hands open and in the air. "I did nothing, Sir Edwin, I swear. If she is injured, it is because she tripped."

But Sir Edwin shouted over Jevon's words, "Sir John was right about you. You are the worst sort of miscreant."

Constantia tried again to defend Jevon. "He was nowhere near Sybil when she fell!"

"Seize her!" Sir Edwin ordered.

A pair of harsh hands locked around Constantia's shoulders. She twisted, trying to free herself, but the man behind her held her fast. Jevon attempted to spring toward the stairs, but the knight with the sword drove a fist into his stomach, doubling him over.

"Next time it will be my blade," the knight warned.

"This . . ." Jevon gasped, "is . . . a mistake."

Sir Edwin gave a snort. "We will see about that." He asked Sybil, with far greater courtesy, "Can you walk, mistress?"

"My ankle," she whimpered. "I fear 'tis broken."

"My men will carry you up the stairs." Sir Edwin gestured, holding up two fingers for two men to join him. Apparently, he judged Sybil's girth too much for one man. "As for you, le Falquet—"

"And his lady," Lady Gwenllian called. "Do not forget her."

"Be assured we will not. Hold on to her, Sir Knight."

The grip on Constantia's shoulders tightened. Sir Edwin moved to make way for the men he summoned to reach Sybil.

Jevon had recovered from the blow. Constantia saw him clench his fists as though longing to respond in kind, but he continued to speak to Sir Edwin.

"Let Lady Constantia go. She has done nothing."

"That is for the baron and your earl to decide." The response came not from Sir Edwin but from the man who so ruthlessly restrained Constantia.

Constantia started, then craned her head to look at her captor. Raimon! What was he doing with the English knights?

"If you need a place to hold them," Sybil warbled while her two knights struggled to lift her out of the straw, "there is an oubliette in the South Tower."

"Oubliettes are for murderers and traitors," Sir Edwin said, "not for thieves, even though I would happily throw le Falquet into one for abusing a helpless old woman. But your South Tower is in shambles, along with its wall. They must go somewhere else for now."

Someone new appeared next to Constantia and Raimon in the doorway, forcing Raimon to edge aside with her. The newcomer wore a padded gambeson like Jevon's, with his earl's badge sewn to the shoulder. The man scrubbed at his ginger beard, a curious contrast to his straw-colored hair.

"I would just leave them in the cellar," he said.

"No one asked you, archer," Sir Edwin growled.

The archer shrugged. "Do as you please. But if you drag them to one of the towers or the gatehouse prison, it is bound to cause a stir and reach the earl's ears. Gunthar will want to know why a woman of the castle is being molested by his knights against his own command. I would not like to be in your place, sir, if the earl feels obliged to interrupt his interview with the baron to demand an explanation."

The archer's words seemed to give Sir Edwin pause. "Very well. Find Sir John and ask him for the cellar key."

As soon as he said it, Sir Edwin seemed to realize the obvious. The "locked" cellar was already open.

"De Cazalet forced my lady to give him the key from her girdle." Sybil sniveled while the two knights summoned to help her linked their hands to form a "chair" to lift her. "He threatened us so violently we were terrified to defy him."

Sir Edwin cursed Jevon again. "Search him," he told the knight with the sword.

Jevon spared him the trouble and held out the key.

It took so long for the two knights to struggle up the stairs carrying Sybil that Constantia was sure her shoulders would bruise from the pressure of Raimon's grip while they waited.

"Why are you aiding the earl's men?" she whispered.

"I am not," he muttered. "They released me when Laurant surrendered. I was in the garrison checking on Franco when I heard Lady Gwenllian scream for help. That is where they took the wounded."

"Franco—wounded?" Constantia tried to twist around to look at Raimon, but he held her firmly pointed toward the yawning cellar door.

"He took an English arrow. Perhaps one from your lover. Was it worth it, Constantia, to lure Jevon back to you at the cost of the entire castle?"

"He is not my lover. And I did not lure him here. I tried to save you all from what was coming, but none of you would listen to me until it was too late."

"I wish I could believe that." Raimon sounded bitter and angry. "All those times I asked you to come with me, I saw in your eyes what held you back. I thought, given time, you would accept the truth about him and open your heart to me. But seven years and you never stopped loving him despite his crime. Jevon de Cazalet, the perfect page, the perfect squire— he would have made the perfect knight to marry." Raimon's sarcasm scraped like an iron file against a steel blade. "But he was not perfect, Constantia. He squandered his entire future in a moment of greed. If he asked you to go with him now that he wears the brand of a thief, what would you do?"

Her heart throbbed for all the tragic misjudgments that had severed her from Jevon. "Had he asked me then, I would have followed him into banishment. But he did not, and he has not come back to Pennault for love of me. He thought *I* was the one who told Lady Gwenllian he stole her brooch. But he was innocent, and I can prove it now."

"How?"

"Lady Heléne found the brooch in the cellar while we hid there. So Jevon could *not* have taken it seven years ago."

Raimon paused. Could he be reconsidering his suspicions of the man he once called friend?

"But someone else could have." Raimon's dismissive scorn burst her hope. "Someone who loved him. Someone who knew neither his father nor Laurant would supply him with the equipment he needed to win glory on the tournament field. Someone who thought a rich brooch might provide what his father and the baron would not. After all, the only thing that could make a perfect knight even more desirable would be a perfect knight with a tournament fortune to shower upon his wife."

She had tried for years to convince Raimon that she could never feel anything for him but friendship. He had chosen to ignore her again and again. Now, his clear sense of betrayal turned his insinuations vindictive—and dangerous.

The two knights carrying Sybil emerged from the cellar, bearing her in the makeshift "chair" between them. They staggered slightly beneath her weight, prompting her to whine, "Please don't drop me!" as they passed Constantia and Raimon.

Sybil's small eyes slid to Constantia with a triumphant gleam.

"Well, Sir Knight?" Sir Edwin called up to Raimon. "Do you continue to stand with Duke Richard or with your chastened baron?"

"I'm sorry, Constantia." Raimon "escorted" her down the steps with a brusqueness that suggested his regret was more cynical than genuine.

Judging from Jevon's clenched fists as he returned Raimon's glare, their new antipathy for one another was mutual. Ignoring the threat of the knight's hovering sword, Jevon's arm lashed out as Raimon released her but he only caught Constantia around the waist and pulled her against his side. Even knowing Raimon and the English knights would interpret her response as an admission that she and Jevon were accomplices and lovers, her head sought the comfort of his shoulder.

"They won't be needing that," Sir Edwin said as the red-bearded archer followed her and Raimon down the steps and set a lantern on one of the barrels. He must have retrieved it from the mural stairs where lanterns hung at intervals to help the servants safely ascend and descend while fetching supplies.

"There is no harm in leaving them some light. She is clearly a lady"—the archer nodded at Constantia—"and she has not yet been condemned of anything. No point in angering her family, whoever they are, and stirring up conflict with Laurant before her case is laid before the earl. We are here to enforce the king's peace, not provoke petty Poitevin quarrels."

Sir Edwin muttered something but left the lantern when he and the others mounted the cellar steps and locked the door behind them.

Silence stretched for a very long time. Jevon pulled Constantia closer and leaned his head against hers. She sighed, wrapped in an irrational aura of safety despite their dour surroundings and uncertain future.

She realized she had closed her eyes to more fully savor the solid reality of his nearness when she felt his fingers beneath her chin. She lifted her face to his, instinctively knowing his intent, and welcomed the sweet caress of his mouth on hers. The years melted away, and they were in the woods again, the air musky with the smell of earth freshly soaked from rain. Notes of late-blooming violets and primrose floated like a gossamer melody through the thick scent of dampened oak as she and Jevon openly confessed their love to each other for the first time, sealing the pledge of their hearts with a tender kiss.

Until, unlike that day, this exchange churned into a release of pent-up passion. She turned into his arms and twined hers around his neck. Every joy she had thought dead and buried when he was banished flamed back to life. Their lips came together again and again in an escalating wave of desire. More than yearning mingled tears with her zealous response. The frank, uncurbed flow of his enduring love hummed all the shattered slivers of her heart into wholeness.

Only gradually did she begin to sense a small but dogged restraint in his ardor. His hands cupped her cheeks and nudged her away so slowly she could taste his reluctance for their lips to part. Even then, he kissed her twice more—slowly, lingeringly, as though to blunt the pain of necessary parting so that he could ask . . .

"Stantia, why are we locked in this cellar?"

He waited patiently for her wits to stop swimming from the ecstasy that swirled her thoughts. When a ray of clarity finally broke through, it flooded her with only one need.

"Do not leave me again." She threw her arms back around his neck. "Whatever happens, wherever you go, promise me you will take me with you."

He drew a sharp breath. "Even to England?" He freed himself, kissed her hands, then squeezed them. Then the lantern light caught the flicker of doubt in his eyes. "Ned says Gunthar was pleased with my help in the siege, but when I interrupted him in the hall . . . One moment I think I am in his favor, the next that he is about to cast me off in anger. I am not sure I can rely on him to keep his oath to me. Certainly not if he learns what happened at the postern."

The dread that surged through Constantia when she remembered their last meeting outside that gate threatened to buckle her knees. "Therri! Did you give him to your earl? Is that why Lord Laurant surrendered the keep?"

Jevon's face reddened in the lantern's light. Had he not thought she would guess the temptation that might seduce him?

"Laurant surrendered because Gunthar's mangon battered a hole through the castle wall and demolished one of its towers," Jevon said. "But I trust that Therri is safe."

"What do you mean you trust? Do you not know for sure?" If his earl had harmed Therri, could she ever forgive Jevon?

"I sent him off with Llygad."

"Llygad?"

"He was listening at the postern and misunderstood my intentions toward the boy." Jevon paused. He slowly released Constantia's hands, then squared his shoulders, the way men did when bracing themselves to receive a blow. "Llygad thought I only wanted to find Therri so I could give him to Gunthar. And, Stantia, I cannot deny that I seriously considered doing so." Jevon ran a hand through his hair, ruffling the waves into engaging disorder. But guilt thickened his voice. "I have lived so long in shame and hiding. I thought I could justify almost anything for the reprieve Gunthar offers. But it was wrong of me to consider breaking your faith and Therri's, even for a moment. That is not the man I wanted to be for you."

No. As Raimon discerned, Jevon wanted to be perfect. At everything. For the first time, Constantia realized how that idealistic drive must have made the shame of being called a thief and banished even worse.

She had trusted Jevon to protect Therri while fearing he might surrender to the very temptation he now confessed. His potential betrayal had tormented her. Now she gazed down at her hands, white and smooth, and cold without the warmth of Jevon's clasp. If she had been falsely accused, banished from her home with a price on her head, potential death lurking around every tree by a traveler or hunter who might discover her and choose to dispatch a branded thief . . .

She saw again the brooch in her palm, heard Beatris's shocked exclamation and Lady Gwenllian's livid accusation. However much Constantia wished to be brave, her courage crumbled like Vere's shattered wall when she thought of the red-hot iron searing a fateful *R* into her flesh.

"It is not wrong to be tempted, Jevon." She hoped he would not interpret the smallness of her voice as the terror that it was. "If Therri is not with your earl, and if you did not take him to his uncle's, then where is he?"

"Hopefully he *is* with his uncle by now. I gave Therri my gambeson with Gunthar's badge to help him pass through the earl's guards unsuspected, with Llygad as his prisoner. Either they managed to avoid Gunthar's men altogether or the ruse must have worked. I would have heard in the camp had they been captured."

Jevon held out a hand as though testing her forgiveness. With a chastened conscience, she readily placed her fingers back in his.

Her gesture lit his face with a smile, though a crease between his brows tempered his relief. "Llygad told me about the attack he ordered on our men in contradiction of Laurant's orders. He is afraid the baron will send him back to Wales, but if he can take credit for protecting Therri, it will exonerate him with the baron. But that was not Llygad's only motive." Jevon's smile faded in pensive reflection. "I could see the affection that has grown between him and Therri. You were right when you told me Llygad has changed. Even if my gambeson protected Therri, Llygad wore Laurant's phoenix on his surcote and risked being seized by the earl's men as one of the baron's knights. Llygad was willing to risk it to keep Therri safe."

Jevon suddenly laughed.

"What is so funny?" she asked.

"Just that I never thought I would say it, but Llygad has grown into a man I respect."

Constantia laughed, too, happy that two men she cared for so deeply finally recognized the worth she had seen in them both all along.

But a new thought turned her serious again. "What about the man who attacked us in the woods? If he found Therri and Llygad before they reached Therri's uncle . . ."

Jevon instantly sobered. "I confess I have worried about that. But given the villain's threat to strew me about in the road for Gunthar to find, I think we would know if Therri or Llygad fell victim to his spite."

She tried to quiet her fears, praying Jevon was right.

"Jevon," she said, her lungs contracting painfully at the news she had not yet shared with him, "they found the brooch."

"The brooch?" It appeared to take a moment for her change of subject to sink in. "Lady Gwenllian's brooch? They found it? Where?"

"Here, in the cellar." Constantia picked up the lantern and led him to the barrel of oats. She stretched her arm across the top, bringing the light closer to the wall. "Heléne discovered it in that crack while we hid here during the siege. Lady Gwenllian has jumped to the conclusion that you and I stole it together."

"Together?" Jevon's brows kinked in an indignant knot. "But that's mad! If the brooch is still here, then the silver they found in my purse clearly came from selling something else. My mother's ring, as I told the baron at the time."

"Then Lady Gwenllian will say I stole the brooch alone. She is determined to blame me for its disappearance all these years, and, Jevon, I cannot prove that I did not."

He gave a short, sharp whistle. "So that's why we are here?"

Constantia nodded. "I was in Lady Gwenllian's chamber all the time. I knew where she kept the key to her jewelry casket."

"So did Beatris and Guia."

"But she is not blaming them. She is blaming me. And you know the baron will heed her. My father will not defend me. He has as good as disowned me in favor of my sister. Now that there is no hope of a fortune for me to bring to Llygad, Lady Gwenllian says I am nothing but a drain upon her husband's house. If she demands it, the baron will banish me from

Pennault the way he banished you. Your earl will not take you to England with him if you bring a wife who is a thief."

She did not mention the baroness's threat of branding. Constantia might find safety from banishment within a nunnery, but a judgment of branding would enrage Jevon. He would try to challenge it on her behalf, and that would anger the baron and further complicate Jevon's own exoneration. Jevon had borne enough. She would not let him suffer one more day by trying to protect her.

He sat down rather heavily atop the oat barrel. "I wish we were there now. Gunthar says in England, they require more than a simple accusation to condemn a man."

Did that generous law extend to women? It did not signify because—

"We are not in England," she said. "We are in Poitou. And at Pennault, Lord Laurant is the only one whose judgment matters."

Jevon did not know how long he and Constantia remained in the cellar, but he felt certain it was more than a day. To pass the time and divert their apprehension over what would happen when someone finally let them out, they sat in the straw and played three-in-a-row, mills, and fox-and-geese, improvising markers with peas and beans they found in the barrels. They dined on the same dried vegetables, fruits, and hard cheese Constantia complained she and the others had consumed for over a week while waiting for the siege to end.

She groaned. "I do not think I can swallow one more shriveled apple slice."

"There is no help for that." Jevon dropped several pieces into her hand. "But since Lady Gwenllian is not here to ration the wine, we can drink to our hearts' content."

Constantia laughed. "You had better weaken it with water from those clay pitchers. No one would be surprised to find a man completely drunk from being locked up with barrels of wine, but a fuddled woman? That would be as ruinous to her reputation as spending the night alone with a man."

Her playful irony did not escape him. He'd doused the lantern three times to save fuel and encourage Constantia to rest. But the darkness lulled him to sleep, too, and although he tried to maintain a discreet distance between them in case the cellar door opened while they slumbered and caught them in a compromising embrace, somehow he always woke to find her tucked snugly in his arms.

She only sought warmth from the cold. But if she'd understood how her nestling nearness intoxicated him more than the wine—He hoped she never noticed the way he pressed her closer with groggy desire before starting awake and abruptly releasing her. She never said anything about either reaction. But then, by the time he found his tinderbox and relit the lantern, she had shifted safely away and subdued any blush on her cheeks.

If he asked her again, would she truly choose him this time? Leave all she loved at Pennault and follow him—where? He knew the answer he ached for, but whether it were still possible . . .

While she ate the apple slices, he cleared a spot on the hard-packed earth floor and arranged some of the straw strands into squares, one inside another. There was no point in wasting this precious time together in morose conjectures of their future when he could weave a hopeful, if unlikely, dream with her instead.

The wine, watered though it was, made him bold. "When I am pardoned and knighted, I shall be the most envied man in all the king's domains for my dazzling wife."

Constantia sat across from him on a "bed" of straw and placed some strands of her own diagonally from the center square's corners and straight from the square's sides to form the lines for another game of mills. She sighed. "Your imaginary bride is not dazzling. Lady Gwenllian is dazzling."

Jevon's heart hitched with encouragement when she chose to join his verbal game. "I suppose if you like eyes that glisten like sapphires and hair that sheens like spun gold and deliciously graceful curves . . ."

She glared at him across their improvised game board, but the lantern light hinted at gilt-flecked twinkles in her glower. "You do not think your beloved's figure delicious? Her curves have blossomed since she was seventeen."

He realized that all too well by now but responded skeptically, "I must reserve my judgment of that for our wedding night."

She leaned across the "board" and punched his shoulder but giggled. He grinned. The wine made them both bold, and perhaps a little giddy.

He counted nine dried peas into her palm, then nine beans into his own before chiding, "Do not interrupt me. I was about to add that I suppose if you like deliciously graceful curves and are content to spend your days being manipulated to within an inch of your life just to boast that, though you were fool enough to marry a shrew, she is a very beautiful shrew."

"While you," Constantia said, setting a pea on one of the intersections of straw lines about the board, "married a dowerless drudge who spent so much time in the sun that her cheeks resemble leather."

"The buttery-soft kind only rich men can afford." Jevon placed a bean on the board.

"And streaky, meandering brown hair." She set down another pea.

"Not meandering. Charmingly defiant of tedious constraint." He positioned another bean.

"Filled with rats' nests." She blocked his attempt to form a three-sequenced "mill" of beans with a third pea.

Fortunately, there were nineteen more placements he could try to win with.

His hands had been perfectly content to cradle her head with its mane of tangled tresses against his shoulder each time they fell asleep, but now he conceded, "Well, the rats' nests will have to go before we marry. Even I have certain standards for my wedding."

Her head tilted inquiringly. "What would those standards be?"

"She must be gowned in blue." The color of purity.

"She looks better in green."

"Did I say blue? I meant green." Even better. The shade would turn her eyes the color of spring, the hue of faithfulness in love.

"And red slippers," she said, blocking his mill a second time.

He frowned at the board and her choice of shoes. "Red? That is a martial color. Everyone will think I am marrying a battle maiden."

"We cannot have that," she acknowledged. "That would be as bad as marrying a shrew." She slid herself around the board until she sat beside him.

Ah, you think to distract me from the game with your womanly charms.

It worked. The heat radiating from her body caused such a kindling in his blood that he slapped his next bean in between two lines and had to nudge it into place with his fingertip.

Constantia smiled. "Nevertheless, she insists on red slippers. But she is not insensitive to her husband's pride. She will embroider her shoes with black for meekness." She placed another pea on the straw lines, then kissed his jaw.

Did she feel the thrill that ran through him? "Black is for prudence—and grief. Does she want everyone to think she mourns her marriage to me?" He swiftly set down another random bean, hoping for a second kiss somewhat closer to his lips.

"Then murrey for meekness."

His hope remained unfulfilled as she studied the board.

"*Murrey* means victory. It would be an embarrassment to my manhood for the wedding party to think my wife held the victory over me rather than the other way around." He dropped a kiss on the top of her head, hoping it might provoke a response in kind.

She completed a three-sequenced mill and removed one of his beans. "Gold, then, for—"

"Stantia, there is no color that represents meekness."

"I know. I just wanted to see if you knew." She giggled again.

No more wine for you. He raised his mug to his lips. As a man, he had more fortitude against the potent drink than she.

"Then you choose the embroidery for her slippers," she said. "Their color will signify her submissiveness to you."

"And begin our marriage with a lie? Let's settle on white for truth. For if there is one truth in my heart above all, it is how very much I love you."

She swiveled and rewarded this reply with a full and heady kiss. Swifter than thought, their arms entwined, and the peas and beans scattered as he lowered her to the floor. She returned his passion so eagerly he could not tell whether he plundered her lips or she plundered his. She flooded him with so much hope it nearly blinded him.

Until his fingers snagged on a knot in her hair and provoked a brief, wincing protest from her. He pulled away. She tried to draw him back, but he evaded her. A deep breath of dank cellar air dissipated the rashness that had engulfed him. What was he doing? They were not yet wed, and with an unknown judgment hanging over their heads, they might never be. Unless Gunthar absolved Jevon of his "crime," he would never be more than an outlaw or accursed mercenary. He was no more willing to drag Constantia through such a life now than he was seven years ago.

He sat up, shoved a hand through his hair, and sucked in more of the stale air. *Fool! No more wine for me either.*

She sat up with him and rubbed his shoulder with a puzzled look.

"Those knots in your hair have got to go," he repeated. "I insist on flowers for our wedding day, not rats' nests." His voice came out too husky for the jest.

To his relief, she took up his bantering refrain. "You are unreasonable, sir. If I must comb my hair to please you, I demand you shave this off to please me." She ran her fingers over his beard.

"But I have grown quite fond of it." He stroked the bristles affectionately. "Perhaps fonder than I am of you."

"Then there shall be no more kisses, for it scratches my palms when I caress your face"—she placed her hands against his cheeks—"and make my lips itch when we do this." She kissed him again, swift and hard, then leaned away with twinkling eyes and scrabbled her fingertips over her mouth as though scratching an irritation away.

"You order me about like a count," he complained. "We may as well drape you entirely in murrey for our wedding, gown, slippers, girdle, veil, and all, to trumpet who will be master of whom in our marriage." He fondled his beard again. It felt silky enough to him. "At least let me keep this until after we speak our vows to spare my pride."

"But I may have grown fond of it, too, by then. I confess, it does make you look . . ." She trailed off, considering him.

"Handsomer? Say handsomer."

She laughed. "Oh, certainly! And older, too, less callow than the foolish boy who asked a dowerless girl to marry him and got himself banished for his trouble." Her face suddenly went bleak and solemn. "You are not really going to take me with you when you leave Pennault again, are you?"

His brows drew together, and he rubbed the taut spot between them. "That depends on Gunthar."

Everything rested on the earl's opinion of Jevon when he and Constantia were released from their cellar prison. But if Gunthar intended to dismiss Lady Gwenllian's accusations, if Jevon had acquitted himself in the last stage of the siege enough to convince the earl once and for all of his worth and faith, surely the door would have been unlocked by now?

"You know I do not care a whit if we live out the rest of our days hiding in the woods together?"

"But I'd care, Stantia."

"I know." She leaned her head against his chest, her arms sliding around his waist. "It will not stop me from following you this time, though. Nothing will."

He held her a little longer until the oppressive shadows swallowed up the last glow of joy that had permeated him with rosy but delusive dreams. When the final spark snuffed out, he released her and stood up.

"I need to stretch my legs."

"I've grown stiff too." She held up a hand to him.

He helped her rise but set her fingers free as soon as he could without offending her. He picked up the lantern and circled the cellar, studying the barrels. She followed him like a shadow, as though fearful he might vanish if she permitted too much space to drift between them. He half-heartedly wished he might, indeed, disappear in a puff of smoke. He had suffered too many partings from her these last few days. He did not think he could endure one more. But if Gunthar gave him no choice, Jevon would walk away again. Anything to protect her from the hunted life he would be forced to resume.

"How much time do you think has passed?" she asked as the lantern illuminated the word *peas* scratched into the barrel from which he had scooped some of their game markers.

"A few days at least. I do not think it has been a week." How long would Gunthar linger at Pennault? He left Vere within a day.

Jevon moved to the oat barrel and lifted the lantern to view the wall.

"You say this is where Heléne found the brooch?" At first he saw only a black crevice in the mortar, the opening perhaps the width of two fingers. Then something glittered in the lantern's flame, so dimly he had to lean over the barrel to be sure he hadn't imagined it. "There is something else in there."

Pushed to the back of the crevice.

He handed the lantern to Constantia, then rolled the barrel away from the wall and slid his finger inside the small gap. The space narrowed, but with some persistence, he encountered something metallic. A ring. Stuck in a position that enabled him to slip his fingertip just far enough inside to snag it and pull it out.

Three narrow bands of gold twisted in a braid formed an elegant circle. The ring bore a fine ruby, but the surface looked scratched, probably from a hasty shove into its hiding place in the wall's broken mortar.

Constantia gave a small gasp. "That belonged to Lady Gwenllian. I have wondered for years what became of it."

Jevon's lip curled. "It must have vanished after I left, or she would have blamed me for this disappearing too. Who bore her wrath in my place?"

"No one. She said she misplaced it and made us swear we would not tell the baron of her carelessness." Constantia lifted her gaze from the crimson jewel to Jevon's face. "Lord Laurant lavishes so many trinkets on her she cannot remember them all. She is especially disdainful of the ones she thinks fail to flatter her, the yellow and purple stones. The baron smiles when she gives those away as a display of her husband's wealth and generosity to visitors who come to the castle, but he frowns when she does the same to his men for trivial services they perform for her. She does not care when her amber and topaz and amethyst jewels go missing, but the rubies and emeralds and sapphires she hoards. It never made sense that she was so dismissive of losing this."

The baroness exploded with rage when her emerald-and ruby-encrusted brooch disappeared. Why the difference?

"Do you think she has taken a lover?"

"I have worried she has taken a lover."

Another time, Jevon would have grinned at the affinity that prompted their simultaneous suspicion. But this was too serious a matter.

Constantia's forehead knit. "I could not help but wonder when the trinkets began disappearing. Lady Gwenllian has always had so many admirers, and she clearly enjoys men's outrageous flatteries. But I never saw any provocative signs from her, no blushes, no furtive glances or enigmatic smiles, no hints of secret rendezvous. We have all watched her closely through the years with men too foolish to hide their open desire for her, but no one has watched her more closely than Lord Laurant. Although he frowns at times, he has never once accused her of infidelity. If she and the baron ever had a row about it, it would have carried to our chamber."

Jevon lifted a brow at Constantia's comment.

"That is how we heard about Llygad's disgrace," she said. "Laurant's roar carried all the way through their chamber door to ours. He would not have shouted any softer if he'd suspected his wife of betraying him with another man."

Jevon observed the baroness for years, too, before his banishment. "Lady Gwenllian is many wretched things but she has never been a ninny. If she gave a ring like this to a lover, it would be to some man who would only dare flaunt it far away from the baron. It would not have ended up hidden in the cellar for—how long did you say this ring has been gone?"

"Years. Almost as long as"—Constantia's eyes widened—"as you, Jevon. Someone took both this and the brooch and hid them here in the cellar. A traveling knight would have taken them with him, so it had to be someone from the castle. Whoever stole them has remained silent all these years and let you suffer for his crime."

Her hands fisted and trembled slightly. With anger?

It was easy enough for Jevon to surmise why both items had been stashed in the cellar. "Likely the thief was too afraid to sell them after he saw how Laurant punished me."

Constantia's forehead puckered again before she turned in a slow circle. "Do you think he hid the rest down here too?"

"The rest? How many of her trinkets remain unaccounted for?" Trinkets. What a ridiculous word for the baroness's jewels.

Constantia took a moment to think. "Two more rings, both silver, one with an amethyst, the other a yellow jasper. A brooch studded with pearls, which she loves, but also topaz, which she despises. And a silver chain without any stones at all. She simply thought that one too dull." Constantia stopped turning when she faced Jevon once more.

He whistled. "If I'd known Lady Gwenllian was so dismissive of her jewels, I might have raided her jewelry casket for every purple and yellow bauble I could find and sold them to the pilgrim for a dowry for you. You and I might have been well married by now."

Constantia's eyes fell from his. "I know you are jesting." Her voice grew small and ashamed. "I should have known you innocent just as surely all these years."

"You could not have known the source of the silver they found in my bag." He said it firmly to comfort her, even though a little, still-bruised part of him agreed with her.

Her gaze remained fixed on the floor. "But after you were banished, there were never any reports of a robber in the woods. You would have been perfectly justified to steal to survive."

"Well, I did steal a few of the baron's deer." Jevon tried to coax her to join his smile, but she would not look at him.

"To eat. That is different. If you had accosted any travelers, we would have heard complaints from knights and pilgrims and tradesmen seeking hospitality or conducting business at the castle. None ever breathed a word of such encounters. You may have poached to eat, but for everything else, you scrabbled by, picking up lost items when you could have stolen them instead. *You burned your own hand* in a bid to live respectably rather than immorally." She gave a half-gulping, half-sobbing gurgle. "You were treated wretchedly and unjustly"—tears streaked her cheeks—"yet still chose honesty. I should have realized that years ago. Instead, I spent seven years doubting you. Seven years!"

It still hurt that she could ever have believed him guilty. But had he been any fairer to her? He stared long and hard inside himself.

"And I spent seven years believing you accused me to Lady Gwenllian. I convinced myself you were a double-crossing wench because I was jealous of the kindness you showed the other squires—including Llygad—when I selfishly wanted your kindness all for myself. I see now what that brash, callow squire I was could not. That generous heart of yours was why I loved you then. It is why I love you now and why I always will. I would not change a single kind, generous hair on your head—even if it were forever tangled in insurmountable knots."

A reflexive chuckle bubbled from her. He slid a finger beneath her chin to force her gaze back to his. Through the tears, her eyes glowed like greenwood kissed by the sun.

She wiped the wet streaks from her cheeks. "You are right. We were too young to think we were ready to wed. But Jevon"—she pressed her palm to her breast, then laid the flat of her hand against his—"my whole heart belongs to only you now. When we are free of this prison, I will go wherever you ask me to, even if I must follow you to your atrocious earl's camp." She wrinkled her nose with distaste and courageous sacrifice.

Jevon laughed. "I cannot ask a higher proof of your love than that."

He kissed her, fervent with forgiveness, repentance, gratitude, and no little pure, straightforward passion. He savored her lips, the caressive strokes of her hand along his beard, her small moan of pleasure when he pressed a kiss to the sweet column of her neck . . . until another uneasy qualm about Gunthar pulled his mouth away. He handed Constantia the ring and took the lantern from her before the flame exposed his worry that her sacrifice might have come too late.

"Let's see if the thief hid the other missing trinkets down here too," he said.

She laced her fingers with his. Starting from the crack where the ring and brooch had been concealed, they searched together bit by bit along the walls. They paused for Jevon to swing the lantern close each time they came across a suspicious blemish in the stones and mortar. Sometimes the marks were scrapes or stains or smears left over time. The cracks they did find were too small to hold a piece of jewelry.

But those were all in the walls above the barrels. What about behind them? Jevon returned the lantern to Constantia so he could move the storage containers.

"Are they not too heavy?" Constantia asked.

A few of them made him huff, but he was not about to confess as much to her. He replied breezily, "Oh no. Easy as— *uhn—uhn—*" This one seemed determined to put the lie to his bravado.

"Easy as an apoplexy?" she quipped. "If your face gets any redder, I am afraid you'll fall into a fit."

He stopped shoving at the barrel and scratched his head. "The lid says *turnips*, but I promise you I could lift a barrel of turnips. What could be in here instead?"

He tried to pry off the lid but failed.

"Be careful," Constantia warned. "Lady Gwenllian has not allowed turnips at the table since a dish of turnip soup made Sir Eudes's lips swell. I think it was something Therri put in the soup, for turnips never made Sir Eudes sick before, and Therri's eyes twinkled naughtily when Sir Eudes ran out of the hall with his hands over his bloated mouth. But now Lady Gwenllian is adamantly averse to turnips, which means these have sat in the barrel for at least three years."

Three years? Jevon balked. He was tempted to abandon the barrel's undoubtedly rotted contents, but spoilage would not account for the weight. He searched the cellar for something to force the lid open, Constantia following with the lantern. Half hidden beneath a small heap of hay in a corner, they found an iron kitchen skewer.

"Some of the castle servants brought items with them for weapons when Sir Baudri locked us in here," Constantia said, "in case your earl's men found us and were not as honorable as you said they would be."

Jevon returned to the barrel with the skewer. "I should be able to break open the lid with this. Stand back. And cover your nose."

Constantia retreated with the lantern, her nose pressed into the crook of her sleeve. Jevon sincerely wished he had something to tie over his face, but since he did not, he braced himself to absorb the inevitable reek like a man.

He had to splinter some of the wood before he could slide the skewer deep enough to hoist up the lid. He took a deep breath, held it, then levered the skewer until the lid popped up.

Constantia cringed as the lid flew open, instinctively shrinking from the rancid blast before it hit her. Jevon recoiled and flung his arm over his nose. Then his arm dropped to his side, and he straightened, staring into the barrel. She cautiously lowered her sleeve. Only stale, musty cellar air flowed into her lungs.

"Why would anyone fill a barrel with this?" he said.

She rejoined him as he lifted an irregularly shaped rock the size of his open hand. The barrel was filled with similar-sized pieces of jagged stone.

She held the lantern over the contents. "I have no idea, but I know where this came from. Lord Laurant anticipated incurring the king's anger when he threw his support to Duke Richard, so the baron raised the height of the gatehouse and some of the walls and towers. This looks like the rubble the workmen used to strengthen the core of the new portions of the wall. There are piles of such stones in the bailey, for the work was not complete when your earl surrounded the castle."

"I saw the changes and the unfinished merlons. But why put such rubble in a barrel?" Jevon stroked his beard with his free hand. "Unless someone did not want it moved."

He held the rock out to Constantia. She set the lantern on a neighboring barrel, slid the ring onto her finger so as not to further damage the ruby, then took the shard and placed it on the floor while he dug out a second rugged stone. Piece by piece, they emptied the barrel of rubble until halfway down, little piles of grain appeared between the shards. Wheat, or perhaps rye.

She saw the questioning lift of her brows mirrored in Jevon's as they exchanged glances. They removed the rest of the shards until only the grain remained. Without the weight of the rubble, he easily rolled the half-filled barrel away from the wall.

He startled her with a shout of laughter before she saw it too. A few inches above the floor, someone had carved into the now-bared wall: *Lady Gwenllian is a witch.*

"It is not funny, Jevon," Constantia said, even as she failed to smother a giggle. "If Lady Gwenllian sees that, she will have Sybil switch whoever wrote it."

He wiped tears of mirth from his cheeks. "But it is true. So is that."

He pointed at an image crudely carved into the wall beside the words: a woman's face with a wiggly frown for a mouth, an inverted V for angry eyebrows, a pair of crossed eyes, and hair that extended in every direction with serpents' heads and forked tongues at the ends of each strand. The artist clearly loathed the baroness.

That described nearly every woman in the castle except for Lady Heléne.

"Do not worry," Jevon said, "I will replace the barrel with the rubble inside so she never sees it."

Aside from the scurrilous depiction and commentary, the wall and mortar were unmarred. Constantia saw no place to hide any jewelry. Jevon looked as disappointed as she. He swiveled the barrel back into place and picked up one of the discarded shards but stopped short of placing it inside.

"What?" she asked when he hesitated.

"Perhaps the rubble was placed here to conceal more secrets than one. Step back."

"Why?"

"Because if you don't, I am going to empty that grain on top of your shoes."

She scurried out of the way as Jevon turned the barrel onto its side, then lifted its base and poured out the grain.

"Oh!" Constantia exclaimed.

As the grain tumbled out, the lantern caught a multitude of glitters and gleams. Together, she and Jevon knelt and dove their hands into the pile of kernels. Jevon pulled out three rings, four chains, and two brooches. Constantia gathered five rings, three chains, one brooch, a pendant, and a paternoster made of smooth, yellow stones with carved ivory gauds. Like the sacred beads, all the jewelry, silver and gold alike, was adorned with gems of yellow or purple.

How had she overlooked so many? She supposed because the pieces Lady Gwenllian disliked usually ended up at the bottom of her jewelry casket, buried beneath her favorites. The baron showered so many gifts on his wife that Constantia had long since given up counting them.

"There must be a small fortune here!" She held up the paternoster. The pattern worked into the ivory beads looked as delicate as lace, while the folds in the gown of the tiny ivory woman dangling at the end looked so real Constantia fancied she could hear the fabric faintly rustle. The woman's hands were poised in prayer.

If the jewelry were gifts, it would not be hidden in a barrel of grain. Someone must have taken them without Lady Gwenllian's knowledge. But how? Besides the baroness, only Constantia, Guia, and Beatris had access to the casket's key, and they were all too afraid of Sybil's switch to do anything so reckless.

A memory checked her. Jevon had also seen where Lady Gwenllian kept the key when he attended her as a squire. After Jevon left, Llygad took his place. Could Llygad possibly have been foolish enough to steal these? Constantia had defended him to Jevon when Jevon suspected Llygad of finding the brooch and letting Jevon bear the blame for its disappearance. But with so many items missing, who else could the thief be?

If Llygad intended to sell the jewels to marry Guia, he either had second thoughts or had simply not yet found the opportunity.

Unwilling for the moment to confide her thoughts and risk a smug, "I told you so," Constantia placed the paternoster in her lap and picked up the pendant. An amethyst three times as large as the ruby in the ring on her finger hung in a frame of silver swirls and tiny diamonds.

"Ho, what have we here?"

Constantia almost dropped the pendant. She scrambled up from her knees, gathering the jewels in her hands, then whirled toward the shaft of light behind her. The cellar door was open, and a man with a torch stood on the next to the last step of the stairs. No wonder she had seen the folds in the saint's gown and the tracery in the ivory gauds so clearly. The light must have streamed over her shoulder and she'd been too engrossed to notice.

Jevon rose more slowly, his deep, steady breathing joining with the hammering of her heart. Raimon. He left the stairs and moved toward them, his gaze sweeping from the rings and brooches in her and Jevon's hands and the chains dangling from their fingers to the spilled grain and pile of rubble on the floor. When his eyes returned to her face, his expression was unreadable.

But the glare he turned on Jevon blistered with contempt. "Some of the earl's men avouched their belief in your innocence before they left, but they were only archers, so no one paid them any heed. Your earl certainly did not. He has left your fate in Laurant's hands. The baron appears unsure how to deal with you, but *this* will settle his mind." Raimon motioned at the incriminating evidence.

"The earl is gone?" Jevon's breathing, like his voice, grew suddenly tight.

"Two days ago. The baron had other matters to deal with, like raising the fine your earl demanded to convince the king Laurant's renewed fealty to him is sincere and arranging terms of safe conduct for the Lady Clothilde to be escorted from Blancaval to Pennault. Muck like you has had to wait."

Constantia fisted her knuckles around the jewels. "Raimon, you are speaking to Jevon." Whatever Raimon thought Jevon had done, they had once been friends.

"I am speaking to a traitor." Raimon's retort clapped the air like the slap of a hand. "Tell me I am wrong, Jevon. Tell me you did not share Pennault's secrets with your earl to help bring down our walls."

Constantia almost threw another indignant rebuke at Raimon, but Jevon's silence stopped her. Of course. Raimon was right. Jevon would have revealed all he recalled of Pennault's defenses. Why wouldn't he after the cruel injustices Laurant had dealt him?

Raimon's lip curled when Jevon did not deny the accusation. "Laurant was merciful when he let you go free with only the brand of a thief on your hand. He said that was payment enough for the loss of a single brooch. But when he sees all of this—"

"Jevon never took the brooch," Constantia interrupted him. "Did not Lady Heléne tell you she found it safe, here in the cellar?"

Raimon's gaze whisked back to her. "Lady Gwenllian gave that story exactly the weight it deserved. None. The silver they found on him"—

Raimon jerked his head toward Jevon—"proves he stole and sold something. So what if he did not have time to sell the brooch too? He was a thief then, and he is a thief now. When the baron sees the two of you dripping with Lady Gwenllian's stolen jewels, this time he will lop off Jevon's hand, if not his head. Your hand, too, Constantia. Unless you convince Laurant you knew nothing about this when the earl's men locked you down here."

Constantia shuddered. She had tried to brace herself for the branding iron, but to lose her hand entirely?

"Constantia had nothing to do with these jewels." Jevon's voice cut like a keen-edged knife. "And I have been gone for seven years. How could I possibly have stolen all of these?"

"You could have hidden them down here before you were banished. And Constantia could have helped you. She knew where the key to the jewels was kept, she must have given it to you. Unless she stole them herself and let you take the blame. Which was it, Constantia?"

"Neither," Jevon snapped.

But Constantia knew neither of them could prove it. She knew some of these jewels had disappeared after Jevon's banishment, but with Lady Gwenllian's negligent interest in these particular stones and her grudge over the missing brooch she *had* valued, she would be ready to jump to the same conclusion as Raimon. Especially now that Jevon bore the added stigma of betraying their castle to the English.

Raimon shifted the torch so that the light flowed over Constantia. His glare softened. "If you reconsider my offer to join me as my wife when I go tourneying in the spring, I will keep you safe from any consequence of this. Laurant will listen to me. He favors me more than any other knight. He will believe me if I tell him you are innocent of conspiring with this despicable cur."

"*I* am despicable?" Jevon said. "What about you when you nearly speared Therri trying to disembowel me outside the postern? But impulsiveness was always your weakness, Raimon. Too impassioned with your sword strikes, too cocky in your lance's aim. It was no wonder I could always best you. I thought we were friendly rivals, but the truth is, you were jealous of me, weren't you? Is that why you want Constantia? If she says she will marry you, will that prove you are better than me now?"

Raimon's features twisted before flattening into a hard mask. "I do not need to prove anything. Laurant knows my value as clearly as he remembers how you turned on him like a rabid dog and bit the hand that trusted you to guard his wife and children. He did not know the true depths of your depravity then, but he will have no doubt of it now. Constantia"—Raimon swung back to her—"what am I to tell the baron?"

She, too, had not forgotten how Raimon's recklessness had come so near to harming Therri. But Raimon had boasted for years how he planned to become a renowned and glorious knight. Despite his envy, perhaps if she appealed to his chivalry, he would live up to its ideals.

"I have always been truthful about my feelings for you, Raimon. However much I have disappointed you, you have always known me to be honest. You know I would never steal from Lady Gwenllian or anyone else. The integrity of the title you bear should compel you to urge the baron to believe Jevon and me when we swear by any oath he asks that neither of us is responsible for taking or hiding these jewels."

Instead of defusing Raimon's anger, her words drew another blazing, injured glare from him. "I will swear to what I saw, your and Jevon's hands full of plunder. Do I even need to wonder how you two have passed the time while locked down here? I doubt I would even find you still a maid if you said yes to my offer. When the baron sees that ruby ring on your finger, he will know you for what you are—a conniving, pilfering harlot who conspired to sell our secrets to Henry the Angevin's English devils to avenge your thieving lover."

Constantia glanced at her hand. The condemning ruby stared back at her like a great accusatory eye.

A loud crack snapped her head back up. Raimon's feet flew out from under him before he hit the ground in an ungainly sprawl.

"Call her a harlot again," Jevon warned, his fist still hovering in the air, "and I will give Laurant something worse than theft to punish me for."

"Jevon, don't." She would have grabbed his arm had her hands not been full of the convicting jewels.

Raimon scrabbled up, more gawkily than gracefully. He scooped up the torch he had dropped, thankfully on the bare patch of earth they had cleared to play mills. As Jevon lowered his fist, Raimon pulled his sword from its scabbard and leveled it at Jevon's chest.

"Are you going to come with me peaceably, or will I need this to persuade you?"

"We will come with you," Constantia said before Jevon could do anything more to provoke him.

It took all her willpower to clamp down her panic. The only thing that terrified her more than the thought of the iron or the knife was losing Jevon again. She felt the brush of Jevon's hand as he tried to catch her arm before she moved toward the stairs.

"Stantia!" he shouted.

Did he guess what she intended? She mounted the steps with a quickened pace to avoid him pushing past Raimon and his sword to stop her.

The great hall's rush-covered floor lay empty of trestle tables save for the still white-clothed table on the dais. The table had been cleared off, but the lingering aroma of roasted meats and savory sauces mocked Constantia's ravenous hunger after the cellar's meager fare. Most of the midday diners had dispersed, but dread pricked over her at the few men who remained. They were the older, most seasoned of the baron's knights, the ones he summoned to council whenever a weighty matter lay before him. The same knights who had condemned Jevon to branding and banishment.

The men stared gravely at Constantia and Jevon as Raimon ushered them into the hall. None spoke. All waited for Laurant's reaction, but the baron did not immediately appear aware of them. He paced back and forth on the dais in front of the table, hands locked behind his back, the long tunic beneath his plain brown surcote swishing against his ankles. Lady Gwenllian saw them though and frowned.

Poised in the elaborately carved chair beside her husband's empty one, she sat as regal as a queen. Rays of sunshine streamed through the high windows, firing the vibrant threads Constantia and Guia spent so many hours embroidering into the silk surcote that hugged the baroness's curves enticingly. The same brilliant sunlight ignited the varicolored jewels in the circlet that held her snowy veil in place over the shimmering waves of gilded hair that trailed over her dainty shoulders.

Beatris stood to the right of the baroness, holding a silver plate of what looked like almond cakes, while Guia, on the baroness's left, held a goblet rimmed with blue and red gems.

When Lady Gwenllian saw the jewelry in Constantia's hands, her bewitching face went white. Constantia knew the baroness would not let loose her fury in front of her husband's knights. Oh no. Before men, Lady Gwenllian ever played the lovely, if strong-willed, enchantress. She drew her husband's abstracted attention with an elegant but distinct clearing of her throat.

Laurant glanced at his wife, observed the direction of her brittle posture, and turned toward the floor beneath the dais.

"What is this, Constantia?" The baron looked genuinely baffled by the jewelry.

Raimon answered before she could. "The baroness's jewels, my lord. Lady Constantia and de Cazalet had all these hidden in the cellar in a barrel of grain."

Raimon nudged Jevon forward with the point of his sword to stand alongside Constantia with his jumble of stolen "baubles."

"We found them," Constantia confessed, "but we did not steal them, my lord." She would do whatever she had to, but if the truth could save them first—

Raimon gave a scornful grunt. "Of course she would say that. But the silver we found on de Cazalet seven years ago was intended to create her a dowry." Raimon looked at Constantia in challenge. "Do you deny that he asked you to marry him before the brooch went missing?"

Constantia had confided Jevon's proposal to no one at the time, and Jevon insisted he'd told no one about his mother's ring. But from the look on his face, she realized he must not have been as cautious about sharing his hope to marry her with Raimon and perhaps with Franco. After all, Jevon had considered them both almost as brothers, something Constantia never felt for Guia and Beatris.

Raimon took her pause as confirmation. "They were undoubtedly in on the theft of the brooch together, along with all of these. They plundered my lady's jewelry casket and hid their spoils in the cellar. The missing brooch led to de Cazalet's banishment before they could sell it with the rest of my lady's jewels. Now he's had his revenge by helping the English destroy our walls and abasing us all before his earl, especially you, my lord. He planned to rub your humiliation further in your face by running off with Constantia and these jewels once and for all."

Lady Gwenllian rose with a rigid grace. "Sir Raimon is right. The English could never have defeated us had de Cazalet not exposed our weaknesses."

Worse than theft of the jewels, Constantia knew the fall of Pennault Castle was a sin the baroness would never forgive. She would do her utmost to make her husband punish Jevon even more brutally than before.

"As for the jewels, no one had access to my jewelry casket except myself, Constantia, Beatris, and Guia." Rather than distorting her delicate features, Lady Gwenllian's quivering anger only made her sparkle more radiantly. "I always suspected that Constantia gave Jevon my brooch to sell, but she averted suspicion from herself by accusing him alone."

Constantia's hands clenched the jewels so hard the edges cut into her palms. "I never accused Jevon. I told you he borrowed your brooch to repair the clasp, but you would not believe me."

She stopped as the shame she could never quite shake choked her afresh. She may not have accused Jevon, but when she saw his pile of silver, she'd allowed the poison of doubt to enter her mind.

The baron frowned. "Bring those jewels closer. Let me see."

Constantia stepped to the edge of the dais. She resisted glancing at Jevon as he joined her, still too mortified she had not believed him from the first.

Lady Gwenllian rustled over to join her husband as Laurant bent down to examine the pieces. Constantia could scarcely breathe as she awaited his thundering anger.

Laurant turned to his wife. "These are all gifts I gave you. You complained when the brooch disappeared but said nothing about these going missing. Did you not even notice?"

Lady Gwenllian looked taken aback.

"My love," the baron said in the pause of her hesitation, "I have never complained when you gave trinkets to my knights for performing services that please you. Largesse is a virtue expected from lord and lady alike." He glanced at his knights below the dais, some of whom wore rings and chains of yellow and purple gems. Despite Laurant's munificent disclaimer, a small pinching of his features contradicted his praise of her generosity before he looked back at his wife. "But if Sir Raimon is correct that these simply went missing without your knowledge . . . well, I should be loath to think you did not receive these with the same affection with which I gave them to you."

Constantia had not expected this reaction. Instead of swift condemnation of the "thieves," Laurant looked honestly hurt that his wife had not valued his gifts enough to remember them all despite their excessive number.

"You have given me so many . . ." Lady Gwenllian faltered, then rallied, "and I *did* notice all these were missing. But however certain I was that Constantia stole them, I could not prove it, and I would never accuse anyone of something as serious as theft without evidence of guilt."

Bitterness made Constantia's tongue reckless. "That is exactly what you did when you accused Jevon. You never had any proof that he stole your brooch. Neither of you did."

"We had the silver." Lady Gwenllian's icy stare challenged Constantia. "You see how pertly she speaks to you, husband. You have been her lord and protector all these years, have fed her, clothed her, and boarded her all at your own expense, and she repays you with audacity as well as theft. What further proof do you need of her guilt, and Jevon's, too, than the evidence they hold in their own hands?"

Instead of replying, Laurant pulled a piece of folded parchment from his belt, opened it, and frowned at whatever was written inside.

Lady Gwenllian watched him with a petulant pout. "You have had your brows knit over that ever since the earl left. Why will you not tell me what it says?"

The baron folded the parchment and placed it back inside his belt. "Sit down, my love."

Lady Gwenllian's mouth crimped with displeasure at having her query ignored.

In a rare moment of annoyance, Laurant's mouth mirrored its scrunch. "I beg you to show me the courtesy of respect before my men."

With an equally rare blush of embarrassment, Lady Gwenllian returned to her chair. Guia tried to hand her the goblet, but Lady Gwenllian waved it away.

"Sir Raimon," Laurant said, "put away that sword. I told you to keep your weapon sheathed unless absolutely necessary."

Raimon returned his sword to its scabbard. Something about the pommel looked different from the last time Constantia saw it, but Raimon rested his hand on it, obscuring the design as he defended his action.

"De Cazalet attacked me, my lord—"

"Attacked you?" Laurant surveyed Jevon, who was clearly unarmed. "With what?"

"His fist—"

"His fists only? You have a perfectly brawny pair of those yourself."

Raimon colored. "And he had a kitchen skewer."

"He lunged at you with a skewer?" The baron's voice sharpened.

"Well . . . no . . ."

Jevon spoke for the first time since entering the hall. "Constantia said one of the kitchen servants left it behind in the cellar. I used it to pry open the barrel because someone had sealed it shut. Yes, I hit *Sir* Raimon because he called Stantia a harlot. If I'd wanted to kill him, I'd have wrapped one of these chains around his neck after I knocked him down. But I did not, did I, *Sir* Raimon? Because I am not a murderer, nor am I a thief. And neither is Stantia."

"But you are a bald-faced liar," Lady Gwenllian said while Raimon flushed still deeper at Jevon's mocking of his knightly title. "Both of you. As though my husband cannot see the evidence right before his eyes. Why do you dither, husband? The two are clearly guilty. Ask your council if they do not agree."

The circle of knights must have observed the baron's earlier disgruntlement, for several of them tucked their hands with the baroness's rings behind their backs. But the chains and pendants on their breasts were impossible to conceal, and Sir Eudes, the gatekeeper, wore one of each.

Sir Eudes scraped his throat awkwardly. "My lord, their guilt does appear beyond dispute. De Cazalet has made it clear he stands with our enemies. He directed the final barrage of English arrows at our men. As for Lady Constantia—well, those jewels she carries speak for themselves. She and de Cazalet should be punished together, else every lowborn scrub in the castle will think they can steal my lady's belongings and who knows what else?"

Joining in the gatekeeper's surly glower at Jevon, the other knights murmured their agreement.

Two stark valleys dug between Laurant's brows as he listened to the rumbling from his council.

Beatris's eyes flared nearly as wide as when she had learned the English were at their walls. "My lord, will you brand Jevon again? And Constantia too?"

Constantia tried to suppress a shiver, but she knew Jevon felt it. She heard him draw breath to withdraw his denial and say something foolish, like, "Constantia had nothing to do with this, the blame is all mine." Constantia inhaled equally swiftly to contradict him, but before she could, Guia dropped Lady Gwenllian's goblet.

Crimson wine splashed across Lady Gwenllian's hem and slippers. Guia hurriedly bent to mop up the spill with the hem of her own gown. Lady Gwenllian leaned forward and boxed her ear.

While Guia sank to her knees, green with dizziness, Lady Gwenllian said with an ominous calm, "If Constantia is a thief, she is not immune from my husband's laws."

Guia whimpered and rocked with her hand clamped over her ear. Laurant slipped the parchment from his belt again.

Sir Baudri slid an uncertain look from the baroness to the baron. "The punishment does seem over harsh for a woman, especially one of Lady Constantia's birth. Perhaps a simple flogging would serve."

Lady Gwenllian stared hard at Sir Eudes and his chain and pendant until he said, "But there is precedent, my lord. It is well known that your grand-father branded an old crone in his village for blasphemy when she cursed the village priest who offered her mass."

Sir Milo nodded. "Petronilla the Blighted. On the night of the branding, her cottage burst into flame, smiting her and her daughter with heaven's retribution."

Three generations later, Petronilla's and her daughter's story still enter-tained the men of Pennault castle and subdued the women. Sir Milo left out the part about Petronilla's daughter having her tongue slit for accusing the same priest of seducing her.

"But Petronilla was a serf," Sir Baudri said, "and Constantia is a lady. It cannot be considered the same."

Lady Gwenllian nudged Guia away with her toe as though Guia were a bothersome dog. Guia curled her body and wrapped her arms around herself. She had lost all spirit since Llygad abandoned her, and now that Constantia knew the truth of his whereabouts, she had no way to tell her.

"Petronilla was a woman," Lady Gwenllian said to her husband, "and so is

Constantia. Did your grandfather's judgment explicitly state that he dealt her the punishment for being a serf?"

Laurant shook his head, his attention fixed again on the contents of the parchment. "The story of Petronilla has only come down as legend. I do not know whether it is true or a tale invented by my father to discourage our serfs from listening to grumblings of heresy." He tucked the parchment back into his belt.

"But, my lord," Sir Eudes said, "you quoted the case of Petronilla when you ruled on de Cazalet's punishment, to which we all gave our assent. If you rule differently now, you will be admitting that you—and we—were wrong in our judgment."

The other knights, even the hesitant Sir Baudri, nodded.

Laurant sent a sour look at his wife. According to Llygad, it had been she who'd reminded the baron and his council of the legend seven years ago and goaded her husband into branding Jevon when the baron initially appeared on the verge of pronouncing simple banishment. Lady Gwenllian's luscious lashes fluttered at her husband, and when they stilled, her jeweled eyes were filled with guileless docility. The baron's irritation instantly dissolved into one of his enamored gazes.

"I know you will judge wisely and justly, my lord," she said, meek but coaxing, "as you did before. Had they admitted their trespass and begged for your mercy, you would have been right to consider leniency. But where there is no penitence, there can be no forgiveness. You must do your duty. Constantia and Jevon are guilty together. They must suffer equally for their crime."

Mindful of Jevon's nearness, Constantia stifled another tremor.

"Precedence has been both set and followed," Sir Eudes agreed. "We are ready to give our assent to your verdict, my lord."

Some of the knights responded more loudly than others, but they all answered, "Aye."

"We are all agreed," Sir Eudes said. "Sir Raimon, go tell the blacksmith to ready the branding irons."

Irons. The finality of the judgment jarred Constantia from her shrinking inertia. If she did not act now, it would be too late to save him. She shoved herself between Jevon and the dais, riveting the baron's attention on herself.

"My lord, Jevon is innocent. *I* stole these jewels years after he left Pennault. Guia and Beatris will witness that these jewels were still in your wife's possession after Jevon's banishment." They would if Constantia convinced them that doing so would bolster their own innocence.

She ignored Jevon's sharp intake of breath from behind her. If this was the sacrifice required to stay with him, she would endure the red-hot iron. But she would *not* let him suffer that agony again.

She stared with ferocious resolve into Laurant's eyes. "Brand me. Send me from Pennault, but let Jevon leave these walls unmarred."

Jevon would embrace the flames of hell before he allowed Constantia to taste the branding iron. He shouldered her aside, flung his jewels onto the dais, then scooped the rest out of her hands and tossed them on top of the others.

"*I* took these," he said. "All of them. I meant to sell them so Constantia and I could marry. You found me out before I could, and I have borne the cost of my theft these seven years. Punish me further however you wish. Brand me again, cut off my hand, hang me, only do not lay any of this guilt on Constantia. She played no part in my crime."

He trusted he could count on Lady Gwenllian's spite for helping the English defeat her castle to override Constantia's "confession," no matter what Guia and Beatris might say.

Constantia sputtered. Amber sparks spit at Jevon from the green balefire in her eyes. "Do not listen to him, my lord. He lies to protect me. He did not know where your lady hid her key. He could not have taken the jewels."

"You mean without your help." The baroness glared down her delicate nose at Jevon and Constantia, but her expression was demurely deferential when she looked at her husband. "She and Jevon could only have planned their theft together. It is only just that Constantia bear the same punishment as he." Lady Gwenllian added a tremulous smile. "I say it to protect your honor, husband, so that no man may call you weak or arbitrary. Do as my lord bids you, Sir Raimon."

Raimon turned toward the exit to obey. Only the sudden appearance of Franco, pale and somewhat unsteady on his feet, forced Raimon to pause to listen to something Franco said.

Jevon swallowed a lump of both guilt for the arrow wound Franco suffered and relief to see him still alive before a motion from Constantia made him glance at her. Her fisted hands slid into the folds of her gown as though retreating from the disfiguring penalty pronounced. She caught his eye and shook her hands back out, lifting her chin defiantly. She was relying on Lady Gwenllian to expel her from the castle with Jevon, thus forcing him to take her with him. But she did not know—truly know—what the brand of a thief would mean.

He seized her hand and squeezed her fingers hard enough to make her wince just long enough to hold her silent. "My lord," he said, "it would be *against* your honor to punish the innocent. You gave me to serve your wife as her personal squire. I frequently received instructions from her in her chamber, and one day I saw where she hid her key. I took it without her or anyone else's knowledge." He gave Constantia's fingers another quelling scrunch. "I alone took the jewels. I hid them in the barrel until I could sell them. I took the brooch to sell first, then—"

"But you did not sell the brooch," Laurant interrupted. "Heléne showed it to us. And you did not sell these." He indicated the jumbled jewels on the dais floor. "Then what piece did you sell for the silver we found in your purse?"

Jevon's mouth hung open, too startled by the query to invent a quick answer.

"Stay, Sir Raimon," the baron said as Raimon pushed past Franco with a brusqueness that almost knocked his wobbly companion over. "And you, Sir Franco, return to your bed. You are unfit to be up and about."

Raimon rejoined the other knights with another nasty glance at Jevon while Franco said, "I heard that Jevon de Cazalet was back. I thought perhaps I might speak with him."

Jevon braced himself for the same glare of betrayal that shone in Raimon's eyes, but Franco's gaze met his with an unexpected anxiety.

"This has nothing to do with you," Laurant replied. "Go."

Franco obeyed with clear reluctance and a swaying tread.

The baron turned to his wife. "My love, pray bring down your jewelry casket. With my chaplain's aid, I have kept a list of every piece in your dowry and each gift I ever gave you. We will count them all and see if any of the pieces are missing. Sir Baudri, pray summon Father Dominic and ask him to bring the inventory of my lady's jewels."

Lady Gwenllian hesitated, then rose, graceful and self-assured. "Guia, Beatris, come with me."

Beatris began to follow, but Guia tightened her self-embrace where she still huddled on the floor. "Please, let me stay here with Constantia."

A pleat of displeasure formed on Lady Gwenllian's brow, but the baron nodded, so she swept from the hall accompanied by only by Beatris. Sir Baudri left to find the chaplain.

When they were gone, Laurant let out a slow, heavy breath and fixed his gaze on Jevon. "Now we will speak frankly."

Laurant's handsome features assumed a command Jevon forgot the baron could possess in the absence of his wife. Perhaps because Jevon's last memory of Laurant had been his nod of assent to the branding iron just before it seared his flesh.

"Seven years ago," Laurant said, "when I pronounced judgment on you, I did so in bitter disappointment of your disloyalty. You were the most gifted squire I ever fostered. You excelled at every sport that makes a man worthy of knighthood. You always fought your fellow squires fairly and were gracious in both victory and defeat. My son looked to you as a mentor and friend. Do not think I never noticed. There were times I believed he loved you more than he loved me."

"Oh no, my lord," Jevon protested.

"Oh, I did not begrudge you for it. I was grateful that if Therri must admire someone other than his father, it was a talented, honest squire. More importantly, though, I trusted you. To help Therri learn courtesy as well as martial skill. To guard him along with Constantia when my wife set her to watch him and my daughters at play. And I trusted you with my wife, to serve her as faithfully and honestly as I believed you served me. When her brooch disappeared, when I saw the silver in your purse, when you could show no proof that you sold some ring none of us had ever seen you with—I admit I felt betrayed."

Laurant walked to the baroness's chair and rested his hand on one of the decorative knobs that extended upward from either side of the tendrils and flowers carved into the arched wooden back. After a moment, he swiveled toward his knights.

"I can issue orders as shrewd as any man in battle. My courage in combat has never been questioned."

To a man, the knights, all of an age to have fought with him except for Raimon, nodded and agreed, "It is true."

"Alas," Laurant conceded, "I have not always been as adept at governing my household. My men know this as well, but if any of them had a wife as beautiful as mine, I should like to see what straits they would resort to never to lose her."

A kindling of accusation lit the baron's eyes. Had one or more of these men sought to lure Lady Gwenllian away from Laurant? Jevon had been too young and too preoccupied by his own love for Constantia to have spared two thoughts for any provocative exchanges between these knights and their lady. Laurant, on the other hand, as a jealous husband, may have caught a good many covert sighs and glances.

Did Laurant think this confession would somehow win Jevon's sympathy for the cruel judgment the baron had meted out to satisfy his beautiful wife? Or mitigate the vicious threat of the same he now threatened Constantia with?

Everything in Jevon wished to call the man "coward", but he forced himself to swallow his swelling resentment. His humility might be feigned, but his urgency was not. "My lord, I will confess to whatever crime your lady wife demands and bear the penalty for it. But I plead with you not to lay my sin at Constantia's feet."

Constantia jerked her hand away so quickly, his squeeze closed around empty air. "My lord, no! It is not just that I should escape your chastisement when I—"

"Quiet!" Laurant shouted. "I will be ruled by no more women this day." He leveled a finger at her, his face flushing as red as autumn apples. "I am not speaking to you. I am speaking to Jevon. And what I want to know is"—he swung back to Jevon—"what is the meaning of this?"

Laurant whipped the parchment from his belt and held it out. Jevon could not make out any insignia on the broken red seal.

"I do not know, my lord," he said. "Who sent it?"

"Who sent it? Read it, then you tell me." The baron flapped the parchment impatiently against the air.

When Laurant remained beside his wife's chair, Jevon mounted the dais. He glanced at Constantia as he passed her. Her lips were locked in mulish resentment of the baron's rebuke, but it would hold her quiet for now.

As Jevon joined Laurant, the baron thrust the parchment into Jevon's hand. The outside was blank, and the broken wax seal bore no device to identify the sender. Jevon opened the tri-folded note and read the single line inscribed within.

Your son is safe, thanks to Jevon de Cazalet.

"What does it mean?" This time Laurant whispered the question so that his council could not hear. When Jevon hesitated, the baron asked, "You recognize the script?"

The baron surely had. He had Pennault's chaplain instruct all his pages in reading and writing.

"It is Llygad's." Jevon matched the baron's lowered tones.

"It is Llygad's," the baron agreed. "I have not seen his face since the earl began his assault on our walls. I thought he fled in cowardice or shame for the stain he placed on my honor when he broke my truce with the earl. What, then, does this mean?"

"He did not flee, my lord. He took it upon himself to risk capture by Gunthar's men to escort Therri safely to his uncle's."

"Llygad? After the curses I flung at him and the threats I made to expel him from my service? It is *Llygad* who guarded my son to my brother's castle?" Laurant's hand wrapped again around the nob on Lady Gwenllian's chair, his knuckles white. "And what part did you play, Jevon?"

"I gave Therri my gambeson with the badge worn by Gunthar's archers. I told Therri to deliver Llygad up as a hostage if they were captured by the men Gunthar left to watch the road. The guards would give Llygad to Gunthar, but they would not suspect Therri so long as he wore the earl's badge. They would leave him free to journey on to your brother's as soon as their heads were turned, never realizing he was your son."

Laurant sank into the chair.

"Safe, safe," he uttered. "Have you any idea of the anguish I suffered when the earl returned Sir Raimon to me after my surrender? How near I came to shouting, 'But where is my son?' After the havoc Gunthar wreaked upon our walls, I dared not risk sending so devilish a man in search of my heir. The way Gunthar stared at me when he forced me to renew my oath to the king —Saints! It curdled my blood. So I have held my tongue, praying that Therri escaped you and made it to safety somewhere, somehow on his own, all the while terrified lest, in fact, he was lost or hurt or even dead."

Escaped you? He means me. "Sir Raimon told you of our encounter outside the postern gate?"

Laurant nodded weakly. "Until then, I did not know you were with the earl. As soon as Sir Raimon told me—" Laurant ran a hand across his forehead, shading his eyes. "I could not blame you for joining my enemy, for returning to Pennault with revenge in your heart for what I did to you. I feared . . . that you had made Therri . . . disappear . . . just to punish me."

To Jevon's shock, a tear rolled down the baron's cheek. The way he uttered the word *disappear* made Jevon shudder. What the baron meant was the fear he had blurted out—"even dead."

"My lord," Jevon said as Laurant wiped his nose on his sleeve and sent an anxious glance at his knights, "I could never hate any man so much as to kill his heir. I confess I considered giving Therri to the earl as a hostage to force your surrender of Pennault, but I changed my mind."

The baron scrubbed more tears away while his knights and Constantia watched. Guia had somehow found her way into Constantia's arms and appeared to be weeping against her shoulder."

"Why?" the baron asked. "Jevon, why?"

"Not because I thought Gunthar would harm Therri. The earl's tongue and stare can both cut a man to the soul, but he is no devil."

From the way Laurant pursed his lips and scrunched his brows, he clearly thought otherwise.

"And not because I have forgiven this." Jevon could not resist thrusting his branded hand under Laurant's nose.

The baron looked away as though ashamed.

"I did it for Therri, and Therri alone. Because I cared for the boy and do not believe children should pay for their parents' sins."

Laurant sat a long while in silence, avoiding Jevon's eyes.

Jevon seized the moment to look at Constantia. Her dark head dipped alongside Guia's. From the way she rubbed her hand up and down Guia's back, she must be trying to soothe the other woman's tears. Kind, compassionate, selfless Stantia. His love. His life. His own soul's twin. Wherever he went, whatever the uncertain future held for him, he would treasure their brief reunion to his dying breath.

It was not until Laurant abruptly stood that Jevon saw Lady Gwenllian had returned to the hall. A pale-cheeked Beatris walked two steps behind the baroness, carrying her jewelry casket. Lady Gwenllian stopped, a startled look on her face. Jevon glanced at Laurant and saw that the baron held up a staying hand.

"A moment, my love," Laurant said with unaccustomed firmness.

"But, husband, Beatris can tell you—"

"A moment," Laurant repeated.

Had he ever spoken so sternly to her? Lady Gwenllian scowled prettily, gathered her features into a soft, aggrieved cloud, and turned her injured gaze upon her husband's knights. They smiled consolingly back, but cautious of the baron's watchful eye, not too consolingly.

"She does not know," Laurant murmured to Jevon. "About Therri."

"How could she not know? She must have noticed his absence from the castle."

"Of course, she's missed him and has not ceased harping at me about his absence, but for now, I have assured her only that he is safe. I have been terrified that it was a lie"—Laurant ran a hand over his face, scrubbing some color back into his pallor—"but now that I know it is true . . . No. I'd best not tell her yet. She has a tendency to chatter confidences she ought not, and if word should reach the earl, it is not too late for him to seize Therri. I was certain he would come tearing back to Pennault to demand Therri's whereabouts when he read that—"

"Gunthar saw this?" Jevon interrupted when Laurant gestured at the parchment.

Laurant made a wry face. "He intercepted my brother's messenger, who'd disguised himself as a holy friar to deliver it to me. When he refused to tell the earl his destination, citing a holy confidence, one of the earl's men seized the letter, broke the seal, and read it to the earl. The messenger told me he was prepared to withstand any torture to protect the letter's intended receiver, but the earl queried him no further. He simply gathered his men and rode off with a frightfully tight set to his mouth. My brother's man waited a day to be certain no one followed him, then brought the message to me."

Jevon had known Gunthar's departure from Pennault without him could not be a mere oversight. Whether Gunthar guessed the letter's destination or not, the one thing the contents had not been cryptic about was Jevon's name.

"There is no place in my camp for a man unsure of his loyalties," the earl had said.

Gunthar did not need to know *how* he was betrayed to know that Jevon had placed some loyalty to another over his loyalty to Gunthar. Jevon did not deserve a pardon or even a humble place among Gunthar's archers. And now he knew he had truly lost both.

At a gesture from the baron, Lady Gwenllian glided with lissome grace to the dais.

"She has some mischief up her sleeve," Constantia whispered to Guia.

Guia quivered in Constantia's arms. She had not ceased sobbing, though softly, since she ran into Constantia's embrace. Either Lady Gwenllian's blow to her ear had been more painful than usual or she still grieved for Llygad.

I must tell her.

"I had nearly forgotten the pendant," Lady Gwenllian said as she joined her husband, "it had been so long since I wore it. But Beatris remembers it."

Beatris scrambled after her mistress, mumbling, "The pendant from her father."

Constantia knew no such pendant existed, but from the threads of pain at the corners of Beatris's red-rimmed eyes, Contantia guessed Sybil's rod had assisted her "memory."

Constantia tried to catch Jevon's eye to warn him of the trap. What had he and Laurant been talking about so secretively? Whatever it was had clearly distressed the baron. Jevon stood near him looking grim and unforgiving, his attention focused not on Constantia but on Lady Gwenllian.

The baroness looked as virtuously offended as a golden queen. She said to her husband, "Jevon and Constantia have insulted my father's house not once but twice, and they have shown nothing but contempt for you, their lord. Justice demands this time they both bear the brand of thief for their crimes."

Laurant stood and took the jewelry casket from her hands. "There will be no more branding."

Lady Gwenllian looked startled. "But, husband, I have proof of their guilt. And your knights have agreed the punishment is just."

Laurant thumped the casket onto the dining table so hard the lid bounced, then slammed down. He frowned at his wife. "No. More. Branding."

Constantia's breath caught. Did he intend mercy or some punishment worse than the iron?

"Join us, Father Dominic," Laurant said to the gray-haired chaplain who entered the hall with Sir Baudri, carrying a scroll, inkwell, and pen. "You, too, Sir Knights. You will stand as witnesses as we check my lady's jewels against the chaplain's inventory."

Lacking an invitation, Constantia and Guia remained standing below the raised platform as the baron opened the casket and spilled its contents across the tabletop.

"Does he mean it?" Guia whispered. "Will my lord truly pardon the thief?"

"He did not say pardon." Constantia's hands felt lighter than they had in days, liberated from her dread of the branding iron, but she dared not relax yet. Branding was not the only penalty for theft.

"I could bear a flogging," Guia mumbled. "It could not be worse than Sybil's switch. Maybe . . . maybe even the stocks."

Was she trying to encourage Constantia with prospects of a lesser punishment? Oh, if only the baron might prove so magnanimous! The whip, the stocks. Constantia could bear those, too, if afterward she and Jevon could somehow be together.

"But the bite of the brand or to lose my hand or my ear—I can't. Oh, Constantia, forgive me, but I can't!"

Constantia stared at the crooked part in Guia's hair. "*You* can't? What—?" She pushed Guia away. Guia shrank, but Constantia held her shoulders so she could not escape. "What do you mean?"

Several of the knights on the dais turned at Constantia's sharpened voice. Jevon raised his brows. Laurant glanced up, but his attention quickly fixed on something else. He nodded at the jewelry Jevon had tossed on the floor of the dais.

"Beatris," he said, "gather those up and bring them here."

Beatris obeyed, heaping the jewels into the lap of her gown. She cast one of her panicked, round-eyed looks at Constantia before hurrying to the table.

Constantia took Guia by the sleeve and dragged her farther away from the dais so they would not be overheard. Raimon stood near the hall's arched exit, his hand on the hilt of his sheathed sword, ready to execute any command the baron gave him. As much as Laurant valued him, Raimon had not enough years or experience to be counted among the baron's council.

Constantia guided Guia to one of the tapestried walls. Guia started to stammer something three times, but each time, her sobbing choked her.

"Guia," Constantia repeated her name as calmly as she could, given the roil of anger in her belly, "why would you fear the brand or losing your hand or ear unless you did something that might earn such a punishment?" She could think of only one thing that "something" could be. "Did you steal those jewels from Lady Gwenllian?"

Guia gasped. "No! Constantia, I swear it! I only took the brooch."

"Only took the brooch?" Guia's face blurred in the flaming mist that swirled before Constantia's vision. "*Only took the brooch?* Do you mean the brooch Lord Laurant *branded Jevon for?*"

"I am so sorry, Constantia." Guia twisted a lock of lank hair around her finger, her face a woeful crumple. "I had no idea what would happen when I picked it up. I was coming back from the laundry hut when I saw some silver coins on the ground in the bailey. I bent to pick them up and found Lady Gwenllian's brooch half hidden in the dirt. I knew she had not been wearing it on her mantle when she left her chamber that morning, which meant someone—you or Beatris, I thought—must have taken it from her casket for some reason."

"Jevon took it to repair the clasp as a surprise for Lady Gwenllian. He lost it when it fell through a hole in his purse. The coins were his too. If you found the brooch, why did you not put it back in Lady Gwenllian's jewelry casket?"

"I should have." A new flood of tears soaked Guia's cheeks. "I meant to at first. But it was as though the coins enchanted me. I had been crying all day because you were aglow with Jevon's love. Everyone knew he and Raimon and Franco planned to go tourneying when they became knights, and I overhead Franco tell Raimon that once Jevon made his fortune, he would marry you even though you had no dowry. I knew no man would ever love me that much and without a dowry, not even a fat old widower would look at me. Then suddenly the silver appeared out of nowhere, right in my path." Guia scrubbed her red, wet nose. "Do you remember how we used to pray to Saint Nicholas for dowries so we could marry, like the three daughters of the poor man the saint rescued from harlotry by secretly giving them dowries for husbands?"

Constantia felt a nostalgic pang as the teasing, thoughtful squire who had befriended her in her loneliness hovered before her vision again, just as he had in each of her prayers.

"Yes, I remember."

"When I found the silver, I thought the saint had answered my prayers as he answered yours. He gave you Jevon, someone who loved you so much he swore to one day dower you himself. But no one loved me that much," Guia repeated with a sniffle. "I was not pretty like you, or clever or lively or brave. No man would even look at me without a dowry. So the saint sent me the silver coins for consolation. 'If I only had a few more like these,' I thought, 'perhaps some man would marry me and take me away from Pennault.' Then I saw the brooch and picked it up, and it entered my head that selling it would bring me *many* silver coins."

However miraculous the coins appeared, Guia knew perfectly well that brooch belonged to Lady Gwenllian. No holy saint would encourage a Christian woman to steal. But there was so much pain in Guia's face that Constantia said nothing.

"I know it was goose-witted of me." Guia wiped her wet cheeks with her sleeve. "Even if I had known how to sell the brooch, I could not have done so before Lady Gwenllian noticed it was missing. Still, I kept the brooch and dreamed all day about what it might feel like to be free. But I dreamed too long. Before I could put the brooch back, Jevon had been taken and accused and condemned to be branded. I was afraid if I confessed that the baron would brand me instead, and I could not bear that. Constantia, I could not! I panicked and hid the brooch in the cellar, and Jevon bore the punishment for me, and I ruined his life and yours, and I am so very sorry, and I can never, ever make it right to you or him. But please, please, *please* do not let the baron cut off my hand or my ear or hang me!"

Guia's image wobbled in the ruddy fumes of Constantia's anger, but she took Guia back in her arms and let her weep against her shoulder.

"Must—must you tell Llygad what I did?"

Llygad. Had he told Guia he loved her seven years ago, how different everything might have been! But at the time, they had all been caught up in moments that seemed like "forevers." *Jevon has asked me to marry him. We will be happy together forever*, Constantia had thought, not realizing how Guia silently grieved, *No man will ever love me. I will be poor and lonely forever.* Even Llygad later confessed to Constantia the worries that had driven his fierce competition in those days with Jevon. *"I taunted you because I was jealous of him. No matter how hard I trained, he bested me at every-thing. He always won, while I always failed. And I am still failing. I am afraid I will be a failure forever."*

None of their "forevers" had turned out to be true. Constantia lost Jevon, while Guia and Llygad fell in love. Constantia understood, as she had not before, that a moment was not the final word on a life. Llygad's courage in guarding Therri from the English would restore his tarnished honor in the baron's eyes. Llygad would be generously rewarded, a reward that would undoubtedly include Guia's hand in marriage if he asked it. And Jevon had come back, giving him and Constantia a second chance to be together. Whether Jevon agreed or not.

"You must decide for yourself if you wish to be honest with Llygad," Constantia told Guia, "but you owe the truth to Jevon."

"Oh, Constantia, I cannot! He will hate me." She snuffled against Constantia's shoulder. "You must hate me too."

"No." The anger dispersed, replaced with sadness and regret, but also the first gleam of hope Constantia felt in years.

She could never excuse what Guia had done, but branding was a terrible fate, and for a woman, banishment even worse. Men like Jevon might turn bandit to survive or use their martial training to join a mercenary band that asked no questions about scarred hands or missing ears. But a marked and unprotected woman would be nothing more than prey for any lustful man whose path she crossed. Suddenly, compassion became easier for the fear that made Guia conceal the brooch when she heard the penalty pronounced on Jevon.

Nothing Guia said or did could remove Jevon's shameful scars or erase the galling years of banishment. But they all had futures again now, possibly bright ones, if they could each successfully navigate their new present moments.

Assuming that truly had been the extent of Guia's sin.

"Tell me truthfully," Constantia said. "Did you take any of those other jewels from Lady Gwenllian intending to sell them for a dowry?"

"No." Guia gulped. "No, I swear it, Constantia."

Constantia pushed Guia away and stared hard into her eyes. Guia's chin remained level, but her gaze slid just off-kilter enough to prevent it from locking with Constantia's.

"Guia, if you are lying . . ."

"I am not lying. I swear."

"Then do you know who *did* steal them?" What else could Guia be hiding? "Was it Llygad?"

Guia's eyes flashed directly into Constantia's. "No!"

Thank goodness! "But you are not being completely honest with me. Why?" Constantia glanced at the dais. Laurant lifted a chain studded with amethysts from the pile Beatris had deposited on the table. He nodded at the chaplain, who ticked something off on the scroll with a pen. Perhaps Constantia was not asking the right question. "Why did you decide to conceal the brooch in the cellar? And how did you know where to hide it?"

Guia's gaze dropped to the rushes, her face so pale Constantia feared she might faint.

"Guia, if you cannot look me in the eye when you lie, Lady Gwenllian will see through you in an instant."

Guia's hands twisted and twisted, then slowly stilled. "After Jevon was punished, I hid the brooch in our chamber, but I knew I could not leave it there for you or Beatris to find. I was trying to think what to do when Cook asked me to fetch some honey from the cellar. When I got there, the cellar door was open. I was halfway down the stairs when I saw one of Lord Laurant's knights. He had moved the oat barrel and was digging at the mortar in the wall at the level of his waist. He must have been afraid someone might catch him and thought he could block their view of his actions more quickly from that position."

"Who was it?"

Guia's hands twisted again. "I daren't tell you. I dare not."

Constantia's foot twitched impatiently. "Did he see you?"

"No. I pressed myself into a shadow against the wall when he glanced over his shoulder. When he finished making the hole, he stuffed something inside it, then put the barrel back in place. I scurried up to the entry space, but I dared not leave without the honey. I heard him muttering as he came up the stairs. He said, 'If she thinks I am going to risk my head for her, she's as witless as she is beautiful. I will tell her I lost it. What can she do, thrash me like one of her wench women? I should like to see her old harpy try to lay that switch across my back.' He laughed just before he stepped out of the cellar and saw me."

The knight must have meant the ruby ring. Had Lady Gwenllian tried to seduce him with it? Were all the gifts she gave her husband's knights invitations to cuckold Laurant?

A somber male voice droned, "The amber crucifix is missing."

Father Dominic's pronouncement drew Constantia's attention back to the dais. The chaplain's pen hovered over the scroll as he looked at the baron. Laurant's forehead creased, but he signaled for the priest to continue down the inventory.

"Guia," Constantia said, "you must tell me who you saw in the cellar."

"I cannot. If I tell Lord Laurant he stole the ring, he will tell the baron I stole the brooch."

"The knight saw you with the brooch?"

Guia's limp curls swished as she shook her head. "When he found me outside the cellar, I pretended I had just arrived. But he must have been worried, for he insisted on accompanying me down and then carried the honey to the kitchen for me. But I went back a few days later. I thought if he could hide something there, perhaps I could too. I could tell something else was inside the crack when I stuffed the brooch in, but I was too afraid of being caught to look to see what it was. I just pushed the brooch in as far as I could and ran back up the stairs, praying no one would ever find it or, if they did, that no one would think to blame me."

And no one had. They had all blamed Jevon.

"He must have gone back at some point to check on the ring," Guia said, "found the brooch and remembered that I had been outside the cellar the day he made the hole in the mortar. One day he whispered to me as I entered the hall for dinner, 'I know you stole the brooch, not Jevon. If you say anything about the ring, I will tell Lady Gwenllian you stole them both. If she demanded a man's hand branded for theft of her father's gift, she will require an entire hand lopped off for gifts from both her father and husband.' He took me so unawares I swore I would say nothing of his crime if he said nothing of mine. Only afterward did I realize he could not have really known where the brooch came from. I gave myself away, and I have never dared tell anyone until now." Guia bounced pleadingly on the balls of her feet. "Please, *please* do not betray me to the baroness. I know the knight will keep his threat, and I cannot bear to lose my hand!"

"Well, Father?" Laurant's voice queried.

Father Dominic set down the pen and leaned back in the baron's chair. He must have finished the inventory.

On a sudden impulse, Constantia grabbed Guia's wrist and pulled her across the floor.

"What are you doing?" Guia said on a gasp.

"I need to see the knights' faces. If one of them stole the jewels and anything besides the crucifix is missing, perhaps he will do something to reveal himself."

"Constantia, no. No!"

Guia's protest confirmed Constantia's suspicion that the thief was in the hall, and Guia knew it. They would likely receive a switching for disrupting the proceedings, but that did not stop Constantia from dragging Guia, heels scraping through the rushes, onto the dais.

Constantia ignored Lady Gwenllian's glower and Guia's frightened whimper as she positioned herself and Guia next to Beatris behind the baroness's chair. From here she could watch the knights over Lady Gwenllian's diminutive stature. The baron sent Constantia and Guia a glance of displeasure but did not order them away. On one side of the tabletop, Laurant had formed a single column of yellow and purple trinkets from the pile Jevon had tossed onto the dais. On the other side, he'd laid out multiple columns of multi-hued gems from Lady Gwenllian's jewelry casket.

"Including the crucifix," Father Dominic said, "there are six missing pieces."

"Seven, with my father's pendant," Lady Gwenllian corrected. "No one could have taken it except for—"

"There is no pendant from my lady's father listed in the inventory, my lord." Father Dominic glanced uneasily at Lady Gwenllian, but he was a priest and must have felt obliged to mention the omission.

"Then we will not consider it," Laurant said.

"But, husband," Lady Gwenllian insisted, "Beatris remembers it. Constantia knew about it too. Only she and Jevon could have—"

"If your father sent you a pendant, you should have told me. I would have had Father Dominic record it like the others. I'll consider no accusation of theft for any jewels not included in the inventory."

Constantia noticed how he avoided his wife's eyes as he said it. He'd made humiliating admissions about his marriage to his knights this day and must fear he would again melt like a snowflake in August if he saw her aggrieved pout.

But Lady Gwenllian was not a woman easily discouraged. "The other six, then. Constantia knew where I kept the key. She took the jewels without my knowledge and gave them to Jevon to sell. If he had not time to sell the brooch as well, that does not mean he did not sell the rest."

The baron pinched the bridge of his nose, either to squeeze back a headache or to further block his wife's beguiling face. "Which ones are missing?" he asked the chaplain.

Father Dominic moved his finger down the inventory and paused near a line without a tick of ink beside it. "A silver collar studded with pearls and amethysts."

Laurant's hand fell, apparently startled enough to look at his wife. "You wore that collar the day I banished Jevon. I remember everything about that day. I had just purchased you a surcote embroidered with violet threads, and I requested you to wear it with the amethyst and pearls, which you did to please me. So Jevon could not have taken it before then, and neither could Constantia."

For the barest instant, Lady Gwenllian appeared uncharacteristically flustered. "Did I? I must have merely misplaced it, then. I will have my chamber searched. But the amber crucifix—"

"I gave that to you for Easter the first year Jevon was absent to serve us at the table."

The fair skin over Lady Gwenllian's high cheekbones tightened, but her face crinkled prettily as though reflecting. "Yes, of course, I remember now. I sent that to Vere with Constantia as a wedding gift for Sir Damien's new wife. I did not think you would mind."

Clearly Lady Gwenllian believed Constantia would not contradict her. Why would she when the lie exonerated both Constantia and Jevon of its theft? But it was still a lie. One of these knights must have been the crucifix's beneficiary. Constantia surveyed their expressions. Sir Guilhem? Sir Eudes? Sir Baudri? Sir—

"What else is missing, Father?" Laurant asked.

The chaplain's finger moved to another unticked line. "A topaz brooch inside a circle of diamonds in a silver setting."

Laurant scratched his earlobe. "I bought you the topaz and diamonds to apologize for churlishly chiding you for smiling too much at Sir Guilhem after he brought you a bouquet of wildflowers when we lost that surly boar who terrorized the village. We would surely have brought the beast down had Jevon's bow and expert aim still been with us."

Constantia watched Sir Guilhem, but the knight gave no flinch at the baron's jealousy. They must have made peace about the flowers. If Lady Gwenllian had afterward given him the topaz brooch, he had no intention of giving himself away.

Laurant nodded at the chaplain. "Go on, Father."

"A topaz ring engraved with a dove."

The baron rubbed his eyebrow, but Constantia sensed it was to shade the worry in his eyes as he now steadfastly weighed his wife.

"That was to cheer you when you grew cross with me for telling Heléne she could sit at lessons with Therri while Father Dominic taught him to read. It was her tenth year, and Jevon had been gone fifteen months."

The sweet corners of Lady Gwenllian's delicate mouth crimped slightly as her gaze narrowed at her husband.

The chaplain finished, "And a string of agate beads fashioned in the shape of hearts."

Laurant looked so surprised he stopped his nervous twitches. "That was to reassure you of my love after you miscarried our fourth child."

The delicate bloom in Lady Gwenllian's cheeks deepened, but her hands knit so tightly together that her ivory fingers turned a pallid gray. "And I suppose you recall exactly how many months before that you banished Jevon?"

"Four-and-twenty."

"It sounds as though Jevon's punishment weighed heavily on you to have marked his absence so keenly." Lady Gwenllian rarely spoke irritably to her husband in public, but she did so now.

"It weighs mightily on me now that I know he was innocent," Laurant replied curtly.

Jevon's gaze flew to Constantia's, as surprised as she at the baron's pronouncement.

"The only conclusion I can draw," Laurant continued, "is that you either gifted the jewels to some of my knights and neglected to inform me—"

His jealous scrutiny swung from his wife to his knights, but all withstood him confidently. They even turned their hands outward again to expose their rings, gifts from the baroness that Laurant had seen them wearing for years.

"Or you lost all but the crucifix and neglected to inform me . . ."

Lady Gwenllian rose in regal challenge from her chair.

"Or the pieces were stolen, indeed, but not by Jevon or Constantia."

Lady Gwenllian thrust up a defiant chin. "No one else knew where I kept the key."

The baron and baroness glared at one another. Jevon had been banished before any of the jewelry went missing. If Constantia had not taken the key, and Guia had not, then . . .

Constantia leaned over to Beatris and whispered, "No one else but you."

Beatris's mouth popped open, but only a hollow whistle of breath came out.

"I should be loath," the baron said, a stony edge to his voice, "to question my men one by one, but unless you have something you wish to tell me, my dear, I am afraid you leave me no choice."

Beatris's face was as ashen as Lady Gwenllian's fingers. "He made me," she finally croaked.

"Do as you please," Lady Gwenllian snapped at her husband. "I gave those jewels to no man. If they are missing, they were stolen just like these." She waved at the column of yellow and purple jewels.

Beatris's gray lips fluttered like a moth's beating wings. "He caught me drawing a picture of Lady Gwenllian behind the empty turnip barrel after Sir Fauke de Vaumâle stayed a few nights with us last year on his way to visit his great-uncle."

Constantia remembered the arrogant, flame-haired knight who boasted himself a trusted confidant of young Duke Richard. She took advantage of Laurant's sharp rejoinder to his wife and Lady Gwenllian's icy response to ask Beatris softly, "What did Sir Fauke have to do with it?"

Through a gleam of tears, Beatris's eyes sparked with anger and anguish. "One of his companions, Sir Walbért, took a fancy to me and hinted to the baron he might consider me for a wife in return for a most negligible dowry. But Lady Gwenllian heard him and laughed. She told Sir Walbért that I was too old and fat. I am not, Constantia! I am only a little plump. But she humiliated Sir Walbért for thinking me comely, and he rode away without me. I was too mortified to tell you and Guia. Instead, I went down to the cellar and drew Lady Gwenllian exactly as she truly is."

The scowling, snake-haired woman with the crossed eyes. Constantia glanced at Lady Gwenllian as the baroness scoffed, "Why in the world would I hide my own jewels in a barrel of grain?"

"Only he came down to the cellar and saw what I was doing."

Constantia's attention snapped back to Beatris.

"He said his knight's honor obligated him to tell the baroness how I had insulted her, but added that if I let him make a copy of the key to her jewelry casket, he might be able to forget what he saw. I told him I dared not, even if the drawing cost me a switching. But then he said he only wished to sell a trinket or two that Lady Gwenllian did not care two crumbs about and that he would share the profit with me so the next time a man thought me pretty enough to marry, I could wed him whether Lady Gwenllian liked it or not. I was so angry and hurt and humiliated that I lent him the key. And then he never gave me so much as a denier."

Dowries. Their wretched lack of dowries lay, yet again, behind Jevon's disgrace.

"Beatris, who is 'he'? Who saw you make the drawing?"

Like Guia, Beatris shook her head, panic flooding out the anger in her eyes. An insulting drawing would win her a switching, but conspiring to steal Lady Gwenllian's jewels would bring down on Beatris's head the same terrible punishment Guia shrank from.

So, Lady Gwenllian had *not* given the jewels to a lover and accused Jevon to conceal her infidelity. Would she shift her outrage to the true thief if he were revealed? Or would vengeance for Jevon's "betrayal" of Pennault Castle so consume her that she would try to weave another lie to convict him instead?

"Sir Raimon," Laurant barked, "summon the rest of my knights. I will interrogate them all until I have the truth."

Raimon bowed and turned toward the exit. The sunlight from the windows shimmered on the folds of his bright-red mantle as it swished around his shoulders. The garment must be new. It had been too dark in the cellar for Constantia to recognize either the color or the fine sheen of silk.

Raimon had never worn silk before. He could not afford it. Just as he could not afford a sword with three bands of gold around the grip and a pommel enameled in yellow and blue, all of which she could see now that he had removed his hand from the hilt.

The chaplain cleared his throat somewhat tentatively. "My lord, there is one more item missing in the inventory."

One more? Of course! Constantia pulled the ruby ring off her finger and carried it to the chaplain.

"This, Father?" She noted how her query checked Raimon and prompted him to look over his shoulder. As Laurant plucked the ring from her palm, she said, "My lord, you need not offend your faithful knights by a demeaning inquiry. I believe the thief is already in this hall."

She prayed she was right. If her suspicion caused an innocent man to suffer as Jevon had, it would haunt her for the rest of her life. But Raimon had resumed his course and was halfway over the threshold. If he failed to return with the summoned knights, it might seal his guilt, but it would also be too late to apprehend him.

"Stay, Sir Raimon." The baron sounded grimmer than Constantia had ever heard him, save for the night he had roared at Lady Gwenllian. He gazed suspiciously at his council. "What do you know of this, Constantia? How do you come to have my wife's ring?"

"Jevon and I found it in the cellar, concealed in the same crack where Lady Heléne discovered the brooch."

Lady Gwenllian's gaze flashed past her husband for just an instant. Her eyes held both shock and betrayal. And the only knight standing exactly where her accusation whipped was Raimon. Unlike the other jewels, the ring must have been a deliberate—and secret—gift.

Laurant thrust the ring under his wife's elegant nose. "How could you not have missed this one? I gave this to you one year to the day of our marriage vows, inscribed 'to my love, Gwenllian.' You said nothing about its disappearance. Nothing!"

Inscribed? Constantia had not thought to look inside the band. No wonder Raimon had been afraid to either wear or sell it! Laurant would be sure to interpret so personal a gift on the hand of one of his knights as certain evidence of his wife's adultery. But Laurant never sent Raimon farther afield than the nearest town. Any buyer there would recognize the uncommon Welsh name "Gwenllian" as the name of Lord Laurant's wife and might blabber the name of the knight he bought it from.

It did not surprise Constantia how quickly Lady Gwenllian rallied. All her peevish indignation at her husband's previous complaints evaporated. The ethereal roses in her soft cheeks quivered. Her delicately petaled lips trembled. Tears welled in her glowing blue eyes. The baron visibly thawed even before she spoke.

"I was afraid you would think you had married a witless goose if I told you I'd lost it." Her voice oscillated pitifully. "Worse, I feared you would think I did not value the gift and the affection it symbolized. But you will admit you have not seen it on my finger since Jevon left. I should have realized it before. It was not my brooch alone he stole. It was that ring. Along with all of these." She indicated the line of gems Constantia and Jevon had found in the barrel. "They also disappeared before he left. And Constantia helped him do it."

So. Lady Gwenllian chose revenge for the humbling of their castle. Caught once more in his wife's thrall, Constantia expected the baron to turn his condemning gaze on her, but, instead, his brow puckered and he looked at Jevon. Her stomach flopped. She had seen at least some of the jewels in the casket after Jevon's banishment, even if Lady Gwenllian had not worn any of them in the last seven years. Unfortunately, Constantia could not prove it.

But . . . she could prove something else.

"There were no turnips in the turnip barrel."

The baron stared at Constantia as though she had gone daft.

"So?" Lady Gwenllian said.

"When Jevon and I found your missing jewels, the turnip barrel was half filled with grain, with your jewelry buried inside it. The top of the barrel was sealed so that no one could easily look inside. When Jevon forced it open, we found the barrel weighted down with rubble. The same rubble you, my lord, used to fill the core of the new fortifications you began raising along the walls a year ago."

Once again, the timeline would exonerate Jevon. And it was unlikely that a woman like Constantia would not be noticed smuggling the heavy shards from the rubble pile in the bailey up the stairs to the keep, then down to the cellar. A man, on the other hand, had more freedom to wander about the yard and castle at any hour of the day or night without raising particular curiosity.

"We had to lift the rubble out to find the jewels," she said. "Sir Raimon must have seen the shards piled on the floor when he came down to the cellar to summon us to the hall. Ask him."

Laurant might be too enchanted by his wife to see through her guile, but he was insecure enough to pursue the theft of his gifts to her like a talbot on the scent of a hare. "Sir Raimon, can you verify Lady Constantia's words?"

As Constantia turned with the baron toward the young knight, a corner of red cloth disappeared through the exit.

Jevon understood how his old friend would be angry that he had sided with the English in their attack on Pennault Castle. He could even forgive Raimon for the envy he concealed in their youth. But if Raimon had just fled from the hall because he'd stolen the jewels hidden in the cellar, along with the brooch Jevon had been branded for, then stood silent while Laurant's council condemned Constantia to the same brutal punishment . . .

Jevon started to lunge off the dais, but a hand clamped on his arm. Laurant's grip dug into Jevon's protesting muscles while the baron's council formed a wall to block his escape.

Then abruptly, the baron released him.

"Go," Laurant said. "Bring him back so we can learn the truth."

Jevon charged out of the hall. He paused at the top of the wooden stairs pushed up to the second-story door of the keep and saw Raimon loping across the bailey toward a trio of riders who had just arrived. While Jevon clattered down the stairs, Raimon signaled to one of the men. The one in the forefront urged his mount over to Raimon and leaned down as though to listen to some question. Raimon grabbed the neck of the man's surcote, dragged him off the horse, then sprang into the vacated saddle and spurred his way into the gatehouse.

Cursing, Jevon doubled his speed, but grudging courtesy forced him to stop and help the sprawled man regain his feet. "Are you hurt, sir?"

The man remained bent at the waist as he brushed the dirt off the skirt of his surcote and hose, granting Jevon only a view of a headful of thick, slate-gray hair. Jevon swept the dust from the soft folds of the man's dark-green cloak, disgusted that Raimon would so maltreat an old man. Jevon glanced at the man's companions. The younger horseman looked the age of a squire, but the other was closer to Jevon's age. He held a sword, drawn too late to rebuke Raimon's rude "greeting." Only a knight would have a sword and horse as fine as those.

Jevon grabbed the knight's reins as the old man grumbled a reassuring answer about his safety.

"Lend me your mount," Jevon said. "Now."

The knight glared down at him. "Who are you to give me such an order?"

"One of the Earl of Gunthar's men." Jevon still wore the earl's badge. He would say anything to gain the knight's horse. Raimon would be long gone if he took the time to fetch a mount from the stable. Jevon pointed at the devastated castle walls. "Do not give me a reason to complain of more Poitevin recalcitrance. Give me your horse."

The knight glanced over Jevon's shoulder. The old gentleman had pulled the hood of his cloak over his head, shadowing his face, but gave a curt nod.

"Leave the bow," Jevon said when the knight started to unstrap the weapon from behind the saddle. It looked like a simple hunting bow with the string loosed for travel. No matter. Jevon could restring it quickly enough, and from the bulkiness of the arrow bag, he judged he would have missiles aplenty.

The knight exchanged places with Jevon. Jevon gathered up the reins, but a slender hand stretched up and grasped the bridle. Constantia must have caught up with him as he helped the old man.

"Take me with you."

Jevon snorted with the startled horse. "There is no time for this nonsense, Stantia."

The golden flecks in her eyes combusted like tiny embers cast skyward in the percussive pop of a bonfire. "I am not letting you out of my sight again. Not now. Not ever. I made that mistake seven years ago, and I am not going to make it again."

He curled his fingers around hers to pry them off the bridle. "Raimon is getting away."

"You are not going without me." She tightened her grasp on the thin strap of leather. "If you do not find Raimon, you will simply keep riding until you rejoin your mercenary band. If you do find him, you will drag him back to Pennault, turn him over to the baron, and still ride away. You will never stay at Pennault—with me—so long as *that* is on your hand."

The *R* stood out starkly amidst the web of white scars in the bright midday light. It made no difference whether the baron acknowledged Jevon's innocence or not.

"It will always be there, Stantia. It will mark me as a thief no matter where I go. I will not drag you into such a life."

If anything, the sparks in her eyes fired more vehemently. Her mouth set like a petal-glossed stone. Never to kiss those adamant, ambrosial lips again tore his soul in half. But with a controlled, determined strength, he peeled her fingers from the bridle one by one, then spurred the horse toward the gatehouse.

"May I borrow your squire's mount, sir? I vow on my honor to restore him to you safely."

Jevon pulled up and whipped his head around. Constantia addressed the old man with the hood. To Jevon's astonishment, the old man not only told the squire to dismount, he gave Constantia the reins and lifted her into the saddle.

"Do try to bring both horses back unharmed, young man," he called to Jevon. "And pray tell your earl that at least one Poitevin house remains loyal to the king."

Constantia threw Jevon a triumphant look as she rode into the gatehouse. He rode after her, silently cursing her and the old man together.

When they reached the other side of the portcullis, Jevon caught her reins and pulled her up short. "Wait."

Her eyes sparked again. "I do not care what you say—"

"No, wait. You will disturb the ground." He knew there was no stopping her now. Later was another matter.

The aftermath of the earl's siege had left the ground outside Pennault Castle an anarchy of trampled grass and churned-up earth. Footprints turned about in every direction, both man's and beasts' jumbled atop one another and crisscrossed with deep crevices from the wheels of the wagon that hauled the mangon. Jevon dismounted and picked his way through the field. His boot prints added to the morass of impressions, but the marks left by men were not the ones that concerned him.

He finally motioned Constantia forward. She guided her mount carefully to where he pointed at three sets of fresh hoofprints.

"Look. You see how these prints are deeper than the rest? That is because they are newer. All three track up to the gate"—he pointed toward the gatehouse—"but only this set with a chink in the right forehoof's shoe rides away again, and the stride is longer, like a gallop. This is the horse Raimon rides. And that chink is what will allow us to track him so long as he does not change horses."

Jevon remounted and flicked his reins. Constantia followed, ranging herself behind his horse so as not to inadvertently disturb the hoofprints that led them to the road. Raimon had gained too much ground on them. Jevon nudged his mount into a trot, but impatience eventually drove him to a canter. A faster pace would blur his eyes to the tracks in the road.

The distinctive hoofprints led them around the bend in the direction of Vere Castle, but just past the curve, the prints cut into the woods. Jevon veered to follow. Raimon must have thought to lose Jevon here, not knowing the skills Jevon had mastered while he'd hunted from hunger and skulked for safety amidst these trees.

Between the fresh compressions in the leafy debris on the forest floor and the chinked hoofprints in patches of bare earth, Jevon stayed on Raimon's trail even when the thickening growth slowed his borrowed horse. The trees would force Raimon and his mount to do the same. Jevon slid out of his saddle and led the horse behind him. Constantia followed his example. The hoofprints became shallower, interspersed with prints that clearly belonged to a man. Raimon, too, had left his saddle as the shrubbery grew more dense.

"You there. Halt!"

Jevon jolted at the shout. His heart abruptly drubbed in his chest as the bright forest daylight dimmed at the corners of his eyes. His mouth went dry, his palms dampened. Without thinking, he rolled onto the balls of his feet to flee before an arrow or spear or dagger could bring him down like a cornered hart by an "honest man" who recognized either his felon's face or brand.

"Jevon?"

Constantia's anxious query pulled him out of the waking nightmare. She touched his hand—his scarred hand—then clasped it in the warm, calming way only she could. He pushed his heels tight against the earth and the betrayed, bewildered twenty-year-old youth he had been out of his heart, reminding himself that, today, he was the hunter, not the hunted.

"I'm fine." His reply came out too thick through the knot of alarm that still clotted his throat. He was glad when a second shout diverted her gaze from his face and gave him time to wipe the perspiration from his brow.

"Let me through! I am on an important errand for the Baron de Laurant."

Jevon recognized Raimon's voice through the trees up ahead. So the warning cry had been aimed at him. Jevon belatedly realized he knew the challenger's voice too.

"Stay here with the horses," he told Constantia.

He strung the bow, slung the arrow bag over his shoulder, then moved with practiced stealth through the shrubbery. He was not ready to reveal his presence, even to the man with the straw-colored hair and ginger beard he viewed through the bushes.

"And just what errand might that be?" Ned Woodville asked Raimon. "Not off to warn some of your neighbors so they can arm their castles against us, I trust?"

"No, of course not," Raimon replied. "The baron merely wants fresh trout for his table. Your earl and his men ate up the last of our store before you left Pennault. I am headed for the river to replenish our supply."

Jevon watched the scene through a screen of greenery. Ned was not alone. Seven other men, some archers like himself and a few men-at-arms carrying swords, traveled with him.

Ned eyed Raimon suspiciously. "I see no rod on your shoulder nor net about your horse. Do you mean to swipe the fish from the water with your bare hands?"

"I leave a rod hidden near the river in a hollowed-out tree." Jevon had to admire the smoothness with which Raimon spoke his lies. "The longer you hold me here, the hungrier and the surlier the baron grows. Pray, be a good man and let me pass."

Ned grimaced at Raimon's patronizing tone, but burly Hamo, the men-at-arms' sergeant, said, "We have already searched by the river and found it clear. There is no one for him to plot mischief with there. The earl wants us back before dark."

"We have hunted through these woods for nigh a week," one of Hamo's fellow soldiers grumbled, "and found no sign of le Falquet's fair-haired villain. I say the Poitevin thief made the whole thing up."

Jevon bristled at the slur.

"Le Falquet did not 'make up' the knife wound in his back." Ned continued to block Raimon. "And I don't like this fellow's look, nor the way he's prowling about on an 'errand' for a man who a mere sennight ago still called the king a usurper."

Hamo planted his beefy fists on his hips. "You are not in charge here," he reminded Ned. Men of the sword always outranked archers. "Laurant has sworn a fresh oath to the king. Whether he keeps it or not is between him and the earl. Our charge was to find le Falquet's mysterious villain, who appears to have vanished like the ghost he no doubt always was. Let that man go. We will search for another hour, then rejoin the earl with our final report."

Ned scowled but stepped aside. Raimon smirked as he prepared to remount. The moment he set his boot in the stirrup, Jevon knew he would make a hard break through the trees. Gunthar's men, all on foot, would not be able to stop him or give chase.

Jevon whisked an arrow into his bow, aimed it in a single instinctual blink, and sent the shaft into the earth inches from the horse's forehoof. The horse whinnied and reared, startling Raimon into backing away. As a squire, Jevon had helped train Laurant's war horses not to panic in the heat of battle, but this was not a destrier. This horse was a young and skittish palfrey. Jevon fired three more arrows in swift succession, whizzing them as close to the horse's ear as he dared without striking the beast. The horse lost its nerve and pitched itself into the trees, leaving Raimon behind.

Only then did Jevon step into the open, a new arrow nocked and trained on Raimon. The moment Jevon appeared, the air around him hissed, the sound so faint he knew he alone would hear it and only because his bow made the same sound when he drew it in haste. He also knew by the prick of the hair on his arms that the arrows drawn by Gunthar's archers were all aimed at him.

The hunting bow Jevon held did not have Hywel ap Ioan's epigram to guide him as he bared his teeth at Raimon. All the better. "Do you really think I cannot send this squarely through your heart before their shafts reach me?"

Ned held up a hand, sweeping it in an arc at the archers in the company. "You may not command me," he told Hamo, "but I command them, and I order my men to hold. Let us hear what le Falquet has to say."

Hamo grumbled when the archers lowered their bows. His own men carried swords but stood too far away to interfere with Jevon's aim.

"And why should we believe anything he says?" Hamo growled. "If the earl still thought le Falquet unjustly judged, he would not have left him behind in Laurant's dungeon. At best, le Falquet is a thief. Who knows what other crimes he has committed? Rape? Murder? Mercenaries are not known for their scruples, especially those with missing noses or ears—or brands."

Jevon ignored the insinuations and kept his arrow trained on Raimon. "The only thief standing among you is him. Tell them the truth. Tell them how you stole Lady Gwenllian's brooch and jewels and let me take the blame."

Raimon's eyes, fixed warily on the tip of Jevon's arrow, widened. "But I did not."

Jevon sent his arrow into the ground next to Raimon's foot. Raimon sprang aside with a yelp. Jevon nocked another arrow swifter than Gunthar's archers were able to point their bows at him again. "What part of the word *truth* did you not understand?"

Raimon's whitened face sheened with sweat. "I am telling it, Jevon, I swear. I had nothing to do with the brooch disappearing."

Ned, looking regretful but grim, did not signal his archers again. Jevon knew he had time to release only one more shaft before their arrows pierced him. Then he had better make it count. The vengeance he had never felt against Laurant swelled as vast as the sea against Raimon. Jevon always knew that Laurant acted in cruel yet honest ignorance of the truth, but Raimon—Raimon had robbed Jevon of the honorable knighthood that might one day have enabled him to marry Constantia. He had consigned Jevon to the desperate choice of either becoming a thief in truth to survive or an execrable mercenary, decried by the church and despised by the very lords who hired him. And Raimon had done it knowingly, standing silent while Laurant's marshal seared the denouncing *R* into Jevon's flesh.

"Jevon."

Once again, it was Constantia's voice that tried to pull him back. He should have known she would not stay where he told her to.

He steeled himself against her. "Go back to Pennault, Stantia."

He did not want her to see him like this. Cold. Ruthless. The flinty mercenary Raimon had made him.

She stepped beside him. He hated that she could view the savagery in his face, but so long as Raimon stood in Jevon's sight, he could not evict the thirst for revenge from his heart.

"He is telling the truth about the brooch," Constantia said. "Raimon did not take it. Guia did."

Her words almost surprised Jevon into lowering his bow. Constantia reached up when his aim wavered and wrapped her fingers over his where they clenched the grip. She steadied his aim at Raimon.

"Guia found the brooch where you dropped it in the yard. She failed to return it promptly to Lady Gwenllian—why does not matter just now—then panicked when she saw you blamed and branded. She hid it in the cellar for fear of being branded and banished too.

From the corner of his eye, Jevon saw her head turn toward Raimon.

"Guia saw you hide Lady Gwenllian's ruby ring in the same crack in the cellar wall where she hid the brooch. You said you would blame both the ring and the brooch on her if she did not keep your secret. Which means you have known all these years that Jevon was innocent."

"I did no such thing," Raimon blustered. "You cannot prove any of it."

Constantia's fingers remained latched around Jevon's on the bow, continuing to support his aim. "And I cannot prove you sold the five pieces of Lady Gwenllian's jewelry that Jevon could not have stolen because he was no longer at Pennault. Or that you were the one who stole her other jewels and hid them in a barrel in the cellar, then weighted the barrel with rubble that, once again, Jevon could not have placed there because the baron did not begin raising the castle walls until after he was gone. But I *do* know that you saw the rubble perfectly well when you released us from the cellar. They proved the jewels were hidden there after Jevon's banishment. Yet you stood mum as the dead in the hall and once again allowed the blame to be cast on him. The baron will piece the evidence together, too, when he goes down to the cellar. Which is why you have run from the castle."

Raimon sent an outraged look at Gunthar's men. "None of this is true. The wench is de Cazalet's lover, the man you call le Falquet. She will say anything to defend him."

Enraged at the renewed jibe at Constantia's virtue, Jevon almost loosed the arrow. He clenched the shaft between his first and second fingers just below the fletching to hold it in place, but he no longer needed Constantia's encouragement to keep his aim steady.

Her hand fell from his on a scoffing huff. "Judge him as you see fit, Jevon. If anyone thinks to stop you, their arrows will have to go through me."

Until that moment, Jevon had not realized that Constantia had positioned herself between him and the earl's archers, but he knew Gunthar's archers would not harm her. One of them would simply dart around her to bring Jevon down. But not before Jevon could send his arrow through Raimon's heart.

Raimon's gaze fixed as tightly on Jevon as Jevon's fixed on him. Jevon's heart warred while his face and body both remained so still he might have been cast in stone. He had to choose. Let Constantia watch him kill a man with remorseless vengeance—or swallow the bitterness of the last seven years of injustice and allow this thief, this liar, to walk away unscathed from the guilt of his crimes. But Raimon had encouraged Lady Gwenllian to implicate Constantia in the missing jewels too. If Jevon let Raimon go, Lady Gwenllian would make Constantia suffer more than Jevon, as a man, ever had or could. Jevon could not allow that. He did not want Constantia's last memory of him to be that of a killer. But he burned for justice for them both.

Poitevin justice, Jevon. Gunthar may have abandoned you, but you have not abandoned your dream of a better way than this to judge a man.

But what was that way? Gunthar never told him exactly how the English settled questions of innocence and guilt, only that the word of one man alone was not enough to condemn. Then how should he deal with Raimon? The rubble, the timing of the thefts, even Raimon's flight from the castle—all remained circumstantial. None of that proved he actually committed a crime. Was Jevon supposed to simply let him go even though Jevon knew in his bones that Raimon was not only responsible for the theft of the jewels in the cellar but held no regret at all for the years Jevon had been banished and hunted for Raimon's silence about the brooch?

If you want to be worthy of Constantia's respect and love . . .

Constantia. That was another riddle. Why was she urging him to loose his arrow when he knew she would abhor such a bloody act? He risked a glance at her.

She whispered, "We need a confession. And he will not confess unless he is frightened into it."

Jevon almost wept at the faith in her eyes. She had trusted him to make the right choice all along.

But how to pull off such a bluff? Raimon was a knight trained in courage and valor. It would not be easy to frighten him. Except . . . when Jevon had launched an arrow that "barely missed" Constantia's toe, Constantia had stared him down bravely. When Jevon had done the same to Raimon . . .

Jevon raised the tip of his arrow from Raimon's chest to his face. "I will be as merciful to you as Laurant was to me. He gave me a mark for men to judge me by. I will let you live, but a mark of your own is the least you owe me. Choose, Raimon. Your eye or your ear?"

Raimon's jaw dropped. "Wh—what?"

"I am certain I can take your eye out safely. It will still leave you one eye to see with," Jevon said as though making Raimon a perfectly reasonable offer, "and it will be a kinder punishment than the baron dealt me. No one suspects a man of being a thief over a missing eye. If I shear off your ear, well, men may find that more questionable. Of course, you can try growing your hair to conceal it."

Raimon's eyes bulged like beckoning targets before vanishing behind his hands. "No. Jevon, please, no."

Did he hear the whine in his voice? Jevon had not mewled like that when he'd faced the branding iron. Men came home wounded, maimed, sometimes blinded from battles all the time. And sometimes from the rough and tumble of the tournament mêlée. Did Raimon not realize that?

"Tell the truth," Jevon ordered. "Here, before the Earl of Gunthar's men, tell them who stole Lady Gwenllian's jewels."

"G-Guia took the brooch they accused you of," Raimon stammered. "Constantia just admitted it."

The scum. Hiding behind yet another woman. "And the jewels we found in the turnip barrel? Did Guia steal those as well?"

"She had access to Lady Gwenllian's key. So did Beatris." Raimon kept his hands over his eyes but fanned them out to view the reactions of Gunthar's men.

Jevon had seen these men in battle. Not one had shrunk at the prospect of death or maiming. They all grimaced when Raimon shoved his palms tightly over his eyes again and bobbed at the knees.

Constantia said, "Guia saw you with Lady Gwenllian's ring."

"So she says." Raimon's voice thinned and rose a few notches, but he stubbornly persisted. "Guia is an embittered, dried-up drudge who hates Lady Gwenllian for not letting her marry. She is the one with a grudge against the baroness, not I. What cause had I to steal anything from her?"

"Have it your way," Jevon said. "I have never put out an eye through a man's hands before"—or ever—"so I do not know if my arrow's velocity will pierce through your flesh to nick your eye or if your hands will stop it short. Let's find out."

"No." Raimon gasped. "No, no, no!" He balled his hands into fists, no doubt to thicken the barrier between his eyes and the arrow. His knees almost collapsed, but the tree he sagged against propped him up.

A part of Jevon hated taunting a man so pathetically afraid. *Poitevin justice.* But Constantia was right. They needed a confession. They were trapped by Gunthar's men. If one of the archer's arrows killed Jevon, they would take Constantia back to Pennault and leave it up to Laurant—and Lady Gwenllian—to determine her guilt and punishment.

"Stop whimpering like a baby," Constantia told Raimon. "After the shame you cast on Jevon, it is a gift that all he wants is your eye. Better that than for Lord Laurant to learn which knight seduced his wife. The baron might send his adulterous wife back to Wales or put her in a nunnery, but the man who seduced her—"

Raimon spluttered. "I didn't—I'm not—I never—"

"True," Jevon said across his protest. "The baron could never stare down his own knights if he let the man who cuckolded him go unpunished. At least the revenge I demand isn't lethal. You can return to Pennault with whatever lie about me you want, Raimon. Just give me your eye in exchange."

"I never seduced her!" Raimon shouted.

"Guia saw you hide Lady Gwenllian's ruby ring," Constantia repeated. "Lady Gwenllian may believe your word against Guia's, but who do you think Lord Laurant will believe after he just confessed his own jealousy of his wife to his men?"

Jevon tilted his head toward Constantia and muttered loudly enough for Raimon to overhear, "His fists are going to slow my arrow down. I will take off his ear before he realizes it is gone."

Raimon gasped. His hands fluttered from his eyes halfway to his ears, checked as though fearing the threat was merely a feint to unveil his eyes, then vacillated between the two, uncertain of Jevon's target.

Jevon's already taut body cinched tighter as Hamo stepped into his line of vision. But Hamo only spat on the ground in front of Raimon, then sheathed his sword.

"I have never seen such a feeble feather-heart in my life. Settle your quarrel however you please, le Falquet. Until King Henry's courts come to this curst land, this is Poitevin business, not ours. Come, men. We've a few hours of daylight left to search for le Falquet's specter before we report to the earl."

"You have not found him?" Jevon asked. Where could the stranger have gone?

"Not so much as a trace," Hamo said. "I am not convinced of your veracity, nor do I know whether or not you're a thief, but this much I do know. I have watched you in the earl's camp, and you are no coward."

The English trailed their sergeant into the bushes, casting contemptuous looks at Raimon as they left.

Ned lingered for a moment. "For what it is worth, I have always believed you," he said to Jevon before he led the archers after the others.

Ned's faith bolstered him almost as much as Constantia's.

The last drop of color drained from Raimon's face as the English vanished. Despite their scorn, he must have thought they would ultimately protect him from Jevon's revenge.

"Jevon, please." The tree against Raimon's back was no longer enough to hold him up. He slid to the ground. "Please, please, please."

The last *please* gurgled on a full-throated sob as Raimon wound both arms across his eyes so that his hands cupped his ears. Jevon had never seen such a pathetic sight. Raimon's misery could have been long over by now had he simply stared his enemy down while that enemy loosed his arrow at him. Raimon's cowardice disgusted Jevon.

But not as much as Jevon's own cruel taunting of him did.

"Keep your aim steady," Constantia whispered. "He is almost ready to tell us the truth."

She did not sound eager in her encouragement, but she did sound determined. She could see no other way to prove her and Jevon's innocence. But listening to Raimon's broken sobs, Jevon knew he could not do it like this.

He lowered his bow. The bushes still bounced where the English had trod through them. They could not have ventured far.

"Ned Woodville!" he called.

It took only a few moments for Ned to reappear. "Yes, Jevon?"

Raimon, perhaps spurred by a fresh hope of safety, scuttled back to his feet.

"If we were in England and not Poitou," Jevon asked Ned, "how would this fellow be dealt with?"

Ned scratched the red bristles on his chin. "What crimes do you accuse him of?"

"Theft of the Lady Gwenllian de Laurant's property."

"Worth more than half a mark?"

"Most certainly."

"That's worth a hanging."

Raimon's hand wrapped reflexively around his throat. "You've no proof that I am the thief."

"That would be for the jury to decide," Ned said.

The curious word turned Jevon's head toward Ned. "What is a jury?"

"Twelve free and law-worthy men of the hundred."

Gunthar had told Jevon about these twelve free men, but Ned must have seen Jevon's puzzled look at the rest.

Ned explained, "The area of the county or shire where local courts are held. The twelve men drawn for a jury would be familiar with any crimes taking place in the area and know both the injured party and the accused. These men are charged with making inquiries into the crime. They report on whether the accused is of good or bad reputation."

Raimon recovered some of his composure. "Laurant himself will witness to the honorable way I've served him."

"Laurant's word would not be enough." Ned rubbed one finger along the ruddy side whiskers that tracked up to his pale blond hair. "The jurymen must seek out the opinions not only of the men of the castle who know you. Such men might be pressured to answer as the baron wants them to. The jurymen must seek the judgment of those in the neighborhood who are familiar with you or have heard reports of your character and behavior."

"Including my enemies?" Raimon shot a half-frightened, half-surly look at Jevon. "They might tell lies of me."

"That's the thing," Ned said. "No one man's word would judge you. The jurors gather *all* opinions of you, as well as striving to learn if you had opportunity to commit the crime and what motive you had for doing so. And they must do so with the greatest diligence and fairness, for when they present their findings before a royal justice, they must do so under oath. One juror, perhaps, might lie, but all twelve are unlikely to risk their souls and the king's chastisement for friendship's sake or even for a bribe."

Had the knights who condemned Jevon been required to cast their votes beneath God's judgment, would they have been so quick to convict him? Had twelve honest men made inquiries about Jevon's character among the young men and knights of neighboring Vere and Belle Noir Castles, might they not have spoken of Jevon's fairness and honesty in his dealings with them?

"But"—Ned quirked a regretful brow at Jevon—"we are not in England."

Once again, irony burned Jevon's throat. No, they were not. Only Laurant's opinion mattered here, and Lady Gwenllian was at Pennault, whispering her venom afresh into his ear.

"I had better be going," Ned said, "or Hamo will leave my men and me behind."

Ned disappeared once more through the bushes.

Jevon stood so long with the arrow and bow held lax while he tried to decide what to do that Constantia finally nudged his weapon back up.

"We must frighten him again," she murmured.

The moment Raimon saw the bow coast upward, he blanched anew. His hands fluttered pitifully, uncertain what part of his head to try to protect.

Jevon dropped the bow to his side. "I can't. Coercing a man to confess, even if it is true—you and I are better than this, Stantia." He might never see the golden land he longed for. But if he lived by Poitevin justice, he did not deserve to.

A faint stain of shame tinted her cheeks. "Then—then what shall we do? Let him return to Pennault with his lies about us?"

"He won't be going back to Pennault." That much suddenly flashed across Jevon's mind. "Not after he seduced Lady Gwenllian."

"I did not seduce her!" Raimon shouted for the second time. He maintained a defensive position, clearly suspecting Jevon sought to trick him into baring his eyes and ears.

"You had her ring." Constantia repeated her accusation. "Guia said so."

"Guia cannot prove that or that I was the one who stole those jewels and hid them in the barrel. How would I even gain access to them?"

"You bullied Beatris into letting you make a copy of Lady Gwenllian's key," Constantia said.

Raimon snorted, seeming to grow in courage the longer Jevon's bow remained slack. "No one will believe a thing that plump hen says. She wanted to spite the baroness for humiliating her over that drunken sot who thought he wanted to marry her." Raimon glanced at the arrowhead pointing at the ground and crossed his arms in a belated show of defiance. "You cannot prove me guilty of a thing." A second glance at the bow prompted Raimon to think better of his brashness. He uncrossed his arms, freeing his hands for defense again. "If Jevon takes my eye or my ear or kills me, it is not I but he whom all of Poitou will decry as a villain fit for hanging."

"If you are so innocent, why did you run?" Jevon asked. "Every man in the bailey saw you. You pulled an old man from his horse, then leapt into his saddle as though the devil himself were at your heels. Do you think Laurant will not ask himself why you fled and connect it with the stolen jewels?" Jevon demonstrated his utter contempt for his old friend by sliding the arrow from the bow into the arrow bag slung on his back. "Keep your ear and your eye, Raimon. You'll need no mark from me to learn soon enough what it is to be hunted as a thief."

Raimon colored, looking torn between relief and offense at Jevon's insult. But he clung to his perverse denials. "I did not steal—"

Jevon waved it away with a derisive hand. "Oh, by all means, continue to stand by that lie. You are right that Constantia and I cannot prove you guilty of that theft. But there were a dozen witnesses who saw you steal the old man's horse. And since you no longer have it in your possession, you cannot give it back to him. How exactly do you mean to explain that to the baron? Or, more importantly, to his guest, who is no doubt pacing Pennault's great hall and raging to the baron about your abuse and theft at this very moment? The gentleman wore a very fine surcote and cloak the equal of anything the baron has ever worn. I know because I helped him up and brushed the dirt from his clothes after you threw him to the ground."

Who would be dressed as well as a baron except another baron? And horse thieves were hanged even faster than lesser thieves, especially by lords who poured small fortunes into breeding and training what they viewed as prized, precious, and often beloved companions.

"What are you waiting for?" Jevon mocked when Raimon hesitated. "The sooner you start running again, the more ground you can put between you and Laurant's hounds when he sets them to track you down."

Jevon saw the panic in Raimon's face again. He had to realize the clothes and other personal possessions he'd left behind at the castle would make it easy for the hounds to pursue his scent.

It was the best compromise Jevon could think of. Still Poitevin justice, of a sort, but one not doled out by his hand.

Constantia bounced with frustration. This mercy of Jevon's was noble, and she loved him more than ever for his magnanimous heart, but his undeserved clemency to Raimon would not acquit Jevon of his own continued stain of "theft."

Raimon's mantle swirled on the air as he sprinted away from the tree. As it had in the hall, the brightly colored silk caught Constantia's eye.

"That rich mantle does not belong to him," she guessed impulsively.

Jevon's arm moved in a blur. He reclaimed a shaft from his arrow bag, whisked up his bow, and discharged the arrow, catching a corner of the mantle and pinning it to the tree. Raimon staggered as the cords that bound the mantle around his neck jerked him back.

Only then did Jevon ask, "What do you mean?"

Raimon cringed, clearly thinking Jevon had just tried to kill him. Constantia took a cautious step toward Raimon to view his mantle more closely. In addition to the richly hued cloth, the cords at the neck were wrapped with gold bands.

"I thought your mantle was silk in the hall," she said, "but I see now it is scarlet. Not *quite* as expensive as silk but still more than any of Laurant's young knights can afford on the wages he pays you."

Raimon plucked the arrow out of the tree with shaking hands. He frowned as he smoothed his thumb over the prick left in the cloth by the arrowhead. "I won this at dice from those merchants in town Laurant sent Llygad and me to purchase saffron from last month. The mantle is worth a good ten livres, and now Jevon has ruined it."

The merchants were long gone from the town, and Raimon did have a passion for gambling. Constantia and Jevon could not disprove his story, especially with Llygad gone. But the sunshine filtering through the trees revealed more.

"Then what about your sword?" She nodded at the weapon strapped to Raimon's waist, exposed while he examined the mantle. "You must have been struck with the luck of the goddess Fortuna for those merchants to have lost both a mantle worth ten livres and a sword worth even more."

Jevon also studied the glossy blue-and-yellow enameled pommel and the three-figured gold bands wrapped around the hilt.

"The swords Laurant provided for his knights when we were squires were nearly interchangeable," he recalled. "The steel blades were well-tempered, but the swords all had identical hilts wrapped in leather between a simple cross-guard and a flat, circular, unadorned pommel. The weapons were so uniform that some of the knights scratched their names or initials on the pommels to tell them apart. Only Laurant carried a sword with the emblem of his house engraved and painted on the counterbalance. Either you have grown uncommonly skilled with the dice since I knew you . . ."

Raimon's Adam's apple bobbed.

"Or you cheated the merchants . . ."

Raimon somewhat nervously dropped the folds of his mantle over his sword during Jevon's elongated pause.

"Or"—Jevon removed another arrow from his bag—"you bought that mantle and sword with the missing jewels."

He nocked the arrow and aimed it at Raimon.

Raimon raised his hands again. "I-I never said I acquired enough silver all in one night. Laurant trusted me with more than one errand in town."

"But never alone," Constantia said. "The baron always sent someone with you, Llygad or Franco or one of the other knights. If one of them can vouch for these dice games and your winnings, just tell us. Otherwise . . ."

"Otherwise," Jevon said, "give us the mantle and sword. We will restore them to the baron as restitution for the jewels. Then you are free to go."

Raimon cursed but offered no witnesses who could verify his extravagant good luck. Glowering, he reached his hand inside the mantle, where it lingered a few moments. Constantia imagined him caressing the sumptuous hilt, reluctant to let it go. But Raimon finally pulled the sword out of its scabbard and made as though to drop it.

"Toss it at my feet," Jevon told him.

Raimon pitched the sword so that it landed next to Jevon's boots.

"Now give the mantle to Constantia."

Raimon untied the mantle and held it at arm's length. The brilliant red fabric trembled as he stared at the point of Jevon's arrow.

Constantia moved to take the mantle. The moment her hand fisted on the cloth, Raimon gave a hard tug and pulled her to his chest.

"Let her go!"

Jevon's shout clapped against Constantia's ears, but it was too late. Raimon's arm was around her waist, smothering her against the breast of his surcote.

"Or what?" Raimon's smug laugh cracked above her head. "You cannot hit me without risking hitting her. If you try"—something pressed through her hair against the back of her neck—"my hand may inadvertently jerk this dagger and spill some of her blood."

Where had he gotten a dagger? Of course! Raimon had not been fondling the sword beneath the mantle. He must have been checking a blade he'd hidden at the rear of his belt, where she and Jevon would not see it.

"Put the bow down, Jevon." This time, it was Jevon's curse that flamed the air, but he must have lowered his weapon, for Raimon said next, "Now, throw down your arrow bag."

She heard a soft thump as Jevon's bag struck the earth.

"Now—break the bow over your knee."

Constantia forced herself to remember that the bow did not belong to Jevon. But after having watched him wield it as naturally as though it were simply another limb, she knew destroying it would feel like lopping off a part of himself.

A crack shivered without hesitation.

"Now—"

Constantia raised her foot as Raimon began a new demand and slammed her heel down on his, grinding with all her might. The dagger flinched away on his gasp of surprise. She shoved against his chest, releasing the mantle trapped between them as she attempted to break free.

Raimon yanked her back against him, his dagger pressed against the back of her neck again.

"Let her go, Raimon!" Jevon's voice was so tight it could have thwanged an arrow into the knight had Jevon still had one. "So help me, if you harm her..."

Constantia did not hear the rest of Jevon's frustrated threat, for without the folds of the mantle, her hand felt something thin and hard through Raimon's surcote. She traced its outline lightly to avoid drawing Raimon's attention. Three loops around a center circle, a narrow stem about the length of her forefinger, and finally the crosswise bits. There was no mistaking the shape.

"Come one step closer and I'll give you her corpse." Raimon spun her around, the edge of the dagger now across the hollow of her throat. Jevon stood closer than before, his fists clenched so hard she could see them quiver.

"She's coming with me," Raimon said. "Do not try to follow us."

Raimon shifted backward, pulling her with him. It gave her a little gratification that he limped as he did so.

Jevon's lip curled with contempt. "You have already exposed yourself as a coward this day. Using a woman as a shield will only confirm to the world that you are the worst kind of craven."

"I am no coward!" Raimon's bellow nearly deafened Constantia, but he paused in his retreat to shout it. "I am Laurant's best swordsman. You are the craven, threatening a defenseless man with your arrows. In a fair fight, I would leave you dead in a pool of blood. Not one of Laurant's knights, old or young, has ever bested me."

"I do not have a bow and arrows now," Jevon said. "And you are wrong, Raimon. None of Laurant's knights ever bested *me*. Including you."

"You have not fought me for seven years, Jevon. You do not know the skill and cunning I have grown capable of."

"Then show me. Let Constantia go, and I will give you your fair fight." Jevon picked up Raimon's sword and extended it toward him, hilt first. "Trade me your dagger. I am more archer than swordsman now, but a dagger I still know how to wield."

Had Jevon gone mad? As soon as Raimon had the sword, he would plunge it through Jevon's breast!

"Come on, Raimon. No one need know besides you and me of our unequal odds. If you kill me, you can go back to Pennault and tell whatever story you wish of my death. There is still a bounty on my head. One hundred livres if I am captured on these lands, dead or alive. That is more than enough to purchase armor and a courser for the tourney." Jevon paused. "That is really why you took Lady Gwenllian's jewels, isn't it? Because Laurant still thinks tournaments are frivolous?"

Raimon's hesitation suggested Jevon had finally guessed his motive.

"Constantia will tell Laurant how unevenly we fought," Raimon said.

"Then do not take her back to Pennault. Take her to Saint Luc's instead. The monks have never seen her. If you tell them she is your sister and you are in search of a convent for her and offer them just a little of the bounty for their trouble, they will find one to bury her in where Laurant and Lady Gwenllian will never hear from her again."

Constantia knew Jevon was trying to protect her in case Raimon killed him, but . . .

Jevon glanced at her, his walnut-brown eyes full of cocky confidence. He ignored her glare and said to Raimon, "Gunthar's soldiers will spread word of your spineless cowering to everyone they meet unless you deliver my head to Laurant." He wiggled the fingers of his empty hand. "Give me the dagger, *Sir* Raimon. Then I will give you the sword."

Jevon's goading and sarcastic inflection of Raimon's title worked. Raimon lowered the dagger but kept his arm across Constantia's chest as he extended his other hand. "Give me the sword first."

"Jevon, don't," Constantia warned.

Jevon pushed the sword's hilt into Raimon's grip, then released the blade.

Jevon waited with open palm. After the cruel way he had taunted Raimon with his arrow, he could not completely fault Raimon for the shameless temptation on his face. One quick jab through Jevon's unprotected breast and his tormentor would be dead. With Constantia sequestered in a nunnery, who would know whether Raimon had dispatched the "thief" fairly or not?

"Gunthar's men will not keep what they saw today to themselves," Jevon repeated. "Sir Raimon Tirell of Pennault Castle will be known as a caitiff knight in all the courts where honorable men hold the noble sport you aspire to. Before you try to prove your courage and prowess to them, you better prove it to yourself. Give me the dagger, Raimon."

The dig at Raimon's pride worked. He shoved Constantia behind him and slapped the dagger's hilt into Jevon's hand.

Jevon barely had time to brace himself before Raimon thrust the sword at him. He scraped the steel tip aside. A derisive smirk replaced Raimon's earlier panic. A dagger was better than no defense at all, but Jevon understood, as Raimon must, the shorter blade's inherent weakness against the longer sweep of a sword.

But Jevon also knew the most dangerous thing he could do was hesitate. He made several swift, aggressive lunges, left, right, right-left-right, then one large bound straight at Raimon's belly. Raimon twisted and turned defensively before parrying the direct attack. Jevon retreated too quickly for their two blades to meet. His explorative maneuvers gave him his first sense of Raimon's improved dexterity. His boasts had not been empty bravado. Raimon's reflexes had indeed sharpened, but had Jevon held a sword, he might still have been able to swoop past Raimon's attempted block to hit his target.

Unfortunately, a dagger would make such a hit nearly impossible unless Raimon's avowed "cunning" had failed to advance with his speed. Jevon needed to test him further.

He attacked again, this time from a flurry of directions, as recklessly close as he dared to make his dagger whistle and clash and sigh and clang against the tip of Raimon's sword and still give himself space to bounce out of reach of each a skewering stab. Even with Jevon's falcon vision, Raimon's movements had grown too swift for Jevon to take advantage of the telling shift of Raimon's eyes before a strike. But Jevon's ability to rhythmically hit and evade the sword proved the coordination between his own eye and hand was still more accurate than Raimon's.

Even so, two of Raimon's thrusts came disturbingly close to spearing Jevon before he dodged them.

Their battle rounded Jevon toward Constantia, who stood in the shade of an elm tree framed by shiny-leafed boxwood dappled by sunlight. Raimon's near misses had grayed her cheeks, but she squeezed off the temptation to scream with fingers so tight against her lips she pressed them wan. She must know that crying out might distract Jevon and allow Raimon to land a lethal blow.

There's my brave, sensible girl.

She locked gazes with Jevon, then lowered her shaking hands and sketched a trembling *X* against her shoulder.

Jevon froze. *You want me to kill him?*

The scuffling of Raimon's foot spun Jevon to rebuff a fresh swing of the sword. As Jevon whirled back toward Constantia, she tapped her fingers against her shoulder and sketched the *X* again. Only then did Jevon register his misunderstanding. Facing her, he interpreted her right shoulder for the left, where the heart lay.

He had no time to try to understand what her gesture meant. He and Raimon resumed pivoting and swiveling around each other, scuffling to avoid being trapped against the trees or shrubs in their path as the clash of their steel staccatoed against the air. Jevon would need an extraordinary bit of luck to slip past that sword and disable Raimon. Unless Jevon could dull Raimon's focus.

"Which are you?" Jevon called over the reverberating battle. "Thief or seducer? Did Lady Gwenllian give you her ruby ring, or did you steal it to buy that sword?"

"Neither," Raimon snapped.

His blade swung a little too wide on the denial but came near enough to make Jevon stumble slightly before swiftly righting himself. His query had nettled Raimon, but Jevon's wobble brought the smugness back to Raimon's face. Perhaps more fumbling would stoke his brash confidence a little *too* much. After all, Raimon would not expect a mere archer to possess the physical stamina expected of knights who drilled every day with armor and swords.

Jevon panted a little, pretending his small shuffle had flustered him, before insisting, "Guia saw you with the ring. It proves you are one or the other."

"All the ring proves is that Lady Gwenllian is the vainest woman on earth. What she is *not* is saphead enough to betray her husband with me or anyone else."

"So she gave you a love token from the baron simply out of the generosity of her heart?"

Raimon's sword whizzed so near Jevon's head that the air sizzled. Jevon flowed his dodge into a full body roll, placing more space between him and Raimon, then sprang to his feet with more "winded" breaths. Again he viewed Constantia. This time her mouth had completely vanished behind her clamped hands. He wished he could signal to her the game he played, but he could not risk disclosing it to Raimon.

His ruse seemed to be working. The more confident Raimon grew in his advantage, the looser his tongue ran. "She freely gave me her ruby ring, but not out of generosity or because she wanted me for a lover. She did it because she wanted a champion who would boast of her beauty through all Christendom."

"A champion?" Jevon clipped aside another swing of the sword with the tip of his dagger. "You mean on the tournament field?"

"Remember the last few months before Laurant banished you? How every knight who sought the baron's hospitality twittered like rhapsodic birds about the growing fame of William Marshal?"

Jevon deflected another half dozen strikes. Marshal's renown as the undefeated champion of the mêlée had only soared since then.

"The young knights speak of him with wonder and envy in Normandy," Jevon said. He envied Marshal, too, and the English knight's freedom to pursue the ambition Jevon and Raimon once dreamed of together.

"Lady Gwenllian took it into her beautiful, puffed-up head that she must have a champion of her own to rival Marshal. You were the better swordsman, but you were no longer at Pennault."

The force of repelling Raimon's next strike shivered all the way up Jevon's arm. It took a moment to unlock his gritted teeth.

Raimon smirked. "I was the only other knight who had defeated all of her husband's best men. But Laurant told her no." Anger sparked in Raimon's eyes. He paused his advance on Jevon as he appeared to relive Laurant's rebuff. "The baron said he'd poured money and years of training into me so I could fight for *him* if need be, not so I could go make my fortune elsewhere. No matter how Lady Gwenllian wheedled and cajoled and wept her beguiling tears, Laurant kept his foot firmly planted against her. I think he feared my victories might spread word of the Fair Lady Gwenllian too far. For, of course, she wanted me to wear her favor and proclaim her beauty everywhere I went."

Raimon appeared lost in his recollections, but that could be a trap to lure Jevon into making a hasty and fatal move. Just to be safe, Jevon continued panting during the "respite" he'd been granted. He knew the baron well enough to guess Laurant's motives. "Doing so might attract rivals for her affections to Pennault."

"Aye." Resentment blurred the heat in Raimon's eyes. "So she gave me her ruby ring to buy my equipment, a ring that meant so little to her she forgot about its inscription. As soon as I saw it, I knew I dared not sell it lest it be traced back to me and Laurant jump to the conclusion that his wife and I were lovers. But I knew she would expect me to show her some purchase I'd made toward furnishing myself for the mêlée before she gave me something more to sell. It was too risky to keep the ring on my person or among my belongings, so I hid it in the cellar until I could decide what to do."

Raimon's eyes flicked at Jevon's breast. Jevon knew the maneuver he intended from the angle of Raimon's blade and the bend of his knees. Jevon began to circle, forcing Raimon to mirror his motion and readjust his strategy for a moving target.

"I made a copy of Beatris's key to Lady Gwenllian's jewelry casket, then took the topaz ring with the dove in place of the ruby."

Jevon guessed the continued "confession" was meant to distract him as much as Jevon had hoped prodding it might distract Raimon.

"I used the topaz to buy this scarlet mantle. Lady Gwenllian never even missed it. It wasn't stealing when I knew she intended to give me more of her jewels to sell."

Jevon increased his pace, flexing his fingers around the dagger's hilt. He thought back to Laurant's inventory. "Six pieces were missing from the collection we found in the barrel, including the topaz ring. Which piece did you sell for that sword?"

Raimon continued turning at the center of Jevon's orbit, but he rolled the sword back and forth, admiring the hilt with its three glittering gold bands.

"The amber crucifix. She gave that to me after I showed her the mantle. Unfortunately, Laurant came back early from a visit to his brother and caught me showing her my new sword. He knew I had no money of my own, so I lied, saying it was a bequest from an uncle."

In a move almost quicker than breath, he drove his sword at Jevon. Jevon swiped the dagger downward and knocked the sword's tip away. "A lie too easily uncovered if you used it with Laurant too often. One inquiry to your father about a well-to-do uncle . . ."

". . . and he'd have found out I didn't have one."

The new sword hissed at Jevon again, but again he deflected it. They shifted in and out of the trees, Raimon striking, Jevon parrying. Their feet cast up clumps of leaves and dirt. Then Jevon saw Constantia motioning at him again. He dove behind a clump of gorse, using it as a shield while he panted another question to divert Raimon from seeing her too.

"What did Lady Gwenllian give you next to sell?"

Raimon leaned the tip of his sword against the ground, a scornful curl on his lips at Jevon's pathetic need for more rest. "Nothing. Laurant came upon us as she praised my gallantry and excellence above all her husband's knights, and, of course, that roused his jealousy. So she said she could give me no more jewels for a while. It was months before Laurant stopped looking warily at me. By then, so many men were beginning to seek the Lady Clothilde's hand in marriage that Lady Gwenllian rather poutingly admitted herself too old for the frivolity of tournaments. She said I might keep the mantle and sword, but I could expect no more gifts from her."

"But you took more of her jewels anyway." Jevon dragged his sleeve across his forehead, pretending to wipe away perspiration while he flicked his gaze to Constantia. The sun had shifted, chasing the shadows from beneath the elm and throwing a rich glow over her.

"I used those to buy my armor, which I had to do piecemeal as I dared not sell more than one or two items of jewelry a year. The only merchants I had access to were the ones who traded in town."

Jevon guessed where Raimon had hidden his ill-gotten mail—in the hollowed-out tree near the river where Raimon told Ned and Hamo he'd left a fishing rod.

Constantia pinched the cloth on her right shoulder, pulled it away from her breast, let it fall back into place, and drew an X over it.

"If I were noticed selling fistfuls of jewels every time the baron sent me on an errand, it might have reached the baron's ears."

She curled her hand against her shoulder, then jerked it downward. Jevon resisted the impulse to frown his confusion.

"I finally had all I needed to join the tournament circuit next spring except for a lance and horse."

Constantia, looking impatient, repeated her series of gestures.

"And I would have had those had you and Constantia not ruined everything by turning over the barrel where I hid the remaining jewels. I confess it worried me that Laurant left the two of you locked up there so long. I did not know what to expect when he ordered me to release you, so I hedged my bets by donning the mantle and belting on my sword."

"In case you had to flee like a coward."

Raimon's breath hissed at Jevon's jibe, but Jevon did not observe Raimon's expression because he fancied the strangest thing—a pair of eyes peering at him in the gilding sunlight of the boxwood's branches behind Constantia. But when Jevon blinked, they were gone. If they had been there at all.

He mentally shook himself and looked back at Raimon. Raimon stood with his sword raised, poised for attack.

"I have lent you quarter enough," Raimon growled. "Let us finish this."

Yes, let's.

Jevon spun out from behind the gorse, gyrating his dagger against the whirlwind of fresh attacks from the sword. He would have been dead long ago had his razor-keen eyesight not allowed him to follow the sword's whizzing, serpentine paths. But he could do no more than deflect each assault—high, low, to the left, to the right. The larger, heavier blade's vibrations pulsated up his arm until Jevon's arm began to ache.

Raimon's blows fell like a barrage of steely hail, his errors too small for Jevon to slip past with the dagger. Jevon no longer feigned the slowing exhaustion in his throbbing arm. He ducked to one side to avoid a hacking stroke, then swung his leg up and kicked Raimon's wrist as it swooped past him with the sword. Raimon's arm flew sideways just long enough to allow Jevon a chance to rotate inside Raimon's reach and slash with his dagger. His blade sliced Raimon's forearm, but the cut was too shallow to make him drop the sword.

Jevon launched into a deep bound to place a safe distance between them before Raimon recovered for a retaliatory blow. He'd left blood on Raimon's torn sleeve, but in the heat of battle, Raimon should barely have noticed so slight a hit.

Jevon braced himself for a fresh attack. Raimon stood, staring at the bright flash of red on his sleeve. He drew an audibly shaky breath, then flew at Jevon again, but his distraction had given Jevon time to shift the dagger to his left hand. No soldier worth his salt failed to train with both hands.

Their blades again clanged and chimed, but within less than a dozen parries, Jevon sensed a change. Raimon's blows grew more hesitant, and between strikes, he glanced at his arm. Had he not realized he was as vulnerable as any other man engaged in a battle with deadly weapons?

Perhaps not. Laurant had never let his knights train with sharpened swords. The baron wanted them skilled for war but not slaughtering one another through hotheaded or accidental mis-strikes. Unlike Laurant's older knights, Raimon must not have fought in actual battle. When Gunthar's troops overran Pennault, Raimon had remained in Gunthar's camp as a hostage rather than a participant in the fight. Raimon's formidable skills had likely never been challenged by a weapon that could kill him. Not even a dagger.

"Is something amiss with your surcote?" Jevon queried.

Raimon's eyes, angry but defensive, darted up to Jevon's face. "Not a thing."

Two strikes swung at Jevon but with considerably less precision than before.

"You are probably right," Jevon said as his dagger deflected both, "that I cannot defeat you with this. I have spent too little time with a blade and too much with the bow these past years, thanks to you. I won several purses in archery contests at tournaments and always stayed to watch the mêlée. A few times, I saw good knights disemboweled in the chaos of the battle."

The sword continued to whoosh and whistle but more haphazardly. So Raimon's skill *was* dependent on his delusions of invulnerability.

"Sometimes mishaps happened," Jevon continued. "Spears slipped through helmets' eye slits and gouged out eyes."

Raimon's eyes momentarily squinted. Was he remembering the threat of Jevon's arrow?

"Swords cut through weakened ventails, hacking through necks."

A tinge of green colored Raimon's pallor. His swings grew wider and more erratic. That was not necessarily to Jevon's advantage as it made Raimon's moves less predictable. But every time Jevon sprang away from a swing or lunge long enough to grant Raimon a breath, Raimon glanced again at his arm.

Jevon pressed on with his graphic recital. "Lances pierced worn links to mangle bellies and rip out entrails. I have seen men retch and even faint at the brutal hazards of the tourney."

Raimon actually released one hand on his sword hilt and started to cover his mouth.

"And that is only a game, Raimon. What will you do when men expect you to turn your tournament victories to the battlefield, where there are no rules at all?"

Jevon's mocking goaded Raimon too far. He clamped his freed hand back around his hilt and glared at Jevon with venomous, deadly hatred.

"I am not afraid of you, Jevon. I am not afraid of anyone."

Raimon's voice was guttural, as though choking back his stomach's heave, but his sword buzzed with a vicious speed. Jevon could do nothing but leap back and back to escape it. The swings were slapdash and wild, but that made them more dangerous, not less, for a man who held only a dagger. Jevon knew what he was doing.

He has thrown himself into an unthinking frenzy, shutting out the gruesome images I raised to overcome his doubt until his enemy is dead.

Any experienced warrior would have known how to defeat such a volatile, undisciplined attack, gutting Raimon with his sword as deftly as a man gutted a fish. But Raimon's mindless velocity drove Jevon and his dagger back toward where Jevon had last seen Constantia. From the corner of his eye, he caught her dart sensibly out of their way. Almost in the same thudding heartbeat, he found himself engulfed in the pool of sunlight that had slanted its warm glow around her under the elm's branches. Between the tree and the boxwood, there would be no room for further retreat.

A dangerous idea lit Jevon's mind. A gamble, but to work, he had to force thought back into Raimon's brain. And fast.

Jevon dropped the dagger as the sword whirred at him again. "Hold, Raimon, hold! You win! I yield!"

Jevon stumbled against the elm, gripping one hand around the other as though cradling a disabling wound. Would Raimon be too inflamed to notice that their blades had not actually connected? Would he wonder why no blood oozed between Jevon's knuckles? Would he even pause at all?

"Stay your sword!" Jevon shouted. Sinking to his knees in a cower might be more convincing, but he needed to maintain some maneuverability. He hunched in fear but balanced on the balls of his feet in case he needed to pivot.

"Why should I?" Raimon's blade hovered over his shoulder, trembling in its eagerness to slice downward at his helpless opponent.

"Because it is what honorable victors do," Jevon said.

He bobbed his knees to keep them loose, hoping Raimon interpreted the movement as pain.

Raimon's lips curled in a snarl. "You may be right. I do not know if I have the stomach for the hazards of the tourney, but I will not let you live to ridicule me for it to the world. I may retch out my guts after I take off your head, but I will still have your head, and no one, not even your English friends, will doubt my courage when I return it to Laurant and claim the bounty on it."

Raimon twisted at the waist to lend more force to his swing. Constantia's scream echoed through the trees, even rustling the bushes near the elm. As Raimon sliced toward Jevon, Jevon launched himself straight up from his crouch, hauling his legs high as his hands found and wound around a tree limb overhead. He heard the woosh of the sword beneath his feet, followed by the *thunk* he'd hoped for. Raimon's blade had hit the elm's trunk, and this time it stuck.

While Raimon wrestled to free his weapon, Jevon swung himself backward, then forward, shooting out his legs to drive them into Raimon's chest. Raimon flew back—without his sword—and hit the ground. Jevon dropped to the grass, scooped up the dagger, and sprang on top of him. He slapped his free hand hard against Raimon's chest to pin him to the ground, hooked the blade into the right shoulder of Raimon's surcote and made three quick slashes.

Raimon screamed. As the fabric tore, out tumbled a key.

35

Jevon turned the key over, then stood and held it out to Constantia. "Is this what you wanted me to find?"

She looked too numb to do more than nod before she flung herself into his arms. With exhilaration still pumping his heart, he lowered his head to reassure her of his safety with the most impassioned kiss of his life. But before he could find her lips, a hand buffeted the back of his head.

"That," a man's voice barked from behind him, "was the most foolhardy thing I have ever seen."

The brisk blow felt disturbingly familiar. Jevon turned. A gray-bearded man with a drawn sword stood in front of the nearby boxwood, its limbs swaying with the man's emergence from the other side.

"Father?"

Seven years had deepened the grooves in his sire's forehead and the lines that fanned from his nose to the mustache of the charcoal beard Jevon last remembered mottled with brown. But nothing had changed in the blunt way his father looked at him.

Another swift cuff, this time to the side of Jevon's head, assured Jevon the image was not a specter.

"That was reckless. Feigning an injury and dropping your dagger like that? What if this nit's sword had been faster than your leap?"

Jevon rubbed the spot where the smack fell, not because it hurt—his father's rigorous mode of "emphasis" always fell with well-aimed control—but in resentment of his perpetual paternal criticism. "But it wasn't faster than my leap."

"But it *might* have been, and then you would be dead and I'd have had to spear that miscreant for killing my son." His father slammed the sword into the scabbard at his side.

"What are you doing here, sir?" Jevon asked, simultaneously irritated and confused.

"I came to save your neck before Laurant stretched it on the gallows." His father gave a jerk of his chin. "I think the pudding has fainted."

Pudding? Jevon followed his father's glare to Raimon's closed eyes and slack jaw. So he had. He must have thought Jevon was about to kill him.

His father frowned. "Who is this?"

He was no longer looking at Raimon.

Jevon did not realize his arm was still looped around Constantia's waist until he felt her squirm to free herself at his father's query. He started to pull her back, casting a defiant look at his father, then realized that nothing, not his aching desire for her nor his father's baffling appearance, changed his situation by so much as a whit.

He let her slip away. It did not surprise him that his father still did not recognize her. "This is Lady Constantia de Ormande, a friend from my days at Pennault. Lady Constantia, my father, Lord Vidal de Cazalet."

Constantia dipped a red-faced curtsy.

"Ormande?" Lord Vidal repeated. "One of Sir Enguerran de Ormande's daughters?"

"Yes, sir," Constantia said, her gaze fastened on the toes of her shoes.

Lord Vidal's exacting gaze raked over her prosaic gown and jumbled hair where strands of straw from the cellar still clung. "One of the younger, undowered ones, I presume? I heard he proclaimed the eldest his heir before she married."

Only the faint crimping of her skirts by her hands belied Constantia's composure. "Yes, sir," she said again. "My father's liege lord, Lord Laurant, took me into his household as a child. Jevon helped me learn my way about the castle. He was always thoughtful and chivalrous, even as a page. You will be most pleased to discover after all these years that the ugly lies that drove him from the castle were exactly that. Lies."

"Hmph," his father grunted, his gaze shifting from Constantia to Jevon and back to her again.

Jevon feared his father guessed too much between them. Hoping to divert Lord Vidal but also curious, he asked, "How did you know I was back, sir?"

"Your earl told me."

"My earl? Gunthar?" Jevon's pulse began to gallop again. Had Gunthar devasted Roquard Castle as he had Vere and Pennault? What had happened to Jevon's mother? And his brothers?

"He rode up to my gate two days ago," Lord Vidal said, "and demanded I declare which lord I serve, Duke Richard or the king. 'King Henry,' I told him stoutly and opened my gates to him and his men."

Jevon released his breath, somewhat chagrined to realize he had never bothered to learn enough about his father's political opinions to know where his loyalties lay.

"While your mother provided the earl's men with refreshment, I heard them speaking of a Poitevin archer Laurant had locked up who bore a scar on his hand. Some of the earl's men thought it was the brand of a thief. When I asked the earl about this archer, he said he called himself Jevon le Falquet. Well, I am no fool. Once Gunthar left, I rode to Pennault to see who this Poitevin called Jevon le Falquet with the suspicious scar might be—just in case he proved to be my long-lost prodigal son."

Only now did Jevon recognize the cloak around his father's square shoulders. The old man Raimon had flung to the ground at Pennault had worn the same one. Jevon remembered how the man had pulled the hood over his head while Jevon dusted him off.

"Why did you not reveal yourself to me in the bailey?" Jevon asked

"You seemed to be in a great hurry, and for all I knew, you were running for your life again. I did not want to slow you down with an ill-timed reunion."

Running. Of course, you've believed me guilty all these years.

Jevon saw the blend of sympathy and envy in Constantia's eyes as she listened to his tense exchange with his father. How many times had Jevon ranted to her about his sire's yearly lectures? And how many times had she wistfully replied that she wished she'd had a father who cared enough to occasionally visit Pennault to lecture her?

Jevon did not know how he felt about meeting his father this way. Lord

Vidal said he'd come to save Jevon's neck, but so far, he'd offered only censure.

Jevon looked away from Lord Vidal's brusque study and handed the key to Constantia. "Is this what I think it is?"

"I hope so," Constantia said. "I felt it in Raimon's surcote when he held me trapped. If it works to unlock Lady Gwenllian's jewelry casket, it will prove to her and the baron that he had access to the jewels in the cellar."

Jevon cast a dubious look at Raimon's prone form. "It will still be our word against his that we found it on his person."

"Laurant will believe me." Lord Vidal planted his gloved fists on his hips. "I saw you cut it out of his surcote."

Jevon clenched his jaw, half grateful, half bitter. "Thank you, sir. I know how sorely you think I have let you down. But your word will not be entirely unprejudicial. Laurant will expect you to defend me as your son."

Still, it meant something that, this time, his father knew that Raimon, not Jevon, was the thief.

Lord Vidal opened his mouth to say more, but another voice cut him off.

"We will lend our witness, then. Laurant will have to listen to *us*."

Jevon spun about, startled to see Ned Woodville. The archer sergeant stood several paces behind him, holding a strung bow with an arrow at his side. Hamo stood near Ned with his sword. How long had they been there?

Lord Vidal acknowledged them with a nod. "I got turned about in these woods looking for you after I spoke with Laurant. I came across these good fellows, and they offered to show me the way to where they last saw you."

Ned indicated his bow. "I was about to loose my arrow at the pudding before he struck you down. You've the reflexes of a cat to have leapt out of his sword's path so fast."

"We saw you pluck that key off the pudding," Hamo added. "We will attest to where you found it."

The "pudding" again. After today, Raimon would never live down Lord Vidal's contemptuous epithet. Jevon gazed at his former friend. Shattered dreams were painful, as Jevon knew all too well. Fear had undone Raimon's. Youthful impatience for Constantia's hand had undone his.

Suddenly it was easier to face his father's displeasure than to look into her eyes. "How did you know we'd ridden into the woods?"

"I knew there was a clip in my horse's shoe. It was easy enough to follow the tracks into the trees, but after that, I lost you." Lord Vidal cast a scathing glance at Raimon, who began to stir. "At least you had the courtesy to brush me off after you helped me up in the yard. Your mother will be pleased to know that seven years of whatever foolery you have been up to did not cause you to forget your manners."

Jevon supposed that was as much of a compliment as he would ever receive from his father. "Is Mother well, sir?"

Had she grayed as much as his father had? Were her eyes still laughing and kind?

"Well enough to tongue-flay me if I do not return to Rouquard with you. To this day, my ears still smoke from her recriminations when I came home empty-handed after Laurant banished you."

"Empty-handed?" Jevon repeated. "What do you mean?"

"My men and I scoured these woods for you after I learned of your punishment. Guilty or not, you were my son, and I had no intention of letting one of our moneygrubbing barons or knights hunt you down for Laurant's bounty. Only every time we glimpsed you, you scuttled off before we could catch you."

Could it be? "Sir, did you all wear brown hoods?"

"To blend in with the trees. We had to be careful. Many searched for you in hopes of claiming the silver. I could not risk the repercussions if Laurant chose to complain to the king that I had given aid to a condemned thief against the will of the lord he had wronged."

All these years, Jevon was sure his father had cursed his youngest son and declared him as good as dead to their family for the shame Jevon's banishment brought to their house. Instead, the brown-hooded hunters who sought Jevon so relentlessly had not been his enemies but his father's own men sent to rescue him? The bitterness vanished, leaving a lump in his throat that swelled so tight he could not speak.

"Sir Pudding is moaning," Ned said. "Hamo, give me your belt to bind his hands before he rouses."

Hamo shoved Raimon over and held him down while Ned secured his wrists.

"Be sure to take his sword with you," Jevon said. "He bought it with some of Lady Gwenllian's jewels."

Hamo stood and tucked the weapon into his belt while Jevon did the same with the dagger. Technically, it belonged to Laurant, but "borrowing" it seemed a fair exchange for the bow the baron's men had taken from him when they locked him in the cellar. It pained Jevon to lose his beloved weapon. He would send the dagger back to Pennault once he had a new war bow. The quick need to replace it meant he would have to settle for common cow-horn nocks instead of antler, without the intricate carvings he had paid so many of his mercenary coins for. But mostly he would miss the epigram carved into his weapon's yew-wood belly by the cunning Welsh bowyer who fashioned it: *Hywel ap Ioan made this bow to bring the evildoer low.* Jevon had relied on those words to maintain his moral moorings among his less scrupulous mercenary brothers.

Ned helped Hamo haul Raimon to his feet. "We will take him to Pennault," Ned said, "and give our testimony of what we saw to the baron before we rejoin the earl."

The two of them dragged Raimon off before Jevon could thank them. He knew from the way Ned suddenly avoided his eyes that his statement did not include an invitation to return to the earl with them.

"Sir," Jevon said to his father, "will you see Lady Constantia safely back to the castle?"

"What are you going to do?" Lord Vidal asked.

"I am going in search of your horse. Lady Constantia will take you to where we tethered the others, but I startled yours into bolting to prevent Sir Raimon from escaping. 'Tis a fine piece of horseflesh. I should not want you to lose it."

"Likely it has already started for home on its own."

"Perhaps, but I should like to be sure. It is the least I can do after the contemptible way Sir Raimon stole it from you." Jevon bent and picked up the broken remains of Lord Vidal's knight's bow. "My apologies to your companion. As soon as I have the means, I will replace it."

More expense for his mercenary purse.

Jevon gave the shards of the bow with its pathetically trailing string to his father, careful to keep his gaze on Lord Vidal rather than Constantia. Lord Vidal's obdurate features seemed somehow softer now that Jevon knew his father had come after him—twice—to protect him.

His father extended his arm to Constantia. She might be lamentably unkempt for a lady, but that would not stop his father from treating her courteously. His father was annoyingly judgmental, but his paternal lectures were always buttressed by chivalry. Constantia could not refuse Lord Vidal's gesture without appearing disrespectful, so she let him tuck her hand into his arm. But as he led her away, she threw Jevon a glance as sharp as the dagger in his belt.

Jevon waited until they were out of sight before studying his scarred hand. Constantia thought Raimon's key solved everything. But it solved only half their problem. Yes, Laurant would now have to admit his mistake. But then what? Jevon could not support a wife with the only honorable skill he held, especially as part of a *dis*reputable mercenary band. A mercenary archer earned a mere two or three denier a day when employed, whereas a knight might demand two sols.

Jevon was not a knight and saw no way of becoming one. The Poitevin barons, many of whom spent months seeking him for the bounty, would not now merely shrug and accept him into their service no matter what Laurant said. Not with this mark of disgrace still in Jevon's flesh and their memory of its meaning. Some lord beyond these borders might be willing to overlook the thinly obscured scar for his adeptness with the bow, but offer him a knighthood? Such a lord would wonder why, if Jevon had been worthy of the accolade, he had not already received it by the age of seven-and-twenty.

He shook his head. His only hope, a full royal pardon and permanent employment by Gunthar as one of the earl's archers, had evaporated. The earl had turned his back on Jevon not because of his brand but because Gunthar suspected Jevon of aiding a valuable hostage, Laurant's son, to escape Gunthar's hands.

"There is no place in my camp for a man unsure of his loyalties."

Of that sin Jevon admitted himself guilty.

He left the scene of his triumph over Raimon, cursorily scanning the ground for signs of his father's horse. He envied Gunthar's undivided convictions. To be so certain in one's mind that nothing could shake him from them, not even friendship or love, must be an uncomplicated way to live. By allowing both to rule his heart, Jevon had cut himself off from the future he'd wanted most of all.

He knelt to examine a mark in the earth, a half-obscured arc with a distinctive clip. A little farther on, the hoofprints became clearer. His father was right. The horse had turned for home. Then Jevon did not need to follow farther. The forests of Brittany should again provide safe haven for him until he could cross into Normandy and rejoin his mercenary band.

He trudged on. Constantia would be safe by now, exonerated by the key and no less than three witnesses from any complicity in theft. In time, the memories of these last few days, both bitter and sweet, would dim. He would look back on this brief interlude with her and Gunthar and wonder whether he had lived it at all or merely dreamed it out of loneliness and a longing for what his life might have been had this or that only been different.

A footstep crunched behind him. He whirled, Raimon's dagger in his hand, remembering the pale-haired stranger who eluded Gunthar's men. He quickly lowered the weapon when he saw who pursued him, but every other tendon in his body remained taut with surprise, alarm, and a touch of wariness.

"What are you doing here?" he asked.

"What do you think?" Constantia said. "I am coming with you."

"Coming with me? I do not need your help to find my father's horse."

"Of course not. Your father already found it where it stopped to nibble on some hawthorn leaves. I slipped away while he was stroking its nose and scolding it for not recognizing Raimon as an ignominious scoundrel and bucking him off." She bent to view the ground. "There's nary a hoofprint in sight here. I thought you a better tracker than this."

If she thought that twinkle in her eyes would weaken his resolve, she did not know the unflinching mercenary he had become.

"Go home, Stantia," he said in his roughest soldier's voice.

She crossed her arms, the twinkle turning to sparks of defiance. "Not without you."

His mouth tightened.

Her fiery gaze seared through him. "You are leaving Poitou again, and I do not blame you. Only this time I am coming along."

Irritation twitched the hairs on the back of his neck. He did not need a surge of longing whipping up false hope for an impossible future with her. He summoned the thickest sarcasm he could to deflate her ridiculous suggestion.

"And if that villain who stalked us comes upon us again? I cannot stay awake every moment to guard you."

"Then we will take turns guarding each other. There will be less chance of him cutting *your* throat while you sleep if I stay awake to guard *you* until we get to wherever we're going."

He huffed through his nose. "And when I rejoin my mercenary band? What am I to do with you then?"

"Well"—her lashes dipped in a charming show of sudden bashfulness—"perhaps you need not be a mercenary. A man with your skill with the bow will always be in demand for some lord's service, and I can make myself quite useful to the lord's lady. Even if you and I cannot share the same quarters, surely they would not object to an occasional"—she blushed—"tryst between us so long as I have a wedding ring on my finger."

Allowing Constantia to join him as a servant? He opened his mouth to blast the suggestion, but she rushed on.

"Lady Gwenllian may have been forced for the sake of my birth to let me dine at her table, but in all other matters, you know she used me as little more than a drudge. I can spin and embroider, mend clothes, and help in the laundry or kitchen. I know how to care for a lady's gowns and comb and dress her hair. And, above all, I know how to smile politely if that lady snaps and snarls at me and calls me a stupid wench."

She touched a finger to her chin, lolled her tongue out the corner of her mouth and crossed her eyes, making silly sport of Lady Gwenllian's belittling insults. Jevon bit the inside of his cheek to stop himself from laughing at her dotty expression. Laughing would only encourage her.

He could poke innumerable holes in her plan if he had time, but the shadows were lengthening. It would soon be dark, and he had no intention of risking another blot on her reputation by spending another night with her, however chastely, outside the castle walls while he martialed his counterarguments.

"We will discuss this tomorrow," he said. "Go back to Pennault, and we will talk it over in the morning."

"Not unless you come with me."

"You cannot honestly expect me to spend another night under the roof of the man who ruined my life with this?" He balled his branded hand.

"No." She forced his hand open and slid hers around his palm. "But there is nothing more for me there. Therri and Heléne are both safe. Neither is under further threat now that Lord Laurant surrendered and renewed his oath of fealty to the king. And surely a humble archer does not need a wife who comes to him with a dowry. Does he?"

She raised up on her toes to kiss him. Letting her abase herself to true servitude, forfeiting her title as lady? What man with a scrap of conscience would agree to that for the woman he loved? Yet, if he let his lips meet hers, every sane argument would fly out of his head and he might never be able to gather them back.

His resistance dissolved when her hands cupped his face. He did not need her urging for his mouth to drift yearningly toward hers. Only the barking voice that forced itself into the infinitesimal space between their lips made Jevon rear back. The fracture of anticipated pleasure left him aching all the way to his core.

"A scruffy mercenary might not require a dowry from a wife, but my wellborn, if foolish son does, even if he is the youngest of my whelps."

Constantia's hands dropped from Jevon's cheeks as though his skin scalded her. Lord Vidal had joined them, leading three horses by their reins.

Jevon turned on his father, defensive of Constantia's embarrassment. "This is none of your concern, Father."

"Wrong," Lord Vidal said bluntly. "When I agreed to let you be fostered and trained for knighthood by Laurant, I trusted you to grow up in an honorable and responsible manner. Perhaps what happened to you was mere misfortune, but the only way to restore your good name is to take you back to Rouquard and show the world that I have embraced you as my son by knighting you and reestablishing you as heir to my lands along with your brothers. And my heirs require wives who bring at least a modicum of wealth to their marriages."

Jevon assumed the touch of solemnity in his father's expression as he looked at Constantia was intended to appear apologetic.

"There is nothing in your birth, per se, that makes me frown on you, Lady Constantia," Lord Vidal said. "Were your father willing to bequeath to you a few jewels, a sliver of land—saints! For the sake of what I see in my son's eyes, even a few settings of silver plate. Is there any chance—?"

Constantia shook her head. "Everything is promised to my sister. Everything except my mother's fifth-best necklace and fifth-best ring. But they are only chrysolite and brass."

From Lord Vidal's disappointed expression, such trumperies were not worth the mention. He sighed. "That is what I feared. Were your sister only betrothed, I might have been able to persuade Sir Enguerran to shake loose a few baubles for you. But now that she is married, her husband has no incentive to forfeit a jot of her dowry and inheritance in your behalf. It is regrettable." Jevon caught more sympathy than he expected in the glance his father sent him. "But for the love his mother bears him—for the love *I* bear him—I cannot, I *will not* let him resume the ignominious life of a mercenary soldier Laurant's deplorable judgment forced him into."

"You are right, of course, my lord," Constantia said, her voice small but poised.

She curtsied to his father. Somehow when she straightened, her bob of deference had shifted her several steps away from Jevon.

Jevon understood what so quickly quenched her spirit. She would fight to stay with him in rejection and banishment, but divide him from his family when they extended their arms to reclaim him? She had wished too long for a kind word or act from her own father to deny that joy to Jevon.

Her lashes batted hard against her cheeks. Beating back tears? "Forgive me for being so bold with your son. He—I—we were foolish to let our friendship grow into something more. I have navigated these woods hundreds of times. I can find my way back to Pennault if you wish to leave for Rouquard at once."

"It is too late in the day for that," Lord Vidal said. "Besides, I intend to give Laurant another scathing piece of my mind before I go. And you, Jevon, are going to stare him down at my side when I do."

Lord Vidal turned himself about, missing Jevon's glare at being commanded like a wayward page. Part of him wanted to tell his father to go to blazes, that he was a grown man who'd survived on his own for seven years and if he wished to marry Constantia and abandon his birthright, that was his decision. But what life would it be for Constantia if he bore her off with him? It was not as though he could choose the master and mistress they served. What if she fell into subjection to a harridan worse than Lady Gwenllian?

"I confess," Lord Vidal said, "I am not as familiar with these woods as you, my lady. Which way is Pennault from here?"

"I will show you." Constantia swept off through the trees.

"Come, son." Lord Vidal looked at Jevon with an unexpected mix of firmness and compassion.

Jevon strode alongside his father until they caught up with Constantia. Lord Vidal considerately lifted her onto one of the horses, then he and Jevon mounted the other two. Jevon knew his father meant well, but even his eagerness to hear his mother's voice diminished to a flicker in the despair that engulfed him. He could not bear to live at Rouquard, so near to

Constantia but unable to wed her. And he would not take her with him into an unpredictable future. Jevon would collect his bow after nightfall while everyone at Pennault slept and be gone before anyone suspected his intentions. His father would search for him, but Jevon had eluded him before. He would do so again.

Constantia entered the great hall with Jevon and Lord Vidal as Raimon was vigorously defending himself to Laurant and his council. She followed Jevon as he ranged himself near the Earl of Gunthar's archer and soldier from the woods. Judging from the perspiration dotting Raimon's brow, they had already avouched for where Jevon found the key.

"I could never have borrowed your wife's jewels had Beatris not given me her key to copy," Raimon blustered. "And I intended to redeem every piece and return them before the baroness noticed they were missing. You have known me nearly all my life, my lord. You know I am not a thief." This insistence failed to banish Laurant's frown. Raimon's swaggering attitude deflated a little. His voice stretched up a notch. "If you refuse to believe me, then the penalty you declare should be dealt to Beatris as well, and Guia, too, for Guia stole the baroness's brooch and let Jevon take the blame for it."

"Miserable cur," Constantia heard the earl's archer mutter to Jevon. "He's hoping to play upon the baron's reluctance to ruthlessly punish the women to lessen his own punishment."

Laurant tersely cut Raimon off. He subjected Beatris, Guia, and finally Jevon each to a long moment of ambiguous study, then ordered Raimon locked up in the gatehouse prison, Guia and Beatris confined to their bedchamber, and abruptly adjourned his council.

"Tomorrow," Laurant said with uncommon firmness when Lord Vidal demanded a hearing. The baron commanded Sir Eudes to arrange quarters for Lord Vidal and "his son" for the night, then strode out of the hall.

With Jevon's father hovering at his side, Constantia retired with Beatris and Guia, without exchanging further words with him.

No one spoke as they prepared for bed. Constantia tried to comb the straw and snarls out of her hair, praying each stinging yank might reduce the torment in her breast. The endeavor proved a dismal failure. She finally blew out the pungent tallow candle and sought her lumpy mattress. Sniffles and snuffles from Guia and Beatris salted the rasps of their creaking beds, but Constantia lay dry-eyed on her back, refusing to seek the false comfort of Jevon's gloves beneath her bolster. Moonlight leaked through a crack in the shutters. Her sleepless gaze watched the silvery ribbon crawl across the floor as the hours dragged by. Laurant would be required to pass judgment in the morning. On Raimon. On Beatris. On Guia. Constantia worried for the women, but it was selfish grief that crushed her chest as though all the rubble from the cellar were piled atop it.

She should not be wallowing in self-indulgent misery. She was happy Jevon's father had found him. She was *joyful*. Never again would she lie in this wretched bed, fearing for his safety, wondering if his brand had betrayed him to the sword or the noose. The mother who had sent him a valuable ring to deliver him from his father's rebuke over a ripped surcote would welcome him home with tears and caresses. His stern father would soon be awed by the brave and chivalrous man his son had become. And when Jevon wed a dowered, soft-skinned wife with hair so smooth a tangle never dared despoil it—well, Constantia could only hope the heart such a wife would win might still remember with a whisper of fondness the friendship he shared with Constantia in their youth.

Despite her despondence, the hectic emotions of the day at length began to tingle exhaustion through her body. Oh, how she would welcome a few hours of blissful oblivion!

Hoo-hoo-hooooo

The stuttering call shook Constantia from the edge of sleep, pooling anguish through her again. Inconsiderate owl. Did it not understand how dearly she needed rest? She would require all her composure to part from Jevon tomorrow without dissolving into tears in front of his father.

Her eyelids drifted.

Hoo-hoo-hooooo

She knew she'd dozed only because of the way her body jerked awake. The ribbon of moonlight slithered across her midriff, and the aggravating owl hooted more persistently than ever. She started to pull her blanket over her head to muffle its irritating call.

Hoo-hoo-hooooot!

Constantia bolted upright. No owl's hoot ended with an emphatic *t*. They didn't have teeth. Jevon! It was the call he used to use to summon her to meet him in Lady Gwenllian's rose garden.

She threw off her thin blanket, ran to the window, and pulled open the shutter. When two breaths sucked in behind her, she knew her creaking bed had awakened the other women, but neither Guia nor Beatris spoke. Jevon stood below, bathed in the moonlight. He pointed in the direction of the garden, then, as always, held his fist a few inches beneath his nose as if sniffing a flower to be sure she understood. Then he disappeared.

"For heaven's sake, Stantia, when did you start sleeping like the dead? Have you any idea how long I stood in the damp, calling you?"

The gallant way he shook off his cloak and tucked it around her worn, patched one robbed his complaint of any sting.

"You are not the only owl at the castle, you know." She bantered to conceal the ambivalent pounding of her heart. Every moment left with him was precious, especially without his father looking on. But . . .

I am not ready for him to say goodbye. I should have stayed in bed. How can I bear to hear him say goodbye?

His hands lingered on the ties of his cloak beneath her chin. She stared at the breast of his surcote to avoid his eyes. Had he glimpsed the white sleeping chemise beneath her cloak before the folds of his own enclosed her? She had barely enough wits to don her slippers before she ran from her chamber to meet him. Although thoughts of his soft-skinned, sleek-haired future bride prompted her to pause at the garden entrance and rub a few rose petals over the backs of her hands and along her neck.

"I was going to go," he said. "While you slept. I intended to be gone when you woke in the morning." His hands nudged up her chin, forcing her eyes to meet his.

Fool. I should have stayed in bed.

The shadows prevented her from reading his expression. A raw swell of tears burned her throat. "I understand, Jevon. I do. If my father wanted me back—"

"You would fly off to his repentant embraces?" The teasing note in his voice surprised her. "Would you really, Stantia? Rather than marry me?"

I will not cry. I will not. "We both heard your father. Are you going to stand there and tell me he has changed his mind?"

"No. He spent some time in our chamber hurling imprecations at Laurant for dismissing him instead of letting him excoriate the baron for abusing me. But Father finally wore himself out and fell asleep." Jevon's hands still rested beneath her chin, but he tilted his head to one side. "I thought I knew him. Growing up, I thought Father arbitrarily critical of everything I did. I could never live up to his high expectations, and when he learned that I had been accused of theft, I knew he would repudiate me. I *knew* it, Stantia. Only"—she heard the catch in his voice—"only he didn't. He came searching for me instead, hoping to protect me. And I never knew it until today."

She instinctively curled her fingers around his. They were cold to her touch, reminding her they stood in crisp night air and that her own hands were warm because he had bundled her so snugly in his cloak.

"He loves you, Jevon. I saw that clearly today. He is proud of you, and he will be prouder still when he learns how deserving you are of the knighthood he gives you."

He loosed his hands from hers to brush a strand of hair from her temple. "A knighthood would mean nothing to me without you. That is why I was leaving."

So he had already said, but not for Rouquard if his father slept. Then where?

"You mean leaving Poitou? You are going back to your mercenary band?" She was ashamed of the excited way her heart leapt but too selfish to rebuke it. "Then I am coming too!"

"No, Stantia."

She bounced on the balls of her feet, eager to fly off with him this very instant. "There is nothing you can do to stop me. If you do not take me with you, I will follow you on my own. I will! No matter how many times Lord Laurant tries to stop me, I will eventually slip away, and however long it takes, I will find you. Who knows what dangers I might fall into without an honorable archer to keep me safe?"

Every nerve in her body quivered with readiness to carry out her vow.

Jevon threw back his head and laughed. "You do not need my bow. Only the most misguided reprobate would fail to think twice at that termagant sparkle in your eyes."

Constantia suddenly realized the reason she could not read Jevon's expressions. He had placed his back to the moon, flooding her face with its light. His chuckles tugged a responsive smile from her lips, but she resisted because she did not know whether he teased or not."

"I mean it," she said. "If I am termagant enough to frighten a reprobate, I am harpy, shrew, and vixen enough to dog your heels when you walk through Pennault's gate."

The world abruptly spun as Jevon caught her around the waist and whirled her around. "You haven't a shrewish bone in your body, Stantia. And I would not dream of ever leaving you again."

The resplendent fragrance of roses floated with her into clouds of ecstasy when his mouth captured hers. She clung to him with all her strength, just in case when she opened her eyes she discovered his baffling capitulation and this heart-thumping kiss had all been an illusion.

Her senses still swam when he eased away.

"You will not have to dog my heels after I dower you," he said huskily.

"Dower?" Had he spun her too hard to think straight? With a blush of both embarrassment and pleasure, she found herself draped over his lap on one of the garden benches.

He rolled his forehead against hers. "Last time, I sold my mother's ring to make a dowry for you. I thought I had nothing to sell for you this time. But it was waiting for me in the chamber Sir Eudes took Father and me to." Jevon drew a slow breath. "I was going to leave because I thought it would be more bearable to be a thousand miles away from you than to live at Rouquard without you as my wife. But when I entered the bedchamber, I found Laurant had restored my belongings, such as they are, my money bag, the pouch with my food rations, and my bow and arrow bag."

He pulled his head away and reached for a shadowy shape leaning against the end of the bench. She knew immediately what it was.

"Remember how Father said he would accept even a few settings of silver plate on your behalf?" Jevon's words clipped with increased speed. "The bowyer mark of Hywel ap Ioan is greatly sought after. Had I been a gambler rather than hoarding my coins through the years, I would never have been able to afford this. The ornamental nocks alone will be worth at least a couple of silver-plated dishes and spoons. And it will bring even more for bearing Hywel ap Ioan's name as the maker."

She tried to slow him. "Jevon—"

But he raced over her. "Last time, I made the mistake of selling my ring without any witnesses, so I could not prove the silver was mine and that I had full right to gift the coins to whomever I wished. I will not make that mistake again. This time, when I sell my bow, I will round up at least a dozen men to witness its sale to an honest buyer, then I will demand they stand by and watch as I give the coins to you and declare you free to use them however you wish. For, Stantia, it would not be a gift if I forced you to give them right back to me in marriage . . . unless that is what you truly, truly wish."

"You know it is." She dealt him a vehement kiss to be sure he had no doubt. "Oh, Jevon, you know it is. But sell your bow?" It was the companion of his banishment, a weapon that had become more than a mode of survival. It had been his protector, friend, and gradually, over the course of his lonely wanderings, part of his very being. "I cannot let you do that, even for me."

"I will not need it in my father's house. He will expect me to put it away for the arms of a knight."

Jevon spoke with a stoic detachment, but she knew him too well not to perceive the hint of pensiveness in his words. As desperately as she wanted a solution, this could not be it.

She slid off his lap to sit beside him. "Jevon. No."

He sighed. "Will it sadden me to sell it? Yes. But could I ever love any bow more than I love you? If you believe that, I will be marrying a goose-brain for a wife, and the one thing you have never been is goose-brained, Stantia. Do not give my father another reason to doubt my judgment by becoming so now."

He leaned over and kissed her. Did he know how doing so would send all her arguments out of her head?

A ripple of cloth swirling on the breeze made them break apart. A bulky shadow appeared a few feet away. The cloak fluttered on a gust of air before falling back into heavy lines around his body.

Jevon rose quickly. "My lord."

His voice was respectful but cold. Constantia noticed he did not bow to Laurant.

"Forgive me," the baron said. "I did not know the two of you were here. I came outside to think without the baroness's—"

He broke off, but Constantia easily imagined the rest. *To think without the countess's harping.*

"To consider what I am to do in the morning," Laurant amended. He took a step closer, his cloak rustling again on the air. "I did not mean to intrude on you, but now that I am here . . . well . . . Jevon, there is much I need to say to you. But if you prefer to wait till tomorrow so you can stand before my knights and hurl my shame in my face, I will not blame you. I deserve every curse you throw at me, every derision you can heap on my head, and I will bear it all without argument in front of all my men. But I want you to know"—the baron made a helpless gesture—"how terribly, terribly sorry I am for what I did to you."

Jevon responded with stiff silence. Constantia rose to stand beside him, her heart as hard as his. At her movement, the baron's shadowy head and attention swung toward her.

"I know nothing I can do or say can ever right the wrong I did you," Laurant continued. "But there is one thing I do have power to do. Provide Constantia a dowry so that your irascible father will have to let you marry her. You can keep your bow despite the grief it caused me during the siege."

So the baron had overheard some of their conversation.

"Lady Gwenllian will never let you dower me," Constantia said. "She always insisted it was her prerogative to choose husbands for me and Guia and Deatris."

"True," Laurant agreed. "But the payment of the bounty remains *my* prerogative to grant. If the thief I banished were discovered still on Poitevin soil, anyone could deliver him to me, dead or alive, and claim a bounty of one hundred livres. I named the reward to encourage him to leave lest he attempt some sort of revenge on me. And he did." Constantia sensed the baron's gaze moving back to Jevon. "You came back to Poitou with the Earl of Gunthar with revenge in your heart. Do you deny it?"

"It was not revenge I wanted. Only justice."

Laurant waved a hand dismissively. "Term it however you wish. But you came to see her too. Will you deny that?" He nodded at Constantia.

Jevon took longer to answer this time. Before he did, he laced his fingers with hers. "No."

"Well, then. It is obvious she took advantage of your affection to lure you to Pennault, hoping to gain the bounty. If things went a bit awry for reasons that became so muddled I do not wish to waste my time trying to unravel them, the simple fact remains that she entrapped the banished thief and has thus earned the reward."

"But Jevon was not the thief," Constantia pointed out.

"But I still thought him so when he crossed Pennault's threshold. At that moment, the bounty remained in force. If he'd wished to avoid the penalty, he should have stayed in Gunthar's camp rather than setting foot anywhere inside Pennault's walls. He ignored the consequences because of you. If I wish to declare you siren enough to have captured him and therefore bestow on you the bounty, will you reject it?"

She exchanged a glance with Jevon. Even in the darkness, she knew they held as much bemusement at the baron's convoluted reasoning as hers. Such a bounty would give her a dowry that was truly all her own and allow her to marry whomever she pleased. But—

"Will you still acquit Jevon of the theft?" she asked.

"Of course. I do not see what one has to do with the other."

Could Laurant truly be that befuddled? Or was he simply that wily? She recalled how his evasive negotiations with Gunthar held off the earl's siege engines longer than Sir Damien's insolent defiance had. Laurant's contorted justification for paying Constantia the bounty would insulate him from his wife's complaints while he simultaneously asserted his independence to his knights, proved himself honest enough to admit a mistake, and assuaged at least a portion of the regret he so clearly suffered over his misjudgment of Jevon.

"And . . ." Constantia heard hesitation return to Laurant's voice. "And if you, Jevon, would consider a knighthood from me along with the decree I shall issue of your innocence—"

"A knighthood? From *you*?" Jevon physically recoiled beside her.

Laurant's dark frame slumped a little. "I suppose your father has already offered you the same. But mine would be proof of my conviction of your innocence rather than paternal favoritism. You need not stay and serve me, though I would count myself most fortunate if you did. You could ride wherever you pleased with honor, serve whomever you wished—"

Jevon held up his left hand, allowing the moonlight to splash its silvery-white light over his brand.

Laurant flinched. "If I knew a way to blot out that part of my guilt, I would." His voice sounded thick with remorse. "I will go to my grave regretting that, but there is nothing I can do to wipe it away. Shall—shall I deal the same to Sir Raimon for his theft and for trying to lay his crimes at your feet?"

If any man had a right to demand such a punishment on Raimon, Jevon did.

"*No*." His answer did not surprise Constantia, though the force of it did. "You said in the hall, 'No more branding.' I hold you to those words."

Laurant blew out a breath that sounded like relief. "What then? I suppose I could leave him shut up in the gatehouse prison or put him in the oubliette."

Constantia insides quivered at the thought of anyone being dropped into the narrow, windowless, stinking confines of that prison pit, sealed up and simply forgotten.

"Let him go," Jevon said.

"Let him go?" Constantia and Laurant echoed together.

She agreed the oubliette was too severe for theft and branding too cruel, but releasing Raimon as though he had committed no crime at all?

"Jevon," she said, "Raimon must be punished somehow."

"He will be, by his own cowardice. Mark me, it will undo him again and again. When he finds himself the butt of mockery and contempt by those knights he most desires to emulate and has nowhere to look for its source but into his own shrinking soul, the ignominy will be worse than any prison or brand we could inflict on him."

Laurant said nothing for a moment. "Well, if that is what you want . . ."

The baron sounded uncertain. But then, he had not witnessed Raimon whimpering and shrinking from Jevon's bow or the way he fainted when Jevon slashed his surcote open.

"Then what about Guia?" the baron asked. "She played a part in your disgrace too."

Jevon looked down at Constantia. "Is it true?"

Constantia nodded reluctantly. "She did not know the brooch fell out of your purse and did not realize you would be blamed when she picked it up.

But when she heard you accused and condemned to be branded, she was too afraid to admit the truth."

"Why did she take it?" His voice came so softly Constantia strained to hear him.

"Because she wanted a dowry to marry too. But she swears she would have put the brooch back if you had not been caught first."

"I can leave her fate up to you," Laurant said, "or I can let my wife decide. The brooch belonged to the baroness, a gift from her father. Thus, the theft touched her as well as you."

"No," Jevon said. "Let *me* choose. Banish her."

Banish? The horrors of an ostracized woman cast defenseless into the world flashed again through Constantia's mind. "Jevon!"

"Someplace safe," Jevon finished. "Let the monks of Saint Luc choose a nunnery for her."

Laurant exhaled another audible breath. "Yes. Yes, that will do. My lady wife cannot complain about that. Beatris may as well go with her for letting Sir Raimon copy my lady's key."

Constantia knew it would please Lady Gwenllian to see the seal of a nunnery squash any hope Guia and Beatris might still nourish of escaping their spinsterhood as Constantia was about to do.

"Well," Laurant said with fresh awkwardness, "I will leave you both to consider my offers. Do not stay out too late in the chill."

Constantia waited until she was certain the baron was out of hearing before she giggled at the irony. "One hundred livres. Your father's jaw will strike the ground when you present me to him with a dowry so grand."

Jevon chuckled. "That is a sight I cannot wait to see. But are you sure you wish to waste the bounty on me? A dowry that handsome could win you a better husband than a lowly fifth son who will never hold land of his own."

"Perhaps a richer husband," she agreed, "with a more respectable past, but never a better one. You are the best man I have ever known."

Confidence in a joyous future burned so bright when he kissed her that its brilliance would have blinded her had her eyes not closed to intensify the sublimity of their exchange. They kissed at least a half dozen times—she was not strictly counting—before he sighed and leaned his cheek on top of her head, while hers nestled against his breast.

"I am happy—*so happy*, Jevon. But . . ." A nibble of poignancy frayed the edges of Constantia's glow. "In spite of her part in your grief, I wish Guia could be happy too."

"Oh, I would not worry too much about Guia. As soon as Llygad learns where she is, I suspect he will snatch her from the nunnery and bear her off to Wales."

"How will he know where to find her?" Constantia eased away to look up at Jevon. "You mean to send him word, don't you?"

Jevon's grin was all the answer she needed.

"Then . . ." Constantia hesitated, but it was his own fault. If he chose to be magnanimous enough to forgive Guia and help her marry Llygad, he had no right to complain if she wanted to help them too. "Then would you mind if I gave some of the bounty—only a little of it—to Guia for a dowry . . . just a small one . . . of her own? Then perhaps she and Llygad would not have to leave Poitou. He has lived here nearly all his life. He told me that going back to Wales would feel like exile."

"Oh? I thought, perhaps if he were in Wales—" Jevon broke off for only an instant, but she sensed a wistful regret in him before he swept on. "But never mind. Laurant will wish to reward him for keeping Therri safe from the earl. The baron is grateful for my part in that too. If I ask him, I am certain he will recommend Llygad to his brother's service, where both he and Guia will be out from under Lady Gwenllian's thumb. As for dowering Guia, the bounty is yours. I'll not question how you want to spend it."

In that case, she would give a few coins to Beatris so that she might marry too.

Constantia's eyebrows pinched together. "I must buy myself a fine gown to meet your mother in. If she frowns on me, your father might reject what remains of the bounty. And there will be the cost of a wedding gown and a veil for my hair. Oh, Jevon, I might be completely out of coins before we even ride through your father's gate!"

"Unless my mother has changed from the generous woman I remember, I suspect she will insist on gifting you a gown and veil. Though it would probably be wise to comb all these tangles from your hair before you meet her." He threaded his fingers through her locks and immediately snagged on a knot. "Honestly, Stantia, I've never known a woman who cared so little for whether her hair looked like a silken ribbon or an unkempt haystack."

He dodged her feigned slap.

"And now you've grown crotchety too," he said. "That is what happens when women stay up too late. You had better go to bed and catch a few hours of sleep to smooth out that scowl on your face."

She sat on the bench and crossed her arms. "You are right. I might be so cross in the morning that I change my mind about using the bounty for a dowry."

He sank down beside her. "That would be a shame if you decided to squander all that money on fripperies and gowns rather than marrying the best man you have ever known."

"And the best archer," she conceded. "But the very worst thief."

"If I had wanted to steal something, I would have been the best at it. I stole your heart, didn't I? But only after you stole mine first. So you were clearly the better thief."

She wanted to argue over who stole whose heart first, but a fresh wave of weariness engulfed her. She yawned. She told her legs to stand, but instead her head drifted to his shoulder. His arm reclaimed her waist. She would go to bed in a moment. A few moments. A couple of handfuls of moments. Just as soon as that thread of a cloud reached the other side of the moon. As soon as she convinced herself that this was not a dream, that Jevon really sat beside her, and that soon she would truly and finally be his wife.

It might take her a lifetime to wake up from this trance. But a lifetime of dreaming with him was all she had ever asked.

APRIL 1175
ROUQUARD CASTLE

J evon recognized her light footstep against the stones of the wall-walk. He'd tried to vary the timing of his visits to this portion of the curtain wall each day so his wife would not notice and wonder what drew him here, but she always seemed to find him.

She slipped her arm into his. "Your father's bailiff would be offended if he knew how closely you watch him. The serfs know how to make their fields prosper without any advice from you."

Clearly he had used that excuse for his presence here over often. "I am not watching the fields today," he said. "I was thinking of the river beyond and wondering if it was a good day to go fishing."

"The river is there." She pointed. "The fields are there." Her finger shifted. "But to be frank, my dear, you are rarely looking at either. You are always looking there. Over the forest. Are you missing your days as an outlaw?"

He grinned. "Unburdened by husbandly and soon-to-be fatherly duties? Every day."

He embraced her thickening waist and kissed her soundly. He had not thought he could love her more deeply than the day they wed, but to his amazement, each day, nay, each hour, his devotion to her quickened and grew. Like the child she carried. The thought that he would soon be a father both terrified and thrilled him.

It felt disloyal to admit to himself that, despite the joy she brought him, some corner of his soul chafed with discontent. Perhaps he would feel less restless once the babe was born, less frustrated to be bound to his father's lands—and his brothers' frowns. Bernart and Nils had done little but grumble since Jevon's return had restored him to a place in their father's inheritance, further diluting the land and wealth they'd expected to share only between themselves when their father died.

Her fingers brushed across his forehead. Had he allowed a crease there to betray him?

"Something troubles you," she said. "No, not troubles. Disheartens? Won't you tell me what it is?"

"It is nothing."

His time as an outlaw had been an ordeal he never wished to relive, but it was true that he found it a little vexing to be confined to Poitou after the freedom of traveling farther afield as a mercenary. Poitou was as far as Laurant's proclamation of Jevon's innocence guaranteed protection for his questionable scar. But it was not Normandy, or Brittany, or even the tournament fields of Flanders and the glory he'd once hoped to win there that called him to the wall every day.

No matter. No far-flung land could compare to the happiness he'd found with Constantia.

He slid his hands beneath the pristine white veil that floated over her silk-clad shoulders and hid her brown, gold-glazed hair. He cupped the two braids coiled over her ears, smiling at the rebellious wisps that escaped the plaits and tickled his palms in spite of the hours she spent trying to tame them with the silver comb his mother had gifted her.

"How could I be anything but completely content with you?" He tilted her mouth up for another kiss.

Despite the honest pleasure that warmed his mouth when he released her, suspicion still lingered behind the reciprocated heat in her eyes. Before she could speak again, another woman's voice interrupted her.

"Jevon!" Lady Pelegrina hurried along the wall-walk in a generous bustle of spring-green skirts, her veil exposing a rim of lightly silvered blonde hair at her brow. "It is one thing to sneak kisses with your wife in the middle of the day in some corner of the castle where no one can see you. It is quite another to display your passion atop the castle wall, where you can be viewed for miles around."

His mother had a point. Several of his father's serfs snickered up at him and Constantia from their fields, though they hid their laughter behind their hands when they realized Jevon saw them. Constantia's face turned as red as he imagined his own to be. Saints! He and Constantia had been married for eight months. He should be sated with her kisses by now. But he could kiss her for a thousand years and it would never be enough.

"Forgive me, Mother. We will be more discreet."

Lady Pelegrina squeezed her endearingly plump form between him and Constantia. It was not until she slipped one arm into each of theirs that Jevon saw the twinkle in his mother's eyes.

"You are too much like your father," she said. "He mortified me more than once after we married by sneaking up behind me when he mistakenly thought we were alone. One time he kissed me in front of a gardener who was pulling weeds behind a bush, another time before a stableboy who just woke from a nap in the hay. I worried I would never win the servants' respect."

His father, a roguish romancer to his wife? Jevon could not reconcile such a thought with the gruff sire he knew. But now that he thought of it, though his father lectured his brothers just as brusquely as he did Jevon, since his return to Rouquard, Jevon had never seen his father lecture his mother. Lord Vidal always listened to his wife with attentive regard.

"From what I have seen," Jevon remarked as he allowed his mother to draw him and Constantia along the wall-walk, "the servants adore you now."

"Oh, most of them were always kind." She replied with a natural cheer Jevon suspected had ultimately won both the servants' loyalty and his father's heart. She released Jevon's arm as they reached the tower. "There is a man waiting in the hall to see you."

Jevon smothered a groan. A restive peace had fallen over Poitou in the wake of the martial campaign that had finally humbled the rebellious barons of the county and brought Duke Richard to terms with the king. During the aftermath of calm, Franco had come to Rouquard, earnest to convince Jevon that he had always questioned Jevon's guilt. Jevon gradually thawed to the initial awkwardness between them. He spent hours answering Franco's eager questions about Jevon's "adventures" as a mercenary, asking in turn about the events of Franco's life since his knighthood. They parted with a handclasp of revived friendship, but so far, Franco had not returned.

Barons and knights, on the other hand, who once hunted a disgraced young nobleman for the price on his head continued to travel from miles around to stare at Jevon as though the exonerated young man were some curiosity at a fair. Ostensibly, they came to assure Lord Vidal they held no grudge for his unpopular support of King Henry. But they always asked after Jevon, and his father always called his youngest son to join them, obliging Jevon to pretend that their covert glances at his scarred hand did not tempt him to hurl his fist into their impertinent noses.

"Who is it now?" Jevon asked.

"The squire your father sent to look for you did not give me the man's name," his mother replied. "I suspected how you and Constantia might be passing the time"—Jevon's cheeks heated again—"so I offered to find you. Go along now. I will keep Constantia company."

Jevon walked ahead down the tower stairs but deliberately slowed his steps. He had already heard his mother regale her new daughter-in-law with too many tales of Jevon's mischief as a boy and feared she intended to "keep Constantia company" with yet another escapade. How could he possibly have engaged in so many outrageous antics before the age of seven and not remember one of them? It felt entirely unfair that he should not have an equal number of girlhood stories to tease Constantia with just because her mother died and her father was bluntly indifferent to his daughter's existence.

Jevon had barely entered the hall before he felt his father's hand scuff up the back of his head.

"Do not look so surly, boy," his father growled as Jevon smoothed his hair back down. "It is one of the earl's men. One look at your sullen face and he will think I harbor a rebel in my castle."

One of the earl's men? Jevon tried to pinch back a sudden pitch of hope. His mother must have misunderstood. Surely any knight sent by Gunthar came to confer with his father, not the archer with conflicted loyalties who had so disappointed the earl.

Jevon surveyed the hall, searching for a knight wearing a fine woven mantle over a blue surcote with the badge of the prancing stallion. But the badge worn by the man seated at the table on the dais in front of a platter of cheese and soft white bread was sewn to a humble homespun tunic.

"Ned!" Jevon exclaimed.

"Jevon! Your pardon, I meant *Sir* Jevon." Ned Woodville stood and bowed to Jevon's new title. "Forgive me, but since your father was kind enough to summon me some refreshment, I could not resist."

"Eat, eat," Lord Vidal said. "Sit back down and eat."

Lord Vidal knew how to treat a great lord's servant even if that servant were a lowly archer.

Jevon tapped his toe while Ned resumed his meal. He caught his father's glare, stopped with the tip of his boot halfway in the air, then quietly lowered it and waited until Ned finished and chased the food down with a goblet of wine.

By then Jevon's mother had joined them in the hall with Constantia, though the women remained just inside the entrance of the wide, high-ceilinged space.

Ned brushed the crumbs from his fingers and stood again. He crossed the dais to Jevon, then drew something from his traveling pouch.

"I asked Gunthar to be the one to bring you this."

He dropped something into Jevon's hand. A delicate gold band etched with leaves and bearing a large, lustrous emerald encircled with tiny pearls.

"What the devil?" his father exclaimed. Lord Vidal glowered at Gunthar's messenger. "What is this fellow doing with your mother's ring?"

Lady Pelegrina swept across the rushes and mounted the dais with a lively step to view the object.

"Oh," she said with a calm that challenged her husband's anger, "I gave that to Jevon years ago to buy a new surcote. Are you a tailor, sir?" she asked Ned.

"No, my lady, I am merely an archer, one who counts himself honored to have had the privilege of calling your son my friend. Gunthar sent you this as well."

Jevon stared so agog at the ring that it took him a moment to see and accept the letter Ned held out to him. The thrice-folded parchment was sealed with a blue wax stamp of the prancing stallion. Jevon broke the seal, but the scratchings inside puzzled him. Were they intended to be words?

Apparently seeing Jevon's confusion, Ned said, "The earl rarely writes himself because—well, as you see, his handwriting is not easy to decipher. He usually dictates his correspondence to a secretary. That he wrote directly to you is a compliment you should not take lightly."

"Read it aloud, boy," his father commanded.

Jevon chewed his lip and pondered the scrawl until at last the marks evolved into words.

"'To Jevon de Cazalet of Rouquard Castle, greetings. Upon diligent search by my servants, we have located a knight of Bavaria by the name of Albrecht Leckeler of Rothenburg Castle. Albrecht confirms on oath that he purchased this ring from a squire called Jevon de Cazalet seven years ago when Albrecht sought hospitality at Pennault Castle on his way to worship at the cathedral of Santiago de Compostela. At my request, Albrecht agreed to sell the ring to me, which I now return to you. In recognition of your honesty and acknowledging your innocence as declared by Lord Aumary de Laurant's own attestment, I send you this writ from the king exonerating you of the crime of theft. Keep this with you and take care not to lose it. It cannot be replaced. Written by the hand of Hugh de Bury, Earl of Gunthar, at Lamhurst Castle, Kent, on Maundy Thursday.'"

Ned held out a second document. The writing on this one had been inscribed with immaculate precision, but Jevon could not read it.

"This one's in Latin," he said.

Ned met his look with a helpless shrug.

"Give it to your mother," his father replied.

Jevon's mother?

"You know Latin?" Jevon asked as she slid the parchment from him. They had always written to one another in Poitevin. What else did he not know about her?

She smiled. "A story for another day. Now, let me see. 'Henry, by the grace of God, king of the English and duke of the Normans and Aquitanians and count of the Angevins to the barons and knights of my realm. Jevon de Cazalet, also known as Jevon le Falquet, has proven himself by irrefutable evidence to be innocent of the crime for which he was accused by Lord Aumary de Laurant of Pennault Castle in the year of our Lord one thousand one hundred and sixty-seven. Jevon de Cazalet le Falquet may hereafter travel safely throughout all lands ruled or held in fief by myself and my heirs.'"

All the lands? No longer only Poitou?

"'Any mark of guilt he may bear on his body,'" his mother continued, "'is to be disregarded. Any man who offends against Jevon de Cazalet le Falquet for said mark shall pay equal penalty to the offense dealt to Jevon de Cazalet le Falquet in contradiction of this writ.' Ah!" His mother looked up. "That means if some man hangs you or cuts off your head when he sees your scar, the king's officials can hang him or cut off his head in return."

As gratifying as that would be, Jevon would not be alive to see the penalty inflicted. No wonder Gunthar warned him to keep the writ with him at all times.

"'Witness: Hugh de Lacy and Philip de Hastings. At Valognes on the second day of April in the year of our Lord one thousand one hundred and seventy-five.'"

She returned the parchment to Jevon. This time the seal was attached at the bottom of the writ, a man on a throne with a crown on his head, a sword in one hand, and an orb in the other. Around the wax rim was written in Latin: Henricus Rex Anglorum. Even Jevon could translate that: Henry King of the English.

"May I see?" Constantia's shoulder brushed Jevon's. He handed her the parchment. She could not read Latin either, but she traced the words almost reverently and did the same with the seal before looking up at him, tears glistening in her eyes. "Does this mean we are leaving?"

"Leaving?" his father said. "Why would you?"

Constantia met his father's gaze. Lord Vidal had treated her with such gruff kindness since her marriage to Jevon that she'd lost all fear of him. "Because Jevon is not happy here. It has nothing to do with you, my lord, or with you, my lady," she added to his mother. "He dearly loves you both, as I do. But Jevon has always wanted to see the world."

Lord Vidal blew a *hrmp*h through his nose. "I should think he had his fill of the world in his mercenary days."

"But he could never travel free of the danger posed by his scar, until now. And I think there is still some land he has not yet visited that he yearns for." She raised her too-perceptive eyes to Jevon's face. "You are always gazing north from the wall. You told me you have fought in Brittany and the Angevin lands and Normandy. The only other place that lies to the north is—"

"I hope your wife is about to say England," Ned interrupted. "Because that is the answer Gunthar desires to know."

Jevon's chest clenched so tight it took him a moment to draw breath to answer. "Gunthar wants me to join him in England?"

"Well . . ." Ned looked awkward. "Not exactly. He told us all that you have been proven innocent in the matter of theft and he'll tolerate no slanders on your name from any man who serves him. But you still chose loyalty to the house of Laurant over your loyalty to him when you helped Laurant's son to slip through his fingers. He has not forgiven that."

Jevon's chest deflated. His loyalty had never been to Laurant. But it *had* been to Therri.

"The earl views the world in black and white," Ned said, seeing Jevon's disappointment. "One day he will learn to see the shades in between, but until then, he will not accept you back into his service. But he will recommend you to a neighbor of his, Sir Alan Faintree. Sir Alan is a faithful king's man, but he prefers to pay scutage whenever he can rather than follow the king's campaigns beyond the British Sea. You are unlikely to see Poitou again should you agree to serve him. So if you are reluctant to leave your family . . ."

Jevon bit his eager, quivering tongue before he answered too quickly. He did not wish to insult his parents, but—

Constantia's fingers curled into his sleeve. "You were disappointed when I told you Llygad wished to remain in Poitou," she murmured so softly only he could hear. "You were hoping Llygad would go back to Wales so you might have an excuse to visit him . . . and maybe some land nearby?"

Her warm, comprehending eyes laughed up at him. He blessed her for sensing what this offer meant to him, even though she could not know why. *My heart's twin.*

She raised her voice for the others to hear. "You must answer as your heart bids you, husband, but I have always wanted to see England."

"The invitation is not open-ended," Ned warned. "Gunthar requires your reply no later than Whit Sunday or he will withdraw his recommendation to Sir Alan."

Yet another test of Jevon's sincerity, no doubt. He had a sudden thought. "But I am no longer an archer. My father knighted me."

"Oh, Gunthar knows that. Just because the earl is back in England does not mean he does not still have ears in Poitou. The earl's recommendation to Sir Alan is, and I quote, 'an honorable knight of Poitou who will serve you with devotion within the realm of England and any realm beyond except his homeland. Keep him out of Poitou, and I'll vouch you will not be disappointed in him.'"

Jevon did not know whether to be flattered or disconcerted by Gunthar's endorsement.

Jevon sought Constantia's eyes again and found all the certainty he needed. He turned to his father. "Tell Bernart and Nils I renounce all claims to your inheritance. Ned, tell Gunthar—"

"Why don't you come with me and tell him yourself? I've permission to wait a few days if you need to settle some affairs."

"But Constantia's baby!" Lady Pelegrina exclaimed. "If you leave now, I will never see my new grandchild."

Constantia—his dear, compassionate, generous Constantia!—took Jevon's mother's hands in hers. "Then you must come with us. Would Sir Alan allow it?" she asked Ned. "I have no doubt we will find his household kind, but they are strangers, and I would like to have family near when the baby is born." She smiled somewhat mistily at Lady Pelegrina. "You are my only mother now."

Jevon's heart swelled with love for both of them as tears welled in the women's eyes.

"Sir Alan is a congenial and hospitable man," Ned said. "I do not think he would object to extending a welcome to Lady Pelegrina."

"Well, I object!" Lord Vidal boomed. "I am not paying for my wife to go sailing off to England without me, and I cannot spare the time away from my lands."

Jevon scooped his mother's hand out of Constantia's and slipped the emerald ring onto Lady Pelegrina's finger. "When you gave this to me, it became mine to use however I please. It pleases me to give it back to you. Sell it for passage to England."

Lord Vidal rammed his fists against his hips. "The blazes she will. Do you think me a miser like Constantia's sire? If your brothers cannot manage affairs without me for a few months, they are clodwits, and I assure you, I do not raise clodwits. No one pays my wife's passage but me."

"But you just said—" Jevon broke off when Constantia kicked his ankle.

His father glared at him. "I know what I said. Do you think me a dotard?"

"Certainly not, sir," Jevon answered, suppressing the twitch of laughter on his lips.

"Hmph," his father grunted again. "Then I shall visit England with you. I intend to look this Sir Alan in the eye before I decide if his household is worthy to raise my grandson or granddaughter. As for that ring, give it back to him, wife. And you," he said to Jevon, "might as well put it on Constantia's finger, where you no doubt always intended it to go."

More or less. Jevon slid the ring onto the third finger of Constantia's right hand. Her wedding ring, a garnet symbolizing constancy in love, already graced her left. Shaped as a heart inside a gold setting, the garnet had been selected by his father from the de Cazalet jewels, and it was understood that in the far-off future when his daughter-in-law died, it would return to the family fortune. But the emerald ring was different.

"When my mother gave this to me," Jevon told Constantia, "it became mine without condition. Now I give this ring to you, and as your dowry is paid, the ring is yours, your very own forevermore, to do with as you please."

Constantia turned her hand this way and that to study the emerald in different angles of the light, then tilted her glowing face to his. "'Because a gift once given no longer belongs to the giver but to the receiver.'" She quoted the very words he had said to her when he'd held her captive in the woods. "Then I belong to you, Jevon de Cazalet. I gave myself to you without condition on our wedding day."

"And I gave myself to you, Constantia de Cazalet." How his heart drubbed with pride to call her that. "Which means we belong to each other."

"Just like this ring. For always and ever. 'Because that,'" she added with a twinkle of remembrance and promise, "'makes perfect, honest sense.'"

Excerpt from
Loyalty's Web

Who was the mysterious quicksilver stranger who tormented Jevon and Constantia and eluded capture by the Earl of Gunthar's men? Learn his identity and the devious part he plays as the Earl of Gunthar falls in love with the Lady Heléne. Enjoy this short excerpt from the quicksilver stranger's point of view in *Loyalty's Web*, Book 2 in my **Poitevin Hearts** historical romance series.

EXCERPT
LOYALTY'S WEB: **POITEVIN HEARTS**

The young lady struck his hand away. "It is a lie!"

He caught his breath at the transformation anger worked upon her. He had thought her drab but curious a moment ago, decked out in what he imagined must be some squire's cast off clothes. Although her hose-clad legs were nicely turned, the too large, knee-length tunic completely swallowed up any hint of womanly curves. He might well have taken her for a tall, lanky youth had it not been for her pale gold braid. Even tumbled over her shoulder as it was, its thick, feathery end brushed against her hip.

Now tiny flecks of fire set her silvery eyes ablaze. The way her cheeks glowed, he thought the whole of her might burst into flames. A calm, critical survey confirmed a sad lack of her sister's bewitching charms. But drab this young lady most certainly was not.

"I assure you, my lady—" he began, only to be cut off.

"Nay, you lie!" She leaned forward, hands on hips, challenging him as stoutly as any battle-hardened knight. "My father has not betrayed his oath to the crown. How dare you slander my house like this!"

"'Tis no slander," he insisted. "I have proof. A letter. One with your father's seal."

He had seen her wariness when he first approached her on the riverbank, fishing with a pole he suspected she had swiped from the same squire whose clothes she now wore. She had dropped the pole when she flared into anger at his initial accusation. Now, though that anger remained bright, the veriest hint of doubt stole into her face.

"A letter?"

He smiled and raised his bone-thin hand to toss back his long, crimped curls. Hair even paler than hers shone white rather than gold in the spring sunlight. But not the white of age. He guessed himself not more than six or seven years her senior. Yet at times, he felt almost ancient. The corruptions and debaucheries he had once found so thrilling had now grown little more than tedious. Gluttony, theft, seduction, even murder. He had tasted, nay, he had gloried in them all.

Only one earthly pleasure—revenge—continued to elude him. Continued to madden him. But with this innocent's help, he would finally glory in its fulfillment as well.

He said nothing more for a moment, allowing doubt to work its way deep into her mind. Then: "Aye, a letter. You might have it, for a price."

Her hostile eyes narrowed. "I do not even know your name. Why should I believe anything you say?"

"Because it might well be the truth. And if it is, your father is courting disaster, thinking he can play both ends against the middle. The Earl of Gunthar is no fool. He will discern the false faith behind this marriage agreement. He will learn, as I did, that your father's oath of fealty already lies broken in the dust."

The lady's long braid swished with the fierce shake of her head.

"I do not believe it. My father would not swear an oath he did not intend to keep. He would not place his family in danger of the king's retribution again."

"Ah." He smiled sympathetically. "It was most unpleasant for your family, was it not, when the earl besieged your castle?" Her bright cheeks paled. "Or perhaps frightening would be a better word."

Her sharp little chin jutted out at that, whether in defiance of him or her memory of the earl, he did not know. He hoped it was the latter. If he could but focus her hostility from himself to the earl, the risk of meeting her here in the open would have gone far to accomplish his purpose.

"Come, my lady, I do not ask so much. A little information is all. If you could only tell me when the earl is due to arrive, perhaps a few other details. . ."

He trailed off. Drat the lass. Her eyes surveyed him too shrewdly. And her defiant chin lifted higher.

"Your name, sir. Your house. And how this dark secret of my father has come to your knowledge. Tell me all of that and then, perhaps, I will see fit to tell you what you want to know."

His admiration of her stout heart abruptly turned to annoyance. He had not time to joust words with her. If he were seen and recognized, his life would not be worth a copper coin.

His voice hardened. "I have the letter. If you do not wish it to come to the king's knowledge—"

"Then show it to me, if it exists. I will know my father's hand and seal. Show me your proof. Otherwise, be on your way."

She faced him boldly. The tension visibly slid from her body when he did not reply.

"I see. Then I shall be on *my* way."

She picked up her fallen fishing pole and turned to leave.

"My lady."

He touched her arm to stay her. She gasped and jerked away so hard she nearly lost her balance. In that instant he saw the fear in her face. She had masked it well until now. But seeing it assured him of the power he needed.

"I have the letter," he repeated, and this time he allowed some menace to slip into his voice. "Meet me here again in a week's time. Only come at night, when the moon is high. Bring me the information I require and I will surrender the letter to you. Fail me, and your father will find himself in chains. And you and your family will learn the ugly fate that awaits a traitor's kin."

He reached out for her again, hoping the strength of his hand about her arm would press his warning home. But before he could touch her, she swung her pole at him. He ducked just in time to avoid a crack to his head, and felt the *whoosh* of the rod in the air.

"You are a liar, sirrah! And if you dare to step foot on our land again a week-night hence, you will be met, not by me, but by my father's guards."

She turned and ran away from him.

He let her go and smiled. Seven days to let the doubts he had sown harrow her mind.

Aye, she would be back.

Continue reading. Download your copy of *Loyalty's Web* now.

She's the daughter of a rebel. He destroyed her father's castle. Can these bitter enemies find their way to love?

Heléne de Laurant can never forget her days of terror when the Earl of Gunthar's army shattered the walls of her home in the name of the king. It does not surprise her that someone wants revenge for the havoc he has wrought in Poitou. When someone tries to murder Gunthar, she refuses to believe her family and friends are involved. The mysterious stranger she meets by the river can hint otherwise all he wants. She will never abandon her faith in her loved ones' innocence, not even for the flint-eyed earl whose unexpected attentions fluster her and make her heart beat a little too fast.

Heléne's fiery spirit stirs Gunthar in a way no woman ever has before. But he is not free to court her. By command of the king, he has returned to Poitou to enter a marriage alliance with the daughter of a rebel baron—Heléne's sister. Gunthar's devotion to the king demands his obedience. Besides, when one assassination attempt turns into more, trusting the wrong person could truly be deadly. And however much Heléne fascinates and enchants him, she is undeniably keeping secrets from him.

Heléne and Gunthar's attraction to one another becomes impossible for either of them to ignore as, despite their mutual suspicions and distrust, they work together to uncover the plot that threatens Gunthar's life.

When the would-be murderer is finally revealed, will loyalty rule their choices or love?

Download your copy of *Loyalty's Web* now from your favorite online book retailer.

Thank You for Reading

I hope you enjoyed reading *The Falcon's Heart*. If you did, would you please consider ~

Leaving a review on the retail site where you purchased this book. Just a few words about what you liked about the story will help other readers find and enjoy this book too,

Recommending this book to a friend,

Subscribing to my newsletter so we can keep in touch about future releases in this series along with other books I'm writing. Continue reading to learn how you can receive a special subscriber-only gift!

Thank you again for reading *The Falcon's Heart*!

Glossary of Welsh Words

Bara lawr: A traditional Welsh dish made from seaweed, also called laverbread, literally "bread of laver." Pronounced BAH-rah (slight roll on "r") LOWR (rhymes with "flower".)

Cregyn gleision: Welsh word for mussels; used in Welsh cuisine. Pronounced KREY-gin (slight roll on "r") GLAY-shun.

Eisteddfod: A Welsh festival celebrating poetry, music, and storytelling, often featuring competitions in the bardic arts. Pronounced eye-STETH-vod.

Gwraig ffôl: "Foolish woman." Pronounced gwr-AIG (rhymes with -EYE-g, slight roll on "r") FOHL (rhymes with "bowl").

Gwenynen fach: little bee. Pronounced GWEN-uh-nen vahkh (as in Scottish "loch")

Hulpan (pronounced as *hilpun* by Jevon): silly woman. Pronounced HILL-pahn in Welsh.

Jadan (pronounced as *jawdun* by Jevon): Harridan or scolding woman. Pronounced JAH-dahn in Welsh.

Merch y Gwynt (pronounced as *merkawit* by Jevon): "Daughter of the wind" – flighty, unpredictable. Pronounced MAIRK-uh-gwint in Welsh.

Neidr bach: "Little snake." Pronounced NAY-der bahkh (the "ch" as in Scottish "loch").

Source: Gweiadur: The Welsh-English Dictionary online. https://www.gweiadur.com/welsh-dictionary

Glossary of Medieval Words

Angevin: One who hails from the Anjou region of present-day France; birthplace of King Henry II of England.

Aquitaine: A region of southwest France that was ruled by Henry II of England in the 12th century.

Arbalist: A man who shoots a crossbow, or a larger version of the same weapon called an arbalest.

Arrow bag: A sturdy tube of strong cloth, usually linen canvas, closed with a drawstring at both ends, and used to carry a sheaf of 24 arrows. Common among medieval longbow archers. Jevon's war bow was a precursor of this weapon.

Bailey: The courtyard of a castle.

Barbican: A walled outwork projecting from a castle's main gate, built to strengthen and protect the entrance.

Battlements: The **crenellated** top of a castle wall.

Bowyer: A master craftsman who made or sold bows.

Bowyer's mark: **Bowyers** sometimes carved a symbol or mark into the bows they made and sold; in a mostly non-literate society, the bowyer's mark acted as the maker's "signature" attesting himself as the bow's maker and to the quality of his product.

Breton Sea/British Sea: Medieval terms for the English Channel. "English Channel" did not come into common use until the 18th century, while the French version, La Manche, was not used until the 17th century. During the Middle Ages, two of many options scribes (and therefore, likely speakers) used for "the Channel" were British Sea by the English and Breton Sea by those who lived in areas now associated with modern-day France.

Chemise: A woman's loose undergarment.

Coif: A hood made from metal rings (i.e., **mail**) worn beneath a knight's helmet.

Courser: One type of war horse also used in medieval tournaments; exceptionally strong, but lighter and faster than a **destrier**.

Crenel: The gap or notch between two **merlons** on the castle wall.

Crenellated: A wall with gaps for firing arrows, etc.

Crossbow or arbalest: A bow-like weapon that shoots horizontally, releasing a small, heavy arrow, called a bolt, by means of a winding and trigger mechanism. Smaller crossbows could be cocked and triggered by hand. Larger versions (called arbalests) had to be cocked against the ground with the foot via a stirrup.

Curtain wall: The outer wall that lies between the towers of a castle.

Dais: A raised platform in the **great hall**.

Denier: The smallest denomination of medieval French coins, equal to an English penny. Twelve deniers equaled one **sol**.

Destrier: A strong, powerful warhorse used by knights.

Drawbridge: A bridge that can be raised or lowered to allow access across a ditch or moat into a castle's bailey.

Fealty: The loyalty sworn by oath by a knight to his lord.

Fortnight: Two weeks (from fourteen nights).

Gambeson: A quilted jacket worn beneath a knight's armor to cushion the blows of battle; also worn as an outer garment or beneath a surcote by medieval archers, with a tunic underneath.

Gatehouse: A heavily fortified entrance to a castle complex.

Girdle: A belt worn around the waist by both men and women.

Hauberk: A long tunic of chain **mail** that covers the upper body.

Hilt: The handle of a dagger or sword.

Investment: The act of laying siege to a castle.

Keep: The central tower and main residence area of the castle.

Lawn: A very fine fabric made of linen.

Liege lord: The king or lord to whom a man of lower rank owed **fealty.**

Mail: A flexible armor made of small, overlapping metal rings.

Mangon or mangonel: A medieval siege engine similar to a catapult, used to hurl large projectiles at a castle wall.

Marshal: A high-ranking officer in charge of a prince's or lord's horses and stables and, during war, his military cavalry.

Mêlée: A mock battle between two opposing teams of knights that formed the tournament of the 12th century.

Merlon: The part of the fortified castle wall that juts up between two **crenels** (gaps or open areas).

Moat: A broad, deep ditch filled with water that formed a defense around a castle; sometimes left dry and lined with sharp stakes.

Motte: A central steep-sided artificial mound of earth topped by a defensive tower or **keep**.

Mural tower: Towers built into the castle walls.

Nocks: Bits of horn fitted to the ends of a traditional bow (not crossbows) where the string was attached; they helped protect the wood from the wear and tear of the bowstring.

Oubliette: A dungeon deep underground with an opening only at the top.

Page: A boy between the ages of 7 and 13 who served as an attendant to a knight, lord or lady; the first step in a male's training to become a knight.

Palisades: A defensive fence or wall of heavy vertical wooden stakes positioned close together, locked to each other with horizontal beams.

Parchment: Material made from animal skins used for the pages of books and other writing.

Poitevin: A resident of Poitou.

Poitiers: The capital city of Poitou.

Poitou: A region of west-central France ruled by Henry II of England during the 12th century.

Pommel: A counterweight, usually in the shape of a circle or ball, at the top of the handle (**hilt**) of a sword or dagger, often intricately decorated; derived from the Latin word for "little apple."

Portcullis: A grated gate usually ending in spikes that dropped vertically to seal off the entrance through a castle's gatehouse.

Postern: A hidden door in a castle's curtain wall.

Sennight: One week (from seven nights).

Singlewoman: Medieval term for an unmarried woman. While *spinster* later became more commonly used, *spinster* derived from the occupation of spinning cloth whereas *singlewoman* simply denoted a woman's marital status.

Smock: A loose, blouselike garment.

Sol: A French coin later called a sou; equal to twelve deniers.

Squire: A boy between the ages of 14 and 20 in training to become a knight. A squire might be knighted at the age of 21, although some men never advanced to knighthood and remained squires all their lives.

Surcote: Also known as the surcoat or super-tunic; a secondary tunic worn over an under-tunic, usually more elaborately decorated; could be worn over a gambeson by medieval archers.

The hall or great hall: The central living space of the castle inside the **keep**; the ceremonial and legal center.

The Great Revolt: A civil war that took place between Henry II and his sons in 1173-74; also sometimes called the Great Rebellion and the Great War.

Trencher: Large slices of stale bread, cut either round or square, and used as "plates" for medieval dining; sometimes made of wood.

Tunic: A sleeved, loose-fitting outer garment worn by both men and women; could be worn alone or under a surcote or gambeson; for a man, could be knee or ankle length, always ankle length for a woman.

Vassal: A man who owes military service to one of higher rank, in return for land and protection.

Veil: A linen cloth draped over a woman's hair held in place with a gold or silken band around the head.

Wall-walk: The walking space behind the fortifications (**merlons** and **crenels**) on the **battlements**; also known as the allure.

War bow: Predecessor to the longbow or possibly an actual longbow. The description "longbow" was first recorded in 1386 to differentiate it from a hunting bow. Actual longbows likely existed and were used before this date. In *The Medieval Archer*, by Jim Bradbury (see Suggested Reading List), Bradbury suggests that longbows at the time of the Norman Conquest likely measured about 5' in length, gradually evolving through the following centuries to an approximate length of 6' by the 1400s. In this story I have chosen to use the term "war bow" for long bows used in war vs shorter hunting bows used in the 12th century.

SUGGESTED READING LIST

(For readers interested in a further study of subjects addressed in *The Falcon's Heart*)

Code of Medieval Chivalry

Medieval Life and Times: Code of Chivalry. Accessed March 7, 2025. https://www.medieval-life-and-times.info/medieval-knights/code-of-chivalry.htm

Conflict between Henry II and Richard Plantagenet

Barber, Richard. *Henry Plantagenet: 1133-1189*. New York: Barnes & Noble Books, 1964.

Warren, W. L. *Henry II*. Berkeley and Los Angeles, California: University of California Press, 1973.

Henry II's siege tactics

Warren, W. L. *Henry II*. Berkeley: University of California Press, 1973, pp 231-232.

Longbow vs. Crossbow; the Mangon; the Oubliette and other features of medieval castles

Bottomley, Frank. *The Castle Explorer's Guide*. New York: Avenel Books, 1979.

Medieval Archer/Archery

Bradbury, Jim. *The Medieval Archer*. Reprinted in paperback 1999. Woodbridge, Suffolk, UK: The Boydell Press, 1999.

Medieval Juries

Warren, W. L. *Henry II*. Berkeley and Los Angeles, California: University of California Press, 1973, pp 354-358

Medieval Sieges

Bradbury, Jim. *The Medieval Siege*. Woodbridge, Suffolk, UK: The Boydell Press, 1992.

Monastic sign language

Monastic Sign Language. Fish Eaters. Accessed March 7, 2025. https://www.fisheaters.com/monastichandsigns.html.

Poitevin Inheritance Traditions

Chaytor, H.J. *Savaric De Mauléon*. Cambridge, UK: Cambridge University Press, 1939.

Hajdu, Robert. "Family and Feudal Ties in Poitou, 1100-1300." *The Journal of Interdisciplinary History* 8, no. 1 (Summer 1977): 117–139. Cambridge, MA: The MIT Press.

Independence of Poitevin nobles

Hajdu, Robert. "Family and Feudal Ties in Poitou, 1100-1300." *The Journal of Interdisciplinary History* 8, no. 1 (Summer 1977): 117–139. Cambridge, MA: The MIT Press.

Warren, W. L. *Henry II*. Berkeley and Los Angeles, California: University of California Press, 1973, pp 354-358

NOTE: Every effort has been made to provide reliable web links. However, because websites are updated or removed from time to time, some links may no longer be active. Readers are encouraged to search by title or author if a link is unavailable.

Acknowledgements

I wish to express my deepest gratitude to The History Quill for their indispensable support with *The Falcon's Heart*. The feedback from their Beta Reader service was invaluable to me in shaping my early drafts. An early edit by Hilary Cohen at Reedsy, along a final copy/line edit by Michele Preisendorf of Eschler Editing are also deeply appreciated.

And then there is Kelly Urgan, whom I first discovered through The History Quill and later worked with through her own editing service, Editegrity. Kelly went above and beyond in her work on this manuscript. Not only did she provide profoundly instructive insights into the story's structure, she spotted a weakness that had been nagging at me all along though no one else had mentioned it. She was right. Brilliantly right! And she knew exactly how to fix it. *The Falcon's Heart* is immeasurably better for her inspiration.

Other Books by Joyce DiPastena

Poitevin Hearts

Loyalty's Web (Book 2)

Illuminations of the Heart (Book 3)

Loving Lucianna (Book 4)

Dangerous Favor (Book 5)

The Loves of Lyonstoke Castle

Courting Cassandry

Stand alone titles

The Lady and the Minstrel

Short Stories

An Epiphany Gift for Robin: A short prequel scene to *The Lady and the Minstrel* (1)

The Girl by the River: A short prequel scene to *The Lady and the Minstrel* (2)

A Candlelight Courting

"Caroles on the Green," in Timeless Romance Anthology: Winter Edition (*2012*)

Non-fiction

Name Your Medieval Character: Medieval Christian Names (12th-13th Centuries)

Some of my titles are listed in separate series but have interconnecting characters. If you are interested in reading these books as they take place chronologically, here is their order:

The Falcon's Heart: Poitevin Hearts 1

Loyalty's Web: Poitevin Hearts 2

Illuminations of the Heart: Poitevin Hearts 3

Loving Lucianna: Poitevin Hearts 4

Dangerous Favor: Poitevin Hearts 5
The Lady and the Minstrel

The Lady and the Minstrel cycle can be read in this order:

Loyalty's Web: Poitevin Hearts 1
An Epiphany Gift for Robin (short story)
The Girl by the River (short story)
The Lady and the Minstrel

About the Author

Joyce DiPastena illuminates the Middle Ages for modern readers through heartfelt historical romance. However many changes a few centuries may bring, she believes that stories of love can unite people across time. Joyce is a two-time Whitney Award finalist. The Historical Novel Society rated her romantic historical novel, **The Lady and the Minstrel** as "highly recommended," while the same title won a Swoony Award for Excellence in Clean Secular Romance.

Joyce grew up in southern Arizona and can easily withstand summer temperatures of 115 degrees, as long as she's sitting in a restaurant, movie theater, or under a ceiling fan—inside an air-conditioned building. She can be bribed with chocolate chip cookies and enjoys attending the Arizona Renaissance Festival every year. She holds a degree in history, specializing in the Middle Ages, from the University of Arizona. Joyce currently resides in Mesa, Arizona with her black cats, Nyxie and Calypso, who bring her good luck every day.

Joyce loves to hear from her readers. Email her at joyce@ joycedipastena.com, visit her website at joycedipastena.com. join her newsletter, or connect with her at any of the websites below.

9 781970 402001